STAR-CROSSED
NEGOTIATIONS

TESSA MCFIONN

To all those who think forever has passed them by… open eyes and an open heart can find love even in the darkest times

Acknowledgments

Let's set the way back clock to 2017. It's summer in Orlando, FL and once again, I am seated before another agent, hoping to make that connection that will launch my career to the NYT Best seller land. I mention my paranormal series and add that I write science fiction romance, giving a short commercial about my soon-to-be releasing book entitled *To Discover a Divine*. The agent gets extremely excited and says, "I want that!"

Crap.

I had that story with another publisher. Refusing to miss this opportunity, I say, "I have another one."

LIE!!! Complete and total fabrication.

The agent passes me her card with a request to see the first three chapters. So on the flight back to San Diego, I flip open my notebook, put pencil to paper, and *Star-Crossed Negotiations* was born.

As time ticks on, the story gets more fleshed out and life hands me a couple of twists. The agent passes on the project, the new publisher goes belly up, my other publisher and I part ways, and this tale heads to the back burner.

Over the years, I occasionally dust off the old story and revisit the Nexxus, chipping away at it. I began to wonder if this tale was ever going to see the light of day. Finally, inspiration struck and the words practically wrote themselves.

But if not for some wonderful and supportive friends and colleagues, this would have sat unfinished on a shelf in a virtual bookcase.

A shout out goes out to my late night readers, Elma and Mary-Anne, who were always willing to glance over random scenes at odd hours.

To Mary Max, thanks for listening to me ramble on to see if the story was worth telling.

To Denyce, thanks for making sure I stayed true to the characters and the worlds in the Nexxus and kept the momentum going.

To Margaret, Pam, CJ, Tami, Dena, Cindy and my awesome SoCalRW peeps, who don't think the voices in my head are that strange. And Deb Dixon, thank you for reminding me about that forgotten twelfth chapter of the Hero's Journey. Now the story comes full circle.

To my wonderful readers and followers who share my stories with others, I owe you so much! Thank you from the bottom of my heart.

To my friends and family, for making me laugh when things got rough.

To my husband, for reminding me to take breaks and see the world around us, and for making sure that I got sleep.

And to my mom, for letting me tell my crazy stories and believing in me.

Chapter One

"Please tell me you did not agree to this mission."

Vanysha Kureen glared useless daggers at her sheepish captain, Fazzian. Hard to believe the giant Drekkan towering over her was capable of blushing, but she definitely spied the pinkish hue peeking around the thick, blue-black muttonchop sideburns on his grizzled face. Even as he knelt beside her nav station, he had her by a foot, easily. Granted, her cramped pod wasn't spacious to begin with; its cozy placement tucked three steps beneath the pilot's console had made for scant breathing room.

"Now don't look at me like that, Van. It's a total milk run. Only a handful of politicos. Six, tops. They usually don't travel in packs of any more than that. This could be the big payoff for us…"

She pinched the bridge of her nose and dragged in a deep, calming breath. The engines hadn't even cooled from their last "big payoff," and Vanysha was more than ready for some down-time. Not to mention, the ever-growing list of projects the ship needed before they took on another contract; the girl could use a new coat of paint, and there was the refurbished air filtration system her contact in Caiguan City on Bayan was holding for her. She waved off the rest of his standard pot-sweetening speech. "Where?"

Faze dragged his fingers through his whiskers, chewing on his upper lip. *Not good.* He only got squirrelly when it was especially crappy news, and today had brought the grand total to twenty-seven. Her stomach dropped as she added to the tally. Preparing for the inevitable bombshell, Vanysha tucked her hands under her armpits. She asked again, her forehead aching from holding her prolonged frown. "Faze? Where?"

"Hexaka."

She blinked deliberately, composure honed by years as a galactic navigator keeping her arms carefully locked across the front of her sweat-dampened jumpsuit instead of strangling her pilot.

Hexaka.

Her burly commander continued to prattle on, his rationale meant to soothe her jangled nerves. "It's on our way to Bayan, which was our next pit stop anyway, and—"

"And in the middle of a total shitstorm, in case you forgot." She tossed her hands up, praying for serenity from the gods. "Do I need to tell you how many ships have been lost in the Crimson Alley during the past month alone? Tell me they are at least going to offer us a military escort."

No pilot worth his flight wings purposefully flew directly into either end of the corridor between Westran Alpha and Hexaka, the route earning its chilling moniker after years of unending hostilities. And if they did, it definitely wouldn't be unarmed.

"Well, now. About that..."

She leaned away as far as her control pod would allow. "You

didn't think to ask, did you? Why can't I get you to understand this is a passenger transport, not a friggin' armed cruiser. If we get caught in the middle of anything, we're screwed."

In recent weeks, rumors had drifted through the vid waves that the new ruler of the dynastic Bharange family on Westran Alpha was ready to negotiate with the barbaric Hexaks. Hard to believe a blood feud spanning nearly a century could be settled with a change in regime; hatred didn't disappear under the rug simply because company was coming.

But, true or not, Vanysha would personally rather not take the chance. Not that she had much to lose; all she owned was her ship. She lived for the *Royal Janstar* and her small crew of three, who were more like family than friends.

She studied Faze as the silence lengthened, delving deep into his guileless golden eyes. He ran a meaty hand through his wild and shaggy, deep-cobalt hair as she pondered her response. Over the past six years, she'd trusted the man with her life and he'd never led her astray. When the universe had dogged her at every turn, he'd opened his home and his heart to a disowned, discarded waif. He treated her better than her own family, and had taught her to chase after any dream, no matter how crazy it seemed.

"We don't fly any colors, which makes us less of a target," he said, resuming his well-thought-out defense strategy. "But if we cruise through, armed to the teeth, they'll nail us for sure. C'mon, it's a day at best, to get there and back."

As she eyed her mammoth mentor, a healthy touch of uncertainty tiptoed up her spine. He did have a point. As a passenger carrier, they usually flew unnoticed along the fringes, avoiding much of the real hostilities. She wasn't sure if she wanted to press her luck, though. Hoping to banish her growing fear, she rubbed her hand along the base of her bare neck and sighed heavily.

His thick arms crushed her in a strangling hug. "You won't regret this, Van. We'll be home before you know it."

The heavy presence vanished as quickly as it had appeared, and she hung her head.

Hell, she already regretted it, and they hadn't even opened the hatch doors yet.

Wouldn't have been the first time they'd entered enemy territory, and she was sure it wouldn't be the last, either. So why did she have the feeling this was not going to end well?

With a pitiful groan, she swung her head around, working out the kinks in her tense shoulders, and crawled out of her confining cubicle. Her body protested the return to activity, joints popping and crackling as she grabbed her go-bag from the overhead bin. She glanced at the chronom on her wrist before realizing Faze hadn't given her an ETA on the new passengers.

Great.

Nothing like flying blind into hell.

Casting her gaze toward the distant skies, she evoked a favor from the entire Nexxan pantheon. Palpable fatigue oozed from her weary limbs, blending with her desire for a serious shower. Hesitantly, she sniffed her armpit, and recoiled in horror.

Their last run had taken them on a two-week sightseeing tour from Central to the farthest reaches of the Nexxus, and her muscles ached from the long hours of disuse.

"Faze?" she called out, coughing in a feeble attempt to push the volume.

Nothing but the winding down whir of the engines met her ears. No way he'd gotten that far in such a short amount of time. She cupped her hands around her mouth and shouted.

"Just tell me I have time to clean up and change before we take off again?"

Two knocks echoed off the wall, and she smiled in relief.

Thank the gods.

One for no; two for yes. They'd recently switched up the universal call and response. Even though they avoided taking on any dangerous clients, that didn't necessarily mean they were safe. Brigands and thieves were known to attack any carrier, regardless of the colors they flew. By altering the call-and-response pattern, crew members would be immediately alerted of trouble. Sounded great in theory, but in truth, they only used their unique code when the comms were on the fritz. The ship's natural harmonics were a perfect conductor, and the *Royal Janstar* never failed them.

Tingles prickled at her legs, and Vanysha bounced on the balls of her feet until the pins and needles had diminished. After a few more seconds of spastic dancing, her body finally responded to her will. She slung her bag over her shoulder and made her way to the exit hatch, rapped her knuckles four times in quick succession against the hull and waited until the responding three thumps echoed through the deserted ship.

The door slid up, and she ducked under the receding barrier.

Deep night still blanketed the sleeping station, and she moved on automatic pilot toward the crew lockers, her gaze darting into shadowed alcoves and around approaching corners. She rested her fingers lazily on the butt of her sidearm as she took purposeful strides toward her ultimate destination. Her worn leather boot heels muffled most of her passing, time having softened the soles to a paper-thin barrier.

On the whole, traders and pilots were a respectable bunch, but sometimes shipments were short or payments were held due to customs. When times were lean, even the best of men could make the worst of choices.

Arriving at the female lockers unchallenged, Vanysha relaxed her guard a fraction. She slotted in her credkey, and the nearest stall door swung open. Muttering angrily, she shook her head as she read the going price for a shower. Westran Alpha's controlling grip on the supply of much-needed water had moved the simple act of bathing from a necessity to a luxury. She unhooked her ammo belt and placed it carefully out of water range yet still in emergency reach. Gritting her teeth, she stripped down quickly and selected the shortest time. With liquid soap doubling as shampoo in her hand, she took a deep breath and stood beneath the narrow nozzle.

She squeaked in shock as ice-cold water pelted her from above. Her hands twitched and skimmed along her bare skin, while a silent curse formed on her lips, and she lathered her hair, hoping speed would bring warmth back to her fingers. But the initial cold snap had lasted only for a moment, shifting rapidly from arctic to tepid. So, with one hand scrubbing the lingering soap out of her shortish hair and the other smearing suds across her body, she ticked off the remaining time in her head. Practice made imperfect, but at least she knew how long to take with each task.

Her mind drifted as she hurried through her routine. For as long as she'd lived, there had never been peace in the Nexxus. Each of the ten planets was abundantly rich in one material, one crucial element in high demand on the other nine planets. Central was mother to every vessel; the liquid metals flowing like rivers beneath its surface provided the bones and skin for space-crafts, trains, and all manners of transport. The oceans on the trio of Westran supplied water to the entire system, and Hexaka's soil was the source of steeleglass, the most prized material for any and all spaceworthy vessels, with its unique combination of elements that created an unbreakable barrier even in its thinnest form.

Treaties had created shaky alliances from time to time, and

the slightest misstep would plummet neighboring homeworlds into never-ending hostilities, as was the case between Hexaka and Westran Alpha. Vanysha remembered her grandfather's story about a tribal princess' death during a celebratory night after a decades-long argument. He'd said the tale had been passed down to him from his own grandfather, so the truth of the actual incident had been slowly lost through the oral tradition. Another rumor mentioned something about the assassination of the Westran Alpha dynasty's eldest son ten years ago, which had caused things to spiral from tense to outright deadly.

Honestly, though, her mind often reeled as she struggled to keep all the whys and wherefores straight in her head. All she knew for certain was: the longer the Hexaks fought against the Westran Alpha Consortium, the tighter the water restrictions grew.

And the shorter my hair gets. She sighed. If this battle kept up much longer, she would end up bald. Before the Crimson Alley had truly earned its name, her silver-white hair had reached past her ass. Now, she struggled every day to convince herself her asymmetrical pixie cut was stylish and sexy.

Dingy white foam slipped past her toes just as the nozzle cut out. She smiled weakly in victory, and her eyes began to drift closed. Falling asleep buck naked in the locker room? Wow, she was tired. With a determined shake of her head, Vanysha dug deep into her energy reserves and yanked the towel off the hook. Maybe Faze wasn't a complete jackass and had told the parties to arrive in the morning. She repeated the mantra over and over again as she dried off.

She kept one ear tuned toward the distance as she whistled a random melody and slipped into a fresh flight suit. The baggy black cargo pants nearly slid off her hips. Damn. She really needed to remember to eat on these long runs. After rummaging through her pack, she found a workable belt, tugged on the clingy, white long-sleeve top, and tossed her sweaty uniform back into her go-bag, then slammed her feet into her boots. She fastened the buckle of the thick, black leather holster around her waist and gathered up the rest of her meager belongings.

No sound, save her own breathing, echoed in the silence and, confident yet cautious, Vanysha ventured out of the communal showers and returned to her ship. Food could wait; sleep could not. All through her short spritz, she struggled to shake the plaguing unease.

It was just another run, she assured herself. Perhaps these politicos were some sort of negotiators sent to barter peace? Wouldn't that be something. Her little ship carrying the voices that would bring much-needed unity to the peoples of the Nexxus.

So why did she have a lump sitting in the pit of her stomach?

Chapter Two

V ice Ambassador Kieran Phaetal stood tall before the floor-to-ceiling vid screen, his hands tightly clasped behind his back.

"I am greatly honored by your faith in diplomacy, Your Eminence, and if the proper mining concessions were made in exchange for stronger water rights, giving a wider possible profit margin for both you and Hexaka, I believe the Prime Chieftain might be willing to come to the table and negotiate a treatise."

"Bah." The sour scoff had filtered in from behind the young face dominating the foreground, and Kieran locked his jaw, ignoring the invisible dissenter in the Westran Alpha royal court. "Those damned savages don't want peace. You've seen what they've done to any ship coming near their planet for the better part of eight decades. Why should they change now?"

A flurry of voices rose and fell, and a static image of the gold-and-purple rising star insignia of the imperial seal of Westran Alpha filled the video screen. Seconds passed in measured heart-beats, but Kieran forced himself to remain calm. While the closed-door argument ensued, he clenched and unclenched his hands behind his back, maintaining his formal posture. He'd spent the past two years preparing for this exact moment. Hours and hours of studying the subtle nuances of the former monarch wasted, because the man couldn't keep his dick in his pants. The newsfeed from Westran Alpha had reported his demise as a result of a fatal heart attack. *That does tend to happen when five inches of steel is plunged into it while you're busy screwing another man's wife.*

That had been two weeks ago. This current conversation was nearly two hours in, and Kieran was beginning to lose faith.

Without warning, the royal crest vanished, replaced by Westran Alpha Grand Magistorum Xyphos Bharange. *Such a grand title for one so inexperienced in life.* Ever since the news had broken, he'd had little opportunity for contact with the new ruling leader of Westran Alpha, the rumored coup having set the all-too-young man onto the throne. The face across from him appeared to be no older than thirteen; no worry lines creased his forehead, and the guise of innocence still lingered in his deep brown eyes, the elaborate gold-encrusted cape swallowing his narrow shoulders. Kieran felt a tug of sympathy, but sometimes the universe didn't care if you wanted to have a normal childhood.

He shut away his own experiences, slamming down the lid on the useless "if only" sentiments as he held his stiff pose and, using this time spent as a statue to his advantage, he replayed his next steps in his mind. The new ruler wished for peace; the whole of his young life had been spent living beneath the shadows of an ancient feud between his world and the savage Hexaks. Perhaps the time was ripe for an end to the hostilities. The universal supply of Hexaka's sought-after steeleglass, used in every building and every star vessel, was dwindling. Even the most peace-loving planets were resorting to piracy and illegal salvage to obtain the sparse commodity. At this rate, it was only a matter of time before the entire Nexxus would be in the grip of an intergalactic upheaval, and the cause would be laid directly onto this new ruler's lap.

"Is the situation truly so dire in the Nexxus?"

Ah, to be so sheltered. No way to break things gently to the young leader.

"It is my firm belief that now is the time to act, Your Eminence. We have not had any direct contact initiated by a Hexak chieftain in decades, until two days ago." Kieran was still reeling from the communique he'd received indirectly, allegedly sent from the elusive Hexaks, which requested a parlay to finally end the nearly century-old feud.

A gray-wreathed head drifted into the picture, whispering what Kieran prayed to be sage advice to the fledgling ruler. *This could be it.* Moments ticked on in silence. When the older man shifted his gaze to the vid screen, Kieran finally recognized him. The death of Chancellor Pretep's brother, the former Grand Magistorum, had taken a toll on the man, but Kieran was grateful to see the even-tempered advisor continuing to work toward peace. The pair exchanged nods, and the young man shifted his gaze back to the camera as his guardian shuffled out of range.

"Do we have your word that you and you alone will be handling the details of the accord?"

Inside, Kieran leapt for joy, though he maintained the proper protocols to the eyes recording his every move. He offered a reassuring smile, then dipped his head as he splayed a gloved hand over his heart. "I will not fail you, Your Eminence."

A boyish hint of a grin formed on the youthful face, pleased by Kieran's response. Outside of the framed scene, someone cleared their throat, and the happy mood immediately snapped back to somber formality. "Under the powers passed to us from the people of Westran Alpha, we charge you to barter peace with Hexaka."

The screen winked out, dousing the room in darkness, and Kieran heaved a sigh as the lighting soon warmed the narrow conference room. He rolled through the thick knots in his shoulders; the combination of anticipation and staunch military training had locked his muscles into inflexible, cramped rigidity. A sharp ding followed by a clattering broke the silence. He shook off the residual stiffness from his fingers, then crossed to the delivery slot next to the blank screen. With a triumphant grin, he removed the sealed tube and tucked the proof of his claim into his inner jacket pocket.

Anticipating a positive outcome, he'd arranged for transport to Hexaka before making the final contact. Easier to cancel the ship if things did not work out, but few pilots willingly ventured into the Crimson Alley without months of advance notice and a hefty retainer due every step of the way. Luckily for him, he had the financial backing to buy almost any throttle jockey, not to mention connections throughout several systems to find a last-minute ride should options run out.

Still smiling, he tapped in the direct code to the Politico General Raejil Phaetal. The wall blinked twice before a stern face appeared.

"Father. You were right." Pride colored his words as he gathered the papers from the table. "Xyphos was all too eager to look for a peaceable solution."

The harsh lines surrounding the steely gray eyes remained firmly in place, resolute and unyielding, and Kieran was all too familiar with the man's customary cruel sneer that hid beneath the meticulous mustache. "I take it you will be heading to Hexaka."

His father never asked. Demanding, he excelled at; the man lacked even an ounce of compassion. His mother had been the peacekeeper and the heart of the family, and Kieran had looked to her often while growing up under the iron fist of Raejil Phaetal. Their combined nurturing styles had honed him into a fierce and eloquent negotiator. Many treaties had been signed because of his influence. But this … this would be a true feather in his cap. To bring an end to so many years of brutal destruction would cement his place for all eternity in the annuls of the Nexxus.

He nodded as he sifted through the sheets, reorganizing the charts and lists of demands. "Immediately," he said, replying to the query. "I have a ship waiting. With Dagda's blessing, this will be signed in days."

"Get the treaty signed, or do not return."

Kieran lifted his head, giving one final glance to the face on the wall before the screen winked out a second time. His smile faltered at his father's words, but he refused to dwell on them. *I'm a grown man*, he mused. Years and experience had made him a successful diplomat. His father's approval was only icing on the cake. The treat would have been nice, but wasn't necessary.

Shaking his head, he grabbed his folio and, tucking the narrow case under his armpit, slipped out of his corner office. Light spilled out from only two other cubicles, where sat young workers eager to make their mark. He tipped his head toward his secretary as he passed.

"Myka," he said, "please hold all my calls. I will be out for the next week."

The young man scrambled to his feet, bumping his knees against the bottom of the desk. His thick glasses were tilted askew on his slender, beak-like nose, and he blinked his magenta eyes rapidly. "A week? Will you be needing an assistant on the trip?"

Kieran shook his head as he shuffled the papers into his folio. "No, thank you. The trip should be boring and short." The locking strap clicked shut, and he slipped the folio into his bag as he retrieved his vid phone.

"Then perhaps an itinerary, or contact point in case—"

Kieran lifted his gaze to his secretary, *tsking* as he arched one eyebrow. "In case?" he said. "I'm a big boy. I believe I can handle things."

"But I'm sure your father, or any others would want—"

His brow furrowed and he glared at his curious underling. "I will be out, and that is all anyone needs to know."

Kieran was in the business of secrets, and business was booming. Right now, the less anyone knew, the stronger his chances of success. The door whooshed open, and he nodded to his secretary as he headed out.

While the younger officer sputtered in his wake, he tapped out a short message to the chartered pilot as his long legs ate up the distance between his office and the exit. Even his quick steps trailed behind his racing thoughts, though. The number of variables involved in this task was astronomical, many of them leading toward abject failure or painful death.

Were either of those truly any different from one another?

His work was his life, foregoing any distractions that could divert him from his ultimate goal. He flagged down a transport as his link flashed.

Prepped for your arrival. Delvan Station. East Hangar. The Royal Janstar. Bay B18.

The Royal Janstar... Kieran tugged his brows together as he climbed into the vehicle. Drumming his fingertips against his fisted knuckles, he sifted through his memories as he drew nearer to the shuttletram hub. *Why did that name ring a bell?*

Chapter Three

"Are plans in place?"

"Yes. The ambassador just left."

"Good. This will make things so much easier. Are the other pieces in play?"

"I wasn't able to get that information."

"You imbecile."

"A thousand apologies. I assume the others have done their parts, but I have not been able to contact them yet."

"Everything must go as we have planned. If any are discovered—"

"The channels have been protected. Of that, I am certain."

"You had better be right about this. If he is planning to leave tonight, we have connections loyal to our cause at every docking bay. Unless he has found an unregistered transport, he will have to depart from one of the anchorage terminals. I see only one ship registered to leave within the hour: *The Royal Janstar*. See to it she never reaches atmo."

"Yes."

"Do not let me down again. You have too much to lose should the peace accord succeed."

Chapter Four

As the shuttletram zoomed along in the dreary night, leaving the political region of Lansdown in the distance, Kieran reviewed his plan of attack one more time. The young leader had given him specific limitations on the concessions to seal the deal. He only prayed the trade agreements would meet favorably with the mercurial Hexaks.

Having never actually met one of these reclusive creatures, Kieran had consulted centuries-old flight records and history vid reports months before he was offered the chance to broker peace. He'd researched every information data bank, hoping to learn all he could about their language and their customs. In truth, the entire project could have taken one afternoon; much of the intel had been spotty at best. Speculations and half-truths punctuated every inquiry, but some information was better than nothing. All history reports on the warlike and merciless denizens of the planet fabled for its steeleglass stalled nearly a century ago, when a dispute over an arranged marriage caused Hexaka to cease any trade dealings with the Nexxus.

When his eyes had begun to cross, he thumbed off his tablet and glanced out the window. The growing lights of Belleraphon, Central's trade and commerce hub, sparkled in the surrounding darkness. Towers of gleaming ebony and shimmering chrome created the recognizable skyline of his home. As a boy, Kieran had hated the glaring sight, despised the mechanized order and rigid regulations of it all, reminding him of his father and the harsh militaristic upbringing he'd endured. Only after growing up and learning about the chaos brought about by the lack of discipline, however, did he come to appreciate the peace of conformity.

Rain began to fall as the train zipped along. Kieran checked his chronom, astonished by the late hour as the clockwork precipitation dotted the glass. The immense heat generated by the planet's molten core gave Central a regularly scheduled greenhouse effect when the sun went down; three hours after midnight, the shift in temperature cooled the atmosphere, resulting in a downpour lasting only twenty minutes, and by the time the sun rose again, only traces of steam lingered as the cycle began anew. He huffed out a faint whistle, unaware of the actual length of his video conference. Originally, he'd booked the passage to depart just minutes from now, but the message from the ship's captain had only arrived moments before he'd boarded the shuttle. Perhaps they were running slightly behind as well? He had yet to hear any response from the Hexaks, though he was not expecting to arrive until later the following day.

A cold, computerized voice announced his destination, and Kieran shook out of his daydreaming. His transport came to a final stop, and he straightened his uniform jacket before stepping out into the surrounding night. No sense in missing an opportunity for a strong first impression.

Only one hangar bay was occupied, and he pointed his feet

in that direction, noting the absence of armed sentries as he crossed the silent expanse. The captain must be quite experienced…. *Or terribly naïve.*

Kieran's gaze roamed the pockets of pitch dark tucked between pools of brightness. If enemies clung to the shadows, they deserved their reward. No one approached, though, and he arrived intact to the required vessel. The snub-nosed passenger transport was in need of some cosmetic repairs, but it seemed adequate for his needs.

A hatch slid open and an immense Drekkan male exited the ship, ducking his massive head to avoid the top of the archway. Standing nearly two-and-a-half meters tall, his broad shoulders blocked out any escaping light, and a tousled mane of blue-black hair spilled down along the man's jawline, bracketing his easy smile. Kieran steeled his spine and confidently approached the gargantuan man, his boot heels clacking a steady tattoo, eating up the distance between him and his voyage to victory. Black fabric with cracked white letters stating "In My Defense, I Was Left Unsupervised" peeked out from the Drekkan's open fight jacket and hinted at the degree of professionalism Kieran could expect from the crew of the *Royal Janstar*.

The captain had agreed with a minimal amount of bartering to this unplanned flight into enemy territory, though. Perhaps Kieran could cut him a little slack.

An immense hand extended forward, the corners of the Drekkan's golden eyes crinkling as a warm grin lit up his whole face. "Vice Ambassador Phaetal?"

Kieran inclined his head in response. "Yes. Captain Fazzian, I trust we are prepared to leave." He paused, gauging the proffered greeting, then reached for the meaty hand, certain his gloves were firmly in place. His knuckles popped within the grasp, but he firmly locked his jaw to hold his tongue. With the firm shake,

Kieran sized up the man who oozed authority, trustworthiness, and determined confidence. *Perfect.* For this endeavor to meet with success, he'd need men of resilience willing enough to go into the mouth of Hell itself.

The burly alien nodded in response, his barely contained mass of curls bouncing as he placed his fisted hand over his heart. "We are, sir. My crew is prepared, and we only await the rest of your retinue."

Kieran stepped around the saluting captain and made a beeline toward the loading ramp. "I will be your only passenger on this trip. How long before we can launch?" He glanced up and down the narrow corridor. To his right, the path led to a spiraling staircase that vanished above the metal ceiling.

"Sir? I was under the impression—"

"Plans changed." He turned to face the captain. "This will not alter your payment, if that is your concern." *Don't tell me the man's going to lose his nerve now.*

Wheels turned behind the golden eyes, and the nervous expression soon crumbled away. "N-no. It's just…"

Kieran remained firm until the broad shoulders across from him shrugged. "As you wish, sir." The Drekkan scooted past Kieran and thumped the ramp controls with his fist. "Allyn!" he called down the length of the corridor, then moved toward the ascending staircase. "My junior engineer will show you to your quarters," he said to Kieran. "Your belongings arrived earlier and have been stowed safely in the hold. We will be off as soon as you are strapped in."

He watched Fazzian scurry up the corkscrewed steps, marveling at the nimble skill of the massive male before a tug on his jacket shifted his focus. A youngster wearing the bright red robes of the Unsought bowed formally, then gestured farther down the corridor. While slavery had long been abolished in the

Nexxus, some families still "donated" unwanted children under the guise of apprenticeships. The true horrors laid with others whose indentured servitude included being sold to brothels for pleasure or to battle dens for pain. Life was brutally harsh and mercifully short for those who found their way into the slavers' grip.

However, this Allyn's garments were clean, and they moved with ease, telling much of their treatment on board the vessel. He recalled the captain referred to him—or her—as a junior engineer, which made him assume the age of the draped person to be an early teen, at best. Many of the smaller ships were often training grounds for various skilled laborers, and if the willing workers came from questionable beginnings, no one was the wiser. Inside the bowels of freighters, anonymity was easy to maintain, as long as they did the job effectively and efficiently.

Kieran followed the silent guide, examining the immaculate interior. "How long have you crewed with this ship, Allyn?"

A hand popped out from the hem of the robed sleeve, two fingers extended before vanishing just as quickly. *A mute?* Perhaps the reason the child had been turned out in the first place. On most of the realms of the Nexxus, any deformity was grounds for disinheritance.

Or worse.

Yet Kieran knew intimately how abnormalities could become advantages, if properly channeled. He pulled on the hem of his gloves and continued his visual investigation of the vessel.

As they rounded each new corner, Kieran grew more impressed. The ship herself was oddly pristine, given the shabby exterior; whoever had owned her previously had taken great pride in maintaining her. His quiet companion halted and gestured to a cozy inset cabin, where two pairs of seats faced each other. With an appreciative nod, he gratefully accepted the high-backed launch chair nestled alongside the padded hull, and a small tray table retracted into the wall beside him, locking itself into place. Geometric designs of bold and vibrant greens and soft grays accented the creamy beige walls and carpet.

No wonder the ship has such a positive reputation. He'd done a little research after booking the *Royal Janstar* and was pleased to discover the reviews' accuracy. He'd nearly forgotten about the young man, until a flutter of crimson crept into his periphery.

"Thank you. This will do fine." The red-clad figure shuffled backwards, then vanished down the corridor.

Kieran wondered if the rest of the ship's crew was as unique as her captain. But he filed away this thought for later consideration and belted in, searching around the nearby console for the intercom switch. A sensual female voice filled the air, stalling his hand.

"Passengers loaded. All crew prepare for lift-off."

The ship's computer? Most likely. He'd charted the vessel unseen, relying on the advice of others. Word of mouth had pinned the ship's captain as one who'd traveled his required route on more than one occasion, and that was good enough for him. Who was he to judge the man if he got off on a sexy computerized voice?

The ionic propulsion drive whirred, and the ground slipped away. Once again, he nodded in approval. Most vessels still relied on thrust drives, making journeys loud and long. Ionic drives were quiet and quick, both factors heavily influencing his choice of transport. Nothing rattled as the ship broke atmosphere, and soon nothing but the unending night was visible from his octagonal porthole window.

"Ground fall successful. Engaging propulsion."

The ship shot forward, and Kieran jolted at the slight kick as white streaks zoomed past, painting bright stripes across the void until their streaming trails formed an all-embracing tunnel. The ease at which they'd reached top speed shocked him. Never before had he been on a smoother flight. When he saw the captain, he'd need to buy him a drink in thanks.

"Cruising velocity attained. Cabin doors unlocking."

Damn, that was one sexy voice. Yet something in it called to a distant memory. Something familiar in the cadence. A soft click met his ears, and, after unbuckling the belt across his hips, he rose to his feet.

"Light refreshments will be served in the dining cabin. Please enjoy. Our final destination should be reached within two standard hours."

He glanced down at his chronom, calculating the time before his meeting. With the fleet dexterity of his ride, he might even arrive earlier than he'd originally expected. Granted, they were flying through one of the deadliest parsecs in the entire system, but he could dream.

Safely en route, Kieran unbuttoned the collar of his confining uniform jacket as he stepped out of his private berth and his personal seat with a view to leisurely examine the craft. He glanced up and down the corridor, counting three inset doors most likely leading to the lodgings for passengers who'd booked extended excursions.

Aside from the obvious fact that Fazzian was the first captain who'd answered his request for transport, Kieran had purposefully targeted commercial vessels to avoid drawing any undue attention to himself or his journey. Under the guise of a charter flight without any military escort, he hoped their chances of arriving at their dangerous destination safely and in one piece would be stronger.

His thoughts wandered along endless paths of possibilities as he strolled through the quiet corridors. Since his trip was designed to be short, he'd only reserved a basic ticket, bypassing the full sleeper cabin experience, but this ship had been clearly laid out for longer cruises.

Curious, he tapped the control panel beside one of the doors and snuck a peek. Inside, he spied a surprisingly spacious cabin with all the comforts of home: a decent-sized bed, a business desk, a personal-sized, yet fully stocked bookcase and an overstuffed chair made up the bulk of the furnishings, and from the looks of the two interior doors, there was a closet and a personal bathroom to boot. If he ever took a vacation, he'd definitely be contacting the Drekkan to handle the trip.

A rumbling in his stomach reminded him of his original course and, closing the door, he returned to wander the singular hallway. A set of stairs leading down veered off from the straight path, and judging from the clicks, whirrs, and buzzes emanating from the lower path, he surmised it led to the ship's engines. He leaned down, craning an ear. The ionic drive was so soft, he could pick out several words the engineer directed to a silent companion, most likely the Unsought apprentice he'd met earlier. Certain food would be in the opposite direction, though, and he continued along his original course, admiring the vessel as he turned the next corner.

The ship was by no means immense, but as of yet, he'd only met two crew members. Many of the newer cruisers were fully automated, with only a skeleton crew of the living on board in case a computer malfunctioned. But there was a sense of life within this metal cocoon. Portholes along the central hallway were large and clear, giving passengers an exquisite view of the universe. He brushed his gloved fingers along the sleek walls, their black tips returning without a speck of dust. Nodding appreciatively, he mentally penned a letter of approval to the ship's meticulous owner as he meandered toward an inviting room at the end of the path.

Well, seems I've discovered the dining cabin. Several round tables dotted the spacious room, with a second archway cut into the far wall. Across from him stood a series of meal generators and one battered, outdated beverage station. One quick sniff explained much. Coffee. Someone on board this vessel must have been either of human lineage or had dealings with the Terran traders and actually enjoyed the vile beverage. Had the burly Drekkan developed a taste for the bitter drink? Doubtful, but stranger things have happened. He'd met a scant few who savored the dark concoction with relish.

As a young man, he recalled his father trying to force the black sludge down Kieran's throat. *"Real men don't sweeten it. Life won't sugarcoat the truth of itself."* Yet one other person had nearly convinced him of its delicious flavor.

A pair of voices filtered in from the distant entryway, cracking through his reverie, and he strode toward the steaming pot to see if there were other drink options. He recognized the captain, and the second speaker sounded a lot like the computer. Was he having a discussion with the ship?

As two figures entered the room, he froze, grateful his fingers hadn't gripped the fragile glass pot filled with the steaming brew. His blood thundered through his veins, racing to his brain as well as slinking below his belt line, and he gave his head a readjusting shake. Certain this was no hallucination, he swallowed back his shock, then found his voice, uttering a word that hadn't fallen from his lips in nearly six years.

"Vanysha?"

Chapter Five

All of the recycled air vanished from her lungs as Vanysha stared agape at the face she'd never expected to see again. Forgotten was the reason for her latest argument with Faze; she vaguely recalled it having to do with the unnamed passenger, but the tendrils of her important point had faded into oblivion.

Kieran Phaetal.

No way was fate that cruel to her.

She blinked to banish the hateful vision, yet when she reopened her eyes, he still stood before her. Her jaw locked, teeth clamped down hard enough to crack molars, but she gave no other outward sign of recognition.

"You two know each other?"

The upbeat inquiry from her mentor only added to her uncharacteristic need for swift violence. A thousand responses fired through her mind, and thankfully, only one made its way to her tongue.

"Not really." She kicked her legs into action and calmly

strode over to her daily vice. Unfortunately, the current target of her anger was between her and her joy. *Some things never change.*

Six years. Six years since she'd last seen his face. Six long and painful years since her heart, her dreams, and nearly her life had been smashed without so much as a word. She wished time had been harsher on him, but he looked just as gorgeous as ever. Even more so, if she were truly honest with herself. But she'd be damned before she'd say it aloud. With a swift glance, she sized him up, praying he didn't catch her ogling stare.

Gone was the gangly youth she'd laughed with, for he had grown into his towering height. She remembered playfully teasing him about his spindly arms, measuring his biceps with her long fingers. Now, although his crisp uniform jacket hid most of his physique, she'd definitely need both hands to span his build. Broad shoulders tapered to a trim waist, and long, muscular legs filled out the somber black ensemble. In his smoky quartz eyes, the boyish spark had dimmed slightly, but those depths still called to her heart. His dark brown hair was slicked down in controlled waves, no longer the wild and beckoning fall brushing across his forehead, and even his jaw appeared wider and stronger, framing his full mouth with its smooth lines.

No, this was not the Kieran of her long-ago memories. Here stood a man, cruel and unforgiving, the true prodigal son of the Central's leading politico family. He'd promised her he'd never follow in his father's footsteps.

That's what I get for believing words spoken in the heat of passion.

She filed away her useless reactions and, returning to her faltered journey, scooted around him to retrieve her mug. It took a couple of extra steps, but she managed to avoid any physical contact. Bad enough she could smell his cologne since the moment she'd crossed the threshold. If she inadvertently bumped against his arm, she feared her resolve would collapse. Her "move out of my way" signals were received, and he shuffled away from her.

"You are looking well."

She quietly scoffed. At least he had the decency to sound surprised.

Again helpless against her thoughts, her gaze bored laser focused beams through her task as she casually filled her cup, adding the precise measure of sugar and cream to render the color to a sweet, pale beige. No matter how much her legs trembled, she refused to break. *Don't listen to his voice. Think of the last thing he'd said to you.*

"No matter what, I will always be here for you, my love."

What a crock of shit.

The rational part of her mind had given her the strength she needed. Emotions once more in check, she downed half the mug in one swallow before she spun about and pointed her nose back to the dining cabin, her gaze landing anywhere except on Kieran. "Thank you, sir. If you will excuse me, I have duties to attend to."

He opened his mouth, but settled back onto his heels instead, giving her a curt nod. "Perhaps we can talk later."

Vanysha sucked in deep breaths to stay calm. His statement had missed the hallmarks of a friendly request, and she forced a cordial smile to curl her lips.

"Perhaps. Sir." She fought to keep the venom out of her voice. Heaven forbid she forget her manners and not attach the required moniker due his regal position. If he chose to, he could make her current life even more of a living hell than his callous actions had done all those years ago. After all, he was the only son of Politico General Raejil Phaetal. A wave of his hand and her beloved ship would be lost.

Before saying anything else monumentally stupid, Vanysha bowed and headed back toward her cramped nav seat.

"Van, wait," he said, his gloved hand touching her elbow. "You know I didn't have a choice, right?"

"We all have—" The little voice in the back of her head began screaming and she heeded its warning, stopping before she lost her teetering control. Her gaze swung from his fingers to his face, then back to his hold. The polished black leather vanished from her baggy jumpsuit, stealing away its imaginary heat as well. "Of course, sir," she replied. "I believe we are getting close to the boundaries of safe space right now. I have duties requiring my attentions. You might want to return to your seat."

After inclining her head once more, she strode out and ignored any other words behind her.

Why the hell did it have to be him?

Her vision blurred as she stormed back to her confining cocoon. She'd been young, and life had been perfect when they'd met. The connection between them had been instant and stronger than steel. Back then, war and politics hadn't even been blips on their happiness radar. They'd spent hours entangled in each other's arms, living for the moment and never planning beyond their next night. Weeks would pass before she'd even learned his last name, and even that knowledge had done little to cool her affections. She'd naïvely believed he was only distantly related to the ruling family who controlled the fates of all inhabiting the Nexxus.

In hindsight, she should've read the signs. But she'd been young ... *and stupidly thought he loved me as much as I loved him.*

By the time she'd reached her work station, her lungs were burning from her short sprint. Dashing the back of her hand angrily across her watery eyes, she ducked her head and slid into the hollow cubicle. The necessary star maps flared to life before her, and the door was sweet inches away from sealing her in … when it snapped to a halt.

Faze knelt just outside of her space, his fingers acting as a brake while she stared at his forehead creases deep enough to need climbing gear to traverse. "Care to explain what that was all about?"

Pointedly ignoring the concern in his voice, she focused solely on the direct words. She swung her head from side to side, "Nope," then tapped at the visible screens, double checking their current location, and the charted course.

Bright light flooded the dim chamber, Faze sliding the hatch open and obliterating the swirling array of captured star systems. "Huh-uh," he said. "I have never seen you that … that civil with a client before." She glared at the blank screens, counting her heartbeats in the growing silence.

He was right. In fact, she prided herself on her cordiality, ensuring to speak with every passenger. She kept a log of birthdays and special occasions—children and grandchildren's names were recorded in her little book, and she made sure to send along well wishes each year. As a result, many of them referred her transport services to others. She might not have been able to afford lavish advert beacons, but a little kindness cost her nothing and worked far better.

Did she risk tarnishing her reputation over this one thorn?

I think the tarnishing happened long ago.

Vanysha swatted at the voice in her head and searched for a viable explanation that wouldn't reopen old wounds. Bad enough her body had leapt back to the memories of his thorough lovemaking; she dare not let her heart follow down the same dangerous path.

"Burned by the political machine?" he asked.

She swallowed hard, shoving down the pain at her friend's

spot-on description of her past experience. "Yeah. I guess you could say that."

Faze patted her knee, a fatherly smile on his broad face. "Don't let it get you down. Those assholes enjoy making life a chore for the rest of us. Did he have anything to do with getting the green slip for the ship?"

Provided with a perfect cover, Vanysha nodded weakly. For a navigator to request ownership of any vessel, she'd been directed from one paper pushing bureaucrat to the next, losing the better part of a week in the chase. Apparently it was not protocol for the title documents to be in a name other than that of the captain. Didn't matter that she'd done her homework months in advance; she'd scoured every contract ordinance and precept, searching until she'd found the one loophole granting her rights to own a ship. But before she was able to cite the specific edict number, she'd be shuffled off to another haughty bean counter. She was determined, though, and finally, one snooty undersecretary hadn't been quick enough with his dismissal and she pointed out the obscure regulation. Ten minutes later, she'd left Central Administration with the coveted green slip in her hands.

She hated lying to her only friend, but she wasn't ready to face the truth while it still lurked around her ship. "Could you…" She paused. Could he what? Make sure to keep him out of her sight? Pound him into oblivion? Accidentally push him out of the nearest airlock?

The ship rocked violently before she completed her thought, and alarms blared as another jolt shook the hull. Faze crawled out of her lap and scrambled up to the captain's seat. She quickly brought up the nav screens as she snapped into her harness.

"Danton? What the hell was that?"

Her engineer appeared on the comm screen. "You're asking the wrong person. It didn't come from down here." Peering beyond the short Bozzan's bald head, her stomach lurched as Allyn scurried around the giant turbines, frantically putting out a handful of small, smoking fires.

Shit. Not good.

"Don't let my ship explode."

The phrase that had originally become a running joke between her and her prickly engineer now took on a sinister tone. Instead of his standard response of a single-fingered salute, Danton nodded feverishly. "That's the plan."

A trio of bright blips zipped across her external sensors, yanking her attentions away from the vid screen. Perhaps it was the speed of the vessels or the damage from the attack, but their ship's computer wasn't able to tag the fast-moving dots.

"Three ships to the port side. Fighters, judging by their speed. Markings unknown," she called out to Faze, slipping on her comm headset. Granted, she didn't truly care if her current passenger survived this ordeal, but she did have emergency protocols in place. Grumbling half to herself, she linked into the ship's internal system.

"Return to general quarters and prepare for emergency landing procedures."

Decoded: We're about to crash.

A second blast sent the ship into a dizzying spiral, and she braced herself against the low ceiling. When her brain had returned to its upright position, she searched for the attacking ship's comm frequency. "Attention, attention. This is the passenger vessel, *The Royal Janstar*. We are an unarmed civilian transport. We—"

A loud boom echoed through the ship's frame, and her head slammed into the side of her nav pod. Her screens winked out. Bile crept up her gullet as she struggled to focus on the sparking panels before her. Something warm and wet tickled her ear. She reached up, her fingers sliding in the crimson trail, while Faze's voice bled through her foggy mind, his deep baritone bellowing over the piercing klaxons.

"...FIVE. FOUR. THREE. TWO..."

The ship screeched as it collided with something vast and solid.

Suspended weightless for a heartbeat, Vanysha wrapped her fingers around her crash harness and prepared for the worst. Another impact, and darkness swallowed her.

Chapter Six

Loud insects buzzed in the numbing white noise surrounding Kieran. He weakly batted away the swarming annoyances, but knocked his hand into a warped wall. The surprising contact refocused his mind, and memories of recent events jumped into clarity.

He'd remained fixed in the dining hall after Vanysha disappeared. Even in her well-deserved anger, she was more beautiful than he remembered, and she'd managed to reignite his dormant heart. Their years apart had changed the innocent girl into a strong, lean woman. Sadly, the long waves of silver silk he used to wrap around his body were gone, the short, asymmetrical cut now framing her defined cheeks and intoxicating almond eyes of the deepest blue-green. His palms had itched beneath his leather wrappings, the desire to cup her face and kiss those plump pink lips nearly overwhelming.

He'd never meant to fall in love with her; she was supposed to be a temporary distraction before he'd begun his politico-military training. Instead, their fairy-tale romance lasted nearly six months. Half a year, living days of bliss and nights of passion. She was like fire; her radiant energy consuming him whole, and he happily burned. Intelligent and wise beyond her years, Vanysha had often woven dreams of owning a fleet of passenger space liners as she'd curled against his chest.

His body tightened painfully as he shuffled back to his quarters. The last time he'd seen her, she'd slept peacefully in their rented room, the sliver of starlight that slipped in from the high window bathing her bare, sun-kissed skin in an ethereal glow. He'd stared as long as he'd dared to, burning the beautiful image into his mind. Even now, if he closed his eyes, that perfect moment jumped into crystal-clear focus. He reached out and clung to the doorjamb leading to his berth, drawing strength from the solid steel cutting into his encased fingers.

Curse the hateful fates and his duties. Why had life barged in and destroyed his happy world?

A loud boom rang through the ship, the floor falling away beneath his boot heels and only his hold on the wall kept him from landing on his ass. Enough trips through unfriendly space answered his unspoken question. Another blast spun the ship, and he stumbled into his cabin. Vanysha's sensual voice betrayed no fear as she calmly issued the "return to quarters" order. As he fastened the crash harness, his mind harkened back to the hours spent in her loving arms, the keening cries and needy whimpers that would spill from her lips. If he survived this, he swore to use this second chance to right the wrongs of his past.

Right after I throw up.

Muffled voices bled through the cottony filter surrounding his senses. He peeled his eyes open, and when he saw only one solid puddle of vomit on the tiled floor, he lifted his head. The shiny silver steel walls were split and blackened while sparks cracked and popped, flying out from broad gashes in the hull. Fingers dug into his shoulders, attempting to drag him out of his broken seat. Coughing past the dust and smoke, Kieran slapped the harness release before staggering to his feet.

"Found him. And Faze, you owe Van fifty creds."

Kieran didn't recognize the voice, but he noticed the hands didn't help him much after he'd regained his rubbery legs.

"Maybe my luck's changing." Fatigue laced Vanysha's once-sweet tones. Had she been injured in the crash? He took one lurching step forward before he paused, snapping his head around.

"Wait. I need my folio."

Not caring about the exasperated sounds filling the crippled cabin, he picked through the debris until he located the slim leather sleeve, its corners singed and mangled. Tugs on the back of his jacket urged him on. A quick visual check showed no real damage; no pages peeked between any invisible slashes, and the airtight seal was still safely latched. In a moment of panic, he clawed at his chest, but as soon as his palm drove the intact info tube into his sore pecs, he heaved a relieved sigh.

"You wanna stop with the groping and get to the getting? Unless you want to become a permanent fixture, huh?"

Kieran sneered and shifted his gaze over his shoulder toward the rude speaker. "Would you prefer this trip be all for naught?" No head appeared in his vision, and he dropped his chin to spy the dried blood matting the wispy, wheat-blond eyebrows on a surly Bozzan's brutish face. Since he'd never met the man before this moment, he didn't know if that was the dwarf's normal expression or residual damage from their hard landing.

The man scoffed, rolling his beady, chartreuse eyes. "I'd rather be home with my children. Which is where I would have been in the first place, if not for your dumb ass."

"Nothing seems to be burning right now, Danton, but not sure how much longer that's gonna be the case."

"Great. More work. Just what I wanted." Grumbles continued under Danton's breath as the unpleasant man turned around and picked his way toward the bright gap in the hull, where wires and jagged pieces of ceiling created a dangerous obstacle course leading toward the impromptu exit. Carefully minding his footing, Kieran ducked and dodged the crackling cables as he followed his rapidly vanishing guide, getting closer to the glaring outside. He squinted and, lifting his aching arm to shield his face from the orange glow, emerged from the wreckage.

The rust earth beneath his feet bore a new thick black scar reaching far beyond his line of sight, while shards of silver littered the trench and the once-pristine vessel lay in shattered agony. Smoke billowed from the silent engines and between bent panels. Metal, twisted and tangled, had been strewn about like puzzle pieces, yet he wasn't sure if even the goddess could fit the slots and tabs back together again.

Kieran shuffled in a tight circle, surveying the surroundings with grim determination. Desolation met his eye in every direction. Angular summits and crests from distant mountains took uneven bites out of the vast and open sky. Sulfur scented the thin air and, after several deep breaths, he concluded it was more than simply burning debris from the crash. The deep, coppery glow of the peaked suns combined with the barren terrain answered his unvoiced question.

Hexaka. No doubt about it.

Thank the stars for small favors.

He dropped his fleshy visor, massaging out the kinks in his shoulders as a stray thought tapped the inside of his mind. He glanced around, panic-stricken, to locate the rest of the crew, finding instead a curved trail of footsteps that led away from the broken nose of the ship. With a quickening pace, he rounded the wreckage then halted, resting his palm on the cracked fuselage.

Three figures knelt beside a blackened and tattered red cloak, their heads bowed in reverent prayer. Kieran maintained a solemn distance, unwilling to disturb the moment of grief.

Vanysha pulled up the end of the cloak, covering the head of their fallen crew member. Her hand rested on the crimson wrapping, crusted streaks of dried blood painting painful patterns on her slashed sleeve, muddying her bronzed skin.

Kieran closed his eyes and added his whispered wishes for passage for the young boy to have an easier path into the next world.

"So, I guess you made it. Gee, aren't we lucky?"

Lifting his lids, Kieran focused on his former lover, dismissing the venom in her voice, attributing it toward the loss of the young apprentice. "I am sorry for your—"

"Save it, sunshine." She sighed heavily, then shifted her gaze away from the bundled remains to pin Kieran with a gimlet stare. "I only hope your trip is worth all … this." Danton gathered Allyn's body into his arms, then moved toward the small grave a few yards away. Kieran watched the silent funeral procession for a moment longer until another sigh, a pained sigh, caught his attention.

Still on her knees, Vanysha aided the burly captain down. Only then did Kieran realize the extent of the man's injuries. A good portion of the Drekkan's insides were close to spilling out, and a wicked gash nearly split his skull in two. Yet a fierce grin still curled the ends of his scruffy mustache.

"Give him a break. I've had worse than this. Remember that brawl on Starbase K'tal?" Faze coughed and wrapped his arm tighter around his exposed midsection. Kieran stepped closer, fingers gripping the edge of his retrieved case.

Vanysha huffed and sat back on her heels. "You took a shot in the shoulder for being a drunken asshole. This is totally different." She wiped her forehead with the back of her hand before returning to stuff squares of white gauze against the captain's oozing wound.

"I thought your people were healers?" Kieran inquired. Throughout the Nexxus, the intuitive skills of the Drekkan were legendary. Rumors abounded that the females of their race could stop plagues with nothing more than a thought, while the males were better suited toward battle wounds or any injury gained by violence. Yet this man appeared closer to death's door than the promise of another day.

"Why? Did you break a nail?" Vanysha spat over her shoulder, keeping her gaze on her current task.

Faze hissed, pain wrinkling his broad face. "Easy, girl." He shook his head in Kieran's general direction. "Just need to recharge my batteries for a minute."

"Which is why I told you I was fine in the first place, you dimwit." Vanysha swore, her anger less than convincing. Kieran noticed lingering evidence of deep gashes tattering her baggy coveralls, two tears in particular gathering his attention—one streaking across her back from shoulder to hip, and the other nearly splitting the inner seam of her pants in two.

"Are you all right?" In retrospect, Kieran realized it probably wasn't the smartest question to ask. And the incredulous stare from his former lover only solidified his imagined level of stupidity. He steeled his spine, embarrassed and offended, and rose to his full height. With his protective shield of protocol firmly back in place, he turned his attention to the grimacing captain. "I am sorry for the loss of your vessel and of one of your crew, Captain Fazzian. I can assure you, you will be fully compensated and a new vessel will be provided to you upon my return."

The Drekkan opened his mouth, when his golden eyes darted toward his kneeling companion.

"Damn right, you will."

Kieran swiveled his gaze, his jaw unhinging in surprise as Vanysha took to her feet, dusting off her ass before marching straight into his space. The crown of her head almost reached his shoulders, but that didn't stop her from glowering at him. "And a new ship is just for starters."

He sputtered, helpless to form coherent sentences as his mind spun. Of course—it was hers. She'd always dreamed of a ship of her own. They had spent long hours discussing every detail, even down to the vessel's name. His stomach dropped as the long-hidden memory jumped to life.

"The Royal Janstar?" He chuckled, licking a tempting bead of sweat trailing down the curve of her lower back. The salty drip did nothing to slake his hunger for her. After kissing his way up her spine, he rolled her over to gaze onto her flushed cheeks. "Where did you come up with that name?"

Vanysha smiled impishly, wiggling her hips as she positioned herself willingly beneath his weight. "Did you already forget the restaurant where we had our first meal together?"

His deep growl blended with her airy sigh as her body welcomed him inside once more. He threaded his fingers through the blanket of thick, silver white curls and buried his nose into the hollow of her neck, slipping deeper into her loving grip. "Restaurant? I would hardly consider that corner cafe worthy of such a noble title."

She arched her back, her taut nipples scraping against his bare chest. The sound of her throaty laughter drove him wild, and he quickened his strokes. "I still like how it rolls off the tongue."

Answering her suggestion, he dragged his tongue along her jaw, nipping her delicate earlobe. "And I love how you roll off my tongue, la'nen."

He had always called her "kitten," but the woman standing before him now was neither meek nor playful. She'd grown into her claws, and he pitied anyone foolish enough to cross her. If he hadn't left, would things have been different? He gathered his composure, shoving the past back into its box. "I promise—"

Her fierce glare froze the words before they fell. "Don't," she said. "Been down that road before." Then she sidestepped him to limp up the sandy knoll, her aqua eyes focusing on something in the distant emptiness. "Well, congratu-fucking-lations. We made it to Hexaka." She glared daggers over her shoulder. "Even when shit goes south, I keep my word."

Chapter Seven

Vanysha shook her head and went back to staring at the vast nothingness. She'd heard rumors of the desolate wastes that covered most of the Hexakan surface, the planet's close proximity to the Nexxan twin suns burning away any vegetation, but never in a million years did she think she'd find out the truth with her own eyes. Jagged, narrow towers of maroon rock poked out of the sandy landscape, dotting the barren ground with haphazard shadows.

The entire landing was a fog after the side of her head had slammed into the pod's frame. Not until Faze had dragged her out of the smoldering ship did the true gravity of their predicament become revealed, and all she could do was sit and stare as her dream lay in pieces on the hostile land. She sucked in a stuttering breath, the slight action sending a sharp twinge across her shoulder blades, and a surprised gasp snuck out as pain shot down her back and across the top of her thigh, catching her off guard.

"Stay with me, Van. Vanysha?"

She blinked the unshed tears from her burning eyes to focus on the bushy face before her. "Yeah, Faze. I'm here. I'm fine."

"No, you're bloody well not." His words slurred in her brain, and her eyebrows tugged together. "Just keep your happy ass where it is. I'm almost done."

Her frown was giving her a headache, or maybe it was from the massive amount of red she spied coating her overalls. She struggled to sit up, but a steady hand pressed against her shoulder kept her firmly in place.

"I said I was fine."

Or at least, that's what she thought she'd said. The droll stare from her mentor sent a much different message. The ache along her back and leg diminished, receding into a far corner, and she craned her neck to sneak a peek at Faze. He slumped into her field of vision, his heavy weight nearly pinning her to the dusty ground. She scrambled out of the way, muscles burning with the motion, and quick reflexes caught him before he completely dropped into her lap.

"All right, that's enough hero shit from you today." She scooted back and eased him to the ground. "What's the count?"

Faze sighed, shook his head sadly, then tipped his chin toward the bundle of red robes off to her left. "Not good."

No. She crawled over to the still figure, but a hand on her arm stopped her from revealing the extent of the young man's injuries. When she and Faze had found Allyn at the slavers' bazaar, her heart had nearly broken. She remembered what it was like to be thrown away like garbage, disowned and discarded for something beyond her control. The crimson cloak of the Unsought had hung on her body, and the weight of the painful betrayal had nearly destroyed her soul. If not for Faze's kindness, the meat grinder of the slavers' guild would have spat her out years ago. She'd been able to put the terrifying stigma behind her, but the horrors she'd endured haunted her to this day.

"Don't know just yet about our passenger," he added, but she was lost in her memories.

"I'm so sorry, Allyn," she choked out, meaningless words that slipped past the lump in her throat. If she had just approached the scene, she would have assumed he was sleeping, only … the lack of movement belied this. She'd vowed to keep him safe. Vanysha's shoulders slumped at her mounting failings.

"Hey, I know that look," Faze barked out, jarring her from her dismal thoughts. "You offered him a better life than his own family. He knew the risks staying with us, and he never balked. Don't you dare dishonor his memory with unnecessary guilt."

"What bunk did our passenger have?" Danton's perturbed voice crackled in, returning Vanysha to their present plight. She dashed her hand across her watery eyes, then glanced over at Faze. She hadn't assigned his seat, so she honestly didn't know. The verdict was still out on whether or not she cared if the asshole walked away unscathed, but she did have a reputation to uphold.

Faze frowned, apparently searching his mind for the number. "Uh … I think he's in Delta Three."

She relayed the message to Danton over her throat mic, adding with a scoff. "Bet he's lost his lunch by now."

Both men chuckled, amused by her crabby response. "He seems like a tough cookie," Faze said. "One of those highly trained military types."

Pure control stopped her lips from curling into an unbecoming sneer. "You read too much into his slick uniform," she replied, touching the talk button again. "Fifty creds says he's yakked on his shoes."

Her friend's laughter morphed into a pained whimper, and she turned her attentions to his wounds. "You're on," he said.

"But no matter who wins, you're gonna tell me why you've got it in for the guy."

She ignored his request and tore off a corner of her tattered undershirt. The cleanest bit she could find was pretty small, but she had to stop Faze's bleeding. Or at least hold it back until he could heal himself.

"Van?"

She hummed while she dug out the med kit from the salvaged supplies, but refused to lock eyes with Faze. His sizable mitt covered both of her hands, stilling her fidgeting fingers.

"This is way more than some bureaucrat who wasted your time. Vanysha, talk to me." His compassionate tone was a balm to her jangled nerves. Unsure how much time they'd have before another interruption, she gave him an abbreviated version of her shattered heart.

"He's part of a past I'd rather forget." Her gaze remained riveted on her task. If she made eye contact with her dear friend, she was sunk.

"Found him. And you owe Van fifty creds."

Danton's timing could not have been better. Hearing her former lover had lost his dignity during their hard landing brightened her day just a fraction. So much had already been lost, and she was willing to take the little joys where she could. She pressed the button on her throat mic. "Maybe my luck is changing."

"Well, hell's bells," Faze grumbled half-heartedly. "Figured he'd have more of a spine than that." He hissed sharply, grabbing on to her wrist as she applied pressure to his chest. "Easy, easy. At this rate, you're gonna shove that cloth straight through me."

"Sorry." She wrapped a binding bandage around his barrel chest, then shifted her gaze to their fallen crew member as wisps of smoke filtered through the stifling air. The acrid smell of burning wires clung to her clothes; tricky to tell if the stench was new or lingering. Better safe than sorry. She hit the talk button on her mic with a final warning. "Nothing seems to be burning right now, Danton, but not sure how much longer that's gonna be the case."

One problem solved, she peered down at her burly friend. "You okay to sit up?" she asked. Knowing Danton as she did, he'd be arriving in a second or two and would demand proper rights for his young apprentice. Faze nodded. A thin sheen of sweat dotted his brow, but together, they eased him into a semi-seated position. Sure enough, her engineer's gruff grumbling gained volume at her back as soon as the heavy lifting was finished. Vanysha huffed out a tired breath and, resting on her heels, waited for Danton to join them.

The Bozzan engineer knelt beside Allyn's still form and Faze began the benediction, murmuring in soothing whispers. As the prayer continued, she dropped her head. Her gut had told her this trip was going to be bad, and she hadn't listened. Now, her ship was destroyed, scattered across the surface of an extremely unfriendly planet, and she'd broken her promise to a kind boy.

Allyn had never once shirked any of his duties, no matter the nature of them. Working in such close proximity with Danton, the boy had had either the patience of a saint or he'd known the Bozzan's acerbic nature had never been directed toward him. Recently, she'd caught a timid smile or two from the shy boy. Even in death, an eerily calm expression cradled his face, an all-encompassing peace only visible from the grave.

Silence signaled the end of the somber ceremony, and Vanysha took to her feet. Her muscles cried out, but she needed the distraction. The charred rubble of her dreams still smoldered, smoky tendrils vanishing into the thin, bitter air. She limped up the slight berm, having turned away from the heart-breaking losses, to eye the harsh horizon.

Footfalls at her back dragged her out of her dark thoughts, and judging by the space between each loping stride, Kieran was uninjured. At this, a tiny part of her was disappointed. *But the day's still young.* Or it could be nearly moonrise. Confused, angry, and aching, Vanysha clenched her jaw to keep her tongue in check.

His presence reached across the distance between them and brushed against her exposed skin. Her treacherous body was on a different wavelength than her broken heart; it yearned for his touch, urging her to lean back against his firm chest. Six years had changed him. He'd finally grown into his height, filling out the slick uniform, while leaving some details to her overactive imagination. Time had altered her as well, only not in the same fashion. Something inside of her had died and she had no wish to resurrect it. Steeling her spirit, she broke her internal deadlock and moved a step away from him.

"What do you want?" she said, telling herself she sounded tired and aggravated, not timid and fragile. Ensuring her defenses were strongly in place, she turned to face him and silently thanked the barren landscape for the slight incline. At least now she didn't have to crane her neck to glare at him, plus she had the added bonus of the sun at her back. In the glaring rays, she spied a fine trail of red sourced somewhere in the neighborhood of his left temple, and a small bruise painted his square jaw. His stern countenance softened as they locked eyes.

That good, huh? She must look a fright to get such a dramatic shift from Mr. Sour Puss.

"Van, I'm—"

"You already said that. Still don't care." She leaned into her good leg and folded her arms across her chest in lieu of wrapping them around his throat. "I'm assuming you have something of note to say."

His smoky quartz eyes narrowed, hardening under the sudden frost, and the company man stood before her once again. "I have urgent business in Cam'Rhan and need transport there."

She barked out a sharp, mirthless laugh. "Well, of course, your high-and-mightiness. I'll get right on it. How about I pull another ship out of my ass for you? Or better yet, I can call you a turbo coach. Oh, wait! On what? The friggin' comm system is in about twenty billion pieces. Sir."

Air burned her nostrils as she sucked in gulp after gulp, and her tirade did little to improve her mood. If anything, her head throbbed more now after she'd bitched him out than it had at the start.

One corner of his kissable mouth curled up into a cruel sneer. "Your vessel is equipped with the required number of oxygen rebreathers, is it not?"

She gawked at his condescending tone. "Sure, sweetie." She poked her thumb toward the smoking husk. "They're right inside, just beneath the extra transport."

A tic started in the center of the purple ring on his jaw, and he dared one step closer. "Well, perhaps if you'd been more concerned with steering that bucket of bolts, then we—"

"Bucket of bolts! Who the hell do you think you—"

"BOTH OF YOU! STOP!"

Faze's booming voice yanked her from her current course of action and she froze. Blinking, she rounded her gaze back to Kieran. Her arm trembled, caught in the fierce grip of his gloved fingers, her hand a breath away from connecting with Kieran's cheek. Shocked by her own uncharacteristically violent response, she stared into the face of the man she once loved, and something sad flashed within his charcoal gray eyes, before quickly vanishing.

With a swift twist of her wrist, she freed herself to escape from the confusing wave of emotions. She favored her right leg, a sharp twinge present from the still-knitting muscles, and she managed only a couple of steps before stopping.

Faze cringed under the effort of his shout, panting as he sat on the sandy ground. "If you two are done swinging dicks," he said, "I thought I saw a major settlement, before we lost all control, somewhere tucked in those mountains. Don't know if it's the place you're looking for, but if not, you should be able to get transport to where you need to be. It appears to be a day's walk to our south." He pinned Vanysha with a perturbed glare. "Possibly less, if you'd both stop screaming at each other and get your asses going."

Vanysha knelt beside her friend, shaking her head as she gave his wounds a second look. "Uh-uh. I'm not leaving you here alone."

Her captain patted her hands with a chuckle. "I'm not completely alone. Granted, having Danton as company is almost the same as solitary confinement."

"I heard that," Danton's voice echoed from deep inside the smoldering hull. The hammering and swearing returned, and Vanysha swiveled her gaze back to her pilot.

"We'll be fine until you get back with some help." He tipped his chin in the direction of the cockpit and smiled weakly. "You know where the rations are. Just leave a couple for us. Make sure you grab water, too, and…"

<Van, do not leave without arming yourself. This is dangerous territory, and I trust you with a gun more than I do him.>

Vanysha nodded, responding to the laundry list of verbal directions. Dual conversations between her and Faze were now the norm, though she still recalled the splitting headache the first time he'd given her two sets of conflicting directions. Months later, and after much practice, she was able to both continue with her physical tasks and follow his voice in her head. His verbal explanations were polite and expected, while his internal monologues leaned more toward the brutal, uncensored truth.

When calm had surrounded her without and within, she took to her feet, the ache across her back and down her right leg returning, but she shrugged it off. Faze had done all he could to heal her injuries, enough to get her from Point A to Point B, hopefully before this hellhole swallowed the survivors for lunch. Bottom line: his skills could only do so much, especially when he, too, was already wounded. Pain, she knew well. She would be remiss to call it a friend, but it was definitely one of her regular traveling companions.

Leaning on her strong left leg, Vanysha hoisted herself into the exposed cockpit. Blood stained the silver walls, painting rusty streaks along the floor. She clenched her teeth, ignoring the lingering gore and gathered the necessary supplies. Above her, a cracked blue-and-white sign clung to the area beside the broken comm unit: *The Royal Janstar. Commissioned 463.94.02 to Navigator Class Prime Vanysha Kureen.*

She had squealed in delight when she'd first opened that parcel, dancing and bouncing around the hangar bay like a child with a new toy, weeping tears of joy as she'd hugged the metal plaque to her chest. Hers. All those years of fighting and she had finally proved them all wrong.

Now, she brushed her fingers across the raised letters, letting the memories wash over her before she carefully pried the proof of her accomplishment off the wall and tucked it into her go-bag.

"Can I carry something for you?"

She swallowed hard, choking down the bitter sting of loss. Kieran's voice had sounded almost concerned, and that was the last thing she wanted. Maintaining a professional distance was a must for the sake of her sanity. She slung her personal pack across her back, balancing the second bag under her chin. She shook her head. "Nah. S'all good."

An exasperated sigh from behind her made her bristle. "You're injured, and if you lug all the bags around, it'll only slow us down."

Now there's the asshole I was looking for. Vanysha ground her teeth. "And heaven forbid anything slow down your precious trip." She spun around and shoved the overstuffed duffle bag into Kieran's chest. "Sir."

Then she shouldered past him, ignoring his sputtering responses. Ire set her legs on their course, and she slipped the small blaster into the front pocket of her coveralls before stopping beside Faze. His paling cheek was only a shade off from his gray jumpsuit, and panic quickened her heart. She knelt to rest her palm gently on his arm. Black eyelashes fluttered up as a weak grin cut across his face. He captured her hand, enveloping her slender fingers with both of his meaty mitts.

"Don't look so scared. Just go. The sooner you start…"

"The sooner you're done," she said, smiling feebly, finishing their standard goodbye. "Yeah, yeah. No dying on me until I get back." She started to rise, but Faze held on to her arm. Her brows knit together, confused by his odd reaction, and a heartbeat passed before Faze pinned her with an impish stare. An edge of uncertainty flowed through her veins as her friend and mentor pressed their clasped hands to his forehead, then placed an uncharacteristically passionate kiss onto the center of her hand. She heaved a long sigh, rolling her eyes at his sick sense of humor.

"Issues, Faze," she muttered for his ears only. "You've got serious issues." She slid her hand free, resisting the urge to wipe her palm across her tattered coveralls. Kieran's title did include the word "ambassador," and Vanysha wondered exactly how much cultural knowledge her former lover had filed away in his memory banks. This could be a dangerous game Faze had started, but she wasn't about to blow the joke just yet.

Abject shock and grief flashed across Kieran's perfect puss, and she smirked. *If only I had a vid camera.* Apparently the barb had stricken true; she swore to carry that image like a treasured souvenir for the rest of the trip. She hurried her steps, lest she laugh her ass off and ruin things. Safely beyond the frozen statue, she called out over her shoulder, "You coming or what?"

<h1 style="text-align:center">Chapter Eight</h1>

Kieran blinked to banish the scene he'd witnessed, yet the damage had been done. Jaw hanging agape, he stared at the giant who now held his lover's heart, the tender pledge not lost on him. Being the best diplomat meant knowing protocols and reverent gestures from every planet in the Nexxus; nothing was worse than extending a hand to a Bozzan, who found the insult unforgivable, while the jovial hosts of Westran Alpha would not talk business until the third course of any meal had been served.

He held tight to one tiny kernel of hope, though: she hadn't responded with the appropriate reciprocation. An admonishing smirk had curved her kissable lips, but she hadn't repeated the loving promise. Perhaps it was his presence that had halted her, or maybe she had yet to accept him as her mate. Without her consent, the captain's affections would be in vain. Ancient history from a distant world had called it chivalry—tales filled with brave men and beautiful women unable to display their passions to the world; pages of unrequited, one-sided love in which both parties usually ended up dead or brokenhearted. Jealousy coiled deep in his gut, its cold burn souring each inhale of acrid air.

Not if I have something to say about it.

He shook his head, jostling his brain to regain his professional composure, then tossed the heavy duffle over his shoulder. With an envious grumble, he frowned and spun on his heels to catch up with Vanysha. The fiercely possessive response had stunned him. After all, he'd been the one who'd done the leaving all those years ago. He followed her in silence, watching the hypnotic sway of her narrow hips as his mind strolled down memory lane.

Having sworn not to become his father, Kieran had dropped out of his strict diplomatic training regimen after two harsh years. He had no patience for the minutia needed to see an opponent's argument. If his point was valid, enough said. Why should he concern himself with someone who didn't see the truth in his side …?

Lost in thought, he nearly bowled over the quiet person heading in the other direction, and he opened his mouth, prepared to chastise the ingrate for not paying attention, but no sound came out. He gaped, entranced, at the slender female, waves of silver-white hair brushing the floor as she knelt to pick up her scattered items. Tanned limbs moved with a dancer's grace, her arms bare, her wrists adorned with brightly colored bangles. A creamy white blouse had slipped off of one shoulder, while her earth-toned broomstick skirt hid her from the waist down. But he was already starstruck.

"I'm so sorry. I should've been watching where I was going." Her soft voice soothed his soul like a balm, made him yearn for something unknown and terrifying. He dropped beside her and added his hands to her task.

"Please, the fault was mine."

Were those his words?

In his grab for an escaping can of soup, he brushed her hand. Their fingers entwined and she raised her head. His heart skipped a beat. Eyes the color of Westran Alpha's deep blue-green seas, spaced perfectly to either side of a pert nose, blinked up at him, while high cheekbones and a pair of full pink lips completed the delicate palette on her sun-kissed bronze face. Her long feathery lashes fluttered down, and a shy smile touched her kissable mouth.

"Uhhh ... hi," he stammered, her unexpected beauty stealing away any witty conversation. Or, it could have been the blood deserting his brain, racing at breakneck speeds toward the growing bulge in his slacks. He wasn't a blushing virgin, and several of his past partners were considered by most to be the pinnacle of sophistication. Yet something about this delicate stranger touched him on a deeper level as he gazed at her authentic, unadorned visage.

But when she laughed ... he was lost. Rich and smooth like strong whiskey, it rolled off of her tongue, and he wanted to wrap himself forever in the melodious sound....

Even now, years after their initial meeting, he would dust off the memory to assuage him in times of doubt and sorrow. She'd been the best part of his soul, and he'd often wondered where life had taken her after his hasty departure.

"If you don't mind, I'd like to hurry up and finish this trek before nightfall. Sir."

Jerked out of his daydream, Kieran lifted his gaze from the sands beneath his feet and leveled his eyes at her. One hand rested on her narrow hips and sweat trailed down her neck. He shouldn't have been thinking of where those lucky drops were headed, but his body knew that path all too well. He returned his study to her face.

He missed her smile. Her eyes were still the same teal blue, but their mirthful glow was sadly gone. Ghosts now haunted their intoxicating depths, and guilt tapped him on the shoulder. He knew in his gut he was responsible for those shadows and a lame "I'm sorry" would not fix the rift.

"I apologize." He tipped his chin and picked up his pace. "And you can drop all the formality. I promise I won't report you."

She scoffed, one corner of her sultry lips curling up into an unladylike sneer. "Yeah, right," she muttered, then turned her back on him. Her lean legs trudged up the steep dune, and he bit down hard on his molars to cool the fires stoking his blood. Already she set a mean pace, yet whenever he caught up to her, she seemed to discover a hidden burst of speed. She also never walked directly in front of him; instead, she zigged for each of his zags, keeping him just off of her left shoulder. Their time apart had changed her, but to what degree, he feared to know the truth.

"You cut your hair," he said, then cringed inwardly at his clumsy attempt to engage her in conversation. Her pack bounced as her shoulders dropped, but she didn't slow.

"Yeah, well, that's what happens when water becomes too expensive."

He'd strained forward to hear her words, her face pointing toward their current path. Her tone had closed the door on that topic, and silence followed them to the top of the grade.

There, desolation greeted them in all directions, and he gulped down dusty mouthfuls of thin air. He wiped away the sticky damp from his forehead using the back of his glove as a makeshift rag. Shielding his eyes from the blinding suns, he scanned the distant horizon, squinting at the jagged peaks miles away. How were they going to find shelter in this vast nothingness?

Opting for a neutral, and much less satisfactory topic, he gestured toward the far mountains. "Is the city there?" he asked. His stomach clenched as he did some unsuccessful mental math. *Half a day? Day and a half, more like it.* No. Those hills were in no way less than a two-day trek. And considering the chilly company … it would be a very long two days.

Chapter Nine

"Is it done?"

"To our knowledge, the ship never docked at Cam'Rhan."

"This is … wait. What do you mean *to your knowledge?*"

"Our sources at the landing docks have not reported their arrival, and given the time it would have taken for the trip from Central, they should have arrived hours ago."

"But that does not guarantee the ship was destroyed."

"The attack was successful."

"Send out our friends. Tell them to scour the planet. If they somehow made it there, there is still a chance we could fail."

"Understood. Do you wish for any proof of the kill?"

"Yes. Bring me Phaetal's head on a platter."

Chapter Ten

Vanysha split her intent stare between her scanner and the faraway mountains. If Faze's directions were correct, the settlement should be at the leading edge of the peaks. *Damn.* The pace needed to make it by dark would be grueling, to say the least. Already her lungs burned with each shallow inhale and dread followed every exhale, and the throb in her leg was getting harder and harder to ignore.

An extended arm painted a cooling shadow over her shoulder, and she glanced away from the tiny screen. The scent of his cologne tickled her senses, sparking fires she struggled to smother. Steeling herself, she pushed his arm away from her face to aim him in a more correct trajectory.

"Close enough," she quipped. Her fingers had tingled at the brief contact, even though her palm had only touched his jacket. The muscle beneath the cloth was strong, and her body hungered for more.

Water. She needed to douse these flames, if only in theory.

She leaned down to rummage through the pack at her feet

and force of habit had her counting the packaged meals and water supply before she drew out two canteens. If they pushed hard, they could make the settlement on the other side of the hills before they used up their meager provisions. She kept her attention focused on the distance, refusing to glance over her shoulder as she passed the container back to him and regained her feet. "We've got the coordinates," she said, the canteen vanishing from her grip. "Let's get going."

"But shouldn't we…"

His pause halted her forward movement and she choked down the mouthful of water, sputtering as her eyebrows tugged together, then tossed a look behind her. Across his rugged face danced a curious expression before slipping beneath a veil of aloof bureaucracy. She blinked slowly, hoping he would finish his train of thought.

"Yes?" she baited, seeing if he'd bite. "Shouldn't we what?" He narrowed his eyes and clenched his jaw. Her brain warned caution, but her mouth wasn't interested. "Wait 'til the sun goes down? Seek some shelter from the heat?" she said. "In case you hadn't noticed, we're kinda stuck in the middle of a whole lot of nothing." She guided his eye toward the endless seas of burnt orange ground. "If you'd done any research at all on your destination, you'd know the twin suns on Hexaka make each day around thirty-eight hours long, with temperatures reaching upwards of three hundred twenty-five Kelvin during the solar peaks. Which means, sweet cheeks, depending on what time we crashed, we could be in for a long wait." She spun back around and tromped off toward the hills. "So unless you want to work on your tan, you'd better start walking."

"I will have you know…" he huffed out behind her, his long legs sadly catching him up with her much more quickly than she'd anticipated. Ugh. How could she forget how strong his body was? She hiked her pack higher onto her shoulder, jolting herself out of her remembered fantasies as he went on. "I have been spending the past two months intensely studying the customs of the Hexaks, and I have … tons of information on our hosts. Language, formal and informal greetings—"

She scoffed, digging into her bag for something to cover her head. "Great," she said. "So when they find our desiccated corpses, you'll be able to say 'Hi.'" Her fingers found the silk scarf buried beneath the ration packs. She yanked it out and, grumbling as she plodded on, sacrificed a short pour from her canteen, dampening the slick material. She focused on draping the wet wrap, pointedly ignoring her prickly companion's sputtering.

Just plain prick is more like it. She grinned privately, amused by her own wit as she set her attention back to the long trek ahead. Before long, a copse of spindly trees crept into view, and she sent up a quick prayer for some shady leaves on the blurry branches. Sands slipped under her feet while she sorted through twisted emotions.

Why did he have to come back into her life after six long years?

And looking even more handsome than I remember.

She hadn't dusted off her memories during the daylight hours, but he haunted her dreams for more nights than she cared to admit. For far too many mornings, she'd awoken to a tear-dampened pillow, her body still longing for his touch. Even the degradations she'd faced had vanished from her mind, while snapshots of simple moments of joy gazing into his smoky gray eyes had refused to fade. She'd experienced heaven in his arms, and nothing could replace that. While she struggled to hold on to her righteous anger, a frightened part of her wanted nothing more than to throw herself at his feet, begging for his forgiveness.

Her father had drilled it into her head that she must have done something horrifically wrong to lose such a catch as the son of the Politico General.

With each footfall, those hateful words swirled in her head: *"What did you do? Did you not fuck him good enough? Were you that crappy of a lay, he bolted from your bed without a word? He was our ticket out of this shithole and you blew it."* Gritting her teeth to drive away the demons, she held firm. No. She'd done everything right. Why would she need to apologize? If she wasn't what he wanted, then that was on him.

"I'm glad you found someone to make you happy."

She faltered, unsure if she had imagined his voice. "What?" she said, daring a glance over her shoulder, brows tugging together to hide her ire. His gaze studied the uneven terrain at his feet, carefully picking out the safest path. His once pristine black military suit glittered with a fine coating of bronze silt that gave him an almost angelic halo. Her body warmed, while her heart iced over.

"You and your captain. How long have you two been … together?" His deep voice had cracked as if he'd choked on the last word, and she swallowed hard past the lump in her throat to force down her turbulent emotions. Her knees locked, surprise halting her forward momentum.

The sudden stop had turned her into a tripping hazard, though, and he careened into her. She shoved him back, staggering away from his familiar embrace.

"Really? That's what's been eating at you?" She tossed her arms skyward, chuckling darkly. "Stuck in the middle of a friggin' desert on the most hostile planet in the entire system, and you want to know about my personal life?"

His black eyebrows drew into a thick line above his stormy eyes. "Am I not allowed to inquire about——"

"No," she said. "You're not." She met his glare with one of her own. "You walked out of my life, without a damned word. You left me to… You don't get to judge how I live now. I can't believe—"

He covered her mouth with his massive hand, then shot his gaze off into the distance. Panic slammed into her hard, and on instinct, she wrapped her fingers around his wrist, muscles trembling as she yanked away his hand, the message to remain silent received. A surprised frown pulled his brows together for a moment and his breath fanned her hair as he returned to scan the skies, his smoky eyes intent in their search. She strained her ears, craned her neck to detect whatever had spooked him.

At first, only their staggered inhales and exhales broke the eerie stillness.

There.

Off to her left, rapid footfalls pounded at the hard-packed ground. Her gaze darted toward the approaching foe. "Jakkavani. Probably here smuggling out sand to make their crappy imitation steeleglass." His voice had poured the whispered words into her ear and as her heart kicked into gear. She fought to convince herself it was due to their impending fight, merely her body preparing for a looming battle. She wasn't turned on being in his arms again.

He shifted his stormy gaze down, and their eyes locked. "Please tell me you have weapons in that magic bag of yours."

What a time for her dormant emotions to decide to wake up.

Chapter Eleven

Kieran stared into the unfathomable pools of clearest aqua, uncertain if fear or anger made their colors spark. He remembered spending hours simply gazing at her, lost in her unique beauty, wondering how he'd managed to get so lucky. Now, with her close enough to touch, he contemplated the universe's dark and wicked sense of humor. Obviously she'd moved on. But she was right; he had no place to pass judgement on her decision to shack up with her own ship's captain. Perhaps that was how he'd earned the job.

His mind continued to fire, each new path churning tendrils of jealousy into writhing snakes in his gut. His body had much different designs, though, wishing to strip her bare and rediscover every inch of her delicate skin.

Too bad life had interfered with another, more sinister matter.

"Let's hope it doesn't need to come to violence," Vanysha said, and she sidled away from him. With her eyes aimed on the horizon, she took off toward the closest rocky outcropping. "We don't have much of value to them, so we should be relatively safe. Come on, sunshine. Unless you want to find out just how desperate those assholes really are."

Her tempting backside swayed as she jogged unevenly away from him, her wobbling gate kicking his own legs into gear. He caught up to her easily and grabbed for the heavy duffle strapped to her narrow back.

"Give that to me. You're injured."

She shrugged her pack out of his hold, continuing her break-neck pace. "Oh, trust me. I've learned how to make my way through tougher times than this in the past six years. I've got it."

Damned stubborn female. Kieran gritted his teeth and gave chase. They trudged along, the only sounds from their footfalls sliding against the shifting sands. In her defense, she did seem strangely accustomed to the relentless climb; not once did she look over her shoulder to see if he was keeping up, nor did her steps falter. She'd grown into a strong woman, and he hated himself for knowing he'd been the cause of it. Was the idealistic dreamer with the disarming smile still inside of her?

He panted hard, dragging in rough breaths while his thighs burned. No sounds of pursuit followed them, yet his companion did not seem ready to slow down. His energy depleted, he did stop, his head hung heavy off his neck as he propped his locked arms onto his knees. "I think we lost them."

The blast blew over his shoulder, sending up a jet of dust a few feet from his nose, clouding his vision. He fanned his hands in front of his face as Vanysha whipped around him and leveled a small blaster, firing a short volley with dangerous accuracy. His jaw hung agape as he pondered the events. She was saving him? His male ego sputtered and fumed, demanding he take charge. Yet as he reached toward her, aiming to pull her behind the safety of his body, she nimbly ducked beneath his outstretched arm.

"Famous last words," she quipped, deftly slipping out the empty clip and slamming in a full charge. "Any other great ideas?" Her gaze focused on their rear, and he turned to add his eyes to the search. The sun shimmered against the burnt orange landscape and he squinted in hopes of cutting down the glare.

A flicker of movement caught his eye. A helmeted head quickly vanished behind a small, jutting pile of boulders. Like the ground dwelling weasels on Bayan, three other dingy yellow targets poked around the rocky barricade before disappearing again.

"Do we want to kill them, hurt them, or just scare them?" he asked.

He shrugged off the heavy bag from his back, grumbling as he tossed his jacket over the top. Breath tickled his nose as he began his own centering ritual, removing his gloves with determined tugs on each fingertip. If only he didn't have to share his vile skill with her this way and in this matter, but time was of the essence. No answer was forthcoming, so he glanced over his shoulder. A confused furrow cut across her forehead, her aquamarine eyes narrowed. If she was concerned now, he could only imagine the horrors that would fill her mind after.

"Just tell me, Van," he barked, and she shrunk back a fraction, blinking rapidly.

"Just scare them," she replied.

He huffed out a relieved breath and turned back to the target. Rubbing his hands together in slow circles, he prepped his talent. He scoffed. *Talent.* He'd first heard the term from his father not long after his return. His "birthright," the man had called it, one that hadn't appeared in generations. Curse was more like it; an ugly curse that had caused him to remain gloved at all times and in nearly every situation. No one could have prepared him for the weeks spent struggling first to hide the strange new ability, much less the growing months afterward to master some semblance of control over it.

Anger had done little to help channel his freakish new reality, but ignoring it didn't make it vanish either. Squashing it away like a skeleton in the cupboard had proven to be the path of least resistance over the past few years. Rather than dwelling on it, he'd spent his mental energies concentrating on more productive matters, such as learning to become Central's most successful negotiator. Not once had he relied on anything except his wits; his power was a secret he kept from all parties.

Until now.

Give it up, he mused. *She already hates you. Might as well seal the deal.*

The tingling started in the center of his palm, heat and cold intertwining and radiating out to his fingertips. His eyelids slipped shut and he silently prayed she wouldn't despise him more than she already did.

Another blast off to his right snapped him back to the moment and he opened his eyes. Focusing on his target, he flicked his wrists and splayed his palms out toward the rocky cluster. A second later, the grouping flew apart, bits of metal and clumps of hardpacked sand raining back down. Shrieks and howls melted into the distance as their attackers retreated back into the safety of the deep desert. Kieran knelt down to retrieve his discarded gloves, carefully avoiding his silent companion.

The weight of her stare shadowed his every move, but he was not ready to face her yet. His memory had conjured up images of her bright smile and laughing eyes. Warm embraces and hotter nights had become armor to him, preparing him for her certain disgust. After one final tug on the hem of the leather wraps, his dignity safely buried beneath layers of self-hatred, he raised his proud chin.

"Well, that's new."

Her voice had held none of the expected emotional responses, and he dragged his gaze up to hers. She'd sunk her weight into her right hip, inquisitive teal eyes regarding him coolly from beneath an arched brow. He held his aloof demeanor in place and donned his coat.

"Nice to know I can still surprise you."

Immediately, he regretted his bitter retort. *Better to just let it end.* He'd destroyed any chance for happiness with Vanysha the moment he'd walked out those doors all those years ago.

Then why did he want nothing more than to pull her into his arms and kiss her with every fiber of his being?

Another silent moment passed before she broke the spell. "The fact you didn't vanish when shit got real just now was enough of a surprise," she said. Without skipping a beat, she slung her heavy pack across her shoulder and returned to their path. Her leg buckled after two steps, and he dashed in to catch her before she hit the ground.

"Dammit, Van. Stop being so stubborn and let me help you." He was certain his growled response had come across as angry, when the truth was much more demanding. From the instant his hands had gripped her waist to steady her, he was immediately thrust back into the pleasurable past. The longer he was forced to hold his growing desire at bay, the more his shrinking slacks threatened to unman him. He clamped down hard on his teeth, fighting the urge to bury his nose into her silver blonde hair. He missed the beckoning waves of captured starlight made real that cascaded down her back and nearly touched the floor. He loved the hours spent combing his fingers through it, savoring the silken texture as it slipped across his palms.

Her frantic squirms to escape his hold confused him, even as it fueled the raging inferno in his blood. "Let go of me—let go!

Don't touch me," she spat out the panic-filled plea, yet before he could respond, the heel of her boot landed hard on the top of his foot. With a yelp, he released her, hopping away, and when she snapped her gaze back to him, her eyes gleamed with a tangle of deep and dangerous emotions.

"No. You don't get to just swoop back into my life and try to play hero now. I…" Her jaw quivered, yet she uttered no more sounds. Terror-driven shadows haunted her aqua pools and his heart ached.

By the gods, what had happened to her after he left?

Chapter Twelve

Vanysha wanted to hate him, more than she wanted her next breath, or even a transport. She needed to hold on to her rage, to use the degradation she suffered after he'd disappeared as a shield, and the despair she'd faced from that morning on as armor. He'd walked out without any warning, leaving her to face the wolves alone. She had learned to survive without a soul, had forced her heart to beat anew with each passing day. Had he even looked for her after sneaking out the door? Did he know the horrors she suffered?

Moreover, did he even care?

"La'nen, you own my heart, and no one will ever take it away from you."

The longer she stared at Kieran, the more his old words surged up from her buried memories, until anger and pain had melded into a toxic and bitter pill that soured her stomach. She was tired of swallowing her pride, and right now, she was ready to explode.

"Help? Now you want to help?" The floodgates opened, and

she was helpless against the rush of emotions. Shrugging off the bulky pack, she shoved it into his general direction, hoping the surprise action would knock him onto his sanctimonious ass. "Sure thing, puddin'. Have at it. Hell, it seems like you just want to pitch in because your neck is on the line."

The bag bounced against his chest, and he managed to catch the long strap before it landed in a heap at his feet. "Hey, I've been offering to help since—"

"Since when?" She limped over and jutted her chin up to glare into his bewildered stormy gray eyes. *Don't do it, Van.* "Since you walked out on me six years ago, or are we talking about current events? Like when you ruined my new life, crashed my ship, and cost me one of my best crew members? The only reason any of this happened in the first place is because of your dumb ass, and now, we're probably going to die on this gods-forsaken hunk of rock because *you* had something to fucking prove to Daddy."

At the last dig, the air between them crackled and sizzled. A tic began along his jaw, and Vanysha immediately regretted her harsh words, even if they were the truth. She knew Politico General Raejil Phaetal had been at the heart of their division all those years ago. She'd only hoped Kieran would have been man enough to stand up to the tyrant back then. Apparently, knights only existed in stories from the long distant past.

She spun on her heel and pointed her nose toward the rocky outcropping on the horizon, before she said or did something either of them would lament later. "The hills should offer some kind of protection," she said flatly, raising her hand to shield her eyes from the harsh sun's rays. "Looks like an hour away, tops. I don't know about you, but I don't care to get stuck out here when it gets dark." She didn't wait for him to respond before she began the long trek.

With her back to Kieran, she could think a little more easily. Her leg throbbed each time she stepped, but standing out in the open was no longer an option. Wincing with every jolt of pain allowed her to focus more on the magic trick he'd just pulled off.

Where the hell had *that* come from? She flipped back through buried memories, hoping to spark some recollection that would explain the deadly light show, and her treacherous body tingled as remembered sensations flooded through her. His touch had always brought such heat to her skin; however, it had never caused her to actually burst into flames.

"Fine," she said. "You wanna talk about it so badly, spill it already." Her sharp tone was colored by the untimely memory as she trudged on. "What's the deal with the fireworks show?"

"It's nothing," he said coolly.

Vanysha scoffed. "Gods, you are such a shitty liar."

Their hissing footfalls broke the encompassing silence and she was ready to give up on her semi-civil conversation starter before he replied, "It's a…" His words were stiff and stilted. "A gift that apparently appears in my family line from time to time."

"Oh." *What do I say to that?* she mused. "So, how long have you, um, had it?"

He groaned behind her. "Dammit, Van. You make it sound like a venereal disease."

The gloves. Since the moment she'd seen him standing in the dining cabin, he'd worn rich black leather gloves, the edges disappearing under the sharp cut of his sleeves. Was that the reason for this antiquated fashion choice? Was he unable to control it? Were his hands burned or disfigured as a result?

Am I caring about any of these answers?

Vanysha staggered at the jarring question, and she grumbled under her breath, blaming the shifting sands as she quickly righted herself. She sensed his presence close, but she wasn't ready to trust him, not prepared to forgive him. Too many scars held her together, and no matter how much she yearned to find comfort in his strong arms, the damage his departure had caused would always haunt her. Would he ditch her at a crucial moment, leaving her high and dry yet again?

Even with the support system of her crew, she feared the aching, bitter loneliness would drive her over the edge this time, and she blinked rapidly, banishing the stinging tears that emerged with that painful memory. All those years ago, she had stood on the slaver's block, clothed only in the garb of the Unsought, and she'd prayed for death as she shivered, abused and abandoned. Had it not been for Faze, she would have ended her own life, if only to escape the next round of brutality.

Some optical illusion made the hills appear to recede with each step closer, and Vanysha glanced in all directions, prepared for another attack. Perhaps it was the all-encompassing, eerie hush blanketing the entire planet that set her nerves on edge. No birds sang in the waning sunlight, nor did she see any animal tracks on the baked ground. Hexaka was a dead and dismal planet, devoid of any thriving life.

She remembered studying each of the ten planets in the Nexxus while in school, yet even back then, little was known about the harsh land and its equally harsh people. The sands were mined for their unique elements, their particular make up ideal for creating glass as delicate as a flower petal, yet strong enough to withstand the impact of a meteor strike. The history books neglected to say, however, exactly how the materials were transported from the planet itself.

And I'm stuck on this paradise with HIM.

He wanted to say something. She could feel it in the dry air, pressing against her skin, wrapping around her body. Maybe it had to do with the reason he had left her all those years ago, and with each step she took, her irritation grew. Part of her hoped he'd simply open up about it and get it over with. Another part, however, the tiny corner of her heart where she stored all of the memories from their whirlwind love, knew he wasn't the sharing kind of guy. Hell, it had taken him three tumbles in the sack before he'd told her his first name, and another a week before he'd added his last name.

"Call me whatever you desire, la'nen, and that is what I will be. For you, and only you."

Vanysha gritted her teeth, channeling her self-loathing into muscle power, and trudged on. Her legs burned, and each new step threatened to dump her on her ass. Faze's healing had slapped her wounds closed, but the temporary fix was beginning to give way. Time was truly needed to allow the mend to set; full rest and recovery would put her in proper working order. She snuck another peek at the distant rocks, groaning in despondent frustration. *How the hell does it keep moving away?* Silently cursing fate and everything else, she slumped her shoulders and forced her feet forward.

The sands slipped away, and her aching leg gave out. She gripped her thigh, hoping to squeeze the muscle back into action, yet before her knee had touched the ground, Kieran steadied her against his side. Instinct and desire warred within; the drive to both shove him away and to hold him tight locked her body in indecision for an instant. Self-preservation, however, finally won out over pride, and she opted to split the difference, partially accepting his aide.

"I'm fine. I got it," she said. In her mind, her words had been strong and fierce, spoken with such determination that he backed away in fear. In reality, though, her pathetic whine had only encouraged him to hold her tighter.

"If you collapse before we find another ship, I'll be hard pressed to find a pilot to get me home."

She tugged her eyebrows together, ferreting out the truth between his harsh words and his teasing tone. His ability to make even the worst news seem palpable had always been one of his charms. When their first rented room had been destroyed as a result of an explosion in a nearby building, he'd procured new furnishings before she'd even finished her classes. Each burning inhale dragged the familiar scent of his cologne deep into her lungs, making it harder to balance the man she'd once loved to the stranger now walking beside her.

As much as her mind wanted to trade witty barbs, her heart was too broken to play. "I sincerely doubt that," she scoffed. "I don't buy that, in all the fancy skills you've got now, you somehow managed to miss flight school."

He stiffened beside her, and she prepared herself to be unsupported. Yet he did not relinquish his hold. On the contrary, he shortened his strides, giving the task of pace-setting to her. She should walk away. In fact, if she had a brain in her head, she'd hurry back to her broken ship as fast as she could limp and somehow jet off of this fucking rock, leaving him to his own damned fate. *Just as he did to me.*

"D-don't slow down," she stammered, the combination of fatigue, pain, and long-buried memories stealing her anger. "We still have far to go."

"We could make better time if you let me carry you."

"WHAT?" Vanysha jerked out of his arm to glare up at him incredulously. The sun directly behind his head had shadowed his face, so she wasn't able to read his expression. His tone had been calm, to say the least, making the true nature of his statement slightly unclear, so she opted to hold on to indignation. "Am I luggage now?"

Although she couldn't see his eyes, she couldn't deny the heat from those smoky quartz pools. "You were injured in the crash," he said. "I saw the blood on your clothes, Van, and you can't tell me you're not in pain."

Vanysha shook her head rapidly, the frantic jostling of her brain designed to dismiss her body's desire to feel his arms around her. "I *am* pain," she said and bit her tongue, muttering under her breath. "I have been through…" She paused to amend her statement. "If you think for a moment I can't make it to those hills, you are about to be sadly disappointed."

"I was never disappointed by you."

His unguarded whispered words threatened to crack her armored heart, but she knew better than to trust him a second time. As the first sun dipped beneath the far horizon, she persevered on, refusing to turn to see if he followed or not. If she did, he might have seen the tears streaking through the dust on her cheeks.

Chapter Thirteen

K ieran swallowed hard, stunned by her callous attitude. *Am I the cause of this?*

She continued toward the suns' setting, her uneven gait proof of her pain, even as she denied it, and he followed after her in mute contemplation, unsure of the best course of action. Without the twin stars baking the surface, the air had begun to cool. The change in temperature was a welcome shift, even though part of him knew the trapped heat would dissipate once true dark fell. Did the heavy bag across his back include some kind of tent? Making polite conversation about sleeping arrangements, though, might not be met with a favorable response.

He'd called her stubborn. *What a crock.* He'd always been the more hardheaded of the two of them. In Vanysha, he'd discovered his better self; with her, he could laugh and weave dreams about happy forevers. Buried deep inside of her and lost in the heaven of her eyes, he was not a son of the political machine. No, during those stolen months, he was just Kieran, the man lucky enough to have captured the heart of an angel.

"La'nen, what did I ever do to deserve you?" He sat up on his elbows to watch her braid her long hair. She glanced coyly over her shoulder, her fingers deftly weaving through her moonlit tresses, creating an intricate plait. She wore nothing more than her dazzling smile, and he yearned to feel her once again beneath him.

"I believe you tried to run me over. Literally."

He laughed at the honest retelling of their initial meeting and, reaching for her across the comforter, wrapped his arms around her narrow waist. She squeaked in playful surprise but did not resist his pull. "I will still stick by my version: that I was so taken aback by your beauty, I was unable to control myself."

She tossed her head back, her deep, rich laughter driving any remaining blood in his brain back into his engorged cock. "And your only defense was to knock me on my ass and have your way with me right there and then?" she said and spun around to plant herself firmly in his lap. The nearness of her hot core was more than he could resist. Holding her gaze, he yanked away the fabric separating them and watched, transfixed, the tempting play of emotions dance across her sun-kissed face as he slid into her welcoming sheath. Her eyelids fluttered down, and a heady whimper slipped from her full lips.

"And allow the universe to see you like this? Never," he groaned. "This, I will never share with anyone." He gripped her hips and slowly inched deeper into her, bringing both of them closer to ecstasy....

His trousers tightened at the memory of their last night together. Not long after she'd fallen asleep in his arms, one of his father's men had appeared inside their place. In his hands was the message that had forever sealed their fates.

Leave, or she dies.

"What happened to you after——"

"Nunya," she snapped, not missing a step.

He paused at the odd word while his treacherous heart reminded him of the show of affection between her and the burly Drekkan captain. He knew little about Drekkan language;

perhaps the man had taught her some phrases in preparation for their marriage? The hairs along the back of his neck prickled as he imagined his kitten in the arms of that beast. Not that he knew much about the ship's pilot, but he hated the man for the place he now held in her life.

"What's that mean?" Venom had poured from his voice, jealousy coloring the bitter words.

Her shoulders dropped, and she tilted her head to glance behind her. "Nunya business," she replied. The silhouettes created by the last rays of Hexaka's second sun cloaked her expression in shadow, and his heart ached as he missed the mischievous sparkle in her aqua eyes when the moon was full. "That's what it means."

The weight of her stare hung on his soul like an iron cloak. He yearned to hear her laugh again, but he feared too much time had passed and too much life now stood between them. Yet a tiny voice in the back of his mind refused to give up. If she was truly happy as the mate of her Drekkan pilot, then he only wanted the best for her. No reason not to attempt to mend the gap separating them, though.

A distant howl yanked his attention away from his planning and he scanned the darkening sky in search of the source, but the nearby rocks created an acoustic, cacophonous nightmare, bouncing the answering barks and growls throughout the approaching canyon.

"Damn," she muttered. "I hoped we'd've had more time before the rhoxxans found us."

"The ... the whats?" He narrowed his eyes, tried to peer into the growing shadows. In all of his studies of the Hexakan culture, he'd neglected to learn about the planet's other indigenous lifeforms. He hoped his lack of information wouldn't put their lives in jeopardy.

"Rhoxxans," she panted out, picking up speed. Kieran gave chase. "They're basically scavengers, but they'll eat things before they drop." The hills were just within their reach; a few more strides would put the solid rock at their backs and cut their worries in half. His companion's initial burst faded quickly and, without missing a step, he ducked beneath her arm and half-jogged/half-carried her the rest of the way. In tandem, they hobbled, until the safety of the mountains surrounded them. The dying light pointed out several possible alcoves before threatening to plunge the planet into night.

"Do those ... those whatevers live in caves?" Catching his breath, he shifted his gaze down to Vanysha, who offered a half-hearted shrug as an answer, but eventually shook her head. Nodding fervently, he lengthened his strides and continued toward the nearest opening.

"Wait. Light."

He'd nearly missed her soft suggestion, almost lost between his labored breathing and her weakened voice. Balancing her along his side, Kieran rummaged with his free hand into his pockets until his fingertips brushed against the handle of his flashbeam. He fumbled with the switch, swearing softly until his gloved thumb slipped the small knob up, and finally the narrow cartridge flared to life. As the bright shaft pierced the darkness of the long corridor and illuminated the cavern's ceiling, a massive flight of winged creatures squawked and took to the air. On instinct, he ducked his head and wrapped his body protectively around Vanysha until the strange cries grew distant and silence had fallen around them.

The sounds of their breathing lingered, but Kieran refused to move, his body quite content to stay right where it was. He inhaled deeply, pulling her sweet fragrance into his lungs. His eyes drifted shut, and in one blessed heartbeat, he was back in that tiny, one-roomed, slice of heaven … and all the world was perfect.

"Vanysha…." He sighed her name, each syllable a prayer to the gods for a chance to undo his stupidity. "I—"

"No. Don't. St-stop." She squirmed in his embrace, her movements frantic and jerky. As much as he wanted to savor the feel of her in his arms again, he had to remember she was now promised to another. He'd had his time with her, and he'd blown it. "L-let me go."

Dejected, he relinquished his hold, then stood stoically as she darted across the cozy cave. He ran a gloved hand through his hair, praying the impromptu scalp massage would encourage his blood to return to his brain. Even those short moments with her in his arms had set his blood on fire; only a sip from her lips would quench the flames. *Dammit all to the five hell realms.*

He lifted his hand, jaw agape, yet no words slipped from his tongue. *How do you apologize for losing the love of your life?*

Chapter Fourteen

Vanysha quickly shrugged off her pack and tossed it down at her feet, gulping down lungfuls of much-needed air. Long-dead emotions had risen to the surface, and she clawed at the rust rocks before her, hoping the bite would clear her head. Seemed his unconscious heroics had already done their damage, though. She'd been content in her hatred, using the horrors of the past six years as fuel to keep her rage burning, especially when he stood so close that her body yearned to lean in, if only to share the same air.

Even though a warm glow filled the space around her, her mind was still trapped in the darkness of her remembrances. During her long exile, she'd drag out the memory of their rhythmic breathing, the savored sensation of his lips on hers as her inhale became his exhale. It used to drive her to maddening peaks. Theirs was more than just sex; it was a profound connection unlike any she'd ever experienced, and neither would again with any other man. Lost in the pure and perfect passion of their lovemaking, she'd known what it meant to be alive. For six blessed months, she was deliriously happy, without a care in the world … then came the six long years she'd suffered, because she'd dared to believe in a dream.

Stay strong and survive, echoed the voice of her friend and pilot, Faze, through her maudlin thoughts. Squeezing her eyes shut, Vanysha used the inky blackness to center herself. Two of her crew still lived; they were relying on her to come back with help. Even her thorn-of-a-passenger was counting on her to get him to his specific destination, and she frowned as the wheels in her mind spun at Mach speed.

She opened her eyes, then aimed a narrowed gaze over her shoulder. Kieran may have physically dominated the cramped confines with his body, but she could have sworn she'd glimpsed some of the hesitant boy of so long ago. His perfectly coiffed hair hung in stiffened clumps as he studied the ground at his feet.

"Exactly where was it you were going?" she asked.

His gaze snapped up, guilt reddening his cheeks. If she wasn't bone-tired, she would have found his squirming entertaining. He looked like a kid who'd just gotten caught with his hand in the cookie jar, and as much as she enjoyed seeing him in the hot seat, she needed an answer more. She dropped her arms and faced him, exasperated.

"No one just up and decides, in the middle of the night, to go and visit the most war-torn part of the entire system," she continued. Her leg throbbed, but the nearest sit-able rock put her directly within arm's reach of him. If she sat on the floor, she'd likely not be getting up from it any time soon. So, she opted to rest her shoulder against the smoothest spot at her back. "What gives?"

The muscle at his jaw bunched and twitched, and he remained silent, eyes scanning the small alcove. Seconds ticked by, so she threw in the towel. "Fine," she said. "Keep your damned secrets."

Vanysha kicked off the wall and limped over to her discarded pack. As she bent down to retrieve the bag, a hand wrapped around her wrist. Surprise recharged her ingrained survival instincts; she yanked her arm back. She'd been expecting more fight from him, but her violent response must have taken him aback. She slipped too quickly from his grip and ended up on her ass, and before she could stop the action, she scurried away until her back had knocked into the solid wall.

Safely out of reach, her heart raced, embarrassment over-riding panic as she cautiously lifted her gaze. Kieran stood frozen, bewildered, rooted to the spot. When he dropped to his knees, clearly intending to crawl closer, she threw her hands up, her splayed fingers acting as a shield.

"No. Please, don't. I'm fine." She hoped her breathless words had delivered their intended message. "You … you just caught me by surprise, that's all. Really, I'm fine."

Kieran sat back on his heels, disbelief twisting his handsome mouth into a condescending smirk. *Arrogant asshole.* Her inner bitch wanted to slap that smug look right off of his face. His opinion of her was no longer her concern. But the Vanysha still buried deep within her from six years ago had a different desire, her palms itching to cradle his jaw, to feel the tantalizing tickle of his unshaven cheek against her skin. Instead, she curled her undamaged leg up and rested her folded arms across her knee.

"So," she said, breaking the ice, "is there something you wanted to say?"

She stared into his pools of smoky gray, watching the wheels turn behind them. The artificial fire's glow bounced off of the burnt orange walls and distorted their true hues, but she'd never forget the hours spent falling into those stormy depths. His eyes had been warmer then. He'd been warmer then, too.

Perhaps too much had happened to both of them since, to ever go back to those simpler days.

He ducked his head, ran a hand through his hair, and in her heart, she yearned to do the same. Actually, she'd wanted to muss up his perfect helmet of hair ever since she'd seen him in the dining compartment. For the first time, she wanted her Kieran back.

"You're stalling," she remarked to derail her treacherous passion.

Kieran lifted his gaze. A sheepish grin tugged at one corner of his delectable mouth. "Am I that easy to read?"

Vanysha refused to give in to his tempting invitation of word play. Instead, she half-heartedly shrugged. "You haven't changed your tell."

"Yeah." His chuckle sounded cold and forced. "Guess I'll have to work on that." He shifted from his crouch, extended his long legs before him.

If she reached her hand out, she'd be able to touch him. Yet, he remained ever the gentleman, staying on his side of the cave, and she waited while he found a comfortable position. Something told her this was going to be a long story and she didn't want anything to distract him.

She promptly reminded him of her original question. "Why are you here?"

"Would you believe," he said, lacing his fingers behind his head and leaning back, "that I'm here to save the universe?"

She scoffed, slowly shaking her head from side to side. "Wow. Delusions of grandeur much?"

At this, Kieran added a light laugh of his own, as well as an answering nod. "It's true," he said. "I finally got Westran Alpha to agree to sit down to the table for real negotiations with the Hexaks."

"Bullshit," she interjected, her smile lessening the sting. "I mean, isn't the new leader on Westran just a kid or something?"

He dipped his chin once, his proud grin on his sensual mouth sending shivers along her skin. "Yup. His father was too busy worrying about his next screw to care about peace. But his son has a decent head on his shoulders so far."

Vanysha edged forward, eager to hear more. "But there's no way the tribal chieftain here is gonna go for any deal, right?"

His confident swagger slipped a notch. "That's what I'm here to find out." He patted his right hand over his heart before he returned to his semi-reclined pose. "I have the peace accord in my pocket, including all the concessions Westran is willing to make. If I can get the Hexaks to agree to even some of them, that could change everything."

"Do you think that's why my ship was attacked?" she said, unable to censure the hateful thought, nor temper the accusatory venom in her voice. She'd skirted the edge of the Crimson Alley, even crossing directly into Hexakan space on several previous runs, yet never had she even seen another scout ship, much less been intercepted by three fighters.

He vehemently shook his head, freeing more loosened strands of his rich brown hair. "Doubt it. I didn't tell anyone the name of the vessel or when I was gonna be leaving, or where exactly I was going. In fact, no one knew I was coming here except for..."

His voice trailed off as his face paled, and a knot twisted in her gut. She straightened her spine. "Except for?" she prompted, the voice in the back of her mind already jumping to its own conclusions.

Kieran heaved a great sigh as he leveled his eyes at her. "My father," he said.

Chapter Fifteen

Not possible.

Kieran repeated the two words as his mind shuffled through all of the known facts, while Vanysha raved in the distance, her tirade punctuated by some colorful and painfully explicit suggestions of where his father could put the entire Nexxan universe. Growing up as the only son of Politico General Raejil Phaetal had never been a picnic, but his father knew the prospect of a peaceful end to the dispute between Westran Alpha and Hexaka would further cement the surname of Phaetal. Derailing the treatise was not beneficial for business.

Kieran's eyebrows shot up after Vanysha let loose with a particularly graphic act, and he laughed in spite of himself.

"Whoa, okay there," he said. "I don't even want to know where you heard that one." He rose and intercepted her during her latest lap, stepping directly into her path, making sure she saw him with enough time to stop. For as long as he lived, he didn't think he'd be able to banish the vision of abject terror in her eyes when he'd touched her arm. Even now, his blood ran cold when he considered how strong she'd been during their time together.

She halted, folding her arms across her chest. "Hang out at enough bars on any given loading dock and you'll pick up all sorts of insults."

He rested his hands on her shoulders, fighting as his body screamed for him to pull her into his embrace. He had no recollection of Vanysha ever losing her temper, much less swearing with such enthusiasm; she'd always been a resilient ray of sunshine, maintaining positivity in any situation.

While he had to know more of the past six years of her life, he first needed to calm her down. He opted for a direct approach. "I know you have no reason to believe me"—her eyes shifted, glaring daggers as she held rigid—"but my father is not behind this."

Vanysha muttered something and dropped her gaze. He couldn't fault her for her hatred. After all, his father's ultimatum had destroyed their happy lives.

"Half of the populace on Central is about to revolt because of all the water restrictions," he said. Hopefully, his logic would help her see reason. "This war is affecting the entire Nexxan system. If it continues much longer, rebellion is a likely outcome."

"Maybe it's time to shake up the friggin' government," she mumbled.

He slid his hands down her arms, his touch light should she pull away. "I'm not going to argue with you on that point, Van. But my father loves his power. Trust me on this one; he's not about to do anything to lose his place in the politico hierarchy."

Gods, she smelled so good. The crown of her head sat mere inches away from his lips. If he dropped his chin, he could nuzzle his cheek against her tresses of captured moonlight. He missed the thick, ropy braid that practically brushed the floor and he wondered if she would grow it out again should his mission be a success. At the mere notion of seeing those long, silken locks again, his blood crept below his belt line, and his eyes drifted shut.

She is no longer yours. Kieran clenched his jaw, using the tense pain to center his hopeful heart. Why was it so difficult for him to move on? Because he never wanted to leave. To this day, his biggest regret had been sneaking away in the middle of the night without a word. She deserved better, and he needed to let her go.

He gave her arms a gentle squeeze before releasing his hold, and he glanced around the narrow cave, trying to find something to occupy his mind while his body returned to his control. "Uhh … so, you hungry?"

Silence met his lame question.

Curious, he turned back to her. Her gaze was fixed on some point just beneath her feet, the vibrant aura that used to blanket her spirit dim as she stood alone, dwarfed by the fire-cast shadows. Had she managed to fall asleep standing up? Kieran had heard tales of ship's pilots who could nap with their eyes open on long runs. Was this her new skill?

"Why did you leave?"

Her soft words had shattered the quiet, and when she raised her eyes to him, they broke his heart.

"Yes, Phaetal," a voice boomed out. "Please tell."

Kieran snapped his arm out to grab for Vanysha, while he slapped in vain at his pockets for a weapon. In his haste to start a fire, he'd apparently neglected to fully check the cave. Soon, the disembodied voice was joined by others, their laughter at his plight unnerving to say the least.

His companion, however, had a different plan—she ducked under his reach, spun about, and aimed her small blaster at the ledge high above their heads, where a group of Hexakan warriors stood on the rocky balcony. Kieran counted half a dozen men cloaked in an eerie combination of shadows and slivered shafts of light, but more could be using the craggy ledge as cover. They almost didn't seem like much of a threat, dressed in ragged clothes and armor cobbled together from metals and swatches of thick leather. That is, until he took into consideration their high vantage point and the arsenal of weapons most likely trained on them from others they couldn't see. He'd learned in his studies they refused to be called soldiers, since they followed no one's orders.

"Aw, dammit, H'reeh," whined a stockier man beside the obvious group leader. "Always gotta go spoiling things. I was hoping to hear the rest of the story."

One look from the burly warrior, H'reeh, silenced any other discussion. Kieran kept his eyes trained on their unexpected company, while he shuffled his feet closer to Vanysha. Well-trimmed, ruddy brown hair framed intelligent sky blue eyes that watched the unfolding scene with aloof indifference. The others stood shoulder-to-shoulder, stern expressions impossible to read, especially at their current distance.

Splitting his focus, Kieran called out to Vanysha, his extending fingers questing for some piece of her. Unsuccessful in his blind search, he dropped his gaze for a heartbeat to orient himself to her position. Only a few feet away, she swung the gun between several targets, her arms locked in an experienced stance.

"You might as well put down your weapon, girlie." The man gestured to the gathered warriors who were visible. "If we wanted you dead, we wouldn't be talking right now."

Good point.

Stare still trained on their visitors, Kieran guided Vanysha's raised arms to a less threatening position. "He's right," he said softly. Years of practice in the art of mediations had taught him how to modulate his voice to both soothe his immediate client and remain at a room-audible level. The open intimacy often removed the fear of conspiratorial whispers or hidden agendas. Vanysha's arms trembled, fighting his lead for a moment as he added, "I think we're safe for now."

He moved in closer, standing by her side, and turned his eyes to her. Her nostrils flared as she sucked in short, shallow breaths, retaining her guarded stance before finally dropping her arms and replacing the gun into a sheath at the small of her back. A flash of skin peeked out as she holstered the weapon, and his brows tugged together as the snippet of an inky design caught his attentions.

A tattoo? She was the last person he could imagine wearing body art. But he'd think on this later, once they were truly out of danger.

Time for the negotiator to take the stage.

Straightening his spine and giving his jacket a light dusting, Kieran lifted his eyes to his audience. "I am—"

"Yeah, yeah." The dismissive wave halted his tongue. He gaped in stunned surprise. "You're the Vice Ambassador who was supposed to land about three hours ago." The man heaved a bored sigh, then tipped his head toward the back of the cave. "C'mon," he said. "We ain't got all day, and it's a hike to get where we need to go."

During the brief meeting, the wall that had enclosed the alcove had vanished, replaced by a trail of bright torches that lit a path deep into the mountain.

Kieran fought the urge to pull Vanysha in tight, to shelter her against his body. But she was the one with the weapon, making her more his protector than he cared to admit. He harkened back to their trip across the dunes and her apparent adversity to having someone at her back. Adding that to the ever-growing list of things he wanted to discuss with her, Kieran took a deep breath and fell into step, keeping her on his right side.

"Wait a minute." He raised his face up to the exiting group. "You… We've been talking. You speak Universal?"

H'reeh rolled his eyes with a guttural scoff as he paused by the arched tunnel. "Now he figures it out," he said to his group. "I'm not sure they really sent their best and brightest on this mission." Chuckles and mumbled agreements filtered through the departing men, fading as the figures vanished into the caverns below.

Kieran's gaze shifted between the warrior and his companion. Vanysha offered him a noncommittal shrug, which did nothing to soothe his bruised ego. "Don't look at me," she said. "I've thought you're an idiot for about six years now." And without another word, she ambled forward to follow the welcome party.

As Kieran chased after them, he wondered exactly how much the records had wrong about Hexaka.

Chapter Sixteen

H'reeh shook his head, grumbling to no one in particular as he led their new guests through the maze. The message his men had intercepted had said the negotiator from Central would bring word from the new Westran Alpha leader that peace would finally be a possibility. Peace? Since his people had cut off all ties to the rest of the Nexxus, they'd been living in peace. Did the new ruler want to apologize for century-old actions not of his doing, in hopes of reuniting the system?

Curiosity had gotten the better of him, though, and he'd agreed to the visitor, so he waited at their landing bay for the contingent to arrive. After three hours, he figured his intel might have been wrong on the timetable.

When his men had reported a flight of night raptors tearing out of the east gateway, however, he'd gathered a small party and set out to investigate. The birds made for an excellent early warning system—they hunted only in the dark of the night and in total silence so as not to alert their prey. If they were out squawking in force, then there had to be a reason.

He and his men had slipped in above the pair in the midst of an interesting argument. Yet when the female had asked what sounded like an extremely personal question, he'd opted to halt the eavesdropping session. His people valued privacy, and he wouldn't jeopardize their intimate moment for the sake of his own curiosity.

During the short prying session, H'reeh had learned snippets about this odd couple. The young male might have been the son of one slick politico, but the boy himself oozed noble intentions, with a healthy dose of ignorance. The female, on the other hand, was wrapped so tightly in agony and sorrow, H'reeh wondered if anything could crack the thick shell. As much as he wanted to simply dismiss their problems, a niggling voice in the back of his mind warned against completely discounting the lover's quarrel. *And if that lovesick boy is the best the political machine has to offer, I sincerely doubt our chances.*

"Give the kid a break," Drexler, his second chimed in, reading his well-telegraphed concerns with ease. *"How was he supposed to know? It's not like we send out tourist brochures."*

H'reeh tossed a glance over his shoulder, half-expecting to see the man stumbling over his own feet along the slender path. Instead, the officer moved almost gracefully, easily keeping up with his warriors, and he walked unarmed and unarmored, right into the belly of the beast, hoping a piece of parchment would save him. His face bore a couple of recent cuts, and fresh bruises marred his jawline, as though from one hell of a fight, or a hard landing. Perhaps he could cut him some slack.

His female, though, had taken the brunt of whatever they'd suffered to get to this moment. With the amount of fresh and dried blood decorating her baggy jumpsuit, by all rights, she should be resting on a slab. She didn't have the aura of a healer, but she was still alive because of the work of another. Someone else must have fixed her up. She favored her right leg, but refused assistance, and neither did she whine about the pace or the steep decline of their journey. The jury was still out on whether she was really strong and proud, or simply stubborn and willful.

They were truly an unlikely pair, yet her fire tempered his ice. An interesting history lay between them, and H'reeh grew more curious by the second. But he had more pressing matters on his mind than to play matchmaker. He returned his attention to Drexler. Inseparable since they were boys, their fathers in similar roles as leader and counsel, H'reeh and his second had forged a friendship that had stood the test of time.

"Remind me again why I keep you around?" H'reeh said and set his eyes back toward their destination.

"Expert advice. Witty banter. A viable alibi for your mate when you stay out drinking too late."

He shared a deep laugh with his second, and the other raiders joined in.

"Is it much farther?"

"Ah, the stuffed shirt speaks," Drexler interjected, and H'reeh glared at his subordinate, waving off his snarky, yet astute observation.

"Quiet." Shifting into Universal, he replied, "Cool your tits, maestro. We're almost there."

"Almost wh—"

H'reeh smiled as the tunnel ended, spilling out to the rock stairs that descended to his home. Someone at his back let out a faint, appreciative whistle, and his cheeks cramped in a wide, boastful grin.

Other planets in the Nexxus may have had starry skies and sunset beaches, but nothing could compare to the hidden spires of Cam'Rhan. Finger-like towers sparkled in the reflected glow of a thousand bioluminescent torches, reaching toward the cave's high ceiling domed in half a foot of the thick, indestructible glass forged only on Hexaka. The cool blue light gave his city a glimmer of perpetual twilight even in the heart of night, with full dark never fully taking over. The rising suns on the other side of the massive skylights kept track of the hours, charging the photo-sensitive living materials, powering the vast and intricate machines that created Hexaka's renowned steeleglass. He took a deep breath and started down the path that led to the beating heart of Hexaka's capital city.

Why the bid for peace now? For nearly a century, his people had lived in peaceful isolation. They didn't fuck with anyone, and no one fucked with them. In all fairness, Hexaka had hidden behind its volatile history, and H'reeh was happy to keep it that way. He hadn't bothered with any of the political machinations of the outer planets. Never cared to. After his father had slammed shut the borders all those years ago, no one had taken the trouble to learn more, and he was content to keep the Nexxus buried in the savage tales of the bloodthirsty Hexaks until the stars winked out.

But something about the latest request to return to the negotiation table had piqued his interest. Mainly because it hadn't been a request at all; it had been a formal announcement, telling him to expect Vice Ambassador Phaetal and a brokered treaty.

"How ... but..." As if on cue, the young man at his back had sputtered incoherent thoughts throughout the trek to the city's major thoroughfare, and his men snickered at their guest's stunned blathering. He waved a dismissive hand over his head, silencing them.

"Let me guess," he said, "not quite what you were expecting?"

Once on level ground, Phaetal caught up to him, matching him stride for stride. "Not by a long shot," he replied, in a refreshing tone of both respectful awe and veiled apprehension.

"None of the chronicles mention anything about an underground city, much less this … this…"

"Level of technology?" he said, filling in the missing words for his guest. Shop owners waved in greeting as they locked up their stores for the night, and with a smile, H'reeh returned their gestures as he led his odd retinue toward their destination. "Did all you condescending assholes think we forge the glass used in practically every device and vessel throughout the entire Nexxus star system with a campfire and leafed fans?"

The man fell back a step, and H'reeh almost regretted his overly harsh words. Almost. Legends surrounding his people and their fierce savagery helped to keep them safe from outside interference for centuries. As long as the universe got its supply of steeleglass, they'd been left alone. Well, at least until some psychotic schmuck on Westran Epsilon believed himself to be above the law. H'reeh rubbed at his chest, the ache in his heart still raw, even after his little sister's murder more than a hundred cycles earlier.

Daughters knew their roles all too well: pawns and bargaining chips to seal territorial disputes when males were too headstrong to see reason. His younger sister, Gizel, had been willing to play her part, as her mother had before her. Neither H'reeh nor his father, Rangatar Kaizaan, had trusted her chosen match. As guests on the groom's home planet, they could only watch the awkward courtship rites from a distance. Something about the man seemed … off. He laughed too loudly, and often at the wrong times. His sister had only smiled and chalked it up to nerves over meeting her menacing family. She'd assured them it was time for Hexaka to take its rightful place among the Nexxan Federation, and a marriage bond with the influential water planet system would seal their destiny.

H'reeh had always wondered if Gizel knew exactly how

prophetic her words had been. Instead of prosperity, death had followed—the morning following the ceremony, she'd been found, still partially clothed in her wedding dress, her body violated, bloodied, and broken, while the bridegroom giggled and stared at his gore-stained hands. H'reeh's father had been inconsolable, his rage worthy of their savage reputation. After father and son had fought their way to their craft, he'd sent the prince, as well as the other three members of the wedding party, to the emperor on Westran Alpha in a diplomatic case.

Some assembly required.

After that, all shipments of their steeleglass had halted. Granted, the necessary supplies were right on the surface, but only their forgers knew the proper techniques to make it truly unbreakable. Thanks to the work of his forefathers, his people needed nothing the other planets had to offer. Underground rivers and lakes provided all the clean water they could ever want, and the metalsmiths could mend any broken machinery. Their fields, nourished by the filtered sunlight, flourished, and corralled animals fed and clothed all of his people.

His father had sworn that until his daughter's honor had been restored, Hexaka would remain off limits to all of the other Nexxus planets, and that is exactly what he'd done. To this day, the legacy of isolation had kept his people safe from outside politics and turmoil.

Until now.

A firm hand gripped his shoulder and dragged him out of his dark memories, and H'reeh exhaled slowly. Drexler was right—one reason H'reeh kept him around was the man did offer decent counsel, sometimes without needing to say a word.

"Look at him," his lieutenant said, tipping his chin back toward their guests. *"This guy's father wasn't even born when that happened,*

brother." At this, H'reeh nodded in somber agreement. *"At least hear what he has to say."*

The path before them turned the final corner, and he strolled up the steps of the Sovereign Tower, the ruling seat of all Hexaka and home to his family for generations. Golden granite mined from deep in the heart of the planet stood as the backbone for most of the structures. While the rest of the universe relied on forested glens for their building materials, the Hexaks were master stone masons as well as glass makers, and wood was suitable only for accentuation—it made nice window frames and interior doors, but nothing could match the longevity of their marbled counterparts.

At their approach, the massive doors swung open, and his entourage split up, his guards returning to their assigned posts along the prime corridor.

"Fengreir? Jazeem?" he called out, his loud voice more for their bedraggled guests' benefit than for his men. "See them to their lodgings. I'm sure a hot meal would be a nice change. Plus, a shower wouldn't hurt, either." The two guards nodded, then peeled away from the group, waiting for the offworlders to follow.

"Wait," said the ambassador, struggling to reach him through the living wall. "It is imperative I speak with your lead—...uh, chieftain immediately. It is of the—"

H'reeh raised his hand, not offering a look back, and paused before responding, "You already have." He swore he heard the man's jaw hit the ground, but the diligent leader turned about to verify his suspicions and bit the inside of his cheek so as not to laugh at his dumbstruck visitor. He stepped in to clasp the man on his shoulder. "Take a breather," he said. "Your people have done without us for this long. What's another couple of hours?"

Then he shifted his gaze to the palace escort and, with a sharp nod, his company was led toward the guest quarters.

"Drexler, organize a scouting party and send them beyond the Loess Sea. I have a feeling their landing here wasn't a soft one."

"Do you think they were attacked?" his lieutenant asked, even as he hastened to follow the order.

H'reeh stroked his short beard in thought. *"That's what I want you to find out. This is already a complete shit show, and I believe too many outsiders have profited from these so-called hostilities for far too long."*

And I'm tired of dealing with the fallout. H'reeh had censored his words, but the unfinished statement was obvious to his trusted ally. Drexler dipped his chin, then waved for two guards to accompany him.

As the small group hastened down the stone steps, the chieftain sent up a silent prayer, though whether it was for a successful hunt or a total failure, even he didn't dare guess.

Chapter Seventeen

"So I take it that wasn't quite what you were expecting."

With surgical precision, Vanysha's direct statement cut straight through Kieran's scattered thoughts. Nothing made sense, and no matter how many laps he made around the spacious chamber, nothing could set his mind right. He nodded and shook his head, dumbfounded, while he continued to reach for a more intelligible response.

"Technology. Sophisticated technology. An … an entire underground city? Fields? Rivers and lakes? And that … that…"

Clear that his mind was in complete overload, Kieran plopped down onto the massive bed that dominated the room. Another surprise. Instead of a resolute brick covered in a scratchy sheet, he sunk into a cushiony mattress, its aroma wafting up clean and soothing.

All of his studies, all of the hours spent poring over ancient tomes and archives and for what? To discover an ultra-modern civilization, complete with their own modes of transportation. He'd been prepared to find some kind of primitive wheeled carts dragged along by teams of slathering beasts, not sleek elevated trains silently zooming by at breakneck speeds. Men, women, and children they'd passed during their short trek through the capital city had watched him with a wary eye, but not one made a move to attack.

Not what he was expecting? *That's putting it mildly.* What else had the historians of the Nexxus screwed up? The words of one of his sage tutors tapped at the back of his mind: *"History is written by the conquerors, not the conquered."*

"Why?" he asked the universe as he contemplated the ceiling above. The rich, inlaid design on the smooth dome depicted trees of soft lavenders and vibrant reds, showcasing craftsmanship that rivaled the artisans of old legends.

"Huh?" countered his current companion, her voice strained and breathy. "Why what?"

Blinking, Kieran returned to the present and pushed up onto his elbows while Vanysha labored toward an open seat on the opposite side of the room. He'd been so lost in his astonishment he'd forgotten about her injured state. His mind kicked his body into gear—he bounced off of the bed and rushed to her side. Sweat trickled down her forehead, and she winced with each step.

He cupped her elbow and placed a supportive hand around her shoulders, unsure if she'd truly accept his help. Her fingers dug into his arm, but she did not push him away. He fought to keep the touch chaste even though his body had a much different reaction. Before all of his blood stampeded below his belt line, he reengaged his brain and responded to her query.

"Hell, where do I start?" he said. "Why are we so wrong about this place and its people? Why would a race so incredibly self-sufficient truly need anything from the Nexxus?" They slowly ambled toward an odd chair placed near a small pair of tables.

Low backed, the bent wooden frame formed a curved X, and a tufted pillow padded the broad seat. Once at their destination, she gingerly eased herself down.

"Well," she rasped, "guess that's what you're here to find out, right?"

Her face was too pale for his liking; her sun-kissed cheeks sat sallow in the soft white glow of the overhead light. Only then did he notice the rust-colored stain on her baggy flight suit had grown since the start of their trek.

"Dammit, Van," he grumbled as he reached for her pack. "Why didn't you say something earlier?" He rummaged around in the collected contents. If she'd kept her wits enough to stow a weapon, she had to have medical supplies somewhere.

"I'm fine," she answered with a growl of her own, and Kieran shifted his gaze up, glaring at her. His icy stare was useless, though, aimed at the top of her head. Ignoring her protests, he continued to shuffle through the bag. A package of white gauze would have to do. Supplies in hand, he knelt down in front of her and reached for the long sleeves acting as a belt for the tattered coveralls.

She slapped at his hands, tried to scoot farther into the chair's recesses. "I said I was fine."

"I know," he replied calmly, returning to his attempts at revealing her wound. "I heard you the first time."

She continued to push away his efforts; however, he was determined. She was injured, possibly gravely so, and… His thoughts stalled, even as his fingers struggled on. Why was he so resolved to make sure she was okay? As she was so fond of reminding him: she was no longer his to worry about. Yet he couldn't deny his soul's stirrings and the poignant emotions unearthed by her mere presence. A fond recollection jumped to the forefront of his mind, one of a similar tableau: She was curled deep in the corner of their lumpy, forest green chair, fending off his playful attack. Her rich laughter had bounced off of the low ceiling, filling the room with mirth and joy. She'd even used her hair as a makeshift weapon to bat away his tickling digits.

The spirited version of his Vanysha sat as a ghostly specter beside her, masking her current incarnation in painful memory. Gone was the innocent passion in her aquamarine eyes, replaced by harsh and turbulent seas filled with mysteries he longed to solve. He'd often wondered what had become of her once his father had recalled him to Central. Had she truly run off with another suitor as their landlord had suggested? Did this new lover treat her like the precious commodity Kieran knew her to be? Was she happy? Yet the longer he'd mulled over these questions from his past, the more he realized something sinister must have befallen his lover between then and now.

Hoping to calm her frantic fighting, Kieran captured her wrists. "Please," he said. "Let me help you."

His gesture backfired horrifically. In his light hold, her trembling arms thrashed wildly out of his grip, and confused, he snapped his elbows into his ribs and sat back onto his heels. Once safely freed, she used her hands as a shield, pressing her shaking, open palms toward him.

"Don't. I … I can manage on my own." Her voice trembled almost as much as her extended arms did.

A bold knock at the door interrupted Kieran's reply, and before he could grant entrance, the door swung open. A young woman dressed in a homespun smock strode into the room, bearing a tray of fruits and smoked meats.

"Heard we had visitors, so I had to come and see for myself." Intelligent eyes of deep amethyst perched on either side of a broad nose showing the evidence of at least one break. Brick red hair fell in haphazard ropes about her round face as she strode to the table beside the bed and set down the food. She held the air of someone used to being in command. Either that, or all of Hexaka's population lacked the tact gene. "Don't get a lot of tourists around here," she said. "But I'm sure you at least figured out that much by yourselves. And whoa! When was the last time you two took a bath?"

Kieran took to his feet as their visitor continued to make herself at home in their room. He'd considered himself to be tall, yet this young girl stood nearly eye to eye with him. No smile lines or wrinkles marred her olive complexion, but something sat cheerful in her demeanor.

His mind struggled to keep up with the conversation, and manners dictated an introduction of some kind. "I beg—"

"For what?" quipped their mysterious guest, pinning him with a quizzical stare over her shoulder. She shrugged off his speechless reply and turned her attentions to Vanysha. "Yeeouch. That looks like a nasty gash there, hon," she remarked and folded her strong arms beneath her ample breasts as she eyed the stain on Vanysha's jumpsuit. "Lucky we found you when we did, huh?"

From the few encounters with his hosts, Kieran had begun to piece together a general picture, and one factor shone through, brighter and stronger than the suns far above them: the citizens of Hexaka were honest—painfully and blatantly so. In them, he detected no ulterior motives or hidden agendas; what you saw was exactly what you got. These people were not warlike, and neither were they bloodthirsty savages. They were people, just like those on any other planet of their system. They weren't running around in animal hides, soaked in the blood of their enemies. Nor were they dimwitted.

The girl before him smirked and tipped her chin in his direction. "Yeah, I figured you'd've read all the old shit about us. I can see it all over you." She gestured toward him. "Yes," she interrupted as his mouth gaped, "I know what you're thinking, so don't bother denying it."

Without skipping a beat, she shifted her gaze to Vanysha. "I'll send by one of our healers to take care of that leg of yours. Eat. It'll help."

Kieran could only stand mute as the whirlwind female made her way back to the door.

"Dad said he'd be ready to speak with you in the morning. I'm Elsabet, by the way. And oh"—she turned back as she grabbed the doorknob—"could you both turn down the 'fuck-me' vibes in here? Thought I was gonna squirt just walking by the room."

Chapter Eighteen

Vanysha blinked slowly. Was her confusion due to the strange storm of information in the past few minutes, or just a general lack of blood making it to her brain? She did enjoy seeing Kieran squirm, certain his ego had taken more than a couple knocks as they'd hiked down into the bowels of Hexaka.

Not to say the discoveries didn't take her by surprise, as well. She'd skirted the planet so many times but had never realized she'd never seen the lights of any large cities or small villages. The buildings she'd seen in the past must have been ruins, remnants from centuries before the indigenous people had taken shelter beneath the ground. She flipped back through the trip. If she had another chance to explore the city, without the excruciating pain, she might jump at the offer.

Aside from the crippling agony of her leg, however, the foremost thought on her mind was the parting comment from their enigmatic hostess. Were the Hexaks empaths as well as telepaths?

Kieran hadn't moved after the door had clicked shut. Grateful to have his back to her, Vanysha could stare in relative privacy. Did he still want her? She'd dismissed all of his actions as purely selfish and had designed only to see him through his quest. Yet in the moments leading up to their untimely interruption, she thought she'd glimpsed traces of the boy she'd loved with all her heart.

Until he left and threw you to the wolves.

Sometimes she truly hated her conscience. That bitch never forgot anything—not one degradation, nor one lashing.

"Let me at least bring you some food. Please?"

Vanysha dropped her hands into her lap, dismissing her latest trip down memory lane. "Why are you so bound and determined to help me now? Are you trying to make up for lost time?"

Her head, along with her aching thigh, throbbed with each pulsing beat of her heart. The Hexak leader had set a grueling pace down to their city, but she hadn't wanted to appear weak in anyone's eyes. *Especially Kieran's.* She lifted her gaze slightly to see if he was still staring at her.

Kieran remained out of arm's reach, yet still close enough to be at her side within two of his long-legged strides. She now noticed the cuts and bruises on his handsome face, evidence from their less-than-dainty landing, and her brows tugged together sharply. Why hadn't she seen them before? Granted, she knew that, as a passenger on her ship, the damage he'd sustained would have been minimal; she'd spent the bulk of her monies on outfitting the guest cabins and the commuter berth with the best safety protocols in the Nexxus. But not once had she asked if he was okay, whereas he was hyper-interested in her welfare.

"Can't you go back to being an asshole? It doesn't confuse things that way," she said, surprised by her own whining tone. While she hadn't expected to utter her internal thoughts, she was more stunned by his response. An impish grin curled the corner of his lips, while the overhead light twinkled in his stormy gray eyes.

Fuck. She needed to defuse the situation, and fast. She might forget how much of a jerk he really was and jump his bones right there and then. Once again, the last words from their hostess echoed in her ears: *"From both of you."* She didn't want to sleep with him … did she?

Her stomach took that exact moment to make its emptiness known, and before she could countermand her rebellious body, Kieran headed over to the generous tray of foods. Her hand lifted off of her leg, but she didn't stop him. If she told him she wasn't hungry, she'd be lying. In truth, her mouth had started watering as soon as the unexpected princess barged in.

A small plate of fruits, cheeses, and slices of smoked meats appeared in her periphery, and realizing her current stubbornness was bordering on stupidity, she muttered a soft thanks, accepting the peace offering. A considerable part of her wanted to devour everything presented, even going so far as to lick the plate clean, but the voice clinging tight to its righteous indignation pouted childishly in the corner of her mind.

A thick silence blanketed the room, punctuated by the occasional crunch of food or sips of water. Vanysha glued her gaze to her vanishing meal, refusing to answer the heated stare from her troublesome companion, and her jaw clenched the longer the quiet dragged on. Tempting fate, she raised her eyes.

Big mistake.

The Kieran sitting in the room reminded her far too much of her Kieran, the sweet and thoughtful man who'd once swept her off her feet and promised her forever. His hair had lost most of its stiffness, falling in soft waves over his forehead, while he nibbled on a slice of cheese. She recalled sneaking peeks at him during meals, thinking he was absorbed in his own food, only to be caught ogling by those stormy gray eyes.

As their gazes locked, his expression's loving warmth seemed to wither, as though he remembered something important. Was he thinking about someone else? Maybe he had a wife he had left to go on his quest for fame? In the span of a heartbeat, the young man she'd loved vanished before her eyes, and once again, the proper politico stood in his place.

"I only want to make sure to return you to your … your mate in one—"

"Are you friggin' kidding me?" she muttered, shaking her head as she set aside her plate. "I can't believe you actually bought that." She climbed out of the chair and her leg threatened to buckle even as she leaned heavily on the sturdy woven backrest, but she needed to move. She snapped one hand up in his direction, stopping any attempts at aid, while she navigated through the room, white-knuckling every piece of furniture along the way. "Faze is just a friend with one fuck of a warped sense of humor."

Great idea. Just blow your only reason for NOT jumping in the sack with your ex. Why did she just tell him that? Perhaps their hosts' blatant honesty was beginning to rub off on her. She never liked secrets. It led to lies, which inevitably led to pain.

"Van, I—"

The door opened, this time without even a knock, and Vanysha jerked her gaze away from Kieran as two men entered the room. New faces, the young man vaguely similar to the leader who had escorted them into the city proper. But the other man had grabbed her attention—an older gentlemen, his deep auburn hair sprinkled with streaks of silver, and his neatly trimmed beard practically all white. Dressed in a somber and quite proper white physician's tunic and a pair of black slacks, he fixed her with an irritated stare.

"Are all the people on the other planets stick stupid, or did you hoard it all yourself?" Instead of his gruff words setting her teeth on edge, his concerned tone reminded her of Faze. Or was it that he dominated the room with his physical presence? He was a giant, ducking to avoid braining himself on the door jamb as he stepped across the threshold. Unlike the warriors who'd escorted them through the city, his attire was completely modern, reflecting the universal markings of all those trained in the healing arts. Even his soft-soled boots were in better condition than her own worn-out footwear. He was definitely in charge, and he didn't seem to be slowing down as he crossed the room.

"You got a death grip on everything you touch, and you're still on your feet?" said the burly man, admonishing her with a disapproving *tsk*. He dropped into a low crouch and tossed her over his shoulder like a wet towel. Vanysha yelped in surprise at his unconventional approach to bedside manner, but was helpless to do more than simply slap at his exposed back.

"What the—"

"Well, if you're not gonna do what's good for you by your lonesome, guess I'll have to give you a hand in that department." He pivoted and marched toward the narrow couch tucked against the wall. "No wonder you're about to pass out. Has she always been this stubborn?"

Vanysha struggled to push herself up and see more than just the floor while she imitated a sack of potatoes. Was this jamoke questioning Kieran about *her*? Airborne for only a second, her ass bounced onto the soft padding, and the sudden drop stole away her train of thought. The unconventional healer knelt beside her and slipped the pack off of his shoulder.

"You know … ? Never mind. Niko?" He rummaged through his supplies, removing rolls of fresh bandages and bottles of antiseptics. "Take Genius Boy into the next room and get him cleaned up. Don't think he needs anything more than a kiss for a couple of his boo-boos, but check it out anyway." A paper-wrapped parcel was added to the pile, and Vanysha scooted away as far as space would allow.

Even on his knees, the man made for a fantastic wall; Vanysha could only hear Kieran's sputtered protests fading off into the distance. He placed a hand on her shoulder, the touch designed to stop her from struggling, yet not forceful enough should she decide to bolt. A soft click plunged the room into silence, and her heart began to pound.

Her grouchy companion looked behind him before letting out a deep exhale. When he turned back to her, she stared into the face of another person—the harsh lines around his sparkling green eyes and mouth had vanished, revealing a kindlier version of the healer. He gave her shoulder a comforting squeeze, then released her.

"I apologize for the theatrics," he said, his tone soft and comforting as he retrieved a pair of pale blue gloves from his bag. "When Elsabet said we don't have many visitors, she was not exaggerating. My name is Weyland, by the way, physician to the ruling house."

Vanysha gaped, searching for a proper response as she stared at him. "Uh, it's okay. I mean it's…"

Weyland chuckled, one bristly gray eyebrow arching. "Your parents named you Okay? Bummer of a birth mark, kid."

"No, that's not my name," she stammered. "I just meant okay for the … the…"

He shook his head, took her trembling hands into his and patted them gently. "You're gonna be all right here…"

After a lengthening heartbeat, she figured out the reason for his hesitation. "Vanysha," she said.

"Vanysha," he repeated, dipping his chin. The regal gesture eased her scattered mind as he continued speaking. "I sent your companion away since I thought you'd want to do this in private." His gaze darted to her right side, then back again. "You have no need to feel shame for what you have endured. A lesser person would have been destroyed by it, and you rose above it."

Vanysha swallowed hard, overwhelmed by his astute observation, as well as his knowledge of the mark she hid from the world. Mute, she managed a weak nod, and was rewarded with a warm and understanding smile. He tipped his head toward the thicker square package.

"Brought you something to change into when you're all cleaned up. But let's get to that wound first."

Weyland encouraged her head to bob in time with his, and then he released her hands. Digging deep, Vanysha untied the tattered sleeve belt holding up the bloodied jumpsuit, and tears slipped down her face as she squirmed out of the baggy pants, physical discomfort not the only source of her current ache.

Only Faze knew of her brand, proof of her slave status during those dark days after Kieran had abandoned her. If not for her captain, she'd have been sold into permanent servitude to one of the thousand brothels dotting the Nexxus system. She didn't know why Faze had seen her as a person, and not just a fuck toy as she stood on the auction block, until much later.

Young and pleasing to the eye, she'd been snatched off the Unsought auction block by Shad'Phan, the vicious owner of a horde of illegal whorehouses, days after her parent's disgraceful disowning. Faze had come in second place during the sale but had been determined to save her. Years later, he'd confessed that she reminded him of his younger sister who'd succumbed to a mysterious illness when he was in his late teens. He'd delved into every legal manifest in the Nexxus, finally unearthing an archaic loophole in the wording of the contract between the slavers and her new master that made the brothel's ownership of her null and void. Though her bondage had lasted less than three short weeks, it had given the beast enough time to mark her as chattel, property with no rights and no hope. Even the legendary skills of both Faze and his wife, Meena, were unable to remove the seared-in design. The shame of bearing it had nearly crippled her battered spirit, but again her savior had stepped in. After Faze had found her locked in the bathroom with a knife pressed to her wrist, he promised her she'd never have to look at the mark as it was ever again.

"If we can't take it away, we'll make it into something beautiful."

Meena had contacted a dear friend who worked as a tattoo artist, and together, they created a living painting to bury the ugliness. But no matter how many colors had been layered onto the scorched flesh, she'd always inwardly hate the source of the intricate ink. It was also the reason for her long-lasting bout of celibacy. Fear of the inevitable repulsion from any partner had steered her away from intimacy, and until yesterday, she was fine with it.

Until Kieran showed up and destroyed her imperfect world.

She sucked in shallow gulps of air as the flood of memories overwhelmed her. She gave one final kick to escape from her ruined coveralls, and with a habitual tug on the corner of her long, dingy ivory shirt over her brand, she buried her face into her hands and sobbed in earnest.

Chapter Nineteen

Weyland hated seeing the young girl in so much pain; only a fraction of it caused by her injuries. News of their guests arriving through the surface caves instead of the landing pad had spread like wildfire through the Citadel. He'd been expecting to be called upon, but when the sentries had mentioned the search party looking for more crash survivors, he'd stepped up his pace. His assistant, Niko, had trailed behind, grabbing all the possible supplies from the med chamber before they'd headed toward the guest quarters of the capitol palace.

If they'd crashed, the gods only knew how long or how far they'd journeyed to arrive at their hidden entrance. As he searched through the cabinets, double-checking his surplus of gauze and sutures, he recalled the conversation with H'reeh only days earlier.

"Do you think this new leader will be more trustworthy than any of the others?" Weyland had given voice to the thought in the minds of all the counselors gathered in the Chamber of the Sun. He swung his gaze around the circular table and was met with the same worried expression on each face.

H'reeh stroked his chin, eyes pensive and introspective. "It's not this young emperor, nor his message, that intrigues me. It's more about his messenger. It would've been easier for him to send an envoy of his own people, yet he's opting to send an official from Central. Why?"

"Could be one of the politicos actually wants to end this bullshit war," Drexlar said. Murmurs both for and against that theory rippled through the room, but H'reeh shook his head slowly, his eyebrows drawing together.

"Stranger things have happened; that much is true. But there's something more. I can't put my finger on it yet, but I will."

He and Niko were halfway down the hall when he bumped into H'reeh's daughter heading away from the guest rooms. Her cheeks were flushed, her thoughts seemingly jumbled as she barreled into them in her haste.

"Whoa, hold on, Princess," Weyland remarked, gripping her shoulders to steady her. "Are they that bad?"

"They're just... Gods, it's too much in there." Elsabet dragged in a slow, centering breath and, shaking her head, she opened up one of the hallway's cabinets to rummage through the stacks of clothes. "Both of them are pushing and pulling at each other, neither of them willing to make the first move at all." She grabbed a rather stylish ensemble that looked to be for a child. "Something horrific, or imagined to be horrific, is keeping both of them from being ridiculously happy with each other. Why can't people just be honest?"

Why, indeed. Weyland shrugged, unable to answer her insightful if rhetorical question. With a quick flourish, she wrapped up the parcel, placed it in his hands, then tipped her head toward the door at her back. She continued to mutter under her breath while she stole a hug and headed down the corridor. Armed with his bundle and a thimbleful of information, Weyland entered the far room to see things for himself.

Upon entry, he understood Elsabet's spot-on commentary of

the relationship between their guests—a deep history sat between them, yet neither were prepared to examine the past that locked their present in a stalemate. The female was more in need of healing, so Weyland sent the courier into the adjoining room with Niko to give her the space for which she was mentally screaming.

Even now, in the seclusion of this private chamber, she cowered in the corner of her mind, afraid of the stigma her past would dredge up. She was a beautiful young woman by all outward appearances, her silver-white hair in complete contrast to her deeply tanned skin and exotic aqua eyes. While he'd sworn an oath to do no harm and to value the secrecy of all he treated, she needed to hear his message of acceptance in order to lead her on the path to heal her wounded soul. In the meantime, he'd focus on her physical damage. He turned his attention to the partially healed gash across her thigh.

"Was it a Drekkan who worked on this?" he asked, hoping idle conversation would help to set her at ease while he slipped on his protective gloves. His people and the Drekkans, it was believed, descended from the same race of strong empaths, harnessing their Lost Arts and mental skills to manipulate the heart, the mind, and even the body. Yet whereas his distant cousins excelled in physical healing, the Hexaks had opted to delve into providing spiritual and mental help.

The quality of the work showed skill, though it seemed as if the task had been interrupted and the job left incomplete. Had she been able to rest up for an hour or two, perhaps her own metabolism would've sealed the wound shut. Old, faint scars crisscrossed along the inside and outside of her thighs, his blood chilling as he recognized the patterns as fingernail scratches. So many questions filtered through his mind, but if he kept the topics superficial, his patient might open up a bit.

He shifted his gaze from her injury, up to her face, which still hid in the palms of her hands, and he caught a nodded answer. "Well," he added, "whoever did it almost got the time to wrap things up." After glancing back at his work, he uncorked a potent astringent, then doused the open gash.

Vanysha cried out sharply, digging her short nails into the meat of his bicep, and her shoulders hunched over in silent suffering, though she did not plead for him to cease his ministrations.

Weyland capitulated, her brave response earning his respect, and blotted gauze gently against the weeping wound. "That was unfair; I should've warned you. But I thought it was the only way I could get you to say anything."

"Ouch?" she mumbled through her sniffles.

Her timid reply struck an odd chord in Weyland, and he tossed back his head in laughter. "Girl, you have a direct way of stating the obvious."

"Sorry," she said, her voice rough from her emotional catharsis. "I guess I am shitty company right now."

Weyland tipped up her chin with a gentle nudge from his knuckles. "No need to apologize. You're in pain. I think you're allowed to be whatever kind of company you want to be."

A strangled, squeaky laugh snuck out, and he glimpsed the self-assured girl who dwelled within her. "In that case, I should injure myself more often," she replied. "Then I could excuse my standard bitchiness."

"Hate to break it to you"—he leveled an amused stare at his patient—"but around here, you're a cupcake."

He added a wink, and she rewarded him with a shy but honest smile. Weyland returned to his initial question from a different pathway, having taken her response as a favorable sign. "So, tell me about the Drekkan."

"That's not what you wanted to ask, is it?"

Once certain the microfine sand on the planet's surface had been flushed from the open wound, he asked, "You part Hexak or something?" and gently traced the gash with his fingers, finding the spots in need of a stitch or two to seal the gap. "All right, then. If you wanna jump right into that pool, it's fine by me. Is that boy the reason for the mark?"

She flinched during his inspection, and he halted, concerned he'd aggravated the still-healing injury.

"The Drekkan is my captain, but he was also hurt during the crash."

Apparently, the internal wound had a great deal to do with her current traveling companion. He noted her quick change of topic and honored her wish. "Which explains why the healing still needs some work," he said and, nodding, returned to his task. "Anyone else with you?"

"Danton; he's my engineer. He got some bumps, but that man's hard-headed, and I don't think much would get through that thick Bozzan skin of his."

Weyland began to stitch closed the gash as she continued to discuss her crew, the innocuous topic allowing her to relax a fraction. His telepathic people prided themselves on never prying into the thoughts and feelings of others; a person's mind was the only true place owned by no one else in the entire universe. The daunting part was dealing with those unaware of how to shield. To a Hexak, unfiltered emotions equated to people screaming a conversation in a crowded room, and while the polite option would be to ignore the arguing couple, some details inevitably managed to wiggle in. In the case of his patient, her thoughts were mainly focused on her shipmates left behind as she searched for aid, with strong undercurrents of conflicting desires directed toward the man in the other room.

"But we did…" Vanysha stuttered, taking in an audible

breath. "We did lose one of our crew: Allyn." He snipped off the last stitch, cleaned away any residual blood, then lifted his gaze. Grief had wilted her earlier smile, and her downcast aqua eyes shimmered with unshed tears. Normally, Weyland would simply pat whatever body part was nearest to offer reassurance; however, considering the current placement of his hand and her lingering scars, he opted for another route.

After peeling off and discarding the thin gloves, he cupped his hands around hers. Her slender fingers trembled, but she didn't shy away. "I am sorry for the loss of your friend."

"He was just a child, you know? Thrown away by family and never given a fair shake in life." Unsure if she was talking about the lost crew member or herself, Weyland sat in silence as she continued. "And he never complained. Even spending hours on end cooped up in that friggin' engine compartment with Danton —and trust me, that's enough to drive a saint to drink."

He joined in her weak laughter. "Sounds like someone too kindhearted for this cruel world."

"Yeah." She sighed heavily, shoulders drooping. "Why do the gods always take the good ones?"

"Not all of them." He waited a moment as his paused statement caught her attention; she sniffed back her tears and raised her gaze. "Sometimes," he said, "they leave an angel or two to help the rest of us along the way."

A timid blush painted her cheeks, and he took to his feet. "C'mon, kid. You look like you need a shower, and it'll help wash off the rest of the blood." Her gaze swung to the closed door Niko and the ambassador had used, and Weyland shook his head, drawing her eyes back to him. He extended his hand. "Don't worry about him. We'll keep him busy until you're ready for him."

She scoffed and reached out for his assistance. With a gentle touch on her elbow, Weyland guided her toward the washroom. She didn't rely on his proffered arm more than absolutely necessary, earning her more points in the badass column. "Hope you guys are entertaining," she said, wincing as she limped along. "I might want you to hold him for a long time."

Chapter Twenty

Kieran glanced up at the door for the umpteenth time since being escorted into the spacious connecting room. Apparently, many of the chambers doubled as bedrooms as well as working spaces; the open sleeping area was fully equipped with a wall monitor and a wireless keyboard, with an enormous bed tucked into the far corner. He could do little more than observe from a distance, because once inside the room, he had been corralled toward an awaiting chair opposite the modern desk setup, while the medical assistant, Niko, had placed himself firmly between Kieran and the object of his attention.

"Would you stop fidgeting?" Niko grumbled, and with a firm grip on Kieran's chin, he once again jerked his head toward the opposite wall. "Geez, she's gonna be fine. Weyland's the royal physician. You, on the other hand, are about to get a song-worthy scar across that pretty face of yours if you don't sit friggin' still."

The ache along his forehead had little to do with the stinging stitches that tugged his left eyebrow upward. "I don't see why I had to be herded out of the room like, like…"

"Like a child?" Niko quipped, and Kieran leaned away as much as the taut fiber would allow to glare at the man. His shoulder length waves of sandy blond hair sat in sharp contrast to his deep amber skin, eyes like bright olivines fixed on his task.

"Are all your people this rude?"

Kieran's insult had failed to hit its mark, earning nothing more than a noncommittal shrug. "We just don't believe in mincing words." The man leaned in, and at first, Kieran feared he was coming in for a kiss. Luckily, his mouth veered off target and he cut the thread with a snap of his sharp teeth. "Besides," he continued, "why bother when you're surrounded by people who can read your thoughts, right?"

He did have a point, Kieran mused as he reached for the newly closed cut, only to have his hand slapped away. Niko leveled a bland stare that lasted another second before returning to his work, his creamy green eyes rolling back as he grabbed a small jar out of his bag. The man's large hands moved with a dexterous grace, easily uncorking the delicate container, and a cooling salve was smeared over the wound, followed by a bandage of some kind.

"There," he said. "Give it a day or so and you won't hardly see the mark."

With a polite nod, Kieran stood, only to be gently dragged back into his seat. "Not so fast there, sparky. Weyland's still working on your friend."

"How is she?" Panic chilled his blood and he waited while Niko cleaned his utensils in silence. But when no answer was forthcoming, Kieran tapped his foot impatiently, clearing his throat as punctuation.

"Are all *your* people this rude?" Niko said, returning Kieran's earlier query, his tone more inquisitive than accusatory, his gaze never shifting from his job.

"Dammit," Kieran growled, and he jumped to his feet. "No. I…" The pacing did little to clear his mind, but at least it got blood moving through his whole body instead of pooling at his crotch. Since they'd arrived on the hostile planet's surface, this was the only time they'd been separated by more than a few steps. Now, every second she was out of his sight, he was filled with turmoil. Was she badly injured? Not once during their trek had she asked for a rest. In truth, she'd even set the pace for most of the trip.

"If you're worried about her, don't be." A bottle was shoved into his chest, halting any forward momentum and, frowning, he slid his gaze from the proffering hand up to the Hexak medic. Niko lowered his own drink, then tipped his chin toward a comfortable-looking pair of thick, leather-bound chairs. Kieran dropped his shoulders and accepted the peace offering, but opted to remain on his feet.

"Weyland'll let us know when it's safe," Niko stated. He plopped down before he kicked his booted feet up onto the squat padded stool. "So, what's your story anyway? Why are you here?"

Kieran shrugged as he took a long drink from the cool beverage. Sweet and strong, it burned all the way down his throat, and the heat didn't stop until it had reached his gut. But instead of clouding his mind, it cleared away the fog and, blinking in surprise, he lowered himself into the nearby chair.

"Yeah." Niko chuckled at Kieran's response. "You get used to it."

"It is … quite good."

Niko drew his tawny eyebrows together, a deep furrow creasing his broad forehead. "Do you ever relax, or is that stick up your ass a permanent fixture?"

The heady beverage was certainly doing its job; all Kieran

could muster against the blunt inquiry was a weak sigh. "You spend most of your life trying to fit into a predetermined mold of political leadership and see how well you chill out."

The gruff Hexak chuckled and grinned, his broad palm splayed against his chest in feigned shock. "Was that a joke? So you do own a sense of humor. Will wonders never cease?"

Taking a page from Vanysha's book, Kieran flipped off the man and tried not to drown in his mouthful of ale as raucous laughter filled the room. He hadn't realized how on guard his life had been until Niko so indelicately broached the subject. The only stolen moments of peace in his life had been found in Vanysha's arms, and now those days lived on strictly in memories.

"Do you still dig her?"

This time, Kieran coughed hard to get the air and liquids to go down their appropriate tubes. "Huh?" he finally croaked out.

Niko tipped his head toward the closed door. "Your girl. Vanysha, right? You still dig her?"

Words refused to fall from his tongue, even as his heart screamed out in agreement, and judging by the sly smile and knowing nod, Niko had intercepted the silent message. "Yeah, you do. She seems kinda cool."

"What she is," Kieran said, "is promised to another." This admission pained his soul, and hearing it spoken aloud simply drove the loss deeper. He sighed. "Which means off limits."

"Bullshit," Niko mumbled around the mouth of the bottle.

"Excuse me?" Kieran arched a brow at the enigmatic response. Was he suggesting he break up her potential happiness to soothe his own broken heart?

Niko waved off Kieran's indignation and finished off the remains of his drink before replying. "I'm not saying go in there and take her by force, but I wasn't getting any 'taken' vibe from her. Don't get me wrong," he added. "You must've done something to seriously piss her off, but she's definitely not completely off your menu."

Kieran blinked slowly, picking apart the man's curious way of speaking. While the method was unconventional, he still took heart at the message. Before they'd been so rudely interrupted, Kieran remembered her mentioning that her captain was only a friend. Was there still a chance?

"So, why are you here? For real?"

The unexpected question wriggled into his romantic musings, yanking him back to reality. As he pondered his answer, he laughed, mirthless, and lifted one shoulder. "Honestly, I thought I was coming here to save your planet from the war tearing it apart and to bring you into the modern age."

He enjoyed the last swallow of his drink in the surrounding silence. After setting down the empty bottle, he locked eyes with his unamused companion. "Hey," he said, "you asked."

Niko shook his head in disbelief. "Does it look like we need saving?"

"I think the only thing that would be saved is the rest of the universe from its current ignorance about you," Kieran said. "Why are you keeping this war going, when you obviously don't need anything in the way of trade?"

"Who says we are keeping a war alive?"

The sudden new speaker took Kieran unawares, and he jumped to his feet. He'd been so wrapped up in his conversation, he'd missed the door open and shut at his back.

No longer dressed in battle attire, H'reeh appeared to be nothing more than a man. He wore no crown or other visible sign of leadership, and his garb was adorned with only a thin braid of woven gold-and-silver threads along the edges of an inky black tunic.

Niko rose and bowed to his sovereign, placing a fisted hand over his heart, and H'reeh rolled his eyes with an odd groan. Curious, Kieran stood as a broad grin split the young man's face. "Hey, Dad," said Niko.

"Dad?" Kieran choked out in surprise, and he quickly sifted through the entire conversation, double-checking to ensure he hadn't committed some intergalactic faux pas along the way. He cringed inwardly, his tactless comment regarding his own upbringing and the burden of leadership biting him in hindsight. The chieftain clasped his son's shoulder and, chuckling, stepped in to join them.

"Seems you've got a lot to learn about this place, Vice Ambassador," said the leader, "the first of which is war has never been our intention. We cut ourselves off from the Nexxus almost a century ago and have kept to ourselves ever since. We're not the ones responsible for any of this."

Chapter Twenty-One

"They made it to the Hexaks."

"You fool. You'd assured me this was perfect."

"Nothing in this life is ever perfect. Stop sniveling. We can still salvage this and keep our arrangement profitable."

"If Phaetal speaks to the Hexak chieftain, too many questions will surface and—"

"Find your backbone. He is only one man, alone in a hostile territory. Besides, we have agents loyal to us.... We do still have agents in play, yes?"

"Of those we have influenced, only one is willing to stay the course."

"You cannot honestly tell me Phaetal's frightened anyone off."

"Not him. It's the Hexak chieftain. All of our contacts are afraid of being liquidated. Apparently, the Hexaks aren't too fond of spies. The man is no idiot, and need I remind you, he can read minds."

"If that damned ambassador gets to him, we'll all be in jeopardy of being liquidated, ourselves."

...

"Is the tracker still intact?"

"Yes. If it had been destroyed in the landing, we would have known."

"It's only a matter of time before the missive is presented. Bide your time, just beyond their radar."

"And?"

"And when you get the signal, kill any who stand in the way between your fleet and the Hexak chieftain."

Chapter Twenty-Two

Vanysha thought she'd died and gone to heaven confined in an eight-by-eight glass cube. Skin-blistering water rained down to wash away fatigue, dried blood, and half an inch of fine orange sand. When was the last time she'd dared to stand under such a stream without hearing someone pound on the door, demanding her head?

She'd finished her habitual washing routine within two minutes. Now, she stood enjoying the warmth seeping into her sore muscles. With her head hanging heavy off of her neck, Vanysha let her eyes drift shut, and in the peace of her watery solitude, memories of a long ago romantic experience tiptoed forward to play in vivid color and captured sound.

Kieran had promised her a special treat to mark their three months of bliss. He was always surprising her with tender gifts; whether a delicate bangle or a scoop of her favorite dessert, his love for her was visible in all the little things he did. That time, instead of a scrumptious meal, he'd had something much more unexpected in mind.

"*Close your eyes,*" *he whispered, his breath tickling her cheek as he stood at her back.*

Giggling, she complied. Her fingers laced with his, and she shuffled her feet, hoping not to stumble while following his lead, though he announced approaching steps leading up or down, as well as turns in their path, not once leaving her side. Others' friendly voices greeted them, and she could only imagine their smiling faces. She reached out her free hand, searching for a hint of her surroundings. Only smooth walls met her questing touch before he captured her extended arm.

"No cheating, la'nen. Nothing is going to spoil this surprise." He placed a soft kiss on her neck, then pulled her to a stop. The soft click of an unlocking door just in front of her stole her attention away from the hushed conversations, and a gentle hand at the small of her back guided her inside. She took two steps forward before the door closed behind her. His presence disappeared, and she shuffled forward aimlessly in the dark.

"Can I open my eyes now?" she chided. Light and delicate fragrances wafted to her nose, and she heard the faint sound of lapping water nearby. Excitement skated along her skin, and she bounced on the balls of her sandaled feet. Though the urge to peek was tempting, giddy anticipation was heating her blood to a delightful temperature.

"Almost," he said, the warmth of his breath tickling along her throat. He trailed his fingertips up her bare arm before brushing back her long braid. She shivered in desire, her head lolling heavy, following the weighty pull of her thick hair. His lips sent fiery jolts along her skin as he slid the thin straps of her dress off her shoulders. Need burned through her veins, pooled between her thighs as he slowly stripped her. He took tender care with the removal of her sandals, placing her hands along his own shoulders as he picked up one foot, and then the other. Tiling, cool and slick, met the soles of her feet, and her brows tugged together while her smile grew and cramped her cheeks. When the last strap had vanished, so did her companion, and she waited, naked and trembling, half afraid that the anticipation would leave reality flat.

"Open your eyes and come to me, my beautiful." Kieran's voice had

bounced off of distant walls. Her eyelids fluttered open, and her jaw swung agape. Pale blue and sea green mosaic waves adorned the ivory walls, while candle sconces scattered throughout cast the room in a delicate glow. But what took her breath away was the massive, sunken tub that dominated the center of the space.

Waiting with arms outstretched, Kieran stood waist-deep in their private pool, tendrils of steam rising up and encircling his chest. His honest, loving smile promised delights and filled her heart with hope and joy.

She extended her hands, and he took hold of her fingers, leading her to paradise.

Vanysha threw back her head and howled out in misery and rage, slamming her palms against the slick shower walls. Why did he have to break her? Even if she'd never been handed over to the slavers, no man would ever be able to bring her to the same peaks as Kieran. She wished she could go back to hating him.

No, that wasn't right. Once she'd no longer lived in fear for her next breath, she'd simply focused on everything that was not Kieran. She'd convinced herself that the nights she'd cried herself to sleep had been because of her ordeal, not the cold sheets beside her ... that the reasons she avoided any intimacy was because of the disfiguring scars and marring marks on her body and soul, not because her heart would forever be locked in the memory of what she'd had and lost.

"You okay in there, kid?"

The concerned question from the surprisingly understanding doctor yanked her back into the dangerous present. While the Hexaks and their self-sufficiency had been a pleasant surprise, it still didn't answer her nagging question: Who shot down her ship and killed one of her close-knit crew?

"Yeah," she rasped in reply. After coughing to clear her throat, she gave speaking a second attempt. "Yeah. Sorry about that."

"If it makes you feel better," he called out, "yell your fool head off. I won't judge." At this, she smirked, wiping away her tears as she shut off the water. "Just wanted to make sure you hadn't tripped in there and tore open your stitches. I hate doing work twice."

"I'll keep that in mind." She snatched one of the thick towels off the stack and, leaning heavily on her one good leg, patted dry the tender gash. *What's one more scar? Not like I'm winning any beauty contests as it is.*

"Don't go getting all dark and maudlin on me now, kid."

Vanysha grumbled under her breath and tore into the packaged outfit, revealing the first item: a long tunic of dark orange, split up both sides. Sleeveless and flowing, it was complemented by a pair of loose black slacks, and to complete the ensemble, she found a camisole bra top and lacy set of briefs, both in silken black fabric. Her mind traveled back to the faces and figures on the other females she'd glimpsed during their journey here, and she gnawed at her lip.

"They'll fit." The chuckled words slid under the door.

"Am I even allowed to worry on my own?" Her brow knitted together as she fought against her amused smirk and she quickly slipped into her new clothes. Now he truly did remind her of Faze. Both men were fiercely protective of her in a fatherly way, and both managed to bring a smile to her face even when things seemed bleak. She'd tugged the top over her head right as a slight knock announced her visitor before the door swung open.

The doctor nodded as he stood in the entryway. "Around here, you're gonna have to learn how to censor your thoughts, or at least shield what you want to keep private."

"Shield, huh?" So focused on the concept of hiding her thoughts, Vanysha temporarily forgot about her injuries … until she took a step. She hissed out as her knee buckled and she reached out for anything to avoid hitting the floor. Luckily, Weyland's arm was within reach, and she muttered apologies between curses while she remembered how to walk.

Weyland responded with a very Faze-like sigh. "And you could also learn you don't have to do everything by yourself, or the hard way."

Her grimace melted into a pained smile. "Where would be the fun in that?" she said, and together, they shuffled across the floor. She wished she wasn't leaning so heavily on the kind doctor, but the pounding waters had done their job all too well and the residual adrenaline that had coursed through her body had spiraled down the drain. "So, how did you know the clothes would fit me?"

"Elsabet, the chieftain's daughter you met earlier, actually picked out the outfit for you. Never known her to be wrong on guessing anyone's size." Weyland's trek had one destination in mind, and she was in no mood to argue. The massive bed welcomed her as she sank down into the thick mattress. Faze had often teased her about her ability to sleep standing up. He couldn't have been further from the harsh truth. To her, sleep meant surrender, and her mind refused to give up complete control; most days, she simply closed her eyes, catching small naps when things slowed enough to breathe. But the comfort of deep and restful slumber was as elusive as it was desirous; too many waking horrors from her past often reared their ugly heads behind the shuttered darkness.

However, recent events had tapped out her energy reserves, and her fuzzy mind dragged her body closer to the beckoning softness.

"Hang on, there." A gentle shake to her shoulder jolted her back to the present. She blinked her eyes open, embarrassed to have found them closed. A glass of a crystalline blue liquid hovered in front of her nose. She frowned and shifted her cautious gaze to the doctor. "Drink this before you pass out," he said. "It'll help you sleep and speed up your recovery."

She accepted the concoction with a quirk of an eyebrow. "You trying to get me drunk and take advantage of me?"

Another rolling bout of laughter poured out from Weyland, and she wasn't sure if she should feel pleased or offended by his response. "Aw, that's so adorable. Kid, I've got shoes older than you."

She chuckled and, after an initial sniff, drank the mystery medicine. It had no real flavor, but she began to feel its effects almost as soon as it touched her tongue. Her arms dropped to her sides, limp and useless, as a cooling, cocooning sensation seeped through her whole body. She was vaguely aware of being eased onto her side while her eyes fluttered shut.

"Rest easy, Vanysha. You've earned a night free from nightmares."

If only the universe would be that kind to me, she mused before she finally drifted off.

Chapter Twenty-Three

Kieran pinched the bridge of his nose and pulled in another deep breath. Part of him wanted to ask Niko to bring him another bottle of that potent beverage, while his rational brain argued against attempting negotiations buzzed.

Nothing was right. He was prepared to use the snippets of Hexakan he'd set to memory to barter for peace with a warring savage beside a primitive campfire. But instead, he sat in a spacious room with lavish modern furnishings, speaking Universal with a well-educated leader. These people were not bent on the destruction of the Nexxus; they'd shut their doors to the politics of the outside, and were better off because of it.

"So when was the last time you had any dealings with any of the other planets?"

A sharp scoff bounced off the walls to his left, and he swiveled his gaze toward his newest friend. Niko kicked up his feet, rested his heels on the low table. "Shit, I don't think anyone has seen an offworlder before you guys dropped in … for, what, forty cycles?"

"Longer actually," the Hexak leader corrected, and Kieran turned back to face the man. H'reeh stood with his back against the wall, arms folded across his barrel chest. He oozed control, the mantel of leadership resting comfortably upon his shoulders. "The last emperor on Westran Alpha stupidly sent an attack force about two cycles after … after that night. Now, they started it"—he raised his hands, palms open—"and all we did was… Well, come to think of it, and in all technicality, we didn't 'do' anything."

Curious at the emphasis on the word "do," Kieran narrowed his gaze and waited for the rest of the explanation. H'reeh shrugged, then tucked his hands behind his lower back.

"We just, ah, left them on the planet's surface. Not alone, mind you. I think they lasted about two days before the rhoxxans finished them off. That was about a century ago," H'reeh said, and Kieran's jaw swung open. "Since then, we've been left to ourselves."

"A hundred cycles!" Kieran jumped to his feet, unable to sit any longer. "But this city is much older than that."

"It is." H'reeh lifted a shoulder. "During the time of my great-great grandfather's people, they learned the third sun was close to a supernova."

"Three suns?" Kieran blinked at the impromptu history lesson.

"Yup." The chieftain nodded. "Now, while the planet's surface was never any kind of tropical oasis, the blast would've killed everyone dumb enough to be outside. So, Mondevar the Elder started to search for places to hide until after the event."

Kieran frowned, confused. "Why not just send out—"

"This was nearly two thousand cycles ago," Niko interjected, leaning forward to rest a forearm on his thigh. "Most of the planets' inhabitants had no idea there was life on other worlds."

Oh yeah.

"Anyway," H'reeh went on, "legend has it, in his travels, he watched a flight of cam'rhans disappear into a crevasse along the Stony Mountains. He followed them, discovered the massive caves, and moved everyone down here to build what you see today." Kieran glanced up, his mind forming images of the epic tale. "Even named the city after the creatures as an homage to their guidance."

One word triggered Kieran's curiosity. "You said 'legend.'"

At this, the chieftain's son barked out a sharp laugh. "Yeah, 'cuz the truth is so much better. Said he saw the mythical half-bird/half-woman creatures flying around? He finally admitted he was drunk and fell down a crack in the mountainside. That didn't make the caves any less real, or any less of a literal life saver, but I always loved hearing that part after the Naming Day celebrations, when it was just family."

"But ..." He shook his head. Something weird about the timelines spun around in his mind, refusing to slow. "Who would tell that kind of secret?"

H'reeh and his son exchanged impish smirks, then H'reeh rubbed the back of his neck. "My great grandfather, Mondevar the Lesser, heard it straight from the horse's mouth. He passed beyond the veil when I was around nine."

"Wait." Kieran raised his hand in surrender. "This isn't possible. Just how old are you?"

Niko thumbed toward the chieftain. "Grampa there"—an offended harrumph cut in—"is about five thousand cycles, while I'm—"

"Five thousand. You little shit. I'm only three hundred and ninety and—"

"Aaaand..." Niko smirked, stretching out his long legs in time with his exaggerated word. "I'm just hitting my stride at seventy-two."

Kieran needed space and, pacing away from the astounding pair, he shook his head as he struggled to wrap his mind around this new information. Then he halted. "Are you people immortal?" he said. The concept was incredulous, and when he heard the words spoken in his own voice, he realized just how crazy he sounded. But before either man had a chance to respond, Kieran waved off any comments and resumed walking circles around the room. "Never mind," he said. "Okay, so, you were around when all this…" He paused, searching for the right word, but came up short. "This … mess started."

H'reeh's eyes darkened to dangerous levels, and Kieran immediately regretted his glib remark. Quickly, he inclined his head and dropped both his gaze and his knee to the floor. "I apologize. I meant no offense."

The air stilled. Finally, a lengthy exhale gave everyone permission to breathe. "Not your fault," H'reeh said. "Let's say it's still a touchy subject." A simple pat on his shoulder was the forgiveness he needed, and Kieran rose again to his full height.

In the warm light of the room, he studied the face before him. Strange shadows haunted the sky blue eyes that had witnessed the events that had started a war. While faint lines traced delicate patterns around his eyes and across his forehead, nothing would have betrayed the man's true age, and Kieran believed he was in the presence of a true leader; intelligent and fierce, one who'd wade into battles beside his men rather than direct from a safe distance.

Kieran knew what he must do.

"I need your help," he said, "to end this violence." He'd surprised himself with his own open admission, but this unfounded war had been waging for far too long, and for the first time in years, he wanted peace for someone other than himself. The people of Hexaka had welcomed him, and something in that acceptance had called to his spirit. Hope blossomed within. Perhaps it was the reunion with the only woman who held his heart that now sparked his drive; if even a small chance existed to win back the love of his Vanysha, he believed anything—including galactic peace—was possible.

A devious grin pulled up the edges of the reddish mustache. "I thought you'd never ask," said H'reeh.

"Now," Niko interjected, "while all these warm fuzzies sound stinking adorable, do either of you know where to look for who actually is behind all this?"

"I got an idea."

All heads swung toward the open doorway and to the newest additions to the gathering. Escorted by the chieftain's second in command and a handful of guards, the remaining members of Vanysha's crew strolled in. The burly Drekkan, Faze, leaned on one of the Hexaks, looking a little worse for wear, but at least he was alive. He had one arm wrapped around his ribs, and the bloodstains on the front of his flight suit didn't appear to be fresh. His cheek was pale, but Kieran chalked it up to the dusty journey.

Danton, on the other hand, was in the same grousing disposition since their small group had split. The dwarfish engineer grumbled and tapped at the small tablet in his hands, ignoring any pretense of civility, veering instead toward the farthest corner of the room, his gaze firmly locked on the flickering screen before him.

Kieran crossed to the pilot and, after a firm handshake, guided him to the closest available chair. "Captain," he said, "it is good to see you again."

"You were right, sire," the lieutenant spoke up, shaking a

healthy amount of rust-colored sand out of his hair as he crossed to H'reeh, removing his thick armored jacket. "Whoever took out their ship was determined not to leave any evidence. I'm surprised any of you walked away at all."

"What can I say? I've got a damned good nav," Faze announced with great pride.

Moment of truth.

Kieran locked eyes with the pilot and, staring into the determined golden pools, he came to realize the love buoying the male's comment stemmed from a different place—a feeling more paternal than romantic. He recalled Vanysha stating that the Drekkan was nothing more than a friend. Hope dared to tap at the doors of his soul, and he pressed his palm flat against his heart, his silent oath only visible to the captain. In reply, Faze dipped his chin a fraction of an inch, but the stern warning was still present in the man's gaze.

"Where's Van?" Faze asked, even as he scanned the chamber.

As if on cue, the door to the other chamber opened, and Kieran snapped his head toward the soft click, though his spirits fell as the doctor stepped through and closed the door behind him. Desperate, Kieran craned his neck from side to side, wondering if his diminutive companion was tucked somewhere within the beefy man's shadow. But when a second person did not magically appear, Kieran hurried to intercept the royal physician.

"How is she? Can I—"

"No." The single word slammed down like an anvil on his heart. "She's resting, and no one's gonna disturb her. Least of all, you." The doctor pinned Kieran with a laser-focused stare, and a raised palm halted any further discussion on the matter. "For now," he added. "Tomorrow might be a different story. Tonight, she needs to sleep."

Faze scoffed. "Good luck with that one, doc. Short of knocking her unconscious, that girl doesn't have an off button." An odd silence filled the room, and a concerned frown creased the captain's brow. "You didn't, did you?"

Niko gave a stifled snicker; nothing more than a soft cough at first, but in the space of a heartbeat, raucous laughter soon echoed off of the domed ceiling. Kieran glanced to the Hexaks, the massive males hanging on each other to remain standing as they all enjoyed a private joke. Even the chieftain had joined in, wiping away tears of mirth as he slowly shook his head.

"Damn, you offworlders are such easy targets," Weyland said, then clasped Kieran on the shoulder, a broad smile on his face. "She is fine." The man's strong fingers gripped tighter, and a wave of relief coursed through Kieran's veins. "And with the sleeping draught I gave her, she'll be out until the suns are up."

Kieran peered over the doctor's shoulder, wishing he could see through the solid wooden door. During the nights he'd spent with her, he used to watch over her until she slipped into slumber's embrace. Did she still prefer to lie on her left side, chin resting on the backs of her hands, arms curled in tight?

The voice of the Hexak chieftain yanked Kieran out of his daydream. "Now that that's settled," he said, "can we get back to the main topic at hand?" The man had returned to his rigid stance, resting his back against the wall, and without waiting for a response, he turned his gaze to Vanysha's crew members. "Who said they had an idea of who's behind the war?"

"I did." Danton moved away from his secluded corner. "While I was trying to piece together the nav system, I found this." He ambled closer, but the bulk of the group chose to meet him halfway. Kieran nodded to the doctor, then joined the others around the Bozzan. For a race of hulking warriors, they stood at a respectful distance from the much shorter engineer. "It's from the outboard sensor array. It grabbed a couple of images of the bastards who blew up my ship."

Faze cleared his throat, leveling a flat stare at Danton. A scowl drew the Bozzan's thick brows together. "*Our* ship," Danton amended with an embarrassed grumble, then spun the tablet around for all to see. The starry background sat frozen, and Kieran began to wonder if he was missing some unseen ship as seconds ticked by with no change.

"Wait for it…" Danton muttered. Kieran lifted his gaze to H'reeh, who looked up and shrugged one shoulder before dropping his eyes back to the monitor. Kieran had only a second to refocus on the screen, when a streak of blackened chrome zipped across the skies. "There!" Danton shouted and pointed a stubby finger at the disappearing streak before he paused the rolling vid feed. With a couple of quick swipes, he rewound the clip, stopping when the sleek fighter sat in the center of the display.

An eerie hush settled in as all eyes rose from the unimaginable image. "Who wants to go first?" the Bozzan engineer prodded the gathered males.

"But … but…" Kieran struggled to form coherent words. "That's a Central ship—"

"Bearing our colors!"

Kieran's truncated declaration was quickly usurped by the Hexaks', and the room exploded in roars of outrage. Threats of retaliation cried out above the din, and Kieran covered his ears to hear himself think. Was this entire trip a ruse?

"ENOUGH!" H'reeh's sharp command cut off any further comments, and his guards took a knee. Kieran felt the muscles in his thigh quiver to follow suit, but he remained on his feet. "This truly proves nothing," said H'reeh, "other than some asshole knows how to paint. Hell, the Jakkavani smugglers will use any vehicle they can steal or cobble together, and what better way to move undetected through enemy territory than in disguise?" The calm and logical statement brought a much needed level of rational thought into the emotional situation. "Now, while I am not discounting the possibility your ship was indeed attacked by raiders posing as Hexaks, I can assure you I did not order any attack, and neither do any of my counselors have the codes to release the locking mechanisms on our vessels. It's—"

"So you guys do have an armada?"

Kieran swiveled his stare over to Faze. The giant Drekkan held his place in the broad chair, and Kieran was certain he'd viewed the vid playback prior to their journey to Hexak's underground capitol. Curious, he shifted his eyes back to H'reeh.

One of the guards nodded. "Sure we do," he said. "But for as long as I can remember, we haven't had a need to use any long-range ships." Muttered assents added to the simple statement. "Most of the time we just use surface skimmers in case we need to go topside for any reason."

"Why do you ask?" Drexler inquired, cobalt blue eyes narrowed. "You think *we* did this somehow?"

Tempers flared, angered words bouncing off the walls once again, and Kieran blinked, processing the various viewpoints as rapidly as the threats were fired off. A couple of the guards demanded blood for the offense, while Danton rambled on about their destroyed vessel. The Bozzan seemed determined to get his teeth kicked in as he continued to place blame on the Hexaks for their part in the events. When it appeared violence would soon be a reality, Kieran stepped between the arguing parties, arms extended to keep everyone at a safe distance from one another.

"Dammit, Danton, stop making things worse," Kieran growled as he struggled to hold back the throng of much larger opponents. His elbow buckled, and Kieran found himself pinned in the middle of the shouting males. Pissed, he tugged off his gloves, then wormed his arms above his head and, with a deep, centering breath, he clapped his palms together, unleashing a mighty blast. The hollow boom sent out a shockwave, bowling over every male in the room.

His own pulse pounded in his ears as he peered out at the sea of astonished faces of the men scattered across the floor.

Oh, shit. What did I just do?

Chapter Twenty-Four

H'reeh levered up from his undignified position sprawled on the floor—*Guess the kid might be the right choice after all*—and, giving his head a brain-clearing shake, lifted his gaze to the only person in the room not on their ass. The vice ambassador lowered his arms, an odd gold shimmer radiating from his hands. Decades had passed since he'd seen such a formidable display of the Lost Art of Energy Manipulation. That particular gift was prolific in races bent on conquest, so very few of his people were born with the skill.

"And here I thought yelling was the best way to get everyone's attention," Drexler said. H'reeh dropped his shoulders, then swiveled his head to his snarky lieutenant. "Damn, bossman. You gotta get him to teach you that trick."

"If it would get you to shut up, Drex, I just might ask," H'reeh groaned out as he gingerly climbed back to his feet. Furrowing his brow, he studied his guest, seeing the man in a new light. Something in his demeanor spoke of his disdain for the ability; Kieran nearly folding in upon himself, his back bowing as if the rare talent burdened his soul. "So," the chieftain remarked, "were you planning on keeping that little tidbit a secret?"

"Please forgive me. I-I apologize for my loss of control and—"

H'reeh clasped Kieran's shoulder, forestalling any unnecessary groveling. "Hey, no harm done. Everyone stopped screaming, and most of the furniture is still intact." Then he pondered his friendly response. Under any other circumstance, he would have bitten off the offender's head and handed the rest of the corpse to his dogs. Maybe the borderline panic in the negotiator's voice had prompted his calm reply. He glanced around the chamber as his men regained their balance, carefully surveying their expressions. True to the warriors' code, all were merely impressed by the display of one of the Lost Arts, some nodding their heads appreciatively toward their visiting dignitary.

Kieran lifted his gaze, and a wave of sympathy washed through H'reeh. Embarrassment had cast dark shadows in the man's stormy gray eyes and regret lined his face. Immediately, H'reeh sensed no one had ever trained Kieran in the proper ways to harness his gifts and that he'd been stumbling around in a haphazard trial-and-error method.

The Hexak people were well versed in the arcane gifts and they still placed high value on the Lost Arts. Prophecy was quite prolific throughout the clans, second only to Empathy, which was found in every child born on Hexaka. Energy Manipulation manifested itself so rarely, H'reeh knew of only a handful with that gift, one being his son, Niko. He shook his head, saddened by the realization. Guess the other planets in the Nexxus had forgotten their own histories.

"Now that the fireworks are over," H'reeh said, "I think we could all use some decent sleep." And his direct words were immediately followed by each of his men giving a quick salute before exiting the room. Niko and Drexler hung back, however, waiting beside the door. Weyland also remained, dusting off the back of his trousers. "Doc, you wanna tend to our new guests?" added H'reeh. "Got a feeling they're gonna want to stay nearby. And it's not like we don't have the space."

The visitor's quarters hadn't been needed for a very long time, the last event being Elsabet's coming-of-age celebration. Now that his youngest had earned her position in the clan, though, the space had fallen into disuse.

Weyland nodded, "Sounds good," and crossed to the Drekkan. "Come, my friend. I think you and I have some talking to do."

Niko grumbled, swinging his head slowly from side to side. "Great," he said and tossed his hands skyward. "How come I get the pleasant one? Again." H'reeh rolled his eyes at his son's glib, yet spot-on, whine. He did have a point, and Danton seemed to have a similar response to his new shadow—the prickly Bozzan muttered as he ambled out the door, and soon, H'reeh was left with the vice ambassador and his second. Drexler rested his shoulder on the wooden frame, his lazy stance designed to set his guest more at ease, yet H'reeh sensed tendrils of misgivings emanating from his friend.

"If I have caused any offense—"

H'reeh shook his head. "Kid, you're gonna need to cut yourself some slack on this one." Kieran opened his mouth, but instead dropped his chin with a feeble nod. "Get some rest. The suns will be up in a few hours, and we still have a shit ton to talk about." And after giving Kieran's shoulder a final squeeze, H'reeh made his way to the exit, a knowing smirk tugging at the corner of his mouth. "I don't think I need to tell you to stay in your own room, do I?" He glanced over his shoulder, and Kieran sheepishly jerked his gaze away from the connecting door. "You heard Weyland. She needs to heal up, and you need to get your head screwed on right if we're gonna get to the bottom of this."

Certain his orders would be followed, H'reeh continued out into the hallway and shut the door at his back. Drexler fell into step and the two headed away from the guest chambers, only their paired footfalls echoing through the empty corridor. Neither needed to speak; both of their thoughts were on a similar wavelength. Yet, while H'reeh was convinced of the pure intentions of the visiting ambassador, niggling doubts still plagued Drexler's mind.

Their path led to the heart of Cam'Rhan, the last of the day's collected rays dimming, the bulk of the city's population having long since turned in for the night. As they journeyed to the private quarters of the ruling family, they passed by the standard handful of sentries patrolling the quiet streets. H'reeh pinched the tense muscles at the base of his neck, hoping the pressure would slow his spiraling thoughts.

"Why now?" Drexler said as he opened the door leading to H'reeh's private council chamber. "I mean, think about it. We've been flying under the radar for what, at least five decades? Are they actually running out of scavenged glass and need a fresh supply?"

Making a beeline to the crystal decanter on the far table, H'reeh silently mulled over his answer as he poured two healthy measures of the potent amber liquid, then handed one to his lieutenant, still deep in thought. "Profits must be slipping somewhere in the conspiracy."

"So do you think the kid is in on it, or is only the messenger?" Drexler lifted his drink in salute before taking a sip.

H'reeh drummed his fingertips against the glass, allowing the heat from his palms to warm the brandy, and after another second of thought, he shook his head, convinced. "Nah. The way he reacted to the energy manipulation? If he were out to annihilate us, he could've done it then. His heart's in the right place. Now, it's a matter of finding out why he'd gotten chosen to be delivery boy. What do we know about him?"

"Aside from being the son of Politico General Raejil Phaetal?"

H'reeh leveled an unamused gaze at his second, groaning. "Yes, Captain Obvious. Besides that."

"Isn't that enough?" Drexler shrugged, finishing the contents of his glass. "Maybe whoever's pulling the strings thought they could use the leader's kid as leverage?"

H'reeh took a fortifying swallow as questions, answers, and ideas twisted and morphed in his mind. Some key piece was missing, and it was seriously pissing him off. *Dammit.* He'd been out of the political game for so long, he no longer knew any of the players. Tomorrow's conversation would seem more like a lesson in recent history as well as current events.

A door opened and closed softly behind him, announcing the latest addition to join in the discussion.

"So, do we need to worry?"

H'reeh chuckled to himself and looked over his shoulder to his loving mate, Tirelle, who stood framed in the archway, one fist resting on her jutted hip. Even though theirs had been an arranged marriage, he couldn't have chosen a better match on his own. The years might have rounded her feminine curves, but he only saw the fierce female who played devil's advocate as well as staunch supporter in every situation. Silver streaks added sparkle to the flowing auburn waves curling around her face, and the lines around her bright golden eyes spoke of hours spent laughing with their five beautiful children. He opened his arms wide and she crossed the room to stand at his side. Once safely tucked against him, she stole the crystal glass from his hands and helped herself to a sip.

"That depends, love," H'reeh said and, placing a kiss on her forehead, he glanced down to read her expression. "How much did Elsabet tell you?"

Tirelle lifted a shoulder in a half-hearted shrug as she passed him back the drink. "That offworlders are… Damn, how did she say that? Oh! 'They're a bunch of tight-lipped, sexually frustrated imbeciles who need to learn to just say what they mean.' … or something like that," she mumbled, waving her hand. "But you know she's always been more about seeing everyone deliriously happy in love." She stepped out of H'reeh's embrace, the mood shifting to somber. "So, should we be worried about this courier?"

H'reeh took a couple of slow strides away from Tirelle, feeling the weight of two pairs of eyes carefully studying him. "No." He turned and raised his chin to meet the concerned stares of his mate and his second. "I don't sense any ulterior motives from the man. He honestly believes he is here to broker peace."

"And her?" Drexler chimed in. "Her ship and crew?"

H'reeh dismissed the notion with the flick of his wrist. "Nothing more than chance. There's definitely history between the two, but I think it was nothing more than dumb luck that had brought them together. Wrong place, wrong time."

"Or right place, right time."

A curious frown tugged H'reeh's brows together at his mate's contradiction. "You think it was planned?"

"Nothing that determined." Tirelle tapped one long finger against her temple as she balanced her elbow on her fisted hand. "You said there's something in their past they are unwilling to face. Perhaps fate put the two of them together to not only help us, but to also help themselves, as well."

H'reeh smirked, his gaze following his mate around the room as she spoke. "Now look who's trying to play matchmaker."

"Oh hush," she muttered. "From what Elsabet told me, all I'd be doing is helping the process along."

Drexler rolled his eyes with a long sigh. "So the messenger and his girl are gonna get back together. Fabulous. I was so worried." Then he paused and scrubbed a hand over his face. "Sorry, bossman," he said, dialing back the sarcasm, "but we need to figure out all the angles on this, and I don't think either of the potentially happy couple have anything to do with it."

"You seem to have an idea beyond the obvious Westran bad guys." H'reeh crossed to stand beside his lieutenant. "Where's your money?"

The surrounding silence was comforting, each person lost in their own thoughts as they created and recreated plausible scenarios. "From what I remember," Drexler said, "Central has their hands busy trying to keep the peace, so I wouldn't see them playing games." He paused again, shrugging half-heartedly. "Or at least I'd like to think so."

"Didn't a couple of our males recently return from scouting missions on the outer reaches of the Nexxus?" H'reeh asked, tugging at his chin whiskers in an effort to spark his mind.

His curious segue drew Drexler's eyes to him like a magnet. "It wasn't *that* recent," he answered sardonically. "I think Bosh and Sylmar have been back for at least ten cycles."

"Well, that's recent, as far as I'm concerned," H'reeh muttered then stalked away, dragging his fingers through his short hair. "I haven't seen any other planet since before Niko was birthed." As he stared at the pale gray wall, his mind fell into the cracks along the window's sill. A soft touch on his shoulder pulled him out of the darkness. Tenderly, he reached back and laced his fingers with his mate's. "Maybe it's time we brought them in for a serious debrief. I've put it off long enough." H'reeh dreaded the next query, even as the words fell from his tongue, and he locked eyes with his trusted advisor. "Do you think they've been compromised?"

No one dared to break the tension blanketing the quiet void.

"They've sat in on council votes for years," Drexler stated, finally voicing the terrifying fact. "If they wanted to hurt us, they would have moved long before now."

"Unless they had to wait until other pieces were set. Fuck!" Growling, H'reeh stormed over to the couch and plopped down. "Why did I ever agree to letting this … this farce of a peace envoy begin?" He cradled his aching head, shoulders slumping under the weight of his frustration.

"Because it's time to stop living in the past."

With the sage words from his beautiful wife, his anger vanished, and he shook his head slowly with a heavy sigh, then raised his gaze. Tirelle casually rested her hip against the windowsill, arms loosely held in front of her. The artificial moonlight bathed her in an ethereal glow, showing him once again her angelic stature.

"How did I manage to have such an intelligent partner?" H'reeh asked, smiling warmly at his loving mate.

"Just lucky, I guess," Drexler replied, beaming. "Oh, you meant her." He gestured to Tirelle. The joke had begun soon after H'reeh's father had arranged his match to Tirelle, while they were still too young to understand love, and even after over a century, the exasperated confusion still brought a blush to his wife's cheek.

H'reeh groaned and took to his feet. "Drex, are you ever going to get tired of that?"

His friend and confidant chuckled as he made his way to the door. "As long as I have a captive audience," he said, "I'm milking that one until they put me in the ground." And with a parting wave, Drexler slipped out, leaving H'reeh to wrestle with his conscience in private. The chieftain strode toward Tirelle.

"Well, I don't know about you," he said, "but I believe I've had all the company I can tolerate for today." He extended his hand to her with a flourish, and when she laid her fingers in his palm, he tugged her into his embrace. "And I have a feeling tomorrow is only going to bring more crap to my door."

"*Our* door, husband of mine," Tirelle remarked, wrapping her arm around his waist as she rested her cheek against his chest. "We share in the good and the bad."

Just don't let this get that bad. But he didn't need to censor his thought as they walked into the sleeping chamber. His wife held the same fears in her mind, as well.

Chapter Twenty-Five

Consciousness slowly crept in, peeling away the comforting warmth blanketing Vanysha's mind and body. The normal background whir of her ion drive engine had been replaced by an eerie silence.

And a tentative knock on the door.

Yawning long and deep, she gradually uncoiled her arms and stretched her toes toward the faraway footboard. Until the slight tug on her thigh reminded her of her current situation, and she hissed out a sharp retort.

"You awake in there?"

I am now, Vanysha replied internally, but before she could voice a response, the door swung open and flooded the room with cool light, announcing the entrance of the chieftain's daughter. Dressed in a similar smock and under-dress she'd worn last night, Elsabet approached the bed with another tray of food. A cheerful smile split her face, and Vanysha found herself returning the gesture, even if hers missed the mark by a landslide.

"Wow. You look a lot better this morning. Let me guess, Weyland gave you one of his famous nightcaps?"

Vanysha scoffed and gingerly levered herself into a seated position. "That thing packed one hell of a punch," she said. "What was in it?" Squinting, she glanced around the room. What was the current hour? A growing glow brightened the base of the slender windows lining the far wall, climbing higher as she encouraged her body into wakefulness.

"Stingy bastard won't tell anyone his secrets," her companion remarked. "Probably thinks we'll start making it ourselves, then he'll be out of a job." She tipped her head toward the inset bathroom door and Vanysha nodded, crawling out of the cool sheets and limped toward the needed relief. She sensed her ragged reflection demanding her attention, but she refused to glance in the mirror and quickly returned to the room. Fragrant steam wafted through the space, the wisps emanating up from the ceramic decanter, and Elsabet filled a mug with the most heavenly substance in the universe in Vanysha's opinion. In anticipation, Vanysha hobbled over to the unexpected supply of her morning ritual.

"You guys have coffee?" Even as the familiar aroma filled her lungs, she'd felt compelled to voice the ditzy question. With recent events having turned her concept of reality on its head, she was desperate for any semblance of normalcy. Her last cup of joe had been on board her now-vaporized ship soon after realizing their passenger was her ex-lover. The flood of memories froze her muscles, her outstretched hand trembling inches away from the offered mug.

Elsabet strode the short distance and placed the steaming cup directly into Vanysha's grip, wrapping her long fingers around both the mug and Vanysha's hand. "We're not complete savages here."

Vanysha squeaked out a feeble laugh, struggling to cram the rising tide of memories back into their appropriate box. "Yeah, I kinda noticed that," she said and dashed the back of her free hand against her eyes, rubbing away any lingering sleep as well as threatening tears. Gradually, Vanysha became aware that the chieftain's daughter still held her hand hostage, and with a couple of rapid blinks to clear her vision, she raised up her apprehensive gaze. "Are we gonna have a hugging moment?" she asked.

Vanysha cringed at the poorly veiled fear in her own voice, and to her surprise, Elsabet heaved a relieved sigh. "Oh, thank the gods you feel that way about it, too." She released her hold with a shake of her head, jostling her tidy mane of curls. "For a second there, I thought you'd gotten all warm and fuzzy on me."

"Sorry." Vanysha smirked, pulled her mug close. "Warm and fuzzy is definitely not me. I was never really good at the girlie stuff." As soon as the awkward intimacy had dissolved, Vanysha relaxed and took the time to truly see her new friend. Even with her shoulders hunched, Elsabet towered over her by nearly a head and a half. Her broad face and open smile hid no secrets but something in the warm light dancing in the Hexak's pale brown eyes gave her pause.

Elsabet sat back on her heels and folded her arms beneath her ample bosom. "With the way that boy was practically licking you with his eyes," she said, "I'm gonna call bullshit on that one."

Heat blossomed on Vanysha's cheeks and she spun away as fast as she could without sacrificing her balance or her coffee. Rolling laughter poured out behind her back as she tottered over to a nearby chair and she ducked for cover behind her raised mug, but the fired porcelain made for a weak wall. Should she put up a defensive front, or simply let the cackling die down? Vanysha opted to sip her steaming caffeinated goodness in silence.

Still enjoying her own joke, Elsabet pulled the food-laden table closer, then retrieved another chair. "Come on," she said. "No man looks at a girl like that, unless he's already seen what's on the menu and wants more of it." At this, Vanysha coughed, forcing the scalding liquid down the right pipe. Her companion patted Vanysha on the back, aiding in the process. "So, what did he do? Call you by another girl's name in the heat of the moment?"

"No," she finally croaked out, shaking her head as a backup response. Once her throat was in proper working order, she took another slow sip, the strong coffee clearing away her long sleep's lingering fog. The weight of Elsabet's eager stare threatened to steal her appetite as she added, "It was much worse."

Why did she feel the need to open up? Perhaps the inhabitants' stark, unfiltered actions were beginning to rub off. She'd buried the truth for so long, she almost believed it would never rise to the surface.

Almost.

"Can you forgive him for it?"

Hearing the question that had haunted her dreams for six long years stirred her inner voices to choose sides. Loud and raucous in the privacy of her head, they screamed and shouted, crying and railing without end, and as the debate raged on, her breathing grew more and more shallow.

Could she? Remembered pain charged through her body, slamming her mind back into those dingy rooms, sloppy hands pawing at her bare skin. If she closed her eyes, then the full-color pictures would play behind her shuttered lids, but the longer she stared into the nothing, the fuzzier the edges of her vision grew.

Gentle fingertips pressed onto her temples, drawing calming circles on her skin. The light touch banished most of her turmoil and centered her raging thoughts. Her eyelids fluttered down as she accepted the soul-soothing massage.

"If you focus on pain, Vanysha, then all you will find is agony."

She squeezed her eyes tight, holding back the impending flood. "It won't let me live," she said. Words spilled out, and Vanysha was simply too tired to fight the necessary release. "No matter how far I run, or how high I build the walls, it finds me."

"What finds you, hon?"

Vanysha couldn't remember the last time she'd dragged out her jagged memories into the light of day. Blaming her loose tongue on exhaustion and the friendly company, she delved deeper into her shattered past.

"The darkness, the torment. I … I just can't get away from it."

"Then let it go." The soft, direct statement speared through her teetering resolve, and tears slipped down her cheeks.

"How? All I can think of when I … when I see him is… He used to be so kind, so thoughtful. And then…" Vanysha didn't care if her words made any sense or not. Perhaps untangling the jumbled thoughts and emotions might allow her to piece together her own truth. She sighed. "And then he just left."

Through her catharsis, Elsabet continued the light massage, the slow pace relaxing Vanysha's tight grip on her emotions. "Has he ever said why?"

Vanysha only shook her head, her wracking sobs temporarily halting any further attempts at speech. "Never had the chance to ask. I've … I've only ever guessed at the reason," she said at last. Broken, she covered her face with her palms, hiding from the flood of memories—the sights, the sounds, the smells … all of it brought into sharp focus on a continuous replay of the darkest twenty days of her entire life.

"Do you know if he looked for you?"

She struggled to control her stuttered breathing as she contemplated the simple question. *Did he?* She didn't know. After the second night on her own, their "kindly" landlord had her arrested for squatting. Apparently, the asshole's fear of Kieran's father's repercussions was the only thing that kept them in their rented slice of paradise. Once it was clear Vanysha was flying solo, the wicked, greedy bastard had swooped in, hoarding the outstanding month's rent for himself.

Her one call had been to her parents, but instead of offering their comfort, they'd wailed and wept for their own loss. Her mother had even dropped to her knees in a fit of hysterical anger in the middle of the protectorate's dome, blubbering dramatically about *their* loss of privilege and position. Both had been so consumed by the promise of having a marital connection to the politicos, they gave not one thought to Vanysha's broken heart, proving the value of blood to her family. When they'd had the chance to post her bond, they'd chosen to disown her, handing her over to the slavers without a second thought.

"N-no," she stammered, her initial breakdown fading, leaving behind an exhausted sense of peace. "Things, um, well…"

"No need to say more. I think I got it." Vanysha detected no judgement in her companion's voice. She remembered Weyland's warning about shielding her thoughts, perhaps a bit too late; every degradation and violation had played out in gory detail in her mind, and now, she had inadvertently shared the entire ordeal with Elsabet. Her eyes popped wide and, recoiling in embarrassment and horror, she scrambled to regain her feet.

Elsabet, however, wasn't ready to release her hold. The burly chieftain's daughter slipped her hands from her temples and placed them on Vanysha's shoulders, rooting her firmly to the cushioned seat. "Now, just hold on a moment, sweetie. First off, you bolt out of that chair, you'll probably yank open your stitches and Weyland will kick both our asses for that."

"Both?" Vanysha asked, her voice rough and gravelly. She sniffled and rubbed away the lingering tears from her cheeks.

"Hell yeah, both." Once convinced Vanysha wouldn't flee, Elsabet reached back and retrieved her own chair, scooting in until their knees bumped. "I've known Weyland for the whole of my life, and any time something goes weird, and I'm in the vicinity, I get blamed for it."

"Really?" Grateful for the conversation drifting away from her own checkered past, Vanysha released the tension cramping up her shoulders by reaching out a trembling hand for her coffee. She cradled the warm porcelain between her palms and inhaled the liquid's comforting aroma. Elsabet's question continued to spin her thoughts as her new friend launched into an animated retelling of an event from her youth. Vanysha half listened, her mind unable to find a suitable pause button. What if he had gone looking for her? Did it make a difference? If she asked and he said no, would she still be angry at him?

A plate of fruits and toasted sweetbreads plopped into her lap, yanking her out of her reverie. She blinked rapidly and raised her gaze to her hostess. Amusement reflected back from Elsabet's crooked smirk. "You're gonna be holding on to that idea like a dog with a bone, aren't you?"

A fiery blush warmed her cheek, and Vanysha glanced away. "It's just that..." Her words dried up as she fumbled to complete her statement. Tossing her hands, she squeezed her eyes shut and instead spoke from her heart. "In a matter of one day, I went from the best time of my whole life, to wishing I was dead. For all I know, he'd just gotten tired of me and—"

"Nope." The single-syllable word halted any further blathering. "Now, I can't say what he did was right"—Elsabet's raised hands cut off Vanysha's retort—"but right now, all you have is half of the tale. Tell me this: what is the worst thing that could happen if you hear him out?"

Vanysha gaped like a fish, mouth popping open and closed, yet no sound passed her lips. Stunned into mute contemplation, she could only stare at the smirking girl. What would happen? Her heart would be broken? Been there, done that. She'd hate him? Yeah, that was covered, too. No matter how she spun the question, she'd already suffered the worst thing.

He could destroy your heart forever. The cold, quiet whispered truth threatened to shake her to her very core, and she mulled over the prospect as she nibbled on her repast. In the past two days, feelings she had long since buried and dismissed had bubbled up to the surface. Memories of happier days haunted her steps, his sensual laughter mocking her peace. Did she dare pin fragile hope on a useless dream?

"So, how's my patient doing this morning?"

Vanysha blinked away her mental wandering to focus on the new guest. The burly doctor stood just inside the threshold, fingertips drumming silently against his folded arms. A brow arched over his sparkling emerald eyes, and his gimlet stare drew a weak chuckle from her.

"Feeling much better, thank you," she replied, sheepishly tucking her hands beneath her legs.

"Am I hallucinating, or is that actually a dress you're wearing?"

Vanysha jumped to her feet at the familiar voice, the empty plate clattering to the floor, and she bounded across the room. "Gods, Faze!" She flung her arms around her captain and mentor, needing a steady anchor in her turbulent, emotional sea. Faze's deep rumbling laugh carried an edge of exhaustion, so she eased off on her enthusiastic embrace. "When did you get in?"

she asked. "Is Danton with you, or did he stay behind? How's my ship? Is she salvageable?"

Her captain chuckled. "Breathe, Van." And he patted her gently on her shoulder. "Our hosts brought her into one of their hangars, and Danton's been overseeing repairs. With the number of hands on her, we might be able to head home in a day or so."

Vanysha gnawed on her lower lip, contemplating the real possibility of being stuck yet another day in the same space as Kieran. What frightened her the most: a growing part of her wished it could be longer. So many questions had run through her mind and her heart after her short talk with Elsabet, questions in desperate need of answers, and only one person could provide those. Someone currently sitting on the other side of the door to her right.

Had he stayed there all night? Had he even given her a second thought? *What is wrong with you?* her inner self screamed in impotent frustration. *He left you to suffer in hell. He doesn't deserve another second of your time.*

"Van? You with us?"

Vanysha shook her head, jostling her brain back into the present. Sadly, her reaction didn't have quite the expected impact.

"Nah," Elsabet answered for her, drawing out the single syllable and a strange nest of vipers picked up speed in the pit of her stomach. "She's busy fantasizing about—"

"No no no." She lurched out of Faze's shadow and scrambled toward the chieftain's chuckling daughter. "I'm right here, paying lots of attention. No fantasizing going on here." Elsabet continued to laugh as she backpedaled out of Vanysha's reach.

"Fantasizing? About what?"

Vanysha shook her head furiously at her friend. "Nothing. Really, it's nothing." She was intent on keeping her secret safe in its box, and that meant putting her hands over Elsabet's mouth. "It's just a joke, honest. Okay, ha ha. Really funny but—"

"Hell yeah," her traitorous friend grinned, easily leaning out of Vanysha's reach, "but it's not a 'what.' It's a 'who.' See, she's having severely impure thoughts about—"

"Is she still talking about strangling that negotiator asshole?" Faze had unwittingly given her the perfect exit, and Vanysha leapt at the opening.

"Yes!" she blurted out, eager for a shift in focus. "That's exactly it. Subject closed." But Faze was more interested in the impish grin and slow head shake from Elsabet. The Hexak female folded her arms across her broad chest, resting her hip against the food-laden table.

"She's thinking about strangling something, but I don't think it's his neck."

An uncomfortable silence filled the room as all eyes swiveled to Vanysha. Suddenly the center of attention, she fumbled for a way to slip out of the spotlight, with no exit presenting itself.

"So you're sweet on the guy." Faze lifted one shoulder coolly. "What's the issue?"

Vanysha swung her gaze from her friend, over to the doctor standing silent vigil just inside the threshold. The Hexak physician knew more than anyone in the room, but in this precarious moment, Weyland's face gave her neither answer nor solace. She could almost hear his voice in her head: *The ball's in your court. What now?*

"I ... I mean, we..." Yet no matter how she tried to start the confession, her brain stalled the thought. She slumped into the nearest chair with a heavy sigh, gripping the arms to ease the ache in her leg. "I can't do it, Faze. I just can't take that chance again."

"Chance?" Elsabet quipped. "Life is all about chance. Every

day, every decision. You toss a coin to choose which dress you wear—the red attracts the man you end up marrying, while the blue one brings you one step closer to unlocking the secrets of the universe. It's all a game of chance, darling. You can't stop the game as long as you're breathing."

Vanysha tilted her head, glancing sidelong at the profound "savage" who, in the space of minutes, had become a confidante, a philosopher and, more importantly, a friend. She pondered the strange connection she felt with the people of Hexaka; not once had she felt unwelcome or unwanted with the chieftain's daughter or with the kind doctor. She opened her mouth, prepared to give in, when a loud explosion rocked the entire building. The door blew inwards, shattered, as strangely clad soldiers poured in.

Ducking the flying shrapnel, Vanysha rolled to the floor, then spun to face this new wrinkle. The uniforms might have been dirtied up, but she knew Central forces when she saw them. The sheen to the shoulder plates set them apart from the rest of the Nexxus. And judging by the Westran Alpha colors, they were determined to keep this war alive.

A primal roar grabbed her attention, as well as those of the invaders. Elsabet charged directly at the stunned forces, her beefy arms wide, and she didn't stop until she'd managed to knock half of them on their asses. Vanysha scurried to her feet toward the fray, quickly snapping up one of the hastily discarded pulse rifles. Certain the chieftain's daughter was more than capable of handling herself, Vanysha focused her attention on the enemy soldiers that had slipped through the net.

Never one to condone senseless violence but trained in the art of survival, she aimed the weapon with lethal accuracy. Whoever they were, their intentions were not friendly, and she was prepared to retaliate in kind. The heat of a blast whizzing past her ear reminded her of her lack of cover. Jerking her head to the left, she dove behind the remnants of a chair before continuing to return fire.

As her latest target vaporized in a haze of red mist, a strange thought swirled around in her mind: *I wonder if Kieran is okay.*

Chapter Twenty-Six

The enticing aroma of freshly baked sweetbreads encouraged Kieran to drag open his heavy lids. After his hosts and all of the guests had vacated his private sleeping chamber, he'd paced around the room until both his mind and his legs had been utterly exhausted. When he could move no more, he'd collapsed in a heap on the cushiony mattress and sank into a fitful sleep. Images of silver white waves of hair had beckoned to him, passion-darkened aquamarine eyes shadowing him around every ethereal corner. At the negotiation table; in misty hallways. His heart cried out for her, and his arms ached to hold her once again, yet his fingers were unable to grasp.

Distant voices crept into his erotic wanderings, gruff and demanding. The ground beneath him shook, and with Vanysha's name poised on his lips, Kieran bolted upright.

"'Bout damned time you woke up," grumbled his uninvited companion. Kieran groped sloppily for a lamp sitting on the nearest end table, only to have a curtain hastily drawn open, bathing the room in a muted radiance. Flinching back from the unexpected daylight, he shielded his eyes, waited until the objects in the room had slipped back into focus. Niko stood beside the floor-to-ceiling window, yawning broadly while he dragged his fingers through his wild and matted hair. "You made enough noise to wake the dead, what with all that moaning. Thought you were going to start humping my leg."

Kieran climbed out from the tangle of sheets, still crawling out of sleep's embrace, embarrassed to realize he hadn't bothered to take his clothes off the prior night. "Yeah," he croaked as he scrubbed his palm against his stubbled cheek. "Sorry about that."

"I'm just glad you didn't torch the place by accident."

Kieran looked down at his bare hands, then shifted his eyes to the gloves still lying on the floor. "Oh shit."

Niko knocked against his shoulder, jogging Kieran out of his panic. "You don't think those things"—he tipped his chin toward the discarded protectors—"can actually hold back that light show of yours? Give me your hand."

Concerned, Kieran tugged his brows together and extended his right hand, while Niko plopped down onto the bed beside him. His fingertips tingled, warning him, and at the last moment, he made an effort to pull his arm back into his body, determined to protect the chieftain's son from a possible loss of control.

But to his surprise, Niko grabbed onto Kieran's wrist, halting the retreat. "Whoa. Hang on there. Trust me, will ya?"

Kieran scoffed and petulantly attempted to yank his hand back. "Trust you? I'm trying to save you."

Niko barked out a short laugh. "And here I thought it was the other way around. Chill out, listen, and follow my directions. You can feel the charge building up in your hand, right?" At this,

Kieran nodded, grateful for any guidance. "Kinda feels like someone with a thousand tiny needles poking your skin?" And Kieran bobbed his head once again. "Cool. So you have the Lost Art of Energy Manipulation. Don't worry," he quickly interjected as Kieran's stomach churned, "it's fairly simple to command, once you get the basics."

"How … what…" Kieran fumbled over the words tripping off his tongue. "How do you know about, well … this?"

The chieftain's son pointed to the top dresser drawer beside the bed, and with a snap of his fingers and a "pew" sound effect, the drawer shot across the room. Kieran jumped to his feet as Niko beamed. "Think of it as insider information," he replied. "Come on, I'll show you. It's all about focus and flow. Shouldn't take a bright boy like you more than a few minutes to get a handle on this."

Kieran listened intently as Niko explained his curse in a positive light, referring to it as "Energy Manipulation," but it was the term "Lost Art" that sparked his curiosity. As the lesson progressed, he learned acceptance was the key to controlling his power.

"Dude," Niko said, "the reason you keep losing your shit with this is because you hate it." He demonstrated a series of gestures designed to either amplify or lessen the rising energy, a flick of his wrists finally extinguishing the glow. "It's a part of you, like that crappy-ass hair of yours." Kieran leveled a glare at the smirking princeling. "Mastery," Niko continued, "now that takes some doing. But when you start to feel stressed or angry, take a slow deep breath, count to ten, or whatever floats your boat, and that'll bring down the charge."

Flipping through his memories about all of the times his gift had emerged, it had been in moments of high emotional distress, and he studied his palms, mulling over this new information. It had been years since he'd dared be in the same room with another person without his shielding gloves on.

A quick jab to his ribs yanked him back to the present and he lifted his gaze to the chieftain's son who wore a devilish smirk. "Oh, and if you use it right," Niko added, "the chicks fucking dig it." Kieran blinked, deliberate and measured, as his brows shot up his forehead. "Better than a vibrator."

A chime sounded, and Niko swore sharply. "Damn. Lost track of the time." He moved purposefully around the room, opening drawers and grabbing a stack of clothes and fresh linens. "My father is planning on bringing the council to see you in a few, so you might want to clean up." He tossed the pile of gathered items in Kieran's general direction, then tilted his head toward an inset door to his left. "The bath's through there. It takes a second or two for the water to heat up, but it'll last as long as you need it."

Kieran gave his head a violent shake, dismissing the latest fantasy of his Vanysha in orgasmic bliss, and returned his attention to the present. "Do you happen to have a razor?"

Niko chuckled. "Why? Got a girl you're trying to impress? But, yeah," he added before Kieran could again trip over his tongue, "it'll be in the stall, along with all the other civilized bathing tools. Like soap and shampoo and—"

"All right, all right." Kieran's heavy sigh blended with his light laugh as he raised his hand in mock surrender. "I think I got it." Some prime negotiator he turned out to be. He seemed determined to make every wrong move in the eyes of the Hexaks.

"Mind if I give you a piece of advice?"

Kieran stopped and turned toward the chieftain's son. In the light of day, the familial resemblance between the two was undeniable; truly, this man was a newer version of the strong leader, and he carried the yoke of authority on his broad shoulders with grace and ease.

"Leave the beard." Niko patted Kieran's shoulder. "Makes you look more like a man. And if you're planning on impressing your lady friend, I think she'd like a little scruff."

Kieran rolled his eyes, then ducked into the side room—*Great. Now I'm getting dating advice from the enemy*—and as steam gradually warmed the glass chamber, he pondered his earlier thought. Not one of the Hexaks he'd encountered had given off any nefarious vibes. In fact, the entire population seemed blessed with a painful honesty. *Painful honesty, and complete self-sufficiency.*

He lathered the rich, fragrant soap in his palms, mulling over his current quandary. Hexaka's capital city was as ultra-modern as any on Central or Westran Alpha, and he filed through the snippets of daily life he'd glimpsed during his journey from the surface. Having used their steeleglass to create domed greenhouses, crops flourished and livestock roamed across golden fields on the distant hills. The people were intelligent and happy. All manner of commerce and industry were present, without the need of assistance from any of the other planets of the Nexxus. And he'd only visited one city. Hexaka was massive; there must have been thousands of such underground strongholds woven throughout the vast network of caves.

"So why keep alive the pretense of war?"

He'd asked the question to the walls and to the water, having needed to get the spiraling words out of his mind. The only feasible answer was: whomever had orchestrated the myth of ongoing hostilities relied on the continued disengagement of the Hexaks. It took two to fight, and with one party silent, the other had complete control over the narrative.

But who? Who did this conflict benefit? He watched grungy suds slip down the drain as he analyzed each potential player.

Central was the hub of the military politico body, and his father's regime. To mount and maintain such a long campaign was not sound. Plus, with an enemy unwilling to come to the table, his advisors would have counseled against such open-ended efforts.

Westran Alpha was at the heart of the original event; it would make sense for them to hold on to the grievance. But it was their shipments of water to the other planets that were often attacked as they struggled to receive their own necessary commodities.

Kieran rubbed his face while Niko's advice whispered in the back of his mind. Chuckling to himself, he slathered the thick, soapy foam beneath his chin and only shaved off the prickly whiskers along his throat. Time would tell soon enough if he'd made the right decision. With each pass of the blade, he returned to his contemplation.

Bayan? Their textile contracts were solid, terms recently fixed, and never had their loyalty come into question. The Palandar agriculturalists seemed to have some divine magics that allowed their water supply to never be depleted, but who knew how much longer that would last? For each planet Kieran named, he could find nothing tying any of them to such a deep conspiracy. While allegiances held between worlds, the assumption of peace remained. Granted, every ruling body was growing weary of the strangling trickle of water and the rising tide of rage from their populace. Revolution was on the lips of many in the lower castes, and unless he could get to the bottom of this new wrinkle, the shift in power could turn deadly.

Kieran shut off the flow of warm water as another realization crossed his mind: the water here never cooled. Perfectly heated, it had maintained both temperature and pressure during his lengthy shower.

Hexaka was entirely self-reliant; they neither gained nor lost from this war. Peace might encourage them to resume their steeleglass shipments, but it was extremely obvious the planets of the Nexxus needed Hexaka much more than Hexaka needed any of them. He dragged the thick towel over his skin, marveling at the quality of the weave as his political brain continued to spiral through mounting evidence. His job was to discover what the parties desired, and to what lengths were they willing to go to reach those ends.

And then it dawned on him: He wasn't there to negotiate peace; he was there to reforge broken alliances. If he could coax the chieftain to rejoin the Nexxus, the instigators of the so-called Crimson Alley would no longer have control over the flow of water. But how? How would he tempt a people who truly gained nothing in the process?

Kieran stepped into the borrowed trousers and, with tunic in hand, he headed back into the main room. "Niko," he said, "who has the most to lose if Hexaka rejoins the Nexxus?"

His sudden emergence from the bathroom startled Niko, the sweetbread in his fingers hovering inches away from his gaping mouth. "Huh?"

"Your people don't profit from this war," he said and continued across the room, covering the short distance in three long strides. "Hell, all the planets need you a whole hell of a lot more than you need any of us. So, if Hexaka were to rejoin the Nexxus, can you think of anyone who would lose?"

"Lose?" Niko screwed up his face. "Lose what?"

Kieran ran his fingers through his still-damp hair, certain he was on the right track. "Power, money, influence," he replied. "I don't know. It could be something as simple as respect, or a high place in leadership." He paced, each step generating momentum for every new possibility. "Is there anyone on your ruling council with outside contacts or connections?"

"You're barking up the wrong tree there, pal. No one, as far as I can remember, has even left the planet."

"Well, you're not entirely accurate on that."

Kieran swiveled his head toward the door, then dipped his chin toward the speaker in a diplomatic greeting. H'reeh and his second, Drexler, entered the room, and judging by the dark circles underneath the leader's eyes, he hadn't gotten much rest, either. "We had two emissaries who'd been dispatched before the hostilities began, who returned about fifteen cycles ago."

Realizing his indecent state, Kieran quickly tugged the borrowed tunic over his head.

"Emissaries?" Niko asked. "I didn't know we still had any off-planet." He grabbed a couple of mugs filled with an aromatic brew and presented his father, as well as Kieran, with a steamy cup.

Kieran gave the beverage a cautious sniff. "Coffee?" he asked everyone and no one. "You guys have coffee here?"

"Wow," Drexler marveled, shaking his head. "Are you ever gonna stop being so dense?"

With an exasperated groan, Kieran waved off the insult and strode the short distance to meet H'reeh and his lieutenant. "I honestly do not mean to sound purposefully ignorant, but so much of your history has been..." He stalled, struggling for the right word. "Hidden," he said at last. "Fabricated. Destroyed. Whatever you want to call it. It's just that, well, I didn't realize coffee had actually made it out this far. It's fairly rare anywhere aside from Central."

H'reeh shrugged and lowered his nearly empty mug. "I think everyone needs to start by putting all of their cards onto the table. I freely admit we have isolated ourselves from the rest of the systems for nearly a century, so let's assume most of your textbooks are working from outdated info."

A sharp knock on the door drew Kieran's gaze away from the chieftain, who beat him to the punch, nodding toward his son, and with an exaggerated groan from Niko, the barrier swung open. A steady stream of irritated males stalked, one by one, into Kieran's chamber, each face bearing a look of either outright disdain or mild annoyance. *And you had to promise to handle things yourself*, Kieran thought, gritting his teeth as he hastily smoothed his hands down the front of his borrowed shirt.

H'reeh held his silence until Niko shut the door behind the last man. "You say you're here to negotiate peace, right?" he said, and Kieran blinked, waiting for his brain to dissect the simple question. He responded with a rapid nod. "All right, then," H'reeh continued, "so who sent you?"

"I received the missive from Xyphos Bharange, the newly appointed Grand Magistorum of Westran Alpha, including terms and conditions to enter a peaceable treaty with the people of Hexaka," Kieran replied, and as he began the opening speech he'd rehearsed during the short flight here, a stray thought had hit him like a punch in the gut. Vanysha. Was she still resting? Would he be able to see her soon? He stumbled on an imaginary wrinkle in the thick rugs as he crossed the room to his satchel. Mumbling and shaking his head at his loss of focus, Kieran retrieved the sealed, undamaged tube and returned to stand before the chieftain.

For a heartbeat, Kieran hesitated. Under Universal protocols, he would have taken a knee to present the message. But the overly grand gesture now seemed wrong, given what he'd learned about his hosts. So he opted to split the difference, extending his arm as he dipped his head.

"Maybe he can be taught."

Kieran almost didn't recognize the lieutenant's voice, the standard hint of sarcasm missing, but he kept his eyes lowered.

"Quiet."

Kieran smiled at the floor, surprised and pleased to hear the chieftain come to his aid. Perhaps things were looking up. The cylinder disappeared from his hand, and he pulled his gaze up from the ground. As H'reeh cracked open the royal seal, Kieran went back to his slowly cooling mug, his eyes traveling to the closed door to his left. Time apart from his kitten had changed her spirited innocence into jaded ferocity. What exactly happened to her after his hasty departure all those years ago?

Nearly two weeks had passed before he'd been able to finally sneak a moment's reprieve, and he'd flown immediately to their little haven. But the landlord had only shrugged, telling him Vanysha hadn't been around for days and had even mentioned something about seeing her with another. Disheartened, he'd turned away and had never again looked for his chance at paradise. Had she met her captain in those early days? How much of her life had he missed?

"Hang on a second here," H'reeh said, jerking Kieran out of his meandering thoughts. "Are you sure you brought the right paperwork?"

Kieran shifted his attention to the chieftain. A pair of guards had moved into position behind him, making for a fierce, imposing wall. Any misstep in this moment could be deadly. Did he have the right paperwork? In truth, he'd never read any of the sealed documents he'd ever received; his job was to merely deliver the terms decided by one party, and to provide clarification if needed. He knew his limitations regarding concessions and how much wiggle room the contract allowed. Yet, the odd question from H'reeh had chilled his blood.

"I can attest to you the royal missive has not left my hand since it was presented to me." The professional in him was slightly offended, but something in H'reeh's confused expression told him to dial back his outrage. Instead, Kieran cocked his head, narrowing his gaze. "Why?"

The Hexak shook his head, a frown furrowing his brow. "Because this is blank."

Kieran's jaw popped open as klaxons split the air.

Chapter Twenty-Seven

H'reeh shifted his gaze from the stunned courier, up to the ceiling, baffled by the strange turn of events.

"What the absolute shit?"

While he agreed with his son's spot-on observation, it didn't change the truth: An enemy's force had entered the caverns and was now attacking his city.

Furious, H'reeh snapped his eyes back to the only influential outsider to gain admittance to their underground stronghold since the entire civilization had retreated from the Nexxus nearly a century ago. Had this all been an elaborate ruse designed to steal their secrets and finally destroy his people? A dangerous hint of red filtered into his vision as he stalked toward the gaping ambassador. Anger glued his molars together, and in one smooth and swift movement, he grabbed the tunic's loose fabric at Kieran's throat and propelled the man backwards, stopping only when the back of the man's head had smacked against the wall with a resounding thud.

"Talk," he snarled, his rage teetering on a knife's edge between control and destruction. "And I warn you, boy, if I hear an answer I don't like, I will redecorate this wall with your brains."

Abject terror oozed from his captured prey, but H'reeh dared not release his guard yet. His arm vibrated as he pinned the negotiator firmly in place, but while Kieran's fingers held tight to his wrist, he made no attempt to escape.

"I assure you," Kieran croaked out, his toes reaching toward the distant floor, "I came with only the best of intentions and—"

"And now you've paved the way to a new hell for me and my people," H'reeh growled. So many sacrifices. The lifeless, gore-splattered face of his little sister flashed into sharp focus in his mind, coupled with the soulful wails of his mother as his proud father carefully cradled her broken body. The wound had truly never healed, only ignored while his people hid from the Nexxus. Now it cried out for retribution.

He could snap Kieran's neck like a twig. In fact, he should, then bury him in the far caverns and be done with this whole mess. Instead, he locked eyes with the vice ambassador, the son of the Central's current lord-high-mucky-muck and inwardly cursed himself for giving the young man an ounce of trust. Answers were needed now, and tact was in short supply. His rage as his guide, H'reeh easily splintered the weak shields keeping the man's thoughts from him. The gray orbs across from him flared wide, the black pupils nearly devouring the smoky ring before constricting to pinpoints. If any secrets were to be found, H'reeh would crack Kieran's mind like a nut to ferret them out.

A gentle hand on his shoulder nearly broke his concentration, a rising flood of serenity flowing into his fractured head, yet H'reeh was not prepared to give up his quest so easily. He continued to delve deep into the ambassador's thoughts, peeling back layers of recent memories—the explosion, the trek across the surface ... all events replayed in reverse order. And while Kieran tried feebly to throw small barriers around selected thoughts, H'reeh was relentless. Only when the image of the female with whom he'd arrived repeatedly shimmered beyond the shield did he veer from those intimate moments. He dug on, stopping when the image of the negotiator standing before a wall of vid screens had scrolled into view. The missive, sealed and intact, was immediately tucked into a satchel, and H'reeh realized the glaring fact.

Damn. Kieran was nothing more than an innocent victim. True to his word, he was just the messenger, having never once peeked inside to verify the contents of his parcel.

"My lord."

Drexler's urgent tone dragged him out of his fruitless search, and with a heavy sigh, he released his hold, grumbling a half-hearted apology. His anger needed a more appropriate outlet and the trembling male before him was nothing more than a target of opportunity. He shifted his gaze over his shoulder to his friend poised to jump on his command, while the council members argued loudly. Regardless, his homeland was in danger and he needed to act—*now*.

"Fucking hell," Niko blurted out, and H'reeh swiveled his head toward his son. The young male rushed to his side, the opened cylinder in hand. "Whoever created this had a tracking signal installed, and it started up when the seal was cracked open."

"I only opened the friggin' thing two minutes ago," H'reeh said, tossing his hands up. "How the hell did a force get here so fast?"

Niko twisted apart the exposed wires, fingers untangling the brightly colored filaments. "Their fleet must have been hanging out, just waiting for it to let them know exactly where to go," he replied, never once lifting his gaze.

Leaving his son to his work, he stalked toward the only denizens of his homeworld to have seen the outside planets in nearly a century. His lingering advisors parted, leaving Bosh and Sylmar standing apart from their group. They'd been trusted by his father to stay in the Nexxus even after his sister's murder, and now it was time for H'reeh to discover if the men had been twisted by the avarice running rampant on so many other lands. He halted before them. "Is there something either of you want to tell me?"

Bosh tilted his head in reverence, gesturing with open hands. "Sire, I am certain I know nothing of—"

"Lies!" Sylmar shouted, pointing a bent, accusatory finger at his bowing companion, his wiry, silver-streaked auburn hair fluttering as his gaze ricocheted between Bosh and H'reeh. "I told him not to listen. The offworlders are fed on greed and vice, and it poisoned his mind. I tried to—"

Silver flashed in Bosh's hand as he lunged toward the old emissary. "You fool! You'll ruin everything!" Drexler yanked H'reeh out of the range an instant before the crimson spray painted the scene, and before he could blink, two of his guards tackled the screaming counselor—Ilvan yanking the sharp curved blade out of the man's hand as Jazeem pummeled him into submission. He managed to catch sight of Niko as his son ran to Sylmar's side.

"Don't kill him yet," H'reeh spat out as he climbed back to his feet and shrugged off his Drexler jacket. His lieutenant's concern for his life was appreciated, though. Now that the current threat had been neutralized, H'reeh turned his gaze back to the room and, judging by the openly stunned expressions worn by the rest of his High Council, he knew he could trust their loyalty. "See what's going on and slaughter any who dare stand against our people."

Orders were shouted as the males poured out of the chamber, and H'reeh squeezed his temples, hoping to banish the rising ache. Exasperated, he dropped his head back. "And will someone please silence that damned alarm."

His simple command earned a series of affirmatives, and soon, the chaotic cacophony waned, sirens fading into the distance. H'reeh slanted his gaze toward the remaining males in the room. His son, stripped now to his waist, had shoved the heavy fabric against the vicious slash on the old emissary's throat, trying in vain to stem the flowing tide. Drexler had crossed to the twin guards and, with his fingers weaved through Bosh's hair, he dragged his prey across the room.

"Niko?" The chieftain kept his gaze trained on his lieutenant and on the dangerous situation. "Is he gonna live?"

Drexler dumped the bloodied, groaning traitor into the nearest chair, snarling as he wiped his hands against his pants. "If this bastard even breathes wrong, *he* won't live much longer."

H'reeh folded his arms across his chest. While he agreed with his friend, the only two males with any information lay in mangled heaps. Still, he waited for word from his son, and he glanced toward Niko, certain Drexler had things under control. Niko leaned over the old emissary, his ear close to Sylmar's mouth. *Crap,* H'reeh thought. *Not good.*

"Niko?" He hated to disrupt, but time was not on his side.

Niko lifted one finger, yet stayed put. Seconds ticked by, counted by each inhale and exhale as H'reeh waited for what he suspected was the inevitable. He'd never been one to believe in the gods of old, but he sent a silent prayer to whichever deity protected secrets, just in case. Too many lives depended on the words of the man bleeding out on the floor.

A gasped and ragged sigh split the silence, and Niko rested back on his heels. "I got a little, but none of it made any sense to me." Wiping his forearm across his damp brow, Niko turned his gaze toward the captive. "Said something about vengeance and broken futures."

The long-forgotten words slammed into H'reeh, stealing the air from his lungs. His father had boomed them as he'd cradled the battered body of his daughter, sealing Hexak away from the Nexxus. Back then, the hall had been sparsely occupied by the remaining members of the Westran Alpha ruling family, and to this day, H'reeh could still recall the horror reflected in the eyes of everyone gathered, save two faces: The crazed expression of the killer, his face painted with gore, had been burned into his brain, while the mysterious and smug counselor beside him had watched his father's anguish with a self-righteous smirk.

"I am now vengeance. For this deceit, your world shall pay a thousand lifetimes. We leave you to your evils and to your broken futures."

Rubbing his hand against his sternum, H'reeh encouraged his heart to return to its rhythm. In the explosive chaos, he'd nearly forgotten about his guest, and H'reeh frowned, his gaze searching the room. To his surprise, he discovered the man exactly where he'd been dropped. Kieran rested with his back pressed against the wall, his ashen face blending in with the ecru paint. The young man's hand was frozen on his neck, his eyes broad and unblinking.

"You still with us, kid?" H'reeh feared he might have permanently damaged the ambassador. After a heartbeat, though, Kieran blinked, and H'reeh let out the breath he was holding.

"Thank the gods. Didn't want to explain to your girl that I got you skewered, just when she was ready to forgive you."

As if on cue, the door separating him from the party in question burst open.

"Dad! What the hell is going on?" Elsabet made a beeline to him, her rainbow-striped curls bouncing in her frantic wake. Red stained her knuckles, and her dress bore the tell-tale signs of a scuffle. "A couple of assholes barged into the room, waving guns around and barking out orders for us not to resist them."

H'reeh arched a brow and ducked his animated daughter's flailing arms as he met her in the middle. "I take it you didn't listen very well," he said.

She scoffed. "Hell no. You taught me better than that. But this guy"—she tossed her chin toward the sheepish Drekkan —"has to jump in and steal all my fun."

Pride welled up in his chest, but H'reeh bit the inside of his cheek to hide his appreciative grin, and instead, turned his attention to the rescued party. The captain looked better after the night of rest, new bruise along his cheek notwithstanding. Vanysha used the long rifle barrel as a crutch, leaning on the solid butt.

Rifle? The weapons in everyone's hands. That was new.

"I tried to apologize for taking out the one at her back," Faze stated, his exasperated tone indicating the number of times he must have made this same explanation. He shrugged as he shouldered the long-barreled gun. "Hate to see people attack from behind."

H'reeh nodded as he draped an arm around his daughter. "I couldn't agree more. Which does bring me to my next question."

The Drekkan raised his hands in mock surrender, taking two shuffled steps back. "Hey," he said, "we already got the third degree from these guys." He tilted his head toward the doctor and two of the guards he'd sent to watch over his guests. "And I'll tell you the same thing I told them: they're not with us."

"Actually…" H'reeh chuckled at the hasty retreat from the giant before continuing. "My question was a little different." He waited until all eyes were on him. "Mind giving me a lift? I think it's time to finish this negotiation face to face."

Chapter Twenty-Eight

Kieran rubbed at his throat and coughed to reengage his aching vocal cords, while his mind frantically scrambled to find meaning in the flurry of lethal activity. As this venture moved on, he realized he did not have the control he believed was his. The ship's crash, the trek across the surface of Hexaka, and the Hexaks themselves. Now, the official missive that supposedly held the promise of peace for all of the Nexxus planets was nothing more than an empty tube. He was simply a pawn; his mission, a fraud.

Hollow and floating adrift on the strange tide, Kieran stood in mute witness as events unfolded before him. Even if he'd been unaware of his role, the attacking forces had arrived because of him. How could he be so wrong? Had he been so blinded by pride, so certain of any outcome, he refused to search for nefarious hands working against him behind the scenes?

Images of the video conference with the young Westran Alpha leader flashed before him, conjured by the prying tendrils of the Hexakan chieftain's mental probing. A shadowy figure had lurked beyond the fringe, howling against the negotiation, but he'd quickly dismissed the lone dissenter. In hindsight, he wished he'd dug deeper to discover their identity.

The doors flung open, and H'reeh's daughter led a battle-weary group of Hexak soldiers inside. He spied the Drekkan captain tangled in the clutch of armed males, and his heart raced as he continued to search for Vanysha. A flash of silver-white hair caught his eye, and he kicked off the wall at his back. Laser focused, he weaved amongst the milling crowd, shouldering his way through the guards, stopping only when he gently turned Vanysha around and pulled her into his embrace. His rational brain warned him to be cautious, reminding him of her recent wounds and of her obvious disdain for the new version of him. But he didn't consider any of that, or even what he'd do if she pushed him away; he needed to feel her in his arms, if only for a moment.

"Vanysha? Are you all right?" The scent of smoke clung to her soft hair, clouding her flowery fragrance as the words poured out. Something clattered to the floor beside him.

"Yeah, I'm fine," she mumbled into his chest before coiling her trembling arms between them. Her splayed palms held him at bay, and Kieran picked up on her confusion. His lips parted, words hanging on his tongue, but he held his silence, opting to wait for a better time, with less of an audience, to continue his investigation.

"So, are we going on a field trip or what?"

Niko's question reminded Kieran of his original purpose and he released his stranglehold on Vanysha. He attempted to hold her against his side, but she hastily slipped away from him, opting to move closer to her captain. Jealousy's fire ignited in his gut, even as the words of the chieftain's son tumbled around in his mind. Running a hand against his head, he tugged on his hair to center his thoughts.

"Just me, kid." H'reeh clasped his son's shoulder. "I need you to clean up this mess and figure out exactly how deep Bosh and Sylmar's treachery ran."

"Not bloody likely," Drexler added plainly. "I think what he meant to say was: 'Just me and Drexler.' Right?" The lieutenant folded his arms across his chest, putting an undeniable period on the end of his statement. Kieran slid his gaze toward H'reeh, gauging the man's reaction. "'Cuz," Drexler continued, "you know you're not going anywhere without some back-up. You tend to pull stupid shit if you're not under constant supervision."

Faze cocked his head. "As much as I'd love to offer you that ride," he said, returning to the chieftain's question, "unless you've got a transport ship we could borrow that doesn't have your markings all over it, we might be stuck here a while longer. *The Royal Janstar* still needs a few months' worth of work before she'll be flight-worthy again."

"Don't you have any faith in me?" Danton groused as he entered the scene, wiping his oily hands down the legs of his jumpsuit, flanked by a handful of equally greased-covered Hexaks. "She can make it as far as you want. I wouldn't suggest setting any speed records, but she'll make it to wherever you want to go. She's juiced and ready."

Vanysha limped over to the scowling Bozzan. "You're telling me my ship is … is… " Hope resonated in her hushed tones. Electricity climbed up Kieran's spine as he recalled other times her voice had taken on that anticipatory quality. A sharp cuff to his shoulder knocked him out of his daydreaming, and he snapped his gaze over to the chieftain's son. Niko's knowing smirk and slight head shake grounded Kieran faster than a bucket of ice water.

Danton shook his head, both hands splayed out like a shield in front of him. "Now, she ain't gonna be winning any beauty pageants, so don't get your hopes up. But all the holes are patched, and we can get her back to Central for a complete overhaul." He narrowed his eyes, sweeping the room with a somber frown. "Unless you want to keep her here in dry dock for a few months and do the job proper."

"She's been cobbled together from what we salvaged, and parts from a couple of fighters," one of the Hexaks added, sweat and grease painting dingy streaks down his cheeks. He shifted his attention to the chieftain. "We'll get things straightened up for you here, sire. Those pussies from the outer planets don't stand a chance on our turf."

"Then what the hell are we waiting for?" Vanysha asked, and all eyes swiveled toward Kieran's former lover as she stood proudly in the center of the group, arms akimbo as she scanned the room. "We sure aren't going to find the answers we need here, and I'm done being the universe's punching bag. Some asshole ruined my ship, and I'm ready for some payback."

The chieftain tossed back his head, laughter filling the air at her bold words. "Looks like hanging around with Elsabet is rubbing off on you."

As the Hexaks discussed the necessary preparations with Faze, Kieran covered the short distance between him and Vanysha, and he caught her elbow before she became too wrapped up in her flight plans with her crew members.

"Shouldn't you stay here?" He'd meant for his words to be a tender request regarding her safety. Her reaction proved very different: She tugged her arm away and pinned him with a determined stare.

"And just what is *that* supposed to mean?"

Now was neither the time nor the place to get into an argument, and Kieran gestured to the chieftain's daughter, assuming he'd receive back-up for his argument. "You're still injured," he said. "I'm saying it would be safer for you to remain here until—"

"Safer?" She rounded on him, hobbling over to stand before him, chin thrust out defiantly. "I am not some fragile flower who needs protection from the likes of any male."

Kieran shook his head. "No, I didn't say you were. But if something happens to you, I—"

The icy flames in her eyes stole away his voice. "Something *has* happened to me, and I survived it." She spun about and, reaching down for the hem of her tunic, she yanked back the fabric to expose the elaborate tattoo he'd glimpsed earlier in the cave before she glared hate-filled daggers over her shoulder at him. "And I've got the scars to prove it."

Then she stormed off, and Kieran stared on, his heart plummeting, having spied the evidence of a slaver's brand buried beneath the intricately spiraled vines.

Chapter Twenty-Nine

Vanysha didn't stop her forward momentum until she was safely tucked in the navigator's pod. Her unsteady hands fumbled with the harness across her chest, though whether they trembled from rage or the embarrassment flooding her body, she couldn't say. The long trails of fabric wadded at her back took some adjusting before she was comfortable; never had she wished for a jumpsuit as much as she did now. Hindsight was a beast, and she should've had sense enough to look for a change of clothes. Perhaps had she been wearing her standard flight suit, she would have thought twice about revealing her shame to the entire room filled with friends, strangers, and her former lover.

What was she thinking?

A soft knock on the roof of the cramped cabin snapped her mind back to the present. Glancing up, she met the confused face of a young Hexak male, thick black hair poking out from beneath the brim of a burnt orange cap as a deep frown creased his forehead.

"Uhhh…" A cautious grin brightened his hazel eyes. "I think you're in my seat?"

"Huh?" Vanysha's gaze darted around the unfamiliar console, brows knitting together. "What's going on? This is my ship, isn't it?"

The boy—Marin, according to the insignia on the front of his flight jumpsuit—rubbed the back of his neck with a sheepish grin. "Well, technically, yes. We had to patch in one of our own pods to make her flight-worthy again. But that's not why I'm here. I've been given very strict orders that you are to rest until we get to Central."

Her eyebrows crept up toward her hairline. "Really?" she quipped. "By whom, if you don't mind me asking."

"Doc Weyland, your captain…" Marin had lifted a hand, ticking off fingers as the count continued. "My chieftain; his wife, Tirelle—who I'd never go against." Vanysha's brows shot farther up her forehead, but he had no sign of stopping the growing list. "Niko, Elsabet, Maveen, Gibran, and Synsha—those are the rest of H'reeh's kids—a couple of the guards … and, oh yeah, that crotchety Bozzan engineer. I've been told that if I even think about letting you steer the ship, and I quote: 'I'll be viewing my nuts in a glass jar.'" He extended a hand. "And I'm quite fond of them being attached to my body, thank you."

Grumbling at the stars and the sea of overly protective people, she unbuckled the safety gear and climbed out of her fortress. Marin guided her up and claimed the vacated seat. "You sure I can't assist you?" she asked. "There's a couple sensors that might flare up if—"

The light laugh behind her stalled any further explanations. "We made sure everything's working well enough to get everyone to our destination in one piece. Look, I'll make you a deal." He paused in his standard pre-flight checks. "I saw that crash site, and only a top notch nav could've allowed anyone to walk away from that. On the return trip, you can take the reins."

Vanysha smiled half-heartedly at the offer, then stepped back as he swiveled the steel harness door shut. "Thanks," she said. *But that won't help me right now.*

Where had her courage vanished to? She crossed her fingers, hoping the bomb she'd dropped would keep Kieran at bay. Perhaps the rumors of what happened to those who bore a slaver's brand would be enough for him to keep his distance until the suns of Hexaka winked out.

"Van?"

Or not.

Vanysha stared at nothing as Kieran called out again, this time, his voice much closer. Her shoulders drooped, the weight of her throbbing head too much for her weary body to bear. She ran a hand through her hair, her eyes drifting shut as she attempted to sort out the best solution for the situation, and in the dark, the last expression on Kieran's face snapped into crystal-clear focus. She silently watched the fast-and-furious interplay of emotions as they scrolled through his eyes. Question was: Where would the frenetic wheel stop? Repulsion? Disgust? Horror?

Pity?

In truth, she'd been too chicken to stay and see the outcome, opting to retreat into the safety of her ship and her nav pod. Now, standing exposed in the open hallway with nowhere to hide, she wished she'd stayed, if only to know what to expect if she found enough courage to lift her gaze.

The shuffling footfalls halted, and she peeled back her heavy lids. The slick black boots in her periphery were covered with a fine layer of rust-colored dust and the brick red drips of dried blood. Her civil, ship-owner brain demanded she ask her passenger if he'd been injured, but the terrified girl living beneath her skin was too scared to speak. So she remained frozen, locked in the moment and lost in the nightmares of her past. Tension thrummed along her arms, and her fists clenched as she waited for him to make the next move.

His audible swallow and heavy exhale kickstarted the resting snakes in her gut, while the floor at her feet began to lose focus. She prepared for the bad news. *Just get it over with. Let me move beyond this.*

"Somehow, I don't think 'I'm sorry' is going to fix things." His voice brushed against her soul, hollow and sorrowful.

She squeaked out a strangled, mirthless laugh. "Gee, ya think?" Using the last remnants of her pride as fuel, she shouldered past him, hastening toward her personal sleeping cabin as shelter. The small entourage of Hexaks were in the luxury quarters, leaving the crew area quiet and uninhabited. She'd managed two steps before he'd captured her hand.

"Van, I—"

"Why, Kier?" Vanysha yanked her arm free, wrapping herself tightly in her shredded armor. She stopped at her room while forcing down the rising tide of tears. "Was it something I did wrong?" she asked. "I have to know. Did you just get tired of me? Of us? Did you care or even come back?" More questions, bottled up for far too long, swirled in her mind as she fumbled with the keycard, her vision blurry. She was powerless to stem the tide.

The light above the wall panel finally flipped to green, and the door slid open. She snapped her head up, chin quivering as she met his anguished expression. "Was the thought of being tied forever to a … a nobody like me—"

But before she could finish the accusatory query, he cupped her face and silenced her with a tender kiss. On his lips, she tasted memories of laughter and joy, and she dug her fingers into the rough-hewn tunic, torn between shoving him away and dragging him closer. Self-preservation kicked in, bowing her back, keeping a fragile cushion of space between their bodies. He broke away, peppering kisses atop the crown of her head, and she almost missed his ragged words. "My gods, *la'nen*, I am so sorry."

Cradled in his embrace, Vanysha held back the waterworks for the blink of an eye before she collapsed against the weight of her burdened spirit, grateful for the strong arms holding her together. Her clenched fists thumped uselessly against his thundering heart, while the floor slid beneath her and she dragged her rubbery legs along. Still, she tried to focus on the gentle whispers of his voice, rather than her own pitiful sobs. Part of her wanted to rail and scream, demanding him to leave her to her pain. Yet that rage was second to her desire to find out the answers that had haunted her soul for six long years. A soothing rocking continued after her feet had left the ground.

Then she caught the words she knew must have been imagined. Sniffling hard to dial back her cascading tears, she flattened her palms against his chest and leaned away from his enticing warmth.

"What did you say?" She cleared her throat, hoping to banish the squeak from her voice, and she stared off into the surrounding dark of the small room, not quite ready to meet his eyes. No light spilled in from the hall; he'd remembered to close the door, which gave them a terrifying amount of privacy.

"What, aside from 'I'm sorry'?" She visualized his confused, crooked grin. Unwilling to believe in miracles just yet, she simply nodded. He stroked her arms, the rhythmic pressure lulling her turbulent mind just as effectively as it had all those years ago. "I did come back for you," he said, and Vanysha squeezed her eyes shut, swallowing down another rising bout of tears as she focused all of her senses on hearing his words. "The ... the night I left," he said. "Gods, I wish I could've done it differently. I had just gotten up to take a piss when…"

Immediately, she was transported back to their tiny apartment. She'd fallen asleep curled up in his arms, as she had done every night. "Two of my father's guards were waiting out in the living room," he told her, and her eyes popped open at his flat declaration. "They had a note with four words on it: 'Leave or she dies.' All that time, I thought I'd been so careful, thinking he didn't know where I was, or didn't care."

So much information in such a short amount of time, and she needed space. She *had* to look into his eyes to see the truth of it all. For the son of a powerful politico, whose schemes toppled governments, Kieran Phaetal had an unyielding loyalty to facts and honesty; never once in their time together, or even in their new situation, had he lied to her.

Wiggling out of his tight embrace, she crawled off of his lap and crossed the narrow chamber to rest against the inset table, while Kieran stayed on the bed. He turned away, but not before she glimpsed the silvery tracks trailing along his rugged cheek that he dashed away hastily with the back of his hand.

"When?" she croaked out, digging her fingertips into the supportive metal perch behind her. His hair curtained most of his expression, and she prepared for the worst.

"I tried to send a message to you as soon as I got back to the capitol, but each one was intercepted. It took me nearly two weeks to slip away from my father." The anguish in his voice touched her heart, and she relaxed her white-knuckled grip. "I knew the room rent was covered through the month, and I hoped—"

"I was arrested by the landlord for squatting the day after you disappeared."

Kieran jolted to his feet, shaking his head slowly. "What? No, that can't be. He told me you'd left with another man within a week."

Vanysha swore softly, spitting curses at the floor. "If I ever get my hands on that bastard—"

"No." She raised her eyes to find Kieran standing directly in front of her. He trailed his hands down her arms, pried her fingers away from the table's edge. "He's mine," he said.

Venom had tainted his words, and she wondered how he'd take the rest of her tale.

Chapter Thirty

Only the illumination from the passing stars lit the room when Kieran glanced down at Vanysha, her skin like silk against his bare hands. The desire to strip her down and worship her body was staggering, but given the volatile nature of her newly revealed past, he would have to allow her to dictate the speed of her forgiveness of him. *If I am even deserving of any.*

"What about—" He swallowed back his rising fear. The image of the chattel brand on her delicate skin had burned into his mind and in his soul. During their long years apart, he'd often wondered about her. He'd hoped some lucky man treated her like the treasure she was. Did they have a beautiful child with her silver-white hair? Had she forgiven him for leaving her like a thief in the night?

She shifted her face, the shadows haunting her eyes encouraging him to complete his query. "What about your parents?" he asked, hating the harsh, blunt edge to his voice.

Her arms tensed, muscles taut in barely restrained anger, telling him more than words. The relationship between her and her parents, especially her gold-digging mother, had been the source of many late-night conversations. Vanysha would voice her worry and she'd fret over the fear that one day the selfish gene would manifest in her. But he knew now, as he had back then, she was nothing like them, her heart pure and full of love. He drew lazy circles on the back of her hand with the pad of his thumb.

"They gave you to the slavers, didn't they?" he said, sparing her from having to utter the vile truth. Actions rather than empty words were needed, and he walked his fingers up her arms, cupped his palms around her elbows. She balked, hesitating, as he counted the beats of his heart. Then he scooted closer, refusing to let her again face the world without him. "I … I will never forgive myself, *la'nen*. I should have—"

"Did you *really* come back for me?" Her whisper had cut through the silence. Within her soft tone, he detected a glimmer of his Vanysha, his gift. He brushed his knuckles under her chin, guided her gaze to his. Her aquamarine eyes sparkled with unshed tears and she held tight to his wrist as she added, "Don't say it just to … to … to tell me things you think I need to hear. Because I … I can't, Kier. I can't g-g-go down that road again. I…"

He wrapped his arms around her and pulled her into his embrace. "I did, angel. I did." He kissed the top of her head, then rested his cheek against her moonlit hair. "I wandered through the whole area for the better part of two days, until my father's guards caught up with me again, hoping and praying you might walk by. I spent nearly four hours each day at that little cafe you liked so much; you know, the one with the ocean scenes painted on the walls and those sweet cakes with the chocolate frosting."

Light laughter blended with the sobs shaking her body, and

he cradled her close. "I am so sorry," he said. "I was a fool to leave you without a fight. I knew my father's cruel streak, and I knew he'd follow through on his threat without a second thought. You were far too precious to me and I … I thought I was keeping you safe. I guess no good deed truly goes without repercussions." He closed his eyes, savoring the feel of her curled up against his chest. A lifetime ago, this simple gesture had given meaning to his existence; now, he prayed he could return the favor.

"Faze saved me," she said softly, and Kieran nodded in the dark, trailing his fingers through her tresses of moonlight. The shorter strands slipped quickly across his palm and he ached to wrap himself once again in her longer waves. "He … he said he saw something in me on the block that day," she went on, "and when he was unsuccessful in his bid, he tracked down my … my 'owner' to broker a deal."

Furious anguish coursed through Kieran's veins, yet he remained silent, stroking her arms to offer comfort. "I…" The pain resonating in her voice was like an accusatory knife strike to his heart. He placed another tender kiss atop her head, and he sensed her relax a fraction before continuing. "I don't remember much of those weeks before he found me. Sometimes, I get flashes during the night, and I wake up either screaming or throwing up whatever I had left in my stomach."

Vanysha gently pushed away and collapsed into the chair beside the small table. Kieran spun about, crouched at her feet as she propped her forearms against her knees. She stared through the floor, her fingers twisting the long hem of her tunic. "All the while, I kept asking myself: Why? Why did you leave without a word, in the middle of the night? Was I as bad of a lay as my father had said I must have been, to drive you away? Could I have done something, anything, everything better? I tried to rationalize things, saying you must have had a very important reason to vanish as you did. But once the gavel slammed down at the auction, that part of me died." She glanced up from the floor, pinned him with a forlorn stare. "I wanted to hate you," she declared. "To blame you for all that was happening to me. Wanted it with every fiber of my being, because I thought something compelling like hate or vengeance would keep me going."

"I deserve your hatred," he said, choking on the shameful truth. "I was a coward, I abandoned you and—" Self-loathing colored his words, but a tender touch on his lips stalled his apology.

Tears slipped down her cheek as she shook her head, her fingertips trembling on his mouth. "I said I *wanted* to hate you. When I asked Faze why he'd bothered to save me, he said it was the hope he saw in me. To him, he said it shown so brightly, and even after he … he found me where he did, he said that light still burned inside me. He said the only force in the universe great enough to survive was … was something stronger than hate. Now, don't get me wrong," she amended, narrowing her gaze at him, "I am all shades of pissed off at you, and that won't be easy to forget. Too much has happened to me, and I am not the Vanysha you used to know."

"Nor am I the timid boy who left you to survive the harsh world alone." A hint of a smile touched her lush lips, and he placed a tender kiss on the pads of her fingers. "When I returned to the capitol after my failed search for you, I guess you could say a part of me died, as well. I … I knew I would never love another." He held her gaze as his long-buried admission bubbled to the surface. "So I focused all my energies on my career."

"All?" She blinked rapidly, a confused furrow cutting across her forehead as she lowered her arm. "Are … are you telling me…"

Kieran gave a sad and solemn nod. "I have not held another

in my arms since that last night with you." He remained still, intent on reading her final expression, unsure of where it would land. He prepared for feigned sympathy or outright disbelief and waited as her eyes roamed his face.

Her lips moved, yet no sound emerged. "But ... but you were always so ... so passionate?" At this, her cheeks glowed with a delicate warmth. There was his Vanysha. He traced the line of her jaw with his knuckles.

"Only with you, *la'nen,* and only for you. I learned that I not only lost you that night, but I'd lost my heart, as well." She cupped his hand with hers, rested her face into his palm, and in a heartbeat, he was transported back to their slice of heaven so many years ago. He'd teased her about the simple gesture she'd become so enamored with.

Thrust back into the present, he leaned close to brush his lips against hers. "I have no right to ask," he whispered, the words welling up from his very soul, "and if you tell me to leave, I will never trouble you again." His eyes drifted shut, and in the darkness, he found his voice. "But would you show me your ... your tattoo?"

"Why?" Fear had tinged her hasty reply.

Pulling away, he opened his eyes and gazed into hers, then swept away, with the pads of his thumbs, the tears lingering on her long lashes. "Because I ... I need to," he replied. "And I don't care what it is hiding. I think it's beautiful, and sexy as hell."

Chapter Thirty-One

Vanysha swallowed down the last of her tears as she stared into Kieran's smoky eyes. She tilted her head, unsure if she'd heard him clearly.

"You … you what?"

He *wanted* to see her tattoo?

A smoldering smile grew on his face, tugging at one corner of his lips, and a warmth chugged through her veins. He trailed his fingertips down her arms, and sparks tingled along her bare skin. "Please?"

Her mouth dried up, all of the moisture gathering at the apex of her thighs. "Wh-why would you … I mean, it's…" The word *hideous* sat on the tip of her tongue, but refused to fall. In truth, the brand was barely visible beneath the delicate layers of beautiful, artful ink. Faze's wife, Meena, had truly found masters when she'd commissioned the piece; each spiral imbued with love, every twisting vine created with kindness.

Yet she'd never openly shared it with another, the secret hers and hers alone. But the heat from his intense stare had bolstered her courage and her trembling hands reached down for the hem of her long tunic.

His rough voice halted her. "Hold on." Had he changed his mind? Was she too soiled, too broken after all? She held his gaze as he took to his feet, then guided her to join him. "How about we find a more comfortable setting?"

"I kinda liked seeing you on your knees," she quipped, his chivalrous action bringing out the playful side of her she'd thought long dead. She'd missed their wordplay nearly as much as she'd missed his touch.

He arched one thick brow, wound his long fingers between hers, and shuffled back toward the bed. Still lost in his turbulent gray depths, she matched his short strides. The edge of the mattress bumped into the backs of his knees, and Kieran sat back, still guiding Vanysha until she stood between his thighs.

"I thought you might," he crooned. "But first things first," he said, sliding handfuls of fabric higher up her body. Balancing against his shoulders to steady her wobbly legs, she watched as he slowly undressed her. As the first blast of air tickled her stomach, she flinched with a light gasp. The urge to yank down her blouse jolted through her arms, and she dug her nails into the meat of his strong muscles. She swallowed down her rising fear and waited in anxious anticipation.

"Beautiful…" The word breathed against her skin, and lightning ignited her blood.

"Do you…" Any remaining thought vanished as he kissed and nipped his way along the inked tendrils that climbed up her side. Heat flooded her core, knees buckling as forgotten pleasures reawakened in her body. Kieran's broad hands splayed across her back, holding her in place as he worshipped every inch of her tattoo.

Frantic, Vanysha tugged the unnecessary shirt over her head, then the bralette before turning her attention to his tunic. His hungry chuckle caressed her bared flesh, and she shoved him back against the bed.

"Clothes. Off. Now."

Her demands were met with a crooked grin. "Are you in a hurry?" Yet his playful tone did not stop him from peeling off the shirt and tossing it across the room. She blinked rapidly, reengaging her brain, as her gaze roamed over the cut-and-chiseled planes of his chest. He'd filled out in all the right places since she'd last seen him.

Why *was* she moving so fast? "Well," she said to his question, "not really." Then she paused, using the reprieve to catch her breath. "But … you said that you, um…"

Kieran tucked one hand behind his head as he extended the other to her. "For you, *la'nen*, I will wait an eternity." A mischievous twinkle lit up his stormy gray pools. "But I wouldn't say no to making up for lost time."

He'd found her beautiful all those years ago. What would he say to the whole picture now? She hesitated, fear cooling her passion, and moved to cover her exposed breasts only to have Kieran sit up and capture her retreating arm. With a light tug, he pulled her to a gentle halt before she could slink farther away. "Van, I know it will take time to earn your trust once again." His tender voice called to the long-dormant part of her soul. "I am not asking for forgiveness," he told her. "For now, I'm only asking for the chance to make love to you."

Mixed emotions churned in her gut, nearly paralyzing her. "I don't know if I can," she whispered, weak and hateful words that fell from her lips, bitter on her tongue. "I'm, ah, I've been…"

Kieran wrapped his arms around her, buried his face between her breasts, his rough stubble tantalizing her sensitive skin.

Memories flooded her soul as fire coursed through her veins, and she threaded her fingers through his thick hair, the silken strands heaven as they slid across her palms. He growled something, his husky voice muffled. Her eyes drifted closed as he continued to repeat the same word over and over again: "Mine."

Tears pricked behind her shuttered lids as the years apart melted away with his one possessive sentiment. Her back arched, a heavy sob fell from her lips, and the world around her spun before something soft and solid met her shoulders just as the cool air kissed her exposed nipples.

"Vanysha?" He'd murmured the gentle plea, yet fear kept her safely buried in her personal darkness. One fingertip traced the shell of her ear, and she couldn't stop the smile tugging up the edges of her mouth. "Van?" he asked again, his breath warm on her cheek, lips following the path of his teasing touch as it moved along the line of her jaw. She giggled in spite of herself, sneaking her shoulder up to hide from his tender torment. *"La'nen?"*

She squeaked out a pathetic strangled laugh, and her lids fluttered open. Kieran lay on his side, his head propped up on one bent arm. She noticed his eyes had focused lower than her face and, smirking, she tipped his chin up to lead his hungry gaze away from her breasts.

"My eyes are up here, mister." So much time had passed since their familiar wordplay; she wondered if he still remembered his lines.

Smiling brighter than the Hexakan suns, he caressed her cheek. "Yes they are," he said before his gaze dropped back down. "But this beautiful, delectable, luscious, spectacular pair demanded my attention."

The embellishments were a new addition, and between each compliment, Kieran had placed a tender kiss across the tops of her breasts, igniting little fires that spread down to her toes, hitting every place along the way. She fought for a deep breath; needed oxygen to clear her addled mind. But with each inhale, her lungs pulled in the wild, intoxicating scent that had brought her comfort all those nights so long ago.

Would there ever be another chance for them?

Chapter Thirty-Two

Kieran watched the delicate tip of her tongue slip across her lush lips. Her mercurial moods were so hard to keep track of, and he still sensed a great deal of self-loathing in her. He yearned to see her smile again; her happiness had always buoyed his soul when dark thoughts of his father and his intended fate would steal into his mind.

Now, while she lay displayed like a feast before his hungry eyes, he studied this new version of his kitten. She'd always been slender, and even though the world had carved muscular furrows into her pale skin, her breasts remained plump, and he resisted the appeal of tasting those soft mounds for as long as he could.

The beautiful tendrils of vines and flowers inked along her back and climbing up her side fired his blood more than he dared to admit. Tattoos had always fascinated him, yet fear of his father's repercussions had always put the brakes on his own impulse. Seeing the intricate work adorning the body of the most beautiful woman of his life, the only one who held his heart, however … he was now determined to get his own mark. He forced the reason for her body art back into the farthest corner of his mind; guilt and shame would not color this moment. He needed to prove to her that his love had not disappeared from his soul as he had physically done from her bed.

He dragged his tongue around her pert nipple, teasing the tight bead before pulling it into his mouth. Her airy gasp spurred him on, encouraging him to continue the seduction. While he wanted to ravish her, plunder her body, take her as he'd done in the height of their romance, he knew she must set the pace. He'd waited six years to hold her in his arms again, what were another few more minutes of painful patience?

As her nails bit into his shoulders, the ability to think fled from his brain, following close behind the blood racing below his strangling belt line. As he kissed and licked his way to the other bared mound, she muttered one ragged word and his brows knitted together, hoping she'd repeat her request. He hummed his inquiry against her skin and was rewarded handsomely.

"More."

With a firm hold on her hips, Kieran rolled onto his back, and she followed his lead, straddling his engorged groin. Even though she was still clothed from the waist down, the mere weight of her on his sex-starved cock nearly unmanned him and he ground his straining erection against her core. Vanysha sucked in a sharp breath, her aquamarine eyes flaring wide, and she slammed her palms onto his chest.

"Is this what you had in mind?" he asked, then groaned, savoring the play of light and shadow across her face as she dropped her gaze. "Gods, Van, I want you so badly right now."

A strange shudder ran down her arms, sending a terrified message to his body as a single tear fell onto his chest. "Kier," she said, "I … I'm afraid." Her hesitation nearly broke his heart. He eased his hold on her narrow waist and trailed his fingertips up and down her spine.

"I won't push you if you—"

Vanysha placed one finger on his lips as she shook her head. "You don't understand. I … I want to…" She paused, a sad smile tugging at the corners of her lips. "I want to so much, it hurts. But I … I'm…"

Damaged.

The unvoiced word hung in the air, thick and stifling. He refused to see her as anything other than the woman he'd once loved—still loved—and with luck, would hopefully spend the rest of his life loving. Tenderly, he kissed the pad of her finger, before twirling his tongue around the digit and pulling it into his mouth. As his eyelids grew heavy, he held her gaze, sending waves of understanding and love through the visual connection.

Her aqua eyes darkened, and a delicate rosy hue painted her cheeks the longer he suckled her captured finger. She scraped her short nails against his chest, fisted her free hand as her hips slowly undulated. He struggled not to explode and flattened his palms between her shoulders as she lowered her upper body to him. Kieran released her finger and, intent on sweeter fare, brushed his lips against hers. Lightning surged through his veins at her tentative touch. With patient care, he traced the seam of her mouth with his tongue, inhaling deeply, dragging in the forgotten scents of jasmine and dark wine that was his Vanysha.

A sigh slipped from her parted lips, and he cradled the back of her head. Slanting his mouth, he swirled his tongue around hers and drank deeply of the forgotten sensation of her intoxicating kiss. While the urge to feel her beneath him fueled his desires, he recalled her violent reactions to any show of dominance. So, quickly dismissing the thought, he focused on the now

—the curves of her body, the heat of her skin, the fragrance of their arousal.

She squirmed within his embrace, grinding her core against him as she slithered her arms farther down his body. She made no move to break off the kiss, so he simply shifted his hand from her waist to higher up her back. He contentedly focused his attention on her mouth, but when a sharp zip caught his ear, he paused. His hesitation only lasted until the next heartbeat, though, timed with her fingertips brushing the length of his swollen shaft.

Growling like a hungered beast, he squeezed his eyes shut as pleasure threatened to push him to the brink before he'd even entered her. He broke the seal of their kiss, nuzzled his nose into the crook of her neck.

"Better be careful with that, *la'nen*," he purred into her ear. "It might go off without warning."

She laughed, deep and rich, and he almost made good on his threat. His cautious words had only encouraged her to stroke him with a feather light caress. Switching from languid to insistent, she masterfully teased him, her grip the perfect blend of pleasure and pain. Had situations been different, he would have asked where she'd learned the erotic trick, but any stray thought regarding the nature of her teaching had been banished by the sheer joy of simply holding her again.

When she reached down to cup his balls, his eyes snapped open, his groan rumbling through his chest, and he slithered down the bed.

She released her hold and she rolled onto her side. "Is something wrong?" A touch of fear lingered in her breathy words. His feet met the floor, and he quickly spun about to kneel at the edge of the mattress.

"Not a thing," he murmured, voice rough as he locked eyes

with her. One corner of his lips tugged up, and he reached for her hips, laying her onto her back while he pulled her closer. Her brows knitted cautiously as he wrapped his fingers around the waistband of her pants. "But I recall you saying that you liked seeing me on my knees."

A delicate blush again painted her cheeks, and he resisted the urge to shred the innocent fabric. She did look damned sexy in the ensemble from their hosts, but right now, he needed to see her out of it. Falling into her dark aqua pools, he peeled off the remaining layers, then kissed his way down each leg as it was revealed to him. The edge of the bandage covering her still-healing wound scraped his cheek, and he carefully avoided the tender area. His eyes drifted shut, feeling drunk on the sensation of her.

He licked his way up the inside of her thighs until he came to their sweet juncture, where thin, pale lines, some short and some long, radiated out from the triangle of silver-white curls, and rage nearly shattered him. *But that is in the past.* He vowed to make amends for the rest of his days, for his childish fear and weakness. Right now, however, he needed to show her exactly how precious a gift she was to him. Burying his nose into the soft folds, he dragged her heady scent deep into his lungs until it filled his soul, and with barely tethered restraint, he delved his tongue into her hot core.

Chapter Thirty-Three

Vanysha's body jolted at his tender invasion, back arching as the long-forgotten feeling of intense pleasure coursed through her veins. He was right; she'd always loved to see him on his knees, because the magic of his mouth on her sex had always brought her to the highest peaks with each pass of his tongue.

An overwhelming fear had nearly threatened to destroy her mood when he'd wiggled out of her grasp. Had revulsion finally taken hold? Was he disgusted by the knowledge of where she'd acquired her new techniques? Granted, her training as a whore had been brief and she'd been drugged for the better part of it, the variety of ways in which to please a client had been beaten into her body and her brain. Terror of his impending dismissal had stolen the fire from her blood, and only when she'd peered into his eyes had she seen the truth of his escape. Pupils like saucers had greeted her, ringed by a halo of shimmering gray; they'd told her how close he was to his release.

A prideful smile had touched her lips while he'd eagerly stripped her bare. What would he think of the scars? Again, the hateful past crept up from the depths of her subconscious, and as he had done only moments ago, he now slayed her evil demons with a single pass of his wicked tongue.

Her eyes rolled back as her hips rolled under his loving ministration. Air refused to stay in her lungs, escaping as needy whimpers, only to be drawn back in, heavy with the intoxicating fragrance of their lovemaking. His strong hands gently kneaded her legs, climbing higher to caress her ass. Relaxation, however, was the furthest thought from her mind, and in the darkness behind her closed lids, she relished each and every lick. His stubbled cheek tantalized her naked flesh, its rough texture adding a new layer to her arousal. As if sensing the shift in her mental mood, Kieran danced his fingertips down the backs of her thighs, tickling their way to her knees. She bit down on her knuckle to hold in a giggle, though it quickly morphed into a strangled groan as he tossed her legs over his shoulders and pulled her swollen clit into his mouth, feasting in earnest on her weeping core.

She threaded her fingers through his thick hair, then bucked and writhed as her orgasm rocketed through her body, and she flung her head back, helpless against the rising storm of ecstasy, crying out as wave after wave raced through her blood. He growled at her response, the vibration of his lips still suckling her hooded nub sending electrified pulses straight to her womb. Unrelenting, he pitched her once again over the precipice.

Time lost all meaning as pleasure washed away the rage entrenched deep in her spirit. Ripples continued to pulse, radiating out from the drenched apex of her legs as he kissed and nibbled his way back up her body. Each pass of his lips on her sensitive skin made her flinch in erotic surprise, earning his deep, rumbling chuckles. Even his breath sent out delightful aftershocks, from the tips of her toes to the crown of her damp hair.

Her heartbeat picked up as his chest scraped against her diamond-hard nipples, panic bleeding through pleasure, threatening to taint her passion. Desperate, she fought to remind herself of the nights spent under his weight, or of waking up with his warm body curled protectively around hers. But with her eyes closed, he was just another man pawing and slobbering over her naked flesh.

"Open your eyes, my love." His quiet plea had sliced through the void, and she grabbed on to the life-saving rope with all her heart. The soft brush of his knuckles against her cheek encouraged her lids to flutter up. Tears she didn't remember crying blurred her vision and her eyes refocused after a few rapid blinks. She trailed her gaze up from his solid and weeping shaft jutting ramrod straight, following along the length of his carved and chiseled torso, to finally come to a halt at his face. He levered away from her on locked elbows, his loose hair curtaining his face, though his eyes nearly glowed with pure, blinding adoration.

"How can you still love me?" she said, the hate-filled question falling from her lips before she could censor them. Hot tears slid down to dampen the sweat-slick sheets, but his compassionate smile burned away her sickening fears.

"That's easy, *la'nen*." He leaned down to lay a chaste kiss upon her forehead. "I never stopped."

His honest declaration gave her courage. She slipped her hands between their bodies, locked with his stormy gray eyes, and eased the bulbous tip of his cock into her quivering folds. They moaned in perfect harmony as she surrendered to the erotic flames deep in her core. Her eyelids fluttered, but she forced her hazy gaze to focus on Kieran. He hovered above her, his arm muscles bunching and flexing as he carefully inched his thick shaft into her tight sheath, and she tilted her hips, wrapped her legs around his, touched by his gallant gesture. Her shift opened her fully to him, and she welcomed him inside her aching channel.

Kieran growled, baring his clenched teeth, and sunk in deeper until his hips bumped against hers. "Gods, I've missed you, Van." His rumbling voice shot like lightning through her, sparking memories of that little slice of heaven where the world consisted of only the two of them.

Vanysha held tight to her recollections, raising her hand to trail her fingertips along his stubbled cheek. As he balanced on one arm with a strength that impressed her, he cradled her hand against his face before kissing the center of her palm. His rhythmic strokes gradually quickened, each roll of his hips pushing her higher and higher. She arched her back, ground her ass against the bed in desperate need.

Ecstasy coursed through her blood, and her keening cries melded harmoniously with his guttural groans. The cool air coupled with her sheen of sweat sent delicious shudders from her head down to her curling toes and, unable to hold against the rising tide, Vanysha threw her head back, his name ripping from her lips and from her very soul as she pitched over the sweetest peak.

With one final thrust, Kieran roared out in his release, flooding her heated channel, touching off tiny infernos along her bared flesh. She dug her nails into his forearm, his strength anchoring her in the moment, until she sensed a tremble beside her head. Curious, she peeled back her heavy lids to marvel at his physical control, yet before she could compliment him, his elbow buckled, and with a tired laugh, he collapsed beside her. He rolled onto his back, carrying her to rest on his chest.

"I'm sorry, *la'nen*," he panted, cradling her loosely against his thundering heart.

Her eyebrows tugged together, and she leaned back enough

to peer up into his face. "Is there something specific you're apologizing for, or is this a blanket sorry?"

Kieran shook his head, kissed the tip of her nose. "For my lackluster performance. I tried to hold out for as long as I could, but…"

His trailing voice left her to ponder his missing words. For a moment, she thought he'd fallen asleep, he was so still; only the gentle brush of his fingertips up and down her spine proved he was awake. "But…?" she prompted, wanting to hear the end of his statement.

He dragged in a long breath, then released it as a heavy sigh. "Have you ever heard guys talk about how if you use your opposite hand, it's like being with someone else?" He dropped his chin and captured her eyes. "Well," he said, "it's a lie." His soothing heartbeat just beneath her cheek called to hers, its comforting rhythm lulling her into slumber's embrace. As her eyelids fluttered down, she curled up into his arms, his whispered words soft against her skin.

"Because … it was never you."

Chapter Thirty-Four

"Have you heard?"

"Heard? Heard what?"

"Anything. I have received nothing but static from our operatives on Hexaka."

"What? For how long?"

"And the fleet has not responded to any hails, either."

"There is no way a force of that size could have met with failure. According to our database—"

"Which is a century out-of-date. It appears we may have underestimated the resources of the Hexaks."

"Impossible. Even their delegates gave no indication of any military presence—ground troops or aerial assault vehicles—capable of pushing back the might of our armada."

"Perhaps your methods of persuasion against the old man were not as effective as you'd assumed. Not every male is motivated by greed."

. . .

"Do we proceed?"

"We must. We have come too far to turn back. Too many other pieces still in play to halt at this junction."

"Do we at least know if any ships have recently launched from that quadrant?"

"No. As of now, we are blind."

"We risk more than our own lives if we are unsuccessful."

"I am aware of the consequences, but we must maintain a balance, and if Hexaka is truly as strong as they now seem to be, they must be dealt with. Swiftly, and without mercy."

"Let us hope the same is not demanded of us should we fail."

Chapter Thirty-Five

A frantic and insistent tapping chipped through Kieran's welcomed cocoon of sleep and he forced one eyelid open. "Go away."

Amused by the grumpy response of his still-slumbering companion, he smiled and glanced down at her. Last night, he'd watched her until his eyes could no longer focus, though whether it had been from exhaustion or the fall of tears, he couldn't say. His Vanysha lay curled against his side, head resting on his chest, and if the world asked him to give his life at that moment, he would die contentedly.

After his rather embarrassing and short-lived performance, he'd half expected her to toss him out without a stitch. Luckily for him, though, she'd been more forgiving and remained nestled against him. He'd scarcely felt the tug of sleep when she'd stirred beside him, shivering against the cool air and murmuring against the dark. With tender care, he'd gathered her drowsy limbs onto his chest and searched for the blankets beneath his ass.

But the more he'd shimmied on the bed, the more awake

Vanysha grew, and she was soon giggling as he softly swore. When he'd finally retrieved the elusive bedding, laughter poured out of both of them. The sound of her joyful laugh had always brightened his spirit, and he'd almost forgotten the peaceful sensation. Bundling her tightly against him, he'd kissed her, carried away by his memories.

Originally, he'd wanted to steal a quick sip from her lips before drifting off to sleep. Vanysha, however, had had a different idea and, deepening the gentle touch, she'd swung her leg over his hips, and round two was on. This time, he'd even impressed himself at his ability to drive her to multiple peaks before finally joining her in nirvana. The smile had cramped his cheeks as he'd cradled her against his sweat-dampened chest before falling into a blissfully sated sleep.

Until someone had dared to intrude upon his slice of happiness.

The silence after Vanysha's mumbled warning had lasted for a mere moment. Whomever stood behind the closed door hadn't been rebuked by her slurred demand, and the raps resumed, but with more force.

"Um, hey, Van?" Faze asked, voice cautious and measured through the shut barrier. "Do you happen to know where the vice ambassador is?"

Vanysha stirred, her long eyelashes tickling his bare chest, and he bit down on the inside of his cheek to keep from laughing and giving away his hiding place. An impish grin tugged up one corner of her mouth, and as she pushed herself into a semi-seated position, she silenced him with one finger across his lips.

"Maybe," she responded. "Why?"

"We only wanted to make sure you hadn't tossed him out the airlock while we were in take-off."

Kieran rolled his eyes. A knowing mirth had colored the

chieftain's words. And while he was by no means ashamed of the pleasurable last few hours, Kieran did feel like a child caught with his hand in the candy jar.

"What, and miss out on some monumental groveling?" she declared. Surprised, he stared, slack-jawed, at her bold question. Vanysha lowered her gaze, heat warming the deep aqua pools, driving away any rational thoughts from his mind. "Not a chance."

His cock jumped to attention, her sexy crooked grin having sparked wicked ideas in his blood, and he cupped her smooth cheek in his hand to gently lead her to his lips.

"Well, if you can let him up off his knees for a minute," H'reeh stated flatly, halting Kieran with a breath between his mouth and paradise, "we got some shit to get working on."

Reality doused the rekindled embers like a bucket of ice water and he heaved a weighty sigh. Vanysha responded in kind, her exasperated groan mirroring his frustrated disappointment, and she dropped her head, resting her forehead against his.

"Looks like duty calls," he muttered. Her mood had shifted from seductress to somber so quickly, he feared regret might have been rearing its ugly head. He wrapped his arms around her bowed back and pulled her against him. She flinched, muscles locking for a heartbeat before she released the tension coiled in her arms and melted into him.

He nuzzled his chin against her soft hair, almost believing they were back in that tiny room where he'd first learned of love and time had stood still. But his mind knew better. She was right; he did have some significant penance. *Six years' worth, to be exact.* While their passionate reconnection gave him a glimmer of hope, it would take time to rebuild the trust shattered by his former cowardly action.

He trailed his fingers up and down her spine. The outside

world had encroached upon their inner sanctum and duty would again knock on the door, demanding entry very soon. Until then, though, he vowed to do all he could to set her mind at ease.

"Yeah…" she exhaled, drawing out the word, "I guess it does." She slipped one arm out and tapped the button on the wall beside them. The room flooded with a gradual artificial dawn.

Kieran stared at the ceiling, narrowing his eyes as the light grew. "We could stay here all day?" he asked.

Her sleepy chuckle sent his blood on a reverse course, depleting his brain as it raced back below his belt line. A faint whimper snuck out from his clenched teeth while she scooted out from beneath the thick blanket. "Don't tempt me, Kier."

He reached for her, hoping to capture her wrist before she moved out of range, but her reactive lurch as she spun away from his light hold reminded him of the horrors she must have faced. Alone. He swung his legs over the side of the bed, the damp sheet draping across his lap, and offered her an honest smile. She remained still, her gaze wary, and he leisurely entwined his fingers with hers.

"Would that be so bad?" He raised her hand to his mouth. "I mean, you said it yourself." Running her fingertips across his lips, he nipped at the delicate pads while his eyes never faltered from hers. "I have a lot of groveling to do."

Kieran led her palm to his chest, pressed it against his heart, transfixed by the confusing array of emotions swirling in her aquamarine pools. Trembles vibrated down her arm, and her eyelids fluttered closed. The urge to pull her into his embrace thundered through his veins, but his logical, chivalrous mind took the reins, halting any advance without her go-ahead.

"I…"

Kieran leaned closer, tilted his head to catch her strained voice.

Vanysha sucked a sharp breath, then released it in a huff. He remembered that signal all too well; whenever news was bad, or when the rent was nearly due, she'd get fidgety, and as if on cue, she shifted her weight from foot to foot before rubbing the back of her neck. Kieran rose to his feet, making sure his fabric shield stayed wrapped around his waist, and placed his hands on her shoulders.

Another knock broke into the awkward moment. "Be right out," she called, then said to Kieran, "I … I just need time."

His mouth opened, though prudence held his tongue. The vast distance between them had shrunken by inches. In his heart, however, he knew true redemption needed more than just a tumble in the sheets. "We can continue this conversation tonight, then," he said.

Vanysha cocked her head, narrowing her gaze in his direction. "Tonight? You so sure that I'll let you back into my room again?"

"Call it a gift."

Her eyes shimmered. Did she remember?

Chapter Thirty-Six

A gift.

Vanysha blinked back the unexpected push of tears at the old term of endearment. *How have I deserved such a gift as you?*

He'd called her, and everything about her, a gift, and she recalled several times when he'd voiced his concerns about being unworthy of such a treasure. Many nights, as they lay in the afterglow of their passions, they'd talk in hushed whispers about the what-ifs: What if he hadn't nearly bowled her over on the street that fateful day? What if she'd been angered by his rude actions? Some nights, he asked the first question; other nights, her irrational fears would take hold and she'd initiate the conversation.

Once all was said and done, they'd curl up in each other's arms and drift off to sleep. Now, all that long-buried trepidation bubbled up to the surface, twice as vile and ten times as harsh as in those playful days.

"Kier, please…" She pulled her hand away from the temptation of his bare chest. He'd truly grown stronger in their years apart, lean muscles having filled out his lanky frame, and her body hungered for more. Even though their first joining did not last as long as she had hoped, he'd more than made up for it in their second tumble, milking orgasm after orgasm from her until she lay spent and limp across him.

In the budding light of a new day, however, her dark and shadowy companions returned, reminding her of how he'd deserted her to a hateful fate. Determined to hold the higher ground, she grabbed the thick robe slung across the back of her desk chair. Apparently, when Danton and his Hexakan crew had made all the necessary repairs to the ship, someone had taken the liberty of putting the garment right where she'd last tossed it. The scratchy fabric on her sensitive skin grounded her into reality, and she yanked her brain back into work mode.

"We both have jobs to do right now," she said, praying her no-nonsense tone matched the words tripping off of her tongue. "And I think our problems can take a backseat on things until the universe is fixed."

She focused on knotting the waist belt, fingers fumbling with the simple task, but she refused to lift her gaze. Her own emotions were still too raw and begging for attention. If she looked up into his eyes, she might capitulate and spend the rest of the day lost in a haze of pleasure, while the world around them burned to cinders.

His bare toes slipped into her periphery and she held her breath for as long as she dared. But the need to breathe tapped her on the shoulder and she gave in, taking a deep inhale. The lingering scent of his cologne blended with the erotic musk of their lovemaking assailed her senses, and she locked her arms down by her sides.

"Haven't we waited long enough?" Kieran stepped closer, and she retreated a fraction, ensuring the distance between them remained status quo. Gathering up her courage, she lifted her face and pinned him with a stern stare.

"If I can wait another few hours for your groveling, you can surely keep it in your pants for that long."

His brows shot up his forehead. Her direct words had been unexpected, but delivered the right punch she'd needed. She dipped her chin to hide her prideful smirk, then scooted away to rifle through her closet for a more appropriate outfit. "There should be an available change of clothes in the passenger quarters that would be more suited to the needs of the day—"

"Vanysha…?"

She pointedly ignored his soft plea and continued to putter around, gathering up his hastily discarded clothing. "The galley, I'm sure, has been completely restocked during the repairs…"

She picked up his slacks and tunic, then glanced around her renovated room. Most of the wall had been replaced, the sprawling patchwork quilt of steeleglass and cadmium-infused tungsten creating an interesting, variegated design. The bed was new; she felt the resilience in the fresh springs when Kieran had first laid her down onto it. At the time, she'd filed away this fact since she had been preoccupied with the cascading sensations of his mouth on her body.

"Van," he said. "Please?" Her hands froze. If she gave in now, he'd win, and she was in no mood to again leave her fate in the hands of any male.

Especially the one who could so easily shatter her soul.

Steeling her spine, she turned to look at him. So many versions of him danced before her eyes as he stood silently in the center of the room, dark blue blanket held in place by one hand.

All at once, she spied the lover with disheveled hair, the confidant with broad shoulders. Yet his rigid stance whispered of the harsh and unyielding politico, masking the lanky young man with whom she'd first fallen in love.

"Yes," she stated, "we will talk more about this later." She quickly raised her hand as his lips parted. "And I do mean *talk*. But we gotta get going." His crestfallen expression touched her heart and, with a mock sigh, she rolled her eyes, dumping his laundry into his arms. "Stop with the puppy face," she teased, turning him about, and gave him a light pat on his firm ass to direct him. "It's not like either of us can just leave."

Before she'd triggered the door release, he spun back around and captured her lips in a fiery kiss. The suddenness of his action snapped her body into survival mode; she splayed her fingers across his chest, her arms flinching as she shoved him away instinctively. While part of her recognized her lover, habits too ingrained refused to vanish.

Kieran broke the seal of their lips, sensing her panicked reaction, and stepped out of her personal space.

"I'm sorry. I—"

She waved off his apology with a trembling hand. As he backed away, he accidentally bumped into the door, automatically triggering the opening mechanism, and he nearly fell into the arms of the waiting Hexak chieftain.

Before she could blink, the barrier whooshed shut, leaving her in a strange silence. Laughter seeped in through the seams, and she hurried to the release button, blushing as she spied Kieran bare-ass naked, the loosely held sheet partially slipping from his hands as he struggled to stay on his feet.

"Damn," said H'reeh, squeezing the words between the raucous laughs. "Guess the groveling needed improvement.

C'mon, kid." He gave her a conspiratorial wink over his shoulder while he led Kieran down the corridor, adding, "I'll give him a few pointers before I give him back to you tonight."

Her eyes popped open, and she quickly sealed the door shut, an embarrassed warmth heating her cheeks in record time.

Chapter Thirty-Seven

H'reeh shook his head, chuckling as he helped the vice ambassador recover some of his dignity, as well as his handful of clothes. After the surprising reveal of the wily female's tat, and her subsequent hasty retreat to their waiting vessel on the landing dock, the chieftain had a fairly safe idea of where the male was. And he was right.

Judging by their flustered thoughts, and their lack of clothing, some degree of separation had been bridged. Possibly now Kieran could get his head into the game. H'reeh waited patiently as Kieran stepped back into his pants and regained a modicum of composure.

"All right, let's go, lover boy." And, with his hand on the young man's shoulder, they traveled along the corridor that led away from the crew's quarters. "I'm sure your performance wasn't *that* bad."

Kieran dropped his head with a pained groan, and H'reeh patted his back. "You at least got to spend the night with her. That's a start, am I right?" He received only a slight nod in answer, so he opted to shift gears back to business. "Good. Now, since we're taking the long way back, I suggest we use the time to formulate some sort of plan."

Kieran stopped in his tracks. "Wait, what?"

Puzzled, H'reeh glanced sidelong at him. "What what?"

"Huh?"

H'reeh turned and pinned the stammering politico. "What did you have a question about?"

"Oh." Kieran blinked, grabbing onto the chieftain's arm. "You … you said 'the long way.'"

"Well, yeah," H'reeh answered. "There is a shit-ton of questions and not a whole lot of answers. We gotta figure out who's behind all this." As they reached the luxury quarters, H'reeh tapped the wall panel. "And I don't know about you," he added, "but I'd rather not walk into the lion's den with just my charming smile."

The door slid open to reveal the waiting entourage, and while he'd originally planned to travel solo, apparently his people were having none of that. Fengreir, the captain of his private guard, leaned against the far wall, while Drexler sat on the low-backed couch beside the awaiting meal. Jazeem; his twin, Ilvan; and Sendak rounded out his retinue of guards. The nearly identical pair stood close enough to the entrances to handle any threat, their relaxed postures a well-maintained veneer that masked their lethal martial training.

"Was he with her?"

H'reeh nodded covertly toward Ilvan, then gestured to the table of food. "So does anyone—"

Drexler swore under his breath and thumped his fist against the table, while the rest of the guards laughed with glee. Jazeem clapped his hands, then rubbed his palms together with a shit-eating grin.

"Pay up, asshole," he said, gesturing toward H'reeh's lieutenant.

H'reeh blinked deliberately, then stared at his men. "You made bets?" Unabashed affirmations filled the space, and the chieftain dropped his face into his open palm. "We're on the brink of entering enemy territory with the gods-only-know-who controlling the strings of this war and you assholes are betting on if he"—H'reeh flicked his thumb toward the red-faced negotiator—"got laid?"

The gathered warriors cheered and launched up from their posts to surround Kieran. They shook his hand, giving him congratulatory thumps on the back.

"The wager was actually for his location," Fengreir, the regiment's moral compass, informed H'reeh. A lazy shrug served as his opinion of the game.

"Yeah," his second interjected. "But the pot doubles if he got any action."

"Children," H'reeh grumbled. "I brought children." He glanced over to Kieran. The young man's discomfort was waning fractionally with each passing moment, but now it was time to shift the spotlight's focus. "If you're done"—he pinned each of his men with a mildly amused glare—"maybe we can try to see how we can unfuck this situation."

The guards returned to their stations, though their smiles lingered. To be honest, H'reeh was pleased with the outcome himself. Something about their visitors had crept into his heart, and he'd wanted to see things work out for the pair. They'd worked as a team when he and his people had first discovered them, each protecting the other on instinct. Only true love warranted such acts of selfless devotion.

Perhaps there was hope for the universe, too. Folding his arms across his chest, H'reeh studied the room. "Drex," he said, "what have you been able to get out of Bosh?"

His second raised one finger, finishing up chewing the sweet roll he was wolfing down. The head shake had given no useful information, and H'reeh waited for his friend to finish feeding his face. But after giving the man time to lick his fingers, the chieftain's patience had worn thin and he cleared his throat to get the ball rolling.

"I'm sorry, but these things are amazing." Drexler wiped the remnants off his hands, then pointed to the tempting table. "You gotta try one. Okay, okay … first off, the years away from Hexaka made that bastard soft. It didn't even take that much torturing for him to start singing like a *hoonau* bird." He rose and crossed to meet his chieftain. "Apparently, the lure of financial gain and a place of higher stature in the Nexxus had turned his heart from his true purpose."

H'reeh snarled, clamping down on his teeth to hold back the vile curses that stole his appetite. His father had prided himself on his ability to read people and he had personally chosen the current delegates to be his eyes and ears in the universe beyond Hexaka's boundaries. After his anger had sunk safely below the breaking point, he tipped his chin for Drexler to continue.

Drexler nodded sharply, then turned to face the room. "It's no big surprise Westran Alpha is still a major player, and they gained a boatload of power since we basically excused ourselves from the Nexxus' governing table. Seems the rest of the universe felt pity for them after … well, we all know the truth of what really happened." At this, the air thrummed with the combined growls of the gathered males.

"They have more than reaped the rewards from sympathetic allies, but over the past few decades, other planets have been getting the shaft because of Westran Alpha's choke hold on the water supply. Guess 'someone' has been using our colors to attack random ships who dare to fly near us, or just about anyone, and well … you don't have to be a genius to figure one of the players is on the Court of the Principe."

H'reeh shifted his gaze to the lone outsider, who was silent as the report went on. "Does that sounds reasonable, Phaetal?"

Kieran narrowed his gaze, seeming to stare at something beyond the walls of their current space. "If this was the case, why was I ask to handle the peace accord?"

"Did you receive the request directly, or through a third party?" Drexler asked, and H'reeh swung his eyes between his friend and the young man in question. His lieutenant was on to something. The negotiator returned to his internal musing, brows knitting together.

"I … hell, I don't know. The pool of possible candidates is pretty thin." Kieran rubbed his chin with his knuckles. "Not that I'm trying to sound arrogant, but the truth of the matter is there are only four vice ambassadors in the Nexxus with the trainings required for negotiations of this magnitude."

"So it could have been luck of the draw," H'reeh suggested, though the words felt disingenuous. "I sincerely doubt it. You, kid, were *meant* to be handling this one."

"*Unferm qozi.*"

Fengreir had whispered the old phrase while the puzzle pieces fell into place within the lengthening silence.

Kieran frowned. "What's that?"

"Sacrificial lamb." Drexler translated. "Do you have any other siblings? An other brother or sister who would inherit your father's title after he dies?"

Hard to tell if the slow shake of Kieran's head had been his answer or an attempt to sort through the massive amount of data. "It's just me," he finally replied. "But I'm no heir apparent.

Leadership on Central is passed down through the military rankings and political experience, not direct bloodlines."

Drexler arched a brow. "You sure about that? The assassination of a negotiator heading to broker peace on a hostile planet would be a strong catalyst for more aggressive measures, especially if *that* negotiator happened to be the son of the current leader."

"Bring in that piece of shit." H'reeh hadn't directed the command to anyone in particular, but judging by the shuffle of boot heels on the metal floor, more than one of his men was now eagerly running the errand. "He must have promised those assholes something." His blood chugged, sluggish, as a sickening thought crossed his mind. "Drex?"

"Captain! I need you to open a channel to Cam'Rhan, STAT!" Drexler had slammed his hand down onto the nearest comm link and shouted the order, even as the horrific idea blossomed in H'reeh's mind. *If anything happens to my family, I will destroy the entire universe.*

H'reeh locked eyes with the paling ambassador, and he pitied the male. Nothing ruins your day more than learning you're nothing but a pawn in the universe's fucked-up chess match.

Chapter Thirty-Eight

Furious activity sprang up, and Kieran felt like a stone statue as his mind struggled to keep up.

A farce. The whole thing had been a sham from the first steps. Peace. Unity. All of it. Lies. He'd placed the lives of Vanysha, her crew, and possibly the entire population of Hexaka directly in harm's way because he believed in a pipe dream. His stomach churned, guilt awakening the sleeping serpents deep in his gut.

A solid knock to his shoulder yanked him off of the nauseous precipice and, swallowing back the rising bile, he raised his eyes to the Hexak chieftain. Within the peacock blue orbs, he detected neither blame nor accusation. "Don't pass out on me," H'reeh said. "We still got shit to get squared." Nodding rapidly, Kieran set his mind to the task at hand, and H'reeh mirrored his action, taking a slow inhale, while Kieran followed suit. "You good?"

"H'reeh? You gotta hear this." Drexler grabbed a hold of H'reeh's sleeve and dragged him to the vid link screen. Kieran quickened his steps and stared at the display. "I got your dad here, Niko. Wanna say that again?"

Smoke wafted into the frame, a chilling halo forming around the soot-smeared face of his friend. One eye was swollen shut, and a weeping gash that sat on the apple of his cheek spoke of a pitched battle, yet Niko's prideful smile perplexed Kieran.

"We met—oh, hey, Kieran. Did you try that trick I talked about?" Two sets of eyes swung in Kieran's direction, and the temperature in the room crept up by a few notches. Kieran's jaw hung agape, his brain wiped of any witty comeback. "Right. Later on that, then. Okay, so I guess that douche wad Bosh thought he could plant a bunch of explosives throughout the capitol and bring us to our knees before the might of the Nexxus military."

Blinking slowly, Kieran sifted through Niko's dripping sarcasm to find the root of the message.

"What were the primary targets?" the chieftain inquired.

"Well..." Niko tossed a couple of orders over his shoulder, then returned. "I think the plan was to destroy the steeleglass factories, but their aim was way off. Remember, we had the operations moved to other chambers with better access to the supplies about forty cycles back. Don't get me wrong; they did some major damage to the pillars of Lower Cam'Rhan, and the Citadel is in shambles—"

"Niko." H'reeh grabbed the wall on either side of the screen, as if shaking his son's virtual shoulders. "How are your sisters? Your brothers? Your ... my...?"

A crushing pain started in the center of Kieran's chest, his heart aching for the anguish in the chieftain's strained voice.

Niko pressed his palm against the monitor on his end. "We're okay, Dad." An eerie silence descended. Did the telepathic skills of the Hexakan race extend into distant space? "Gibran got hurt pretty bad," Niko said. The gravity of the news hit, not only the chieftain but also the gathered men, like a fist. Kieran glanced over to Drexler, whose head was bowed as soft and desperate words tumbled from his lips. "Mom hasn't left his side." Niko's soothing tone reached across the stars to bring comfort. "And Doc Weyland is certain he's gonna pull through. He'll have a limp and one hell of a scar, though."

Grumbles drifted through the room, venom in each hushed voice holding a promise of vengeance and retribution. Niko took a moment to dash away a stray tear before continuing. "The casualty list is growing," he said, "but it could have been a lot worse. Sylmar had left a kind of confession letter in his chamber, telling where the explosives were set and when they would be triggered. Must have written it just before you gathered the elders; figured it was time to clear his conscience, regardless of what Bosh did."

The door slid open, and two guards escorted in the afore-mentioned delegate, the man looking quite a bit worse for wear.

"Anything about who put him up to it?" H'reeh kept his stare trained on the newly arrived group. Kieran shifted his gaze between the chieftain and the prisoner; the confining space thrummed with a rage that simmered barely beneath the surface.

"Nah," Niko responded with a heavy sigh. "Just a bunch of apologies. Kept on saying they were too long from home and had lost their way."

Sensing an impending confrontation, Kieran set his back beside the vid screen. H'reeh dipped his chin a fraction. "Stay sharp, son." Niko gave a brusque nod, and the image winked out. Kieran followed the laser targeted focus of the chieftain's eyes, wondering if the smug male knew what was in store for him.

Bosh's haughty expression lasted for only a heartbeat. With determined strides, H'reeh ate up the distance between him and the shutting door, and Kieran flinched sympathetically as the chieftain wrapped his meaty hand around the startled man's throat. Momentum propelled him on until he slammed his captive against the nearest solid surface.

"You take your last breath today, Bosh. That, I can guarantee." The guards returned to their posts without batting an eye at their leader's explosive reaction. "The only input you have is how you leave this world: in peace, or in pieces."

Silence cocooned the open space; the overt promise of violence had stolen the voice from the gathered males. All, save one—the traitorous Hexak delegate sputtered and wheezed, clawing uselessly against the thick arm pinning him to the wall like a bug.

"I'm sorry." H'reeh tilted his head closer to the flailing man. "I couldn't quite make that out."

"Y-y-your ... Em-m-m—"

Kieran gawked at the pure strength of the Hexak leader, his prey's toes straining to reach for the floor.

The chieftain inched in. "Hmmm? I'm sure you were telling me the names of your puppet masters on the outside, right?"

"He might be able to say more, if you weren't crushing his larynx," Drexler suggested, pointing out the obvious.

H'reeh scoffed. "Details." His arm muscles flexed, tightening his grasp, and Kieran half-expected the suspended man's eyes to pop out of their sockets. "He's a bright boy. I'm sure he'll figure out some way to tell me."

"We ... we only dealt with couriers and—"

"Liar." The chieftain's angered growl sent chills down Kieran's spine, even at his safe distance. "Sylmar was right. You *have* been away from your own people for too long." H'reeh pulled the dangling man toward his snarling face, before throwing him to the ground, scowling as Bosh slid against the smooth metal floor. "Did you think I wouldn't smell the lie on you?"

Kieran sidestepped the delegate's hand reaching out to grab at his ankle.

"You know it was the right thing to do, don't you, Vice Ambassador?" the sputtering male asked. "Your father must have told you this alliance was never going to come to fruition."

"Why would my father wish for this war to continue?" Kieran said, refusing to rise to the bait and calling on his training as a negotiator.

Please, trust me. The Hexaks were capable of telepathy, so Kieran took a chance of sending a message as a preemptive strike. He kept his gaze leveled on the delegate at his feet, though he caught the chieftain's movement out of the corner of his eye, halting any interruption. Swallowing down his sigh of relief, Kieran waited for an answer.

"He leads the military, does he not?" Red-faced, Bosh slithered to a crouch. "Who better to wish a pointless war to linger on?"

"An intelligent leader understands keeping the people appeased is vital to keeping control. If the masses are frightened or angered, they will demand change, and it is nearing time for the next election cycle." Rapid blinks warned him of an impending falsehood. "Any Politico General worth his salt would broker for treaties at this junction to maintain the balance of power."

"Balance." Bosh sneered as he climbed to his teetering legs. "As long as Pretep holds the ear of the—"

Too late the man realized his slip, and he dashed toward the door. Kieran snapped his gaze over to the chieftain, as the guards easily stopped Bosh's feeble escape attempt. "Pretep is the brother of the former Grand Magestorum of Westran Alpha and was slated to take over, but a loophole was found in the line of succession and it fell to Bharange's son, who's still only a child."

Kieran recalled the older man whispering words into the boy's ear; pieces continued to shuffle and slot into place. He paced in a slow circle around the broad room, needing to get the ideas out of his head. "He had the boy send out an envoy with the missive that held the locator beacon so their armada waiting in the hyperlanes would know exactly where to strike." He tossed a hand over toward the subdued delegate. "His plan was to cause as much damage as possible and, amidst the chaos of the raining destruction, annihilate any remaining vestiges of your family"— he pointed directly to H'reeh—"thereby seizing control of your planet's resources, all while manipulating the young Westran Alpha leader into believing that Hexaka still wished to continue the war."

One of the guards chimed in, confusion coloring his words. "But what would …"

"Don't you see?" Kieran spun to face the gathered men. "With Hexaka in their hands, they could resume production of steeleglass on their own terms, create new ships fortified with hulls nearly indestructible, and continue to raid the Crimson Alley. As I'd said before, this is an election cycle on Central, and an angry populace will scream for a new regime, which means—"

"Which means," Drexler interjected, "whoever would be the next high mucky-muck must be in on this scheme."

Kieran felt the heat of a half-dozen pairs of eyes glaring at him. Shaking his head, he waved off their accusatory stares. "It's not me," he said. "Remember, the leadership on Central is not passed down through bloodlines; it's based on both military *and* political service. I have military training, but not service. My experience is only in the political realm, which takes me out of the pool of contenders. Currently, only two possible candidates are on this docket: Vice Legion Kha Ru'Jan and Prime Adjunct Bokka Ho. Both have served under my father for decades, but I wouldn't put it past either of them to reach beyond their stations. I know little of their private stances, since the party censors any speech that does not conform to my father's wishes. But I'm not sure if they'd make such an open and public move against him…"

Kieran took a moment to breathe, his gaze narrowing on nothing as he searched his spiraling mind for more links in the conspiracy chain. He rested his elbow on his crossed arm, fisted knuckles tapping against his upper lip. A firm hand clasped his shoulder and jolted him out of his thoughts. He met H'reeh's eyes, a strange degree of pride in the male's easy grin.

"I stand corrected," H'reeh said, and Kieran stared, confused, waiting for the chieftain to continue. "I guess they did send their best and brightest to handle this one, after all."

Kieran shrugged in a weak attempt to hide his embarrassment at the unexpected praise, though he found himself smiling, pleased by the man's honest admiration. "Now we just need to figure out which of them is involved."

H'reeh chuckled, patting him on the back. "After all of the mental gymnastics you did in the past couple of seconds," he said, "I think that'll be the easy part."

Kieran tugged his brows together, puzzled, and the chieftain winked. "They'll be whoever greets us at the gate when we arrive. C'mon, kid." And with a friendly nudge, H'reeh pointed Kieran toward an inset door across the room. "Get cleaned up while I wrap this up. Don't worry," he assured, before crossing over to the guards. "Your girl will never know what happened in here."

Kieran nodded and, without hesitation, sought the solace of the luxury washroom connected to the suite. The door slid shut behind him, sealing out the bloodcurdling screams in the nick of time.

Chapter Thirty-Nine

After staring at the shut door for what felt like hours, Vanysha unfolded her legs and slid off the bed. She'd never spent so much time in her own cabin on a voyage before. Most excursions, she was lucky to sneak in twenty-minute catnaps once the trip was fully underway. Her standard routine included mingling with the guests, acting as tour guide to the Nexxus hot spots, and generally doing her job.

Only now did she realize just how boring her living space was. Glancing around the barren walls while ignoring the patches of shimmering steeleglass covering the hull breaches, she had little in the way of personal items displayed: a few image captures of her crew, cards from thankful guests, but nothing of her.

She closed her eyes, banishing herself to the inner darkness of her thoughts. Yet instead of a welcoming emptiness, Kieran's smoldering smile sat waiting. In her mind, both the young boy and the strong man phased in and out of focus, though each version bore the same loving expression.

Damn you, fates.

Growling to no one in particular, Vanysha dashed the back of her hand against her leaky eyes, then punched her legs into one of the jumpsuits she'd salvaged from her charred closet. Moping around wouldn't solve anything, and if she continued to stare at the vast nothingness that currently represented her life, she'd run screaming to the nearest airlock. Maybe since the ship had escaped from the Crimson Alley, she could wrestle the nav pod from the Hexak.

"I could take him," she mumbled to herself as she zipped up the front closure before grabbing her boots up off the floor. A thousand scenarios replete with a million different outcomes whizzed through her mind while her fingers tightened the lacings. She wasn't sure what had pissed her off more: the fact that she found herself right back in her cabin at the end of each of them, or that she found herself right back in her cabin with Kieran in nearly all of them.

Determined to outwit her subconscious failings, Vanysha slammed her hand on the panel to open the door, then stormed out. Her momentum propelled her directly into Faze's chest, the impact practically landing her on her ass.

"Whoa," he said, laughing as he held on to her elbow. "You got a particular destination in mind with all that energy?"

Huffing in frustration, Vanysha tossed her hands in the air. "Anywhere but in there." She tipped her chin toward the door at her back with a groan. "How can anyone stay in those … those coffins for an entire voyage?"

With a slow head shake and a knowing grin, her pilot diffused her un-directed anger. "C'mon, that's not what's got you on edge." Faze nudged her shoulder and guided her away from her Spartan space. "Plus, I know for a fact you demanded we install the highest of luxury chambers for our guests, and you didn't scrimp on our crew accommodations, either."

"But that doesn't mean I want to be cooped up in—"

"Now, just hold on." Faze pulled her to a stop as they passed the threshold into the dining cabin. He rested one meaty fist on his hip. "Your nav pod is smaller than a friggin' closet. You 'coop' yourself in there for days on end, but you're telling me your room is too cramped?" Vanysha shifted her eyes to the floor, unable to meet his piercing gaze. "Van? Talk to me." She sorted through her thoughts, trying to decide which version of the abridged truth would fall from her lips. "And if you even think about lying to me," he added, "I will stop ordering coffee."

Her jaw popped open. "That's cruel and unusual punishment," she whined, and as a precaution before he could carry out his threat, Vanysha crossed over to the half-full pot.

Faze kept pace with her sudden jolt of speed, and much to her surprise, he snatched her mug up off the rack, then held her gaze. Tension coated the ticking seconds as their silent standoff continued. His thick brows knitted together and, growling, he poured her a measure of the necessary go-juice. She lurched for the cup, only to have it yanked slightly out of her reach.

"C'mon—"

"I mean it," he said.

Never had she outright lied to him, or to anyone, for that matter. She knew the dangerous price attached to keeping secrets, and the resulting pain when they were exposed. His expression softened, the deep furrows losing their sharp edges. "I made a promise to you all those years ago I wouldn't pry into your past and to what brought you to that slavers' block." He placed the mug into her waiting hand, then guided her to the small table tucked in the far corner of the room. "But I need to know if whatever it is between you and that boy, be it now or in the past"—he raised a hand, forestalling her interruption—"is it going to put me or mine in danger?"

"Danger?" She plopped down into the chair and cupped her hands around the warm porcelain, hoping its heat would banish the growing chill in her blood.

Faze tipped his chin toward the passenger lodgings on board. "Remember, he was sent to broker a peace treaty we all thought would end the hostilities in this whole quadrant. Things might have gone sideways since then, but I don't doubt for a second that the politico in him still has his eyes on that prize."

Vanysha stared at the rising tendrils of steam, mulling over his astute observation. In all of the recent craziness, the true purpose for their trip had nearly slipped her mind.

"And if he's too busy thinking about you to do his job," Faze went on, "that could put all our asses in a sling."

"Don't worry about that," she stated. "I'm sure I'm the farthest thing in his mind right n—"

Faze's sharp laugh halted her tongue. "Do you think I'm that dense?" he said. "From the moment he said your name in this very room, I *knew* something was between you. I kept hoping you would open up about it, but then…" He shook his head, waving off the unnecessary thought completion. "So I pushed and tried to make him show his hand, and he did. Might have taken longer than I thought, but once you flashed your tat, he definitely tipped his cards. You left in such a hurry, but I saw the look on his face after you showed your mark. Only one thing can make someone take the plight of another so personally, and that is love."

Her vision blurred. Only Faze's large hands pressing against the sides of her head steadied her focus. "Deny it all you want," he said, "but you can't change it. He loves you, Van. So, that makes the question of the hour…" He paused, and dread slogged through her veins. "Do you feel the same about him?"

"I…" Her jaw swung uselessly, sounds refusing to come. "I can't."

Faze screwed up his face. "Can't? What the shit kind of answer is 'can't'?"

"Right now, it's the only one I've got," she muttered over the lip of her mug. Caffeine would be required if this conversation continued to delve into an uncomfortable realm. The bitter sting hit her tongue, and she choked down the strong and tepid brew. Heat from Faze's unwavering stare threatened to bore through her brain while she quelled the sudden urge to flip him off. "Why can't you just let this one go?"

"Because I honestly think the guy is good for you," he said, "if you'd crawl out from under that thick armor of yours. Now I know"—another gesture preempted her interruption—"you're gonna say you need it, but do you really *need* it all the time, and with everyone?"

Gaping like a fish once again, Vanysha huffed in petulant frustration. "You don't understand—"

"Well, I might, if you'd friggin' tell me."

"Dammit, Faze." She clenched her jaw so tight, her teeth nearly cracked. "We were young. I was stupid enough to think he loved me, and after he left, my life turned into a shit show because of him."

Faze rolled his eyes, and he shook his head slowly. "Van, that's a lie and you know it. Did your life have a horrible turn? Yes. Was it your fault, or even his? Fault would mean it was done purposefully and with ill-intent."

"Faze, you saw how he left me. I—"

"No," he said, and Vanysha swore under her breath yet again. *Why the hell did he have to be so intuitive?* He tipped up her chin, riveting her to the present. "I saw how a set of parents abandoned their own child because of their selfish greed." Hot tears slipped down her cheek, but she held his stare. "I got a little from the conversation this morning. Seems like he left thinking he was, what, probably protecting you or something? Vanysha, we all know the road to Hell is paved with good intentions, but that doesn't mean he still can't love you.…"

His calming voice tapered off, and the rest of his statement hung thick in the silence. *Or I can't love him.*

"But do I forgive him?" she said. "Can I?" Thoughts spun in her brain so fast, she struggled to keep up with their hasty escape. "Six years, Faze. It's been six years. People change a lot in that time. What if this was nothing more than … than a fling, because I was convenient? What if, after scratching the itch, he feels he's done his act of kindness and can now go back to living his life with a clean conscience? I know, I know, I know!" She slammed her hand onto the table, the impact vibrating through her arm to jolt her wandering mind. "Gods, I can hear the bullshit in my own words. I know I'm scared. I know I'm just making up scenarios so I don't have to face the possibility of the truth."

"Yo, Drekkan? Where are you?"

Vanysha sent a relieved prayer of thanks up to the heavens at the timely interruption. The voice wasn't the chieftain's, but it was definitely Hexakan, and something was vaguely familiar about it. Faze rose and crossed to the comm unit on the wall.

"Dining cabin. What's up?"

"H'reeh wants to know if we can jump. He says they've figured out who's behind all the shit and he wants to see if we can throw them a surprise arrival party on Central."

Faze shifted his gaze to Vanysha, question upon question layered in his golden eyes, although the hint of a devious smile soon sealed the answer. "Hell yeah. I think it's time for some serious payback. Hit it. I'll be there in two."

"Outstanding. Oh, and you can tell your nav an extra set of eyes might be advantageous on the way in? Just in case, I mean."

At once, Vanysha tossed down the last swallow of coffee, then bolted out of her seat and beat Faze to the exit.

Chapter Forty

"I assume you have interrupted my sleep to tell me of the success on Hexaka."

. . .

"You cannot be serious."

"We don't know what happened."

"I believe that was the same excuse you'd used in a previous message, after you had assured me the Hexak ruler would be killed in the attack by our armada."

"The trap was perfect, and the net—"

"Failed to catch the prey we desired, and now—"

"No."

"No what?"

"This … this can't be possible."

"What? What is happening? What do you see?"

"The vice ambassador just arrived with an entourage of Hexakan males."

"WHAT!"

"It's *The Royal Janstar.* Somehow she survived the attack, and just made an unscheduled landing at the cargo terminal port."

"You fool. Stop them. Detain them. Something—anything! My transport will arrive tomorrow, but whatever you do, they cannot reach the Court of the Principe before me."

Chapter Forty-One

Just keep walking.

Kieran sensed the heat of a dozen hidden eyes trailing each member of their very odd-looking party, but he refused to veer away from his current path. The deserted commercial transport station had provided the perfect backdrop, allowing them to easily slip between the banks of shadows. Two of H'reeh's guards had taken up point positions to either side of him and one measured step ahead, while the other two brought up the rear. Even their boot heels fell in perfect synchronicity. He recalled reading about the savage, untrained brute forces serving as Hexaka's military. Now, he marveled at the deeper truth he was learning first-hand.

"Ex-excuse me, sir?" a timid voice called out from a lone pool of light. A single, pattering set of rushed footfalls snapped the Hexaks to full, lethal attention, and before Kieran could blink, they'd drawn their weapons. Kieran lifted his hand to forestall any outbreak of violence.

The nervous transport official skidded to a halt. "D-d-d-do you have…"

Kieran almost pitied the poor man. Sweat poured off his round, pale face, and by the rising stench, he would need a change of shorts before continuing his shift. "I believe our captain has provided all of the necessary landing codes and customs documents. *The Royal Janstar,* with diplomatic envoy, Vice Ambassador Kieran Phaetal, and members of the Hexakan royal family." Kieran did not break eye contact with the frightened employee. "If you update your records," he said, "you will find everything is in order."

Beady orange eyes ping-ponged between Kieran and the menacing faces of the men with brandished weapons. Seconds ticked, each one adding to the growing unease, but after a few guiding nods, Kieran managed to encourage a similar bobbed response. "There's a good man," he said. Breathing a quiet sigh of relief, he clasped the man on the shoulder before gesturing the group forward. To his surprise, each Hexak retinue member murmured a "thank you" to the trembling worker as they passed by. *Perhaps this was how the void would be crossed,* he thought.

Small steps.

As they continued past the empty spaces and awaiting vessels, Kieran shuffled through the events of the past few hours, seeking out more strings to firmly bind the pieces together.

Moments after ducking into the shower earlier, he'd felt the ship lurch forward, gaining speed, and he'd followed suit, rushing through his routine, trying to stay one step ahead of his rocketing thoughts. No longer was there any doubt about the dark influence of Westran Alpha's snubbed heir in this scheme. Now to find the other puppeteer.

When he'd emerged into the main chamber, he found no visible signs of a struggle, just as H'reeh had promised. However, one less Hexakan male occupied the space. Swallowing hard against the bitter truth, Kieran finished buttoning up his borrowed dress shirt, as a plate of food was shoved into his chest.

"Eat," said Drexler. Kieran juggled the overflowing dish as a chair bumped against the backs of his knees. "We can't have you passing out from hunger when we roll up onto Central."

"Central?" With an unceremonious *oof*, Kieran plopped into the seat, somehow managing to save his meal from ending up on his lap or on the floor. "I thought we were heading to Westran Alpha first." The aroma of smoked meats and buttered sweet breads wafted up from the heaping plate, and in truth, Kieran was in no state to turn down a hot meal. So he filled his fork, determined to work even as he filled his belly. "Why the change in plans?"

Drexler snatched one of the sugary rolls from Kieran's plate and dragged a chair over to join him. "Because," he said, "that is exactly what we would be expected to do. Either that"—he shrugged—"or return to Hexaka with our tails between our legs."

One of the guards scoffed, offended. "Like *that's* gonna happen."

"Others would." Murmurs rumbled through the gathered males at H'reeh's spot-on comment, and Kieran raised his eyes to find the chieftain staring at the blank vid screen. "But they're not us," H'reeh added. "I will continue to move forward on this because I know my people demand blood from those who attack without warning."

H'reeh's blatant honesty put a damper on Kieran's appetite. He set the half-finished plate back on the table.

"Oh no, you don't." Kieran looked up to find Jazeem glaring at him, beefy arms folded across his barrel chest. "Don't you even think about shouldering the blame for any of this."

Crestfallen, Kieran huffed out a tired breath. "But if I hadn't—"

"If *you* hadn't accepted this"—H'reeh stepped toward the picked-over plates—"someone else would have. These fuckers have been moving pieces for years. And that other someone probably wouldn't have been half as smart or as lucky as you."

"Lucky?" Kieran jolted to his feet. "How can you think any of this is lucky?"

Drexler leapt up and laid a hand on his shoulder. "Think of it," he said. "I know it's gonna sound cruel, but it won't be a lie. You charter the ship your ex happen to pilots. You manage to survive the attack meant to kickstart a rebellion." Drexler counted out each statement on his fingers. "You figure out who's behind this shit, and that alone saved the goddess-only-knows how many lives. And, you got laid!" Kieran stumbled forward a fraction, the sudden cuff to his back taking him by surprise. "By definition, that *is* lucky, am I right?"

"What my second is trying to say," H'reeh had stated, shaking his head slowly, "and purposefully sucking at is, while you may feel like the catalyst into this new hell, you are also the only real chance we have to bring these bastards down."

Now, as he approached the tram station, Kieran held those words in the forefront of his mind. He only wished Vanysha walked by his side. His rational mind understood she needed to stay with the ship to oversee any additional repairs; his heart, on the other hand, raged against their growing physical distance. Hadn't he done enough for peace? He'd brought the chieftain of the Hexaks to Central. That went above and beyond his original mission, as far as he was concerned. He should just hand off the rest of the details to his father.

A firm knock to his shoulder jolted him out of his thoughts, and Kieran locked eyes with the Hexak chieftain. "I know you feel like you're so close to the finish line, but we don't know who to trust." H'reeh gestured to his people, grounding Kieran into the crux of the problem. "I'm sorry," he said. "Generally, I don't like to pry into the minds of friends, but right now, you are the only offworlder I trust. I don't plan to let you out of my sight until all of this shit gets sorted."

Kieran dared another backward glance, and the chieftain wrapped his hand around Kieran's head, guiding his eyes to their forward direction. "Relax. Jazeem is still with the crew and he'll know where to find us. Besides"—he gave a conspiratorial wink—"your girl will be along sooner than you think. My men did a much better job on her ship than we led on to."

Kieran scoffed and, having led the group to the waiting transport tram, ushered them inside the dingy compartment. "She'll still demand to have it checked over again," he said.

After the last day spent in the pristine caverns on Hexaka, Kieran began to see the flaws of the so-called "hub" of their own modern civilization. Hidden graffiti had popped into his field of vision, as well as discarded papers and other trash kicked under the seats. "All this time I thought we were the height of … of everything—technology, commerce, you name it. But now…" He shook his head. "Now I'm not so sure."

"What do you mean?" Fengreir chimed in.

What do I mean? Kieran blinked, then gestured to the dilapidated reality of his homeworld. "Look around. This rail is falling apart, and I remember when it was first opened to the public five years ago as the 'cutting edge in transportation.' How old are your trains?" he asked, scanning the gathered faces.

The younger guards shrugged and shifted their gazes to Fengreir, so Kieran waited as the older warrior contemplated his response. "I think the last time we replaced the cars was long before we bid our farewell to the Nexxus."

Kieran barked out a sharp, mirthless laugh. "Over a hundred years old. Not looking any worse for wear. Everything here pales in comparison to all I saw on Hexaka."

"What can I say?" Drexler stretched his long arms over his head in a prolonged, put-on yawn. "We got the coolest shit." At this, Kieran rolled his eyes, though he added a nod of agreement when the lieutenant nudged him with his shoulder. "And it's not like you can't just stay with us."

The surprise invitation was tempting, catching Kieran off guard. "Seriously?" he said with a touch of both apprehension and excitement. Had the offer been made on behalf of the chieftain, or simply words spoken in haste? Kieran's gaze ricocheted from face to face, searching for any signs of hesitation.

H'reeh lifted a shoulder in a casual shrug. "Why not? The palace could always use another pet."

Silence fell in perfect time to his gaping jaw. Seconds later, soft snickers broke the spell until the entire train car had erupted in peals of raucous, good-natured laughter.

As much as he despised being the butt of any joke, Kieran found himself smiling, even as he mentally crossed his fingers to see this possibility come to fruition. The chieftain's earlier praise, coupled with the warm camaraderie amongst the members of the Hexak party, had given him a glimpse into a life where he could be exactly who he was, where both his accomplishments and shortcomings would not be a constant source of ridicule.

But would she come? Dare he ask her to give up on her dream to share in his?

A bump to his arm scattered his daydream. He met H'reeh's eyes while the man tilted his head back slightly toward the landing bay. "You'll never know until you try, right?"

"How about we make sure we all have a home to go to before we start building any cozy cottages, okay?" said Drexler.

Kieran shifted his gaze to the lieutenant, nodding at his astute point.

"Fine by me," H'reeh added as the rail drifted into the station. "Hey, kid … got any decent places to eat around here?" Soon, talk of food had filled the air while Kieran led the group out and onto the streets of Lansdown.

Chapter Forty-Two

Vanysha rolled through her shoulders as she shuffled the final distance toward the address Faze had given her at the landing bay. Seemed like the Hexakan delegation had decided to live it up— they'd booked three floors' worth of suites at the poshest hotel in all of Lansdown. She imagined the looks on the hotel staffs' faces as the chieftain and his men filed into the lobby, and she laughed in spite of herself. Then she shook her head and returned her mind to the simple act of walking.

Exhaustion had long since tapped her reserves, and after her eyes had drifted shut on more than one occasion while "overseeing repairs," Faze had demanded she call it a day.

Fine by me. She'd been more of a hindrance than a help anyway, as pointed out several times by Danton. Now, in her head, she ticked off her upcoming to-do list: shower, food, bed. Hell, at this point, she didn't care in what order those three simple luxuries occurred.

The elevator's gentle rocking sapped her remaining energy,

but the ride wasn't long enough for her to sneak in a real nap. A soft ding sounded through the fog in her mind, and the doors slid open. Groaning, she ambled out before the lift took its return journey back to the lobby. She scanned the keycard then stepped inside.

Just beyond the threshold, she froze, blinking slowly, her lips parting, yet nothing witty fell from her tongue. The soft glow of dozens of candles scattered on every flat surface bathed the room, while muted starlight filtered down from the thick glass ceiling. Two silver serving trays dominated the small oval table standing against the wall, while two delicate crystal flutes waited beside an unopened bottle chilling in an ice bucket.

"Oh, hey," Kieran stammered, looking up from the final batch of candles. "I thought I'd have a little more time to get—"

"What are you doing?"

During her trip to the hotel, she'd had several mental conversations with Kieran, and in each, she had taken complete control, explaining why they should just part ways. She'd argued her points to perfection, every possible angle covered without fail, and at the end, he'd agreed with her assessment without much of a fight. Certain she was prepared to bid him a fond, final farewell, she'd entered her room, spine steeled and resolve solid.

Apparently, though, he'd been preparing a strategy of his own, his tender efforts touching her heart and sucking all of the wind out of her sails. She rewound her brusque query, then shook her head to dislodge her frozen tongue.

"I'm sorry," she muttered, dialing back her aggressive entrance. "I, uh, didn't mean to—"

Kieran rose, a compassionate smile greeting her. "How's your ship?"

"Huh?"

"Your ship," he said, tossing the spent match into the cozy fire burning in the inset hearth. "Did the repairs go well?"

Vanysha blinked, struggling to process the question while she drank in the surrounding picture. Kieran had lost the starched appearance from their first meeting on board her ship; now, he looked more like *her* Kieran. He crossed over to the chair, slipped his muscular arms through the sleeves of the ecru linen button-down shirt, the open front leaving his chiseled sun-kissed skin on glorious display. Loose black slacks hung low on his hips, and his bare toes peeked out from beneath the hem of the pant legs. His hair fell in a tempting, disheveled disarray, and Vanysha twisted her fingers behind her back to quell the urge to run them through the silken waves.

He approached with measured strides, his smile unfaltering. *Ship. Right.* He'd asked about her ship. Yet with him close enough to touch, she cared for nothing outside of this romantic setting.

"Uh, ship," she said, fumbling with her words. "Yeah, she's fine. The, um, repairs are still holding."

Kieran extended a hand, mischief dancing in his stormy gray eyes, and the edges of her lips tugged up at his valiant gesture. She reached over to him, but instead of him pulling her into his arms, Kieran stepped in and wrapped his arms lightly around her. Reacting on instinct, she coiled her own between them, even as she turned her head to rest her cheek against his chest.

"That's good." He kissed the top of her head. Vanysha took a deep breath, then exhaled slowly, reining in her survival response. She forcibly relaxed her shoulders and savored the tender embrace.

"I thought we were going to talk," she said. His chest bounced from his light laughter, and a comfortable memory flared to life, sending her to a different time and place. He seemed to always sense when she'd had a bad day and knew just when she needed one of his cure-all hugs. Some skills apparently stayed sharp with time.

"Can't we have a meal while we talk?"

She lifted a brow at his innocent attempt at deflection. "In a candlelit room?" she remarked.

"Saves energy," he replied, shrugging. "Besides, after being in those caves, I kinda got used to softer lighting."

"We were only there for a day."

"I know, I know…" Kieran trailed his fingers against her back. "This is … I don't quite know how to explain it. I just had this strange sense of…"

"Of what?" She waited for him to complete the thought, even though she knew exactly where he was going with this whole thing: It felt like home. Even with the explosions and the fire fight, Hexaka had been oddly welcoming. Perhaps because all of her citizens approached every situation with a brutal honesty. Chances were, though, it was tied to the man now holding her so tenderly in his arms that made her want to return to the comfort of the Hexakan caverns.

That is, if any of them survived the next couple of days. A giant bullseye had been painted on their small company, and until the villains bent on their destruction were found, her dreams of happily-ever-afters would need to take a back seat.

Kieran cleared his throat and released her. "It's nothing," he said. "Sorry. Lack of sleep, I guess."

He made to move away, but Vanysha retained her hold on his arm. By rights, she should have let him go—*That was going to be your game plan anyway, right?*—but even as she agreed with her inner voice, she truly wanted to hear him finish that sentence. Kieran turned to face her, a shadowed sorrow casting a veil over his stormy gray eyes.

"Kier, you are still such a crappy liar." At this, a weak chuckle escaped his lips as he hung his head. The temptation to step back into his embrace hummed through her veins, warming her blood, but she opted to resist his little boy charm and gave his arm a light shake instead. "Just say it."

He lifted his head to fix his gaze on some distant point. "It felt like home," he said. "Like a real home, the one that happens only in dreams or stories." She slid her hands down his arm and laced her fingers with his, encouraging him to continue with a comforting squeeze. "The people weren't savages; they were kind and honest. And … and they didn't make me feel like a freak."

Freak? Her brows tugged together. "What do you mean?"

Kieran raised his free hand, and then it dawned on her. The gloves. He wasn't wearing those gloves. Her mind quickly backtracked to the hours spent in his arms. He'd held her, skin to skin. She stared at his fingers for another moment, then a soft blue glow began to emanate from his palm. Narrowing her eyes, she peered deeper into the strange light, caught the fine tendrils arching and sparking up from his bared flesh, and she watched, transfixed, awed by the dazzling light show.

"Niko, H'reeh's son," he whispered, "he showed me how … well, he basically showed me how it works." The uncertainty in his voice drew her gaze up to his face. He was intently studying his own hand, and her eyes followed the same path down again. "Seems their people still know about these things, strange skills and abilities that most of the other races in the Nexxus have forgotten. He said they're called the Lost Arts." He flexed and curled his fingers; the smoky waves shifted and danced—colors ebbed and flowed: blue became gold, then spiraled into red. "And the people on Hexaka who possess them aren't ostracized. In fact, they use them in their everyday lives without fear of reprisal."

Temptation proved too great to deny and she hesitantly reached toward his luminous digits. "Does … does it hurt?"

He brushed his lips against her forehead. "Nah." His single syllable answer ignited the embers deep in her heart, and her eyes drifted shut. She pictured the crooked grin she heard in his voice as he added, "It's more like … like a tickling sort of sensation. I don't know. It's hard to describe."

She smiled. "Show me."

<h1 style="text-align:center">Chapter Forty-Three</h1>

Blinking deliberately, Kieran shifted his gaze down to Vanysha, brows tugging together as he studied the top of her head. "Say again?"

At first, he'd thought the pounding of his heart had diminished his hearing. Sounded like she'd asked him to share his gift with her, to touch her? But that couldn't have been right. She should have been running away in terror or staring at him with the disdain he'd seen in the eyes of so many others.

She wiggled out of his embrace, stood in front of him, unafraid and bold. "I want to know how it feels for you." Curiosity sparkled in her aqua eyes.

Niko's words slammed into the forefront of his mind—*Chicks dig it*—and the blood quickly vacated his brain. Panic followed in its wake, though, stifling his rising passions. What if it was too much for her? What if he lost control?

"Uhh, I..." He balked, outstretched arm vibrating in response to his spiraling fear. "I'm not sure that's such a great idea just yet." Other rational reasons popped into his mind: the meal laid out in wait, plus the looming threat of imminent danger jumping out as the current leaders. "M-maybe after we eat?"

"Oh."

Vanysha lowered her hand to her side as she turned away, but not before he'd caught her crestfallen expression. He extinguished the glow, then laid a gentle hand on her shoulder, hoping to halt her retreat.

"No, please. It's just…" He scrambled for the right words. "I-I don't want to accidentally hurt you." Swallowing down his grief, he added the hardest word: "Again."

She stilled, the slight sizzle of the sputtering candles cutting through the heavy silence. "I…" He sighed. "I don't know if I trust myself enough yet, *la'nen*."

"I get it," she said. Her veiled disappointment hid beneath a pleasant smile. "It's okay."

Now or never.

"Wait." Kieran took a deep breath and ran his fingers through his hair, tugging on the short strands. Even as he argued with himself, he wrapped his hands around her waist, easily lifting her off her feet and set her down onto the corner of the table. "If it's too much," he said, "just … just—"

She nodded eagerly, eyes dancing with anticipation. "I'll kick you in the shins if it comes to it."

"Gee, don't sound so excited about it," he declared flatly. His sarcasm fell on deaf ears, though, and when he met her joyful grin, he was powerless. Answering with a smile of his own, fingers crossed that his own apprehension wouldn't spoil the moment, Kieran nodded. He prayed Niko hadn't been pulling his leg.

"Okay…" He'd breathed out the word in one slow, calming exhale. Then he nervously wiped his palms onto his pant legs, the silky material only smearing around the gathered sweat, and extended his right hand toward her. She didn't waste a moment, her own hand resting on his before he completed the gesture of invitation. With a chuckle, he inhaled deeply and called on his gift.

"You have the power to control it, Kieran. It obeys you, not the other way around."

Buoyed by the confidence of his friend and the complete trust of his lover, Kieran brushed the tip of his glowing finger across the back of her hand. Vanysha gasped, and his body immediately reacted to the familiar sound. *Guess Niko was right after all.* He trailed his touch along her arm toward her shoulder, then lifted his gaze to her face. Some time during his mental preparations, or perhaps after the first connection, her eyelids had slipped shut.

Kieran split his focus as best as his body and mind would allow, eyes glued to the subtle signals playing across her sweet face while he carefully held the reins on his power. Her lashes fluttered against the apples of her flushed cheeks, her lips parting slightly before she pinched her bottom lip between her pearly white teeth. A soft growl rumbled in his throat as he basked in her sensual enjoyment.

"You like?" he asked.

Vanysha purred, her head lolling as she bowed her back. "Oh, gods, yes," she sighed, elongating each word as a visible shiver raced across her bare arms. Kieran stepped in and placed a tender kiss against her forehead. The faint odors of engine grease and traces of recycled air couldn't hide the blossoming fragrance of her building arousal. Her free hand gripped the waistband on his loose trousers, and she snaked her legs around his. His erection tented the silken fabric, and he seriously began to rethink his choice of attire. Believing Vanysha would have been occupied for another hour working on her vessel, he'd planned on cleaning up and dressing in something more formal for his dinner date.

The idea of putting the brakes on this moment for a wardrobe change, however, bordered on stupid. Instead of allowing his thoughts to stray, he continued to savor the stark intimacy, nuzzling his nose into the hollow behind her ear as he cradled her face with his glowing hand. Needy whimpers tumbled from her lips, poured down his chest, her warm breath stoking the inferno in his blood with its promise of ecstasy. He tunneled his fingers through her hair, then pulled her flush against him.

Slanting his mouth over hers, he greedily swallowed her keening cries, fed on her rising passions, and once certain he retained control over his power, he trailed his hand down the line of her throat to cup her breast. She latched on to him, her hips bucking and grinding against his. Dear gods, he wasn't sure who was going to reach their peak first, and both of them were still clothed. He filed away his thank you message to Niko, opting to live in this perfect moment.

Higher and higher they climbed, locked in pure sensation, until Vanysha threw her head back, crying out as she writhed against him, lost in her release. Her nails bit into his shoulders as she crashed over that exhilarating precipice. With a thought, Kieran slowly pulled back his gift, then cradled her to his chest, listening to the thundering beat of her heart.

"Good thing I planned a cold dinner," he mumbled, smiling as her warm breath fanned his cheek. "Thank you."

"Th-thank me? F-f-for wh-what?"

Kieran leaned away and tipped her chin up with his knuckles. "For your trust, for starters. I know I have a lot to make up for"—he placed a finger on her lips as they parted—"and so much has happened since … since we were last together."

"Did I miss something yesterday?" she quipped.

Kieran groaned and rolled his eyes, though nothing could stop the smile tugging up the corners of his mouth. "Yes; your joke missed its target."

"Then why are you laughing?" With a playful grin, Vanysha hooked her ankles behind his legs, trapping him willingly.

Resting one hand on her waist, he ran his free fingers through her hair, still as soft as silk. He watched the strands of captured moonlight slide across the back of his hand. There once was a time he'd fall asleep cocooned in the length of her tresses.

"Hey?"

Kieran shook his head, clearing his maudlin memories to level his gaze at her. She cupped his hand in hers, laid her cheek in his palm. A ghost of a smile lingered on her kiss-swollen lips. "Don't go getting all dark on me."

"I thought I was supposed to be the insightful one," he declared.

She lazily lifted one shoulder. "I've picked up a skill or two along the way."

"Has your cooking improved?"

Too late Kieran snapped his mouth closed as Vanysha's aqua eyes flared and her jaw hung agape. He raised his hands in mock surrender while she sputtered half-formed rebukes. Then, laughing in earnest, he cradled her face and placed a loud yet chaste kiss on her lips. She snaked her arms between them and pushed him away, even as she joined in the mirth.

"Yeah, you think you're funny," she said, chuckling as she bounced off the edge of the table and onto her feet. "Comments like that might get you barred from my bed ever again."

Vanysha turned her back to him, and Kieran wanted so much to pull her into his arms and press her lush ass into his aching groin. Only his knowledge of her unspoken fear halted the romantic response. He cleared his throat, both to dislodge his heart and to announce his movements, and he crossed to the banquet he'd laid out for their meal.

At once, the vid screen to his left pulsed rapidly, and he froze, his brows tugging together. After two long strides, he tapped the comm link on the wall. The face of H'reeh's second in command popped into view.

"Yo, kid." An odd twinkle gleamed in the man's deep green eyes. "Hope you're up for some company."

Before Kieran could ask for more, the image winked out, and a forceful hand banged on the door.

"Stay there," he said, and he raised a hand toward Vanysha, wishing he was better equipped to protect her should things go badly. He punched the release button on the wall, and the opening portal revealed a curious gathering of faces. Drexler was strangely missing from the group, but in his stead, was the Hexak chieftain plus a pair of his guards. Yet it was the final member of the group who took him by complete surprise.

"Myka?"

Chapter Forty-Four

H'reeh snuck a peek over the top of Kieran's head. Damn. The boy had set out candles and everything. Romantic moment completely fucked over by bureaucracy. He filed it away, determined to make it up to them once the current fire was out.

He'd known as soon as Drexler had sent their guards out into the city proper, it would only be a matter of time before some interested party had turned their gaze in the right direction. He thought it would have taken more time, but his friend had made an effective point.

"Boss, ain't no one living on this planet who's ever seen our people, and all they know is what's in those ancient history vids. They're expecting savages, so let's give it to them."

He'd given his men strict orders to only speak in their language, but they weren't to harm any civilians or to cause too much damage. Jazeem and Ilvan had volunteered a little too happily for the mission, so he'd opted to split the difference, sending only one of the young hotheaded pair with Fengreir. Older and wiser, Fengreir would control Jazeem's knack for mayhem, plus his sheer size would be enough to cause the locals to run for the hills. Luckily for the population, their search didn't take long.

H'reeh tossed his thumb to the trembling man sandwiched between his guards. "You know this guy?" Dwarfed by the hulking Hexaks, Myka, as Kieran had called him, smoothed his jacket for the tenth time in the past four seconds, fidgeting fingers adjusting and readjusting the lapels on the obviously expensive fabric. He was thin and wiry, and the designer suit enveloped his spindly limbs. Yet even with the slick package, H'reeh had sensed something rotten dwelling just beneath the surface.

"Yes." Kieran nodded and scooted back to allow their group to come inside. "He's my secretary. Do I even want to know where you found him?"

Jazeem scoffed. "Well, let's say if you were trying to train him up as a covert operative, you seriously need to work on your tactics."

Kieran screwed up his face. "Huh?"

Apparently his guard's jab had hit its mark. Eyes an eerie shade of deep pink enlarged behind unneeded oval lenses, edges nearly peeking around the bronze metal frames. "I … I had heard a delegation from Hexaka had landed, and I—"

Jazeem interrupted the man's fabrication with a harsh, guttural outburst. "Oh, I call bullshit on that one, pal, 'cuz I sincerely doubt your media service announced us as 'delegates' from anywhere," he said, two fingers of each of his hands bracketing the word while he glared at the flustered secretary.

"Degenerates maybe," added Fengreir, his mild, whispered tone at odds with his stature. "Plus, he's been following us since we docked."

Jazeem nodded as he swiped an apple from the basket on the table. "Like I said: crappy tactics."

H'reeh read the offworlders in the room. Kieran seemed authentically stunned by the subterfuge of his trusted aide. Myka gaped and gawked, obviously scrambling hard to find a way to cover his tracks with his empty words, even as his eyes darted toward each corner in search of some possible exit strategy. Which left the final member, the female, as the lone outside observer. Her cool gaze scanned their faces, yet continually returned to the man in the hot seat. She sat apart, one leg tucked into her chest as she perched on the farthest table, but H'reeh doubted she missed any detail. Something in her demeanor caught his attention, though. Fear had paled her cheek, an odd sense of recognition perhaps.

Retrieving the pilfered fruit from his guard's hand, H'reeh crossed to Vanysha and presented the apple to her.

"Sorry for wrecking your night," he said. "Looks like your boy had quite the feast planned, too."

Vanysha accepted the peace offering with a despondent shrug. "Don't worry. If it makes you feel any better, it's not the worst evening I've spent."

"For the record, kiddo, that actually makes me feel worse." With a friendly knock against her shoulder, H'reeh managed to earn a timid smile. "Do you know this guy?" he asked.

She shook her head slowly, though her narrowed eyes whispered another answer. "I've never met him before, but … I can't help feeling like I should, I don't know, know him somehow."

"I'm sure your boy will figure it out." He leaned in closer, cupped his hand to her ear. "Past idiocrasies aside, I think he's a smart one." At this, he added a mischievous wink, then turned back to the gathered group. "So," he announced, and the room fell silent, "any idea why your aide was following us?"

Every head swiveled toward Kieran. *Come on, kid, you've got this.* Given the miraculous way the negotiator had pulled together all the pieces up until now, the chieftain was certain he'd figure it out soon.

Kieran lowered his gaze, contemplating the floor. "Myka has been in my service for years. If he'd wanted me gone, he could've poisoned my food long before this…"

Kieran's voice trailing off sparked H'reeh's curiosity. "I sense a 'but' coming on."

"Before I left for Hexaka … he was quite adamant about getting an itinerary for this trip." The vice ambassador began to pace in slow and stilted steps. "I didn't think it strange until just now. Normally, I would give him a detailed account."

"Have you left him out of the loop before?" Vanysha's question rerouted Kieran's path, leading him directly to her, and H'reeh swung his gaze between the two lovers. Her vocalized query had mirrored his own thoughts. *They make a good team. Cute one, too.*

Kieran nodded deliberately, as if sorting through memories. "On occasion, if I felt it was not truly business related, or deemed confidential by the client. And he never seemed to care about it at the time."

"I don't understand all of this scrutiny," Myka said. "Haven't I served you faithfully?" He sidled between the guards and approached the vice ambassador. With a practiced flourish, he rested his fingertips on his chest and dipped his head in reverence. "I have been a loyal employee and—"

"That ring."

H'reeh slipped out of the sputtered blathering, shifting his focus to the stunned whisperer, Vanysha's rapt stare never wavering from Myka's left hand. Curious, H'reeh narrowed his eyes, then carefully studied the source of her intense fascination. Myka wore an ornate gold-and-red signet ring on his index finger. Peering in closer, H'reeh picked apart the emblem of a strange four-winged bird, its head thrown back and talons flared as if ready for battle.

"I know that symbol," she said, unfolding her leg as she took to her feet. With unsteady strides, she crept closer, while still remaining distant. "That's Shad'Phan's brand."

The name held no sense of familiarity, so thus made no immediate connection to H'reeh. He glanced over to his people, each one offering up the same perplexed shrug. Judging by the visceral shift in the negotiator's expression, though, the clan in question was the final puzzle piece, and it had just slotted into place.

Kieran spun around, quickly maneuvering Vanysha out of his aide's reach. "But that is also the crest of the Ru'Jan family? Are you sure? Absolutely sure?" Panic had laced his normally calm voice, kicking H'reeh's men into protection mode.

In the ensuing silence, H'reeh sauntered toward the secretary, his movements smooth and kept out of the man's line of sight. He locked eyes with Jazeem, the receipt of his message evident in his guard's blink. Then, with every precaution and contingency covered, H'reeh directed his attention back to Vanysha. Her deep aqua eyes had glazed over while revulsion and anguish poured off of her, souring the surrounding air. She slipped her hand behind her back and, nodding slowly, rubbed at the mark H'reeh knew marred her flesh and her soul.

"Yeah," she muttered, the word hollow and spiteful, "the lines aren't as sharp, but I'm sure." Her sad eyes lifted to study the man's face. "Now I know why he seemed so familiar. He has to be Shad'Phan's son."

"NO!" Myka howled, and he lurched forward, snarling and clawing his way toward Vanysha. "You've ruined everything!"

As quickly as it had started, though, the threat of violence vanished. The man had managed to move only a fraction of an inch before H'reeh's meaty hand clamped around his spindly neck, halting any real progress. At the same time, Kieran wrapped himself around his female, even as Jazeem shielded the pair.

A quick rap on the door caught H'reeh's ear before the door slid open to admit Drexler, Faze, and the rest of his guards. His second swung his head back and forth in a slow, scrutinizing arc, brows pulled together in an inquisitive frown.

"Damn, looks like we missed all the fun," he quipped, nudging the Drekkan captain. "Please tell me we got something useful from it."

H'reeh lifted one shoulder, then tossed his chin toward the vice ambassador and his companion. "Ask them. Seems like this scumbag"—he shook the captured man like a rag doll—"is the key to all of this shit, and he's really excited about spilling his guts about everything." Chuckling darkly, the chieftain leaned in, mouth inches from the man's ear. "Unless you want me to spill them for you."

"Y-y-y-you wouldn't dare."

"There's no need for that," Kieran said, stealing away H'reeh's momentary joy. H'reeh let out a disappointed huff and relaxed his strangling hold. "I have all the information I'll need. I'm more disappointed in myself," the negotiator continued, "for not reading the signs earlier."

The air inside the room stilled, waiting for his explanation. H'reeh caught a sly movement from his lieutenant, and with a humorless glare, he halted Drexler's hand a fraction of an inch away from connecting with the back of Kieran's head.

"There were always rumors that one of the ranking officials in my father's cabinet had deep ties to the Slavers' Guild, but nothing had ever been able to be proved." Kieran retained his tight embrace on his female, as if his presence could somehow banish her past. "Since there was no proof to the tales, and all parties received their fair cut of the profits, it was brushed under the rug." His gray eyes snapped toward Myka. "So Vice Legion Kha Ru'Jan and Shad'Phan are … what? Brothers? Making you the vice legion's nephew and the go-between for the Slavers' Guild and my office."

Drexler shifted his stare between the two male offworlders. "But, what does this have to do with us?" And H'reeh shrugged in reply, unclear of the connection, as well.

"Power," Kieran answered with a heavy sigh. "It's all about the balance of power. If Ru'Jan held control of the governing cabinet on Central *and* the water rights and supplies on Westran Alpha, while his brother had dominance in the Slavers' Guild…"

Jazeem whistled low, echoing the rest of the Hexaks' mumbling. "Holy fuck. These bastards could do whatever they wanted throughout, what"—he tossed a broad gesture toward the skies—"the entire Nexxus system?"

"With no one to challenge them," added Kieran, dejection coloring his voice.

"No," H'reeh stated calmly, his gaze pausing on each face. "Not 'no one.' I plan on challenging all of them." At this, his men rose to their full height, one by one, and moved in unison to stand at their chieftain's side. Drexler fell into line at H'reeh's right, arms folded across his chest, while a proud grin split his face. "And they are not prepared for the hell about to land on their doorsteps. We've been hiding for long enough, buried in history and living in the shadows. Time for Hexaka to reclaim its place in the Nexxus."

Chapter Forty-Five

This can't be happening.

Vanysha forced air in and out of her lungs while her mind struggled to process the recent events. When she'd first seen the sniveling man squeezed between two of H'reeh's bruisers, her blood had run cold. During the time of her servitude, she rarely saw the faces of her "clients," and she'd done everything possible to wipe away the drug-addled memories of the few images that refused to vanish.

But no amount of time or drink would banish the truth that had been burned onto her skin, and onto her soul.

Moments ticked by. Vanysha was dimly aware of the world continuing around her. She shuffled back until her ass bumped against the far wall. Figures drifted in and out of her field of vision, mouths moving, arms gesturing, yet the fog of her past was too thick for sound to penetrate through. Only the pounding of her own frantic heart reverberated in the cocooning silence. Ice chugged through her veins, and she wrapped her arms around herself to drive away the chill.

She'd done everything right. Once she'd been freed from the shackles of the Slavers Guild, she'd rebuilt herself; with the help and guidance of Faze and his loving wife, she'd learned a reputable skill, and had even bought a ship under her own name. She'd done all she could to let go of the past, and not let it define her. In her naïveté, she assumed the universe would forget all of the atrocities she'd endured to reach this moment.

First Kieran, and now this. She squeezed herself, hoping to stop herself from flying apart. *What will it take for me to be free from my demons?* Silent screams ripped through her mind, and she felt violently ill.

A shadow fell over the floor at her feet, and she lifted her head, swallowing hard against her churning gut. Kieran stood before her, as if he'd been conjured by her thoughts, a comforting smile on his handsome face. His full lips moved, forming words that didn't reach her ears. He ran his fingers through his hair as he tipped his head toward the departing crowd. The Hexaks and her pilot waved as they exited, taking the funhouse mirror version of her former slave owner with them. Myka glared at her, venom dripping from his hateful gaze, and after a less-than-friendly shove from one of the guards, he disappeared into the hall.

Alone with Kieran, Vanysha swiveled her face back to him, craned her neck to peer into his turbulent eyes. The edges of his grin had wilted as he spoke once again, the sounds too distant for her to pluck apart. Then he leaned down and extended a welcoming hand. It took a moment for her brain to send the signals to her rigid limbs, but she finally reached out and gripped his offered hand.

She hadn't remembered sitting down, but he easily brought her to her feet, and with one arm draped around her shoulders, he guided her through the room, dousing the candles along the way. His warm breath fanned her hair, but she remained trapped in the terrifying quiet. Soon, his steps led to a door, opening up to reveal a spacious bedroom, and she nodded, following his gentle lead. Sleep did sound tempting to her body even as her mind screamed in fear of the horrors the darkness would awaken.

Caught between the warring parts of her psyche, Vanysha stumbled toward the center of the room and plopped down onto the soft mattress. Kieran, holding on to her hand, knelt before her. He rested her fingers on his shoulder before he lifted each of her feet, removing her clunky, grease-smeared work boots. She stared on, locked within her world of silence, as he rose to his feet and peeled back the sheets for her. She dutifully snuggled back into the bedding, her eyes glued to his every move.

Would he leave her in her solitude? Or would he stay?

Which of his reactions did she want more? Panic climbed higher until he slipped beneath the covers and settled in beside her. Fully clothed, he laid the thin fabric over them, then pulled her in close. His touch was gentle, fingers trailing up and down her bare arms as she rested her head on his chest. The beat of his heart pulsed against her cheek, leading her lungs in the steady rhythm. She dragged in sharp, shallow puffs through her nose, counting the pinpricks of light as they multiplied before her unblinking eyes … until an unending white filled her field of vision and something inside her snapped. Her entire body tensed, clenched muscles shuddering. Distant wailing, harsh and enraged, pierced through her muffled cocoon, and yanked her back into the world.

Strong, solid arms held her tight and fought off the receding darkness.

"It's all right, *la'nen*. I'm here. I've got you. I'm here. You're safe."

Kieran's voice broke through the cacophonous din, the

comforting words like a balm to her battered soul. She continued to shake, her throat aching as tears raced unchecked down her face.

Am I ... am I the one screaming? Second by second, Vanysha slipped back into her own skin. Heat radiating from Kieran's hands drove away the frost clinging to her spirit, while the soft press of his lips against her hair anchored her further into the now.

"Breathe with me, Van." The desperate whispers had poured into her ear, and she struggled to follow the simple request. She gulped in greedy mouthfuls of air, blinking rapidly to stem the flood of tears. With his palm, Kieran drew slow, broad circles across her back while he took in long and deep inhales. "That's it, that's it..." Exhaustion weighed heavily on her shoulders, each intake of the much-needed oxygen a labor.

"They took him away. He's gone. It's only us, *la'nen*." Her mind picked apart his words.

Him.

That hateful face surged into the forefront of her mind, yet the version that had just left the room was not exactly the same. Everything was similar: beady, sickly mauve eyes; cruel slash of a mouth; a haughty nose to look down upon all. But time had not ravaged the man dressed in the expensive suit, proving it hadn't been her former owner. Not the vile creature who'd branded her and had forced behavior-altering drugs into her to make her docile and compliant toward the fiends who used and abused her for their pleasure.

Her breathing grew shallow and short, a sour taste building in her saliva-coated mouth. Wave after wave, unbidden memories crashed into her mind—all the shit she thought she'd buried now surged to the surface, and Vanysha was drowning in the trials of her past. She slammed her hand across her lips and scrambled to free herself from the tangled sheet. As if choreographed, her feet hit the floor, and a small bin appeared before her, just as her stomach unloaded its meager contents.

She heaved until her sides ached, and after she'd disgorged everything she'd eaten in the past two days, her body had finally ended its purge. A peaceful ease descended, as if the dizzying weight chained to her soul had finally evaporated. She took stock of her body and spirit, while her lungs practiced the art of breathing. Her knees pressed down into the carpeted floor, the rough fabric of her jumpsuit offering little padding. Sweat trickled down the back of her neck to soak her flimsy tank top.

The stench wafting up from the trash can inches away from her face threatened to start vomit round two. Shakily, she lifted her head and tumbled into a semi-graceful seated position.

A glass of water was pressed into the palm of her hand, cool and comforting, and she attempted to cough out a reply, but her raw throat refused to function.

"Don't try to speak," Kieran said, his own voice strained. Had he sat with her the entire time she was throwing up?

Embarrassment spiraled through her, followed quickly by the forgotten sensation of gratitude. She swished around a couple of mouthfuls of water, then spat out the dregs into the small bin before daring a full swallow.

Kieran removed the grisly evidence, rising up to set it out of reach. He returned to her side, gently picked up her arm and, with a damp cloth, wiped away the clinging sweat. She watched in rapt attention as he cleaned her up, his head bowed in concentration, his touch hesitant. With his kind and loving gesture, she was thrust back into that tiny apartment, before the outside world had intruded and destroyed their slice of heaven.

Vanysha set down the empty glass and grabbed his hand,

stilling his movements. "Kieran?" she whispered, ducking her head with the hope of capturing his downcast gaze. He trembled, the vibrations racing down his arm, making his open shirt flutter in the small created breeze. She glimpsed flashes of his tense neck as the silken fabric shimmied low on his broad shoulders.

"I know I have no right to ask this," he said, and Vanysha craned her neck to hear his soft words. "But if you give me the chance, I promise I will do everything in my power to make up for all the time we've been apart, and for all that you've suffered."

"That's a pretty tall order," she croaked out, the hinted mirth in her raspy voice drawing his face to hers. Guilt and remorse shadowed his stormy gray eyes, and with all of her remaining strength, she lifted her hand to caress his stubbled cheek. In that moment, he was no longer her phantom tormentor, responsible for all of the violent twists and turns of her life. Here, in the quiet of the night, he was only a man who'd sought to keep her safe through a selfless act.

Chuckling weakly, she tilted her head and pinned him with a resolute stare, even as she fought against her growing smile. "Just how much power do you think you'll need for that task?"

An impish smirk warmed his face. Tenderly, he cupped her hand cradling his cheek, then placed a fiery kiss on her wrist. "With you at my side, *la'nen*, I would tear the suns from the sky."

"Wow…" The word had been a mere exhale of her breath, his smoldering stare boring straight to her heart, banishing her fears. "Be careful, though. Might just hold you to that."

"I hope you do." Kieran trailed his fingers through her short hair, and for the first time in years, Vanysha tossed around the idea of letting it grow out. Her heavy eyelids drooped the longer she savored his soothing touch. Before long, she sensed movement, the floor vanishing beneath her legs, but she was too tired to protest. In her weightless moment, her cheek pressed against his chest.

Is the universe giving us a second chance? she dared to hope, and within seconds, she drifted off to sleep, lulled by the steady beat of her lover's heart.

Chapter Forty-Six

"Where are you? Hasn't your ship docked yet?"

"Disembarking now. I have—"

"So you haven't heard the news?"

"News? What news?"

"We have a problem. The Hexak chieftain is waiting in the foyer to speak to the Enclave right now."

"That barbarian? Who would believe—"

"Apparently he has a witness. It's—"

"He will not be seen until the whole of the High Council has arrived. Meet me outside the Enclave gates in five minutes. Are the assassins in place?"

. . .

"I say again: Are the assassins in place?"

. . .

"Dammit."

Chapter Forty-Seven

Kieran canvassed the strange mix of faces gathered in the Enclave—representatives from every royal family or ruling body from every world in the Nexxus system sat in terrified silence, all bearing the same nervous expression, their sidelong glances or outright stares encouraging him to stand a little taller. He had, after all, entered the Court of the Principe flanked by a pair of fully armed Hexakan guards, the clan chieftain at his side. The trio, who were dressed in shimmering ebony armor spun from finely processed steeleglass, and ceremonial regalia bearing the deep obsidian and copper dragon emblem of Hexaka, dwarfed nearly all of the other delegates. Their sheer presence alone buoyed Kieran's confidence. They held all of the cards and—

<Don't get cocky, kid.>

H'reeh's words had filtered through his head, matching the somber gaze of the pensive leader. *<Just because we've got the answers, doesn't mean shit can't still go sideways.>*

A quick nod pulled the reins on his thoughts. With so many

positive developments over the past day, he'd almost forgotten they were still deep in enemy territory.

After Vanysha's cathartic breakdown, he'd tucked her into bed and disposed of the evidence. Panic had raced through his veins, and he'd nearly spilled the trash can's contents across the bathroom floor in his haste to get back to her. Yet when he'd returned, she was fast asleep, her calm, easy breathing sweet music to his ears. His smile stayed firmly in place, until a rough hand on his shoulder had jarred the two of them awake later. How long had he enjoyed the serenity of the night? He didn't know. Neither did he truly care. Until the universe had settled down around them, he'd simply carry the memories of those quiet hours holding her in his heart and use them as fuel to stoke the fires of peace.

Now, firmly rooted in the present, Kieran shifted his gaze back to the gallery high above the seated assembly. Somewhere in the distant sea of faces, Vanysha, along with her Drekkan pilot and one of H'reeh's men, meandered through the throng. The thought of his lover acting as their lookout had made his stomach turn, but he hated even more the idea of a weapon trained on the back of his or the chieftain's heads as they faced the members of the Court.

Every possible scenario had been discussed in the early morning, the what ifs and what abouts spinning thick in the air, coiling with the rising steam from the carafes of coffee and plates of sliced meats and toasted breads. Drexler and Jazeem had been tasked with keeping their witness safe and concealed until the opportune moment arose. It had taken some fancy footwork from H'reeh to convince the men it wasn't babysitting, and soon everyone eventually knew and had accepted their jobs. The board was set.

Now, time to begin the game.

Three sharp gavel pounds echoed off of the marble walls, drawing all stares away from Kieran's party to focus on the massive double doors swinging open. Chair legs squeaked, and the entire congregation took to its feet. Kieran smoothed his hands down the front of his jacket, abruptly halting in the familiar action as his palms brushed against the ornately embroidered tunic. The gift from the Hexak chieftain had taken him by surprise, but refusing the vestment had been clearly out of the question. The light fabric draped across his somber black wardrobe, the bold pop of color visually allying him to the men standing at his sides.

"All rise to—"

"Who has dared to enter the hallowed halls of this Enclave uninvited?"

Kieran recognized the booming voice and condescending tone of his father. Under normal circumstances, he would have bowed his head, shoulders drawn up to his ears to hide from the ever-present disappointment. But he was no longer that timid, uncertain boy, and he no longer feared the loud blustering of the old man. Instead, he proudly held his chin up as his father entered the chamber, flanked by his retinue of advisors. At seventy years old and with half a century of politico-military service, his father still cut a foreboding figure, his salt-and-pepper hair, cropped close in the standard military style, having receded farther since Kieran had last spent time with the man. Icy chips of black diamonds bore straight into his soul, but Kieran did not back down.

He took a calming breath, yet before the well-rehearsed and required response fell from his lips, the Hexak chieftain beat him to the punch.

"Oh, I got your invitation." H'reeh stepped toward the raised seat of judgement on the dais, and the room gasped. "I just don't think anyone really expected me to show up at the soirée."

"They speak our tongue."

H'reeh narrowed his eyes to glare at the sputtering senators in their gallery boxes lining the walls. "Of course I do, you jack-holes. We speak all your languages, as a matter of fact." And he flung his arm toward the room. "Just haven't given two shits about trading words with any of you for a long time." He paused, leveled his gaze at the figures on the great dais. "Until now."

"A proper degree of decorum is expected by all representatives," said the bristling man to the left of Kieran's father. Many years had passed since the vice ambassador had been in the presence of the fully convened Court. Somewhere in this room, possibly even on the platform before him, stood one of the architects of this phantom war. Would they move openly, here and now, or bide their time until the Enclave dispersed?

"Exactly what is *that* supposed to mean?" asked Ilvan. The guard had leaned in close to Kieran and used his hand as a makeshift shield, even though his staged whisper had easily reached the farthest seats in the chamber.

"Means no swearing," Kieran translated, never shifting his gaze from the staring contest with his father. Ilvan muttered something along the lines of "party pooper," and only his years of training had stopped Kieran from verbally agreeing. Apparently, both of the guards were identical in more ways than just their appearance.

H'reeh folded his thick arms across his chest, narrowing his eyes at the gathered dignitaries, and dared anyone else to interrupt. Once it was clear curiosity held sway over the room, he spoke. "I am Rangatar H'reeh, only son of Gran Rangatar Kaizaan, first of my name and leader of the outworld called by the ancients as Hexaka." Kieran arched his brow in surprise.

He'd only heard of the lengthy formal introductions, which were required for any being who wished to be recognized on the floor of the Enclave. "I stand before the Court of the Principe to demand—"

"You demand nothing here, savage!"

Outraged voices rose and fell, its tide buoyed by decades of destruction and violence. To his credit, the Hexak chieftain ignored the heckling and firmly held his ground. "I demand the heads of Vice Legion Kha Ru'Jan and Chancellor Pretep Bharange for acts of piracy, murder, extortion, and for conspiracy in the attempted genocide of my people."

And so it begins.

Chapter Forty-Eight

Vanysha shouldered her way to the edge of the balcony to find out what was causing all of the commotion. She had a pretty clear idea, but she wanted to see it with her own eyes. From grumbles around her, she'd picked out snippets and partial conversations, yet one thing was certain: the appearance of the Hexak chieftain had surprised the hell out of everyone.

Finally in the clear, she leaned against the marble banister and took stock of the proceedings below.

Kieran stood alongside H'reeh and two of his Hexakan guards, Fengreir and one of the twins, who all never flinched, even as insults were hurled from nearly every level of the vast chamber.

"Who does that barbarian think he is?" muttered a woman to Vanysha's left. Dressed in yesterday's finery, time having taken a toll on both the once-lustrous gown and its wearer, the condescending noble sneered and scoffed at the gathered Hexakan representatives. Vanysha blinked, then swung her gaze from the elite citizens passing judgement high above the situation to her friends standing proud on the floor below.

No, she corrected herself. These people were more than just her friends; they were her lifeline to happiness.

"Maybe he thinks he's his people's leader," Vanysha replied, tipping up her chin in defiance, "and has every right to be treated with proper respect due a man of his station." The woman, clearly not expecting Vanysha's response, fluttered her weathered fan in front of her face, and in her haste to distance herself, bumped into the man beside her. The unnecessary theatrics egged Vanysha on. "And maybe," she added, "just maybe, you should check your surroundings before you open your mouth next time. Never know who's standing beside you."

A meaty hand rested on Vanysha's shoulder, and judging by the pallor of the woman's cheek, either Faze or the Hexak guard had joined her.

"Need any help here, little sister?"

Must be the guard. She'd never known Faze to refer to her by anything other than her name. If she were honest with herself, though, she rather enjoyed the idea of having such protective adopted brothers with whom she'd traveled across the stars. Before the world had caved in around them once again, Kieran had spoken of the sense of home and family he'd felt while on Hexaka. No matter how much she wanted to deny it, she echoed his sentiments.

Perhaps it was the fierce way in which all of the Hexakan people had protected each other when the invasion had begun. But it went deeper than that. Their brutal honesty and warm friendship had easily stripped away the layers of armor she'd built up for so many years, and within the intricate network of caverns, she'd discovered a serenity she'd never believed could be hers. Even a sister in whom she could confide secrets.

While she loved her ship and her crew, the burden of keeping the single-vessel company afloat taxed her. She couldn't remember the last day she'd had to herself; her life was consumed by her job and by the struggles to make ends meet. But was she truly ready to find a permanent place to call her home?

She shook her head, dismissing her wandering mind, then glanced over and up to meet the stern, icy peridot eyes of the Hexak warrior. Sendak was his name, and she bit the inside of her cheek to stop from giggling, his now-grim countenance in sharp contrast to the easy smile he'd worn throughout their journey.

"Nah," she said, patting her shadow's hand resting on her shoulder, "I think I made my point. Don't you—" But when she'd turned back, her snooty companion had mysteriously vanished into the crowd. "Huh. Guess she had somewhere else to be."

"Who had somewhere else to be?" Faze asked, and Vanysha spun around as her pilot approached. With the influx of delegates and lookie-loos curious about the first sighting of a Hexak in almost a century, neither of the boys in her party had drawn much attention. Plus, since Sendak had pulled his dark auburn hair into a slick ponytail and tucked the length beneath the collar of his long coat, he could almost pass for the Drekkan's brother.

Vanysha waved off his question. "Have you found anything?" she asked.

Faze growled, dragging his fingers through his beard. "No," he said. "The damned chamber is locked up tighter than a Bozzan's wallet, so they're on their own inside."

"But there is no real vantage point for an assassin in there," added Sendak. "The inset booths for the delegates line the walls and their only access points are from the front. No place to sneak in."

H'reeh's men had done a thorough recon of the Enclave

chamber, as the rest of their party had decided on the plan the day before. Hard to believe they'd only been planetside for less than two full days. Too much, too soon. Too many horrific memories running through her mind, all eager to derail her mission. Vanysha clamped down on her teeth, shoved her demons back into their cages, and refocused.

With the news of the Hexaks' arrival now public, Kieran had been certain more open attempts on the chieftain's life loomed on the horizon. The engineers behind this atrocious war could not afford for their plans to be revealed so near the finish line; they'd be desperate, and they'd be sloppy. But that didn't make the threat any less real. As much as her heart wished for her to cower in the shadows, she'd made the decision to search for possible assassins in the crowds that would surely gather along the walkway looking into the sunken rotunda known as the Enclave.

Guards filtered through the curious patrons, their gleaming golden helmets easily identifying them to the law-abiding citizens, though Vanysha knew the deterrent was wasted on their opponents. She tapped her finger rapidly against her lower lip as she scanned the masses.

"We have to assume anyone can be the killer," she said, the words tumbling out of her mouth hastily. "It would be just as easy to pose as one of the sentries; they're obviously armed, and no one would bat an eye seeing a weapon in their hands." She narrowed her gaze, searching for some beacon broadcasting *assassin* across someone's forehead. "Dress well, hide the gun. Fuck"—she tossed her hands skyward—"we don't even know what kind of a weapon to look for."

"It has to be a subsonic round," Sendak said flatly, and Vanysha cocked her head to stare up at the solemn Hexak. "There's a force shield over the opening." Her eyes darted to the empty space just beyond the banisters, then back to the giant, whose lazy shrug served as the first answer. "I can smell it," he explained. "It's like a combination of dry lightning and four-day-old sweaty socks."

Vanysha curled her lip as Faze shuddered, shuffling away from the edge.

"Well, that paints a disgusting picture," Faze said, and he wiped at his hands as if brushing away the offending, unseen odor. "Although, it does narrow down the list of possible weapons." He paused, but Vanysha knew what her friend's next words would be.

"We need to split up."

She blinked at the perfect synchronicity of all three voices.

"Well," she remarked, "that was easy."

Sendak winked, his smile returning for a brief moment. "Great minds," he said. "Okay, kids, stay in contact and keep your head on a swivel. I've got a feeling time is running out."

Vanysha opened her mouth, but the Hexak guard had turned and vanished into the crowd. So, she angled her gaze up to Faze, and the Drekkan nodded solemnly before he, too, made a hasty exit. With a deep breath, she eyed the shifting tide of faces, searching for a possible killer.

If I were an assassin, where would I hide…?

As she meandered, she pondered her own would-be actions, but in truth, there were too many possible answers, which made the task that much harder. Her eyes were constantly drawn to the stiff soldiers as they strolled in pairs through the gathered crowd, and she halted her steps, spun about to rest her back along the ornate railing.

In plain sight would be my instinct, she answered herself. *But not a guard. Someone who is supposed to be in a place but not really noticed.* A sinking feeling sat heavy in her gut as a janitor dressed in a baggy jumpsuit pushed his cart of brooms and mops between the onlookers. She followed the man's movements, unblinking while her mind churned. Not a single patron paid any attention to the lowly worker, all too engrossed in the proceedings happening on the Enclave's floor.

She kicked off the banister and trailed after her quarry, certain she was on the right track. Hunched over, the man never raised his gaze from the floor, yet something in his manner had set off all the bells and whistles in Vanysha's head, and as he reached into his cart, his sleeve pulled back to reveal a familiar, flamboyant tattoo of a crimson phoenix.

Her hands shook as she touched the mic at her throat. "The janitors," she said, the words rushing out in a harsh whisper as she ducked behind a decorative tree to better spy on her prey. "They're here now. They—"

A sharp prick to the back of her neck had lasted only a heart-beat before a strange weightlessness slogged through her limbs.

"There you are, my pretty one."

The voice from her darkest nightmares had poured into her ear, carried along by fetid breath, and then everything went black.

Chapter Forty-Nine

<B *oss. I think we've got a problem…>* H'reeh had heard Sendak's voice as clear as if the man had been standing beside him. Not good.

<Talk to me. What exactly do you mean by problem?> H'reeh tapped Kieran's shoulder to get his attention. Then, as covertly as possible, he glanced up to the gallery far above their heads, hoping the vice ambassador understood the message.

<Vanysha said something about janitors, then went silent.>

The corner of H'reeh's lip curled, a growl slipping between his clenched teeth. Time to bring out their ace in the hole. *<Kill anyone you have to. But find her.>* Knowing his orders would be followed without question, the Hexak chieftain tossed back his head and howled, the force of his anger echoing off of the walls of the Enclave.

At once, silence slammed down, as if the air itself feared to make itself a target of his wrath. Even Kieran was taken aback by his outburst. He'd apologize later, but time was not on their side and the game pieces were shifting faster than the sands of the Loess Sea.

"Now that I have your attention," he stated, coolly smoothing a hand along the front of his tunic, "are we ready to get this shit show underway?" And with a nod to no one in particular, he approached the stunned trio seated at the raised dais. "Nearly a century ago, my people pulled away from the political machinations and devious intrigue of the Nexxus. We had a valid reason and—"

"You slaughtered the rightful prince of Westran Alpha!" a voice shouted from the rafters.

"After the meaningless and violent murder of my sister at the hands of that maniacal madman!" H'reeh roared back above the muttering and grumbling. Once again, an uneasy quiet descended and he turned his gaze toward the delegates seated high above as he stalked through the chamber with long strides. "She entered her wedding chamber fully aware of her responsibilities and obligation to act as a bridge between two worlds. She was…"

A red haze crept in from the edges of his vision, an old hatred stealing his voice, threatening to take hold of his heart as the image of her shattered, lifeless body swam into his mind. Taking a measured breath, he forced down the pain, banished the rising ire with a calming exhale.

"Since that day," he went on, "we have stayed silent and separate, contrary to what your leaders wish you to believe." Again, he cranked up the volume of his voice to be heard above the slowly rising din. *No wonder nothing ever gets done around here,* he mused. *No one ever listens to anyone.* He lifted his hand, the gesture stopping all of the wagging tongues. "But we will play the villains no longer. We of Hexaka have had no need of any of you long before we split, and nothing has changed for us."

"Nonsense!" interjected another haughty speaker. "You live on a lifeless rock, surviving in mud huts and—"

"Wow." H'reeh chuckled, shaking his head. "Do you think before you speak, or are you just as surprised as the rest of us by the shit that flows from your mouth?"

"He is telling the truth," Kieran declared, and a flash of pink blossomed on the young male's cheeks. Ilvan barked out a sharp laugh, and even Fengreir coughed to hide his chuckles. "I mean, about their need of the other planets in the Nexxus," he quickly amended. "I have seen Hexaka firsthand. Like many of you, I was expecting to meet with the barbarians of our outdated history records, yet what I'd witnessed, I dare say, proved just how wrong we have been."

The vice ambassador tilted his head up to ensure his voice filled the vast chamber. "I marveled at their advanced technology, all built underground in the massive system of caverns that rest below the planet's surface. I saw fields of grains warmed by domed steeleglass shields, flowing rivers of clear waters running beside a mag-powered rail system. They are completely self-reliant, living in harmony. If anything"—he swiveled his eyes up to pin his father with a determined stare—"we need them far more than they will ever need us."

"Bah," scoffed the balding male sitting on the far left of the raised trio, and H'reeh arched a brow, filing away his reaction. "He could be—"

"Vice Ambassador Phaetal is many things," boomed the voice of the Politico General himself, and H'reeh narrowed his eyes, curious as to how this father-son moment would play out. His gaze swung between the two, struggling and failing to find familial similarities. Really, only the timbre of their resonating voices linked their blood. If H'reeh got a better look at the leader, more similarities would possibly become evident. In the meantime, though, he waited, as did the others in the Enclave, to hear the end of the man's sentence. "But a liar he has never been."

With an appreciative tip of his chin, H'reeh reclaimed center stage. "I have come to speak my piece, to get out from under the shadow and misconceptions you've had about my people for far too long, then I'm gonna take my toys and get the fuck home."

Offended gasps filtered through the chamber. H'reeh waved off the impending admonishment. "Yeah, yeah. More decorum. Got it. Anyway," he continued, "power is a dangerous drug, and you've got a couple of serious addicts posing as representatives of two major players. For nearly a century, Westran Alpha has been milking the so-called *'hostilities'* at our hands." He bracketed his sarcastic delivery with air quotes before relaunching his speech. "Even had fighters painted in our colors, hoping to fool everyone into believing we were the aggressors. Warships from Central."

"Preposterous!" roared a voice from the dais; the same bald man who'd earlier tipped his hand. *Ah, there you are.* "You have no—"

"Don't even think about saying I have no proof," H'reeh cut in, pausing before adding, "Vice Legion Kha Ru'Jan. Do you really think I'd drag my ass here with nothing but conjecture and theory? And let's take a moment to ask why you are the first one to jump up and cry foul?" And H'reeh stabbed his finger toward the politico general's chief advisor as Drexler and Jazeem stepped forward, their bargaining chip shuffling between the pair of armed men.

Inquisitive whispers followed the trio, and the advisor's face turned a lovely shade of grayish green.

"What's the matter?" the chieftain asked softly with a knowing smirk. "Cat got your tongue?"

Kieran tugged on H'reeh's sleeve. "Wait," he said. "I thought we were going to bring him in when Vanysha's team found the assassin."

H'reeh paused a beat as his soldiers continued toward the center of the chamber. *Fuck.*

"They're close." The chieftain gave a heavy sigh, and he shifted his gaze to meet with the unsettled storm gray eyes of the vice ambassador. "But they ran into some trouble."

Kieran paled a fraction as he inched away. "What kind of—"

A shot rang out, and H'reeh lurched to his right, dragging Kieran with him behind one of the ornate pillars as chunks of marble flew into the air.

"That kind," the chieftain answered. Shouts and the screeching of chair legs erupted in the confined space, adding to the cacophony, burying any clue as to the assassin's location. Another blast came in from a different vantage point, followed by a third, all ricocheting off items in their immediate surroundings. Two targets seemed to be on the hidden snipers' radar, and only blind luck kept them from accomplishing their mission.

"Keep that little worm alive, Jazeem!" H'reeh called out above the din as he slid his own weapon from its concealed holster then activated the shielding woven into the ceremonial cloth. He hadn't had time to explain the true nature of the garment he'd presented to both of the offworlders, but he'd refused to let them go into the battle without any protection.

"But who's gonna keep *me* safe?"

H'reeh groaned, rolling his eyes at his petulant guard. A flash at the edge of his periphery nabbed his attention, and he leveled his gun in the general vicinity. "Jaz, you're a big boy," he replied, staring intently at the possible hiding hole far above their heads. "I'm sure you'll figure something out." Light glinted off of a blast rifle's muzzle and H'reeh smirked, exhaling smoothly as he pulled the trigger. The air hummed as a slow beam lanced through the open space to carve a perfectly level trench in the would-be assassin's head. "And you were right, Drex," he added over his shoulder, "the aegis designer didn't account for other subsonic weapons."

Somewhere off to his left, his lieutenant scoffed. "Amateurs. How's the negotiator holding up?" A distant blast from the gallery followed by cries of terror announced the demise of another sniper. Two down, hopefully only one more to go.

"Dunno," H'reeh answered. "Yo, kid?" A chilling gurgle bubbled up from behind him. "Kieran?" Shit, if he'd gotten himself killed…

"H'reeh?"

He knew that tone all too well—panic and desperation blended into a sorrowful cocktail. Preparing for the worst, the chieftain glanced over his shoulder. "Dammit. What the hell went wrong?"

Back hunched, Kieran knelt beside Fengreir's prone body. The vice ambassador shook his head, arms trembling as he pressed down to stem the flowing crimson escaping from the man's neck. "I-I-I don't know what … it all happened so fast and … and I only looked away for a second—"

H'reeh crawled closer in the shadow of an overturned table. "Ilvan? You need to get here." Beneath the grizzled beard, Fengreir's complexion paled. One final scream rang out, and then silence descended, declaring the end of the firefight. H'reeh rested his hand on his captain's shoulder. A slight flicker of light remained in the man's milky lavender eyes.

"Sorry, your majesty," Fengreir rasped. *"Guess I'm slowing down in my old age."*

"Don't try to speak, old friend." H'reeh sensed Ilvan at his back and scooted out of the way. *"You have honored your oath."* The chieftain paused, refusing to continue the traditional blessing for the

fallen. *"But I'm not gonna let you off the hook that easily."* Switching to Universal, he gave the captain's arm a light squeeze. "You still owe me twenty creds."

Fengreir's weak smile served as a response, and H'reeh pulled Kieran away from the gory scene. "Stay with me, kid." Sobs and hushed voices began to filter in, now that the immediate threat had been neutralized. Kieran dropped his gaze to the blood smeared across the once-vivid jewel tones of the gifted tunic. H'reeh gripped the vice ambassador's arms. "You did all you could," he said. "Ilvan will take over from here. You have another task."

As much as H'reeh hated to teach a crash course in life, now was not the time for coddling. "Your female is in danger, and you are the only one who can find her."

Chapter Fifty

Kieran snapped his gaze up from the red slipping off of his fingers, swallowed past the rising bile, and pinned the chieftain with a worrying stare.

"What?"

His brain shifted through the man's cryptic message: *"Your female is in danger, and you are the only one who can find her."*

"You're gonna have to trust me on this one, Kier. We ain't got a lot of time." H'reeh rose and carried Kieran along. Movement danced on the edges of his periphery, but the intense focus of the Hexak's sky blue eyes refused to let him go. He followed the chieftain's lead, entranced, and stepped farther away from the grim activity. "I know Niko gave you some quick pointers about your Lost Art, but these skills, these energies, also create tangible connections and I'm gonna need you to tap into it. I know there's a deep, unbreakable bond between you and Vanysha."

Kieran opened his mouth to protest, yet the lie refused to pass his lips. H'reeh smiled slyly. "Yeah, nice try. That reason alone is how you can locate her. Close your eyes and connect with her."

His brows tugged together, even as his lids slipped down. *How the hell am I supposed to do that?* Confused, Kieran struggled to picture her hair, or even the color of her eyes until the jolting slap of a broad hand against his chest yanked him away from the failed visuals.

"No," H'reeh said. "Go deeper. Think visceral, possessive. Primal."

Primal. The single word echoed through his mind and fired up his blood. Images of Vanysha laid out like a banquet before his feasting desires exploded behind his closed eyes. Her sensual voice and her needy, keening whimpers rose up within his memories.

"Reach for the tether and find her."

Before Kieran could ask what H'reeh meant, a silvery filament of aquamarine flared to life, and his eyes flew open. He blinked rapidly, then focused on the ethereal path, clear and visible, while a friendly shove to his back urged him on. And so, with steady, determined strides, Kieran followed the trail, slow at first, but soon picked up the pace as each twist and turn shifted the brightness of the tether. Driven on by his quickened speed, Kieran dashed up the grand staircase, shouldering his way through the fleeing crowds. The light stream pointed toward a set of double doors, but appeared to stop at the barrier.

His feet skidded to a halt, and as he gradually caught his breath, he leaned in, pressed his ear to the seam and strained to hear more than the sound of his own blood thundering through his veins. *I can reach her. I have to.* His eyelids drifted shut and, once again, he tapped into the powerful and passionate memories. Three voices filtered through from the space beyond, yet he counted four heartbeats, and judging by the cruel laughter that stole the heat from his skin, Vanysha must have been unconscious. Or worse. Rage made to spur him into action, yet a calming touch in his mind cooled his anger.

"You rush in half-cocked, kid, and you might get both of you killed." The chieftain's timely warning froze his fingers a scant inch above the rounded knob, and with a controlled exhale, he gripped the handle, slowly spun it about. A faint click gave him permission to push open the door. While the animalistic part of his brain demanded he rush in and slaughter everyone inside, the logical voice advised a more civilized, more strategic approach. Boxes and shelving units provided cover, as well as a labyrinth of possible pathways. Sticking close to the shadows, Kieran crept toward the pair of speakers oblivious to his stealthy advance.

"How did you find this bitch again?"

"You are kidding? I'd never forget that hair."

"You mean you'd never forget the back of her head."

Kieran locked his jaw to hold back his furious and repulsed growl while the unknown culprits chuckled. Peeking between two skewed piles, he spied two men dressed in gray jumpsuits who surrounded a familiar figure bound to a chair and gagged by a thick band of cloth. One eye was swollen shut, but even from his distance, Kieran could read the smoldering anger in her expression.

They would pay for touching her, but whether retribution came from his hands or hers, that was the true question.

"Seems fate has brought us together once again, my pretty," came a voice from the other side of his hiding place. Vanysha swung her head, nostrils flaring as she squirmed in an attempt to escape the approaching speaker. "Had I known how much income I was going to lose by allowing that Drekkan to sever your contract, I would've refused." The two underlings backed away, and Vanysha's frantic thrashing gained momentum. "Did you know, even after all these years, I still have clients ask for the girl with starlight hair."

When the slaver gripped her chin, Kieran exploded into action. He roared, channeling the power of his Lost Art, and demolished the barricade between him and the stunned kidnappers.

"Get your hands off of her," he growled as he stalked through the smoldering debris. Four pairs of eyes stared in shock, but the quiet only lasted a second before blasts filled the air. Kieran raised his hands, sent return fire of his own creation, his gaze fixed on Vanysha as his targets dove for cover. Screams sliced through, smoke rising in thick plumes, adding to the chaos. The male nearest to his bound lover ducked behind her, pressed a wickedly curved blade against her exposed throat.

"Well, well, well," the slaver crooned, lips too close to Vanysha's cheek for Kieran's liking. "Is this the one you used to cry over in your sleep, my pretty?" Kieran narrowed his eyes and studied the cowardly man using a female as a shield. Dishwater blond hair surrounded hawkish features wrapped in shimmering amber skin, yet his magenta eyes undeniably confirmed the familial relationship to his former secretary. Must have been Shad'Phan. "Do you think he'll still want you, knowing what you've become?"

Kieran glanced toward Vanysha, hoping his tender gaze would soothe her terror. "I know what she is," he stated, keeping his voice even. He sensed the heat of curious stares, but he refused to break contact with his lover. A wary frown pulled her brows together, and he offered a loving smile to set her mind at ease. "She's mine."

In the next heartbeat, the world took a surprising turn. Sprinklers popped out of the ceiling to rain fire-retardant ash onto the pockets of blazes. Kieran jerked his arms up and, aiming his barely contained anger toward the two hidden assailants, instantly vaporized one of the men. His aim was off on the second target, though, and a blast knocked into his shoulder before another slammed into his chest, spinning him about, a dull pain radiating through him. He hissed out as the floor raced up to meet his face.

A crash and a muffled cry from behind him chilled his blood, and he pushed his head up off of the floor. Vanysha, still tied to the chair, had apparently used the back of her own head as a weapon; blood trailed down the front of her shirt, and the guild master staggered on wobbly legs, hands attempting to stop the gushing red from his shattered nose. Before the man could regain his composure, Kieran launched himself toward the slaver and tackled him around the waist, stopping only when they'd slammed against the nearest wall.

Even if he lost his life in this moment, he'd die knowing his Vanysha would never again suffer at the hands of this monster. *But*, he thought as he balled up his fists, *I'm not about to make the taking easy.*

Chapter Fifty-One

Vanysha shook her head, hoping to make sense out of the surreal scene. At first, she'd thought it had been the lingering effects of the drugs Shad'Phan had injected into her, ensuring her submission after she'd discovered the familiar faces among the custodial staff. But unless her eyes deceived her, Kieran had come to rescue her. *How the hell did he find me? I don't even know where I am.*

When the fireworks had begun, she'd found her spine and had slammed her head into that cruel face as hard as her body would allow. The cold blade at her throat had clattered harmlessly to the floor, and now, she rocked her weight from side to side, determined to free herself. But her efforts were both thwarted and aided by steam engine Kieran. With an animalistic roar, he barreled headlong into her former owner, and in his haste, his knee knocked into her chair. She perched on one wooden leg for a terrifying moment, until gravity took over and she toppled, the flimsy frame cracking on impact.

Meaty thumps and guttural grunts filled the air behind her,

giving urgency to her struggles, and tears streamed down her cheeks as she fought against the constricting bonds. She thrashed, broken splinters cutting into her arms and legs.

He was here. Kieran was really here. Not just a figment of her drug-addled imagination. Both hope and fear fueled her muscles, and her continued action helped to burn through the lethargic narcotic. But while she sang internal praises to the gods for the timely arrival of her savior, she was well versed in Shad'Phan's treachery and had to get free. Her arm flailed and she nearly punched herself in the face, surprised by the sudden freedom, then she twisted around, using her now-freed hand to rip at the unwavering ties.

New voices called out, adding to the cacophony, and the screeching alarm fell silent, though the sounds of the two men locked in furious battle still raged on. Kieran had been shot; she knew the blast had hit him. How much longer would he last with such an injury?

A nearby scream pierced the air, followed by a sickening thud.

Please, goddess, no. Vanysha scrambled to her knees and turned. Two bodies lay on the ground, her former owner sprawled across Kieran, a crimson pool spreading out from their still forms. The hilt of a blade poked out, caught in the seam of the men's sides and clutched in Shad'Phan's stubby fingers.

"NO!" Dread had poured forth through her shout as she scooted closer. Forcing her own pain away, she yanked out the blood-smeared knife, raised it high above her head, blinding rage and a vengeful grief driving her on. To her surprise, Kieran lifted his head and struggled to slither out from beneath Shad'Phan's body.

"K-K-Kieran?" Her voice trembled and the blade slipped from her fingers to clatter harmlessly onto the concrete floor as

Kieran levered himself into a seated position. "I thought … I thought you…" She flung her arms around him and, crawling into his lap, wept.

"Shh," he whispered, strong hands holding her gently. "I'm here. You're safe now."

Countless questions spun in her mind, and instead of savoring the peace of the moment, Vanysha shoved away his comfort to pop him solidly on the shoulder.

"You scared the shit out of me," she croaked through her tears. "Don't ever do that again." She'd beaten her fists against his chest with each word, her confused swirl of emotions needing some logical outlet. Judging by the laughter pouring down her back, Kieran was not offended by her weak, violent response.

"Okay, okay," he chuckled, capturing her wrists in one hand. She lifted her head to gaze at him. The blood streaked along his cheek did not detract from his handsome features, and the proud smile across his face sent the butterflies in her gut into a frenzy. Raising her hands to his swollen lips, he brushed a soft kiss along her knuckles. "It's a deal."

"Geez, you two…" The new speaker reminded Vanysha of their current surroundings. "How 'bout finding a more romantic spot for this kind of thing?"

"Piss off," Kieran replied with a wink before shifting his gaze. "Is he still alive?" he asked, tipping his chin toward the slaver.

Footfalls grew closer, slowly encouraging Vanysha to return to reality. She stared at the figure lying off to her left, watched as booted toes kicked the man in the ribs, and she waited, holding her breath. Was this nightmare finally over?

A weak groan rose up from the prone body. "Alive enough," said the Hexak guard. Sendak bent down, picked up Shad'Phan by the back of his neck, and tossed the man like a rag doll over his shoulder, ignoring the deep crimson puddle on the steel gray floor. "C'mon," he added, cocking his head back to the gaping entrance, "H'reeh only knows so many jokes, and I'm sure he exhausted them about ten minutes ago."

Vanysha nodded and, gathering what strength she could, slid off of Kieran's thighs. The emotionally charged burst seemed to have bottomed out; she was quite content to stay seated on the cold floor for a while longer. But when Kieran struggled to climb to his feet, she found her reserve and, kneeling beside him, she ducked her head under his arm and they managed to rise up together.

"I should be carrying you, *la'nen*," he muttered into her ear, even as he tightened his hold around her waist.

"You can carry me next time," she quipped, splaying her fingers against his chest to keep him upright.

Their pace was slow and uneven as the trio shambled out of the antechamber and made their way toward the grand staircase. Vanysha eyed the descending steps. *This is gonna suck a lot*, she mused.

"Holy shit!"

"There you are!"

Relieved voices had called out an instant before the burden of Kieran's weight was lifted from her shoulders. The loss of ballast nearly took her to the floor; only a strong grip on her arm kept her vertical. "Thought we'd lost you there, Van."

Vanysha faked a laugh and shook her head as she patted Faze's hand, grateful to see her friend once again. "Not for lack of trying, I'll tell you that."

The giant Drekkan chuckled. "You look like shit. Can't leave you alone for a minute, can I?" Faze cupped her cheek, and with a pass of his thumb, the throb along her jaw diminished and her vision sharpened, both eyes now open and in working order. Before she could properly voice her thanks, though, he jogged off to catch up with the others, gesturing for her to follow down the marbled stairs, calling out behind him, "Well, be sure to tell me the whole story once we're done inside."

"Inside?" she echoed, gaze bouncing from the steps to the flurry of chaotic movement at the base of the staircase. She narrowed her eyes, stared at the back of the Hexak lieutenant's head. "What the hell did I miss?"

"A lot," replied Drexler as he led her through the whimpering crowds. "Assassination attempt, shots flying around." He glanced over his shoulder, and Vanysha caught a veneer of sadness beneath the half smile. "Screams, death," he said. "Good times."

Death. The word landed like a fist and her gut tightened. The hulking Hexak shrugged and shouldered his way toward the massive double doors. Vanysha recognized the twins bookending the locked entryway. Neither smiled as their group approached. A quick exchange in harsh, guttural words between the Hexaks brought an unexpected tear to her eye. She had no idea what any of the men were saying, yet her heart ached. Had the assassin reached his target?

Sendak bowed his head, the body of the unconscious slaver tumbling off of his shoulder, falling like a stone onto the hard floor. Jazeem crossed to his friend, touched his forehead to the other man's, his fingers resting on the back of Sendak's neck. Grief floated up from the brief gesture. Looking away, Vanysha trained her gaze on the duplicate still-standing guard.

"Oh no," gasped Kieran. "Fengreir?" Vanysha scooted away from her pilot, wrapped her arm around her lover's waist, unsure if she was giving or taking needed solace.

Ilvan closed his eyes, his audible swallow answering the painful inquiry. Vanysha brought her fingers to her lips as the silent guard gave his head a sharp shake, and before she could ask more, Ilvan pushed open the grand doors.

Never in her wildest dreams would she have imagined herself walking into the Enclave, to stand in the presence of the Court of the Principe, but she was reasonably sure the smoldering wreckage of shattered chairs and broken marble columns was not the usual decor. Many of the delegates had vacated the impromptu battlefield; only a handful of officials had bravely remained.

H'reeh stood in the center of the room, arms folded across his barrel chest as he spoke to an older man. Kieran's secretary, as well as two other men, on their knees and trussed up, finished out the strange tableau. Set apart was a prone figure, a scarlet-stained linen draped over him.

Fengreir. Closing her eyes, she sent a small prayer to the heavens, and her steps slowed instinctively as the group continued forward. Even though she'd never met the constipated-looking official standing beside the Hexak chieftain, a huge part of her knew this had to be Politico General Raejil Phaetal, the man who'd started her life on its downward spiral.

Kieran's father.

Oh, boy. Won't this be fun. Taking a deep breath, Vanysha lifted her head and strode proudly at Kieran's side.

"About time you guys decided to join us," said the chieftain. Streaks and splotches of red covered the once-vibrant tunic, but the burly Hexak appeared uninjured. "You brought the rest of the evidence. Good. He still alive?"

Jazeem nodded, the burden of delivery transferred to him while his friend paid his respects. "Yup. That's the rumor." He dumped Shad'Phan's body at the politico general's feet, and it landed with a sickening thud in complete silence. "Whoops," he amended. "Better make that a no." Vanysha coughed to cover her improper giggle as the leader recoiled from the gift. "Hope you didn't need him to say much."

H'reeh lifted one shoulder, then gave a dismissive wave of his hand. "Meh, I can make this work. All righty, then," the chieftain said, and he gestured toward the three men on display before returning his gaze to the elder Phaetal. "They say every conspiracy needs three sides. To sum it up: Pretep wanted to keep the perks his people had gained so many years ago after we stepped away from the table." He circled behind one of the trussed-up delegates and rested his hands on the man's shoulders. "He and your buddy, Ru'Jan, there"—he tipped his chin toward the bound vice legion—"had grown fat off of the side income from the Slavers' Guild run by his brother, Shad'Phan, combined with the profits from the raids on all the vessels along the Crimson Alley. Together, they concocted a plan to knock my entire race off the board without anyone's knowledge and create whatever narrative they wanted, keeping alive the myth of the savage Hexaks with continued attacks, and holding the Nexxus in their greed-fueled stranglehold." He glanced over at Kieran. "Might have succeeded, too, if not for your kid here. He was the one who pieced it all together."

Vanysha glanced up at her lover, his eyes veiled in shadow as he looked toward the Hexak chieftain. Would he refuse the spotlight he had struggled so hard to reach? Hoping to avoid the focus, she made to slip away from his side, only to have him capture her hand before she could fully retreat, and as he intertwined his fingers with hers, he stepped toward the dais. She dug in with her heels, even as her feet followed.

What are you doing? She didn't know if she was asking this of herself or her partner, but the die was now cast. She had to see this to its ending.

Chapter Fifty-Two

Kieran could feel the heat of several dozen pairs of eyes on his face, but he still held his head up. Even the incredulous, judgmental stare of his father couldn't diminish his spirits, though he had opted to face the enemy with his Vanysha at his side. Lacing his fingers with hers, he approached the dais as he drew energy and strength from their tender connection. The ache in his shoulder throbbed, pulsed with each step, but he pushed away the pain. With any luck, this feigned and fleeting bonding moment with his father would play out to its inevitable ending, and he could return to forging a new life path with friends and a chance at love.

"You?" The disappointed tone Kieran had grown up with was now masked by an unexpected layer of pride. Even his father's dour frown had perked up along the corners of his mustached mouth.

Kieran dipped his chin, then winced slightly as he lifted his head. "The pieces in this game had been on the board for years, and once the young Westran Alpha leader dreamed of finding peace with Hexaka and bringing an end to the hostilities, they were forced into action. Ka'Jun had swayed the Hexak representative still on Central after their homeworld had cut ties with the Nexxus, and sent them back with orders to destroy the steeleglass factories, as well as the ruling family."

"Which would have given him the opportunity to control production on Hexaka," mused the politico general as he rested his chin on his knuckles, thick black brows pulling together over diamond gray eyes. "But how does this one play into this?" he asked as he toed the dead slaver at his feet.

"Shad'Phan is—sorry, *was*—the Prime Warlord of the Slavers' Guild, and Ka'Jun's brother. Through his network of brothels and gambling dens, they funneled money and ill-gotten goods to every end of the Nexxus without a second glance from…" Kieran paused, thinking over the best way to finish the statement without accusation. But, coming up short, he shrugged and charged forward. "Well, from you, and the others on the Council."

"Bribe the right people," H'reeh added, "and anything is possible."

Kieran nodded in agreement. "And with the worsening restrictions on the water supply to the other worlds, Ka'Jun believed you'd be ousted and he'd slip into the role of Politico General by a landslide vote."

Silence drifted in, a calming balm that threatened to steal Kieran's waning energy. "If not for some luck on our part," he said, "they might have succeeded in following through with their plans, as well as the genocide of the Hexak people."

"Luck?" H'reeh chuckled and shook his head, his grin firmly in place. "You reading the signs, your girl recognizing the link between the two crests? I say it was more like friggin' divine providence."

"After what we've all been through," Kieran added, pulling Vanysha close, "I am willing to believe in a higher power." He glanced down at her as she stumbled against him, her gaze furtive and unsettled. Hoping to reassure her, he wrapped his arm around her shoulders, then leaned over to brush a kiss atop her head. A wistful smile touched his lips as he inhaled the scent of his Vanysha—his heart, and the only woman he would ever love.

Locked in her deep pools of exotic aqua, he held her fingers lightly in his and found his voice. "Vanysha?"

"Vanysha?" The familiar disapproval now sat in his father's tone. "The same worthless, common girl who—"

"I'd watch what you say next." Kieran swiveled his gaze toward his defender, surprise breaking the momentary spell. Drexler had folded his beefy arms across his chest, glaring daggers. "We're all kinda fond of her, and we don't like people who insult our sister." The Hexak lieutenant nodded. "Go on, kid. Let's get this proposal done so we can go home."

"Proposal? Home?" Vanysha squeaked in disbelief, and Kieran grinned as he turned back to face her. "What the … Kieran? Is he … I mean, are you serious?"

"I have never been more serious, or more sure of anything in my life." He pressed her palms against his chest, then covered her hands with his. "Six years ago, I found paradise with the most beautiful woman, but I was too afraid to fight to keep it. The universe was kind enough to give me a chance to redeem the cowardice of my youth." Everything around him melted away, until only Vanysha remained, proving she truly was the center of his world. Caught in the magic of the moment, and lost in her beauty, he took a knee before her. "Vanysha," he said, "if you say the word, I will stay by your side until the stars fade."

Her eyes glistened, her lips parting, though no words fell.

Smiling broadly, Kieran leaned close. "Say something," he whispered overtly, caressing her cheek and wiping away the escaping tears with the pad of his thumb. "I'll take a nod. We can work on the words later, *la'nen*."

Laughing through her sobs, she bobbed her head, then threw her arms around him. Kieran joined in the joyful moment, cradling her against him, reveling in the peace only her presence could deliver, and with a contented sigh, he rested his cheek against her soft tresses.

A polite cough brought Kieran back to reality. "Well," H'reeh said, "I think we've done all we needed to, and I for one am ready to get the fuck outta here."

"Same here," echoed Drexler, stretching his arms above his head, groaning as his spine popped and cracked. "I haven't had a decent meal the whole time we've been here."

Mutters of agreement filtered through from the Hexak contingent, and as Kieran took to his feet, the men crossed over to their fallen friend and lifted him off the cold ground in solemn reverence. Kieran tightened his arms around Vanysha, the warmth of her embrace chasing away his grief, and with the bower set, the quiet procession moved toward the grand doors.

H'reeh reached the entry and turned, a mischievous grin on his face. "So, you two coming or what?"

Kieran huffed out his held breath, the speech he'd prepared vanishing with the Hexak chieftain's direct question. He peered down at his beloved as he mentally crossed his fingers.

"*La'nen*? What do you say?"

Vanysha slipped out of Kieran's arms and lifted her gaze. A spark of hope twinkled in her teal eyes, and she squeezed his hands with a shy nod. Kieran cupped her face, elated, and kissed her soundly. He wanted to put as much distance between his old life and the start of a new forever, so he broke the seal of their lips and strolled after the Hexaks, arm wrapped possessively around Vanysha's shoulders.

"Now just where do you think you're going, Vice Ambassador?" sputtered Raejil. "There are protocols in place regarding matters such as this, as well you know. More is to be done. The trial must be set and—"

"You can handle the rest without me. Consider this my official resignation, Politico General," he called back to his father. "I've had my fill of this place. It's time I lived my own life."

He tuned out the harsh words flung at his back, attention focused on the friends before him and his betrothed by his side. Peace washed through him as he strolled arm in arm to meet the Hexak entourage.

Smiling, he accepted the warrior's handshake from the Hexak chieftain, while the guards thumped him on the back. "You had me worried for a minute there," H'reeh said. "How were we gonna get back without the best nav this side of the Nexxus?"

Laughter and playful banter flowed easily amongst the Hexaks as the group began their trek once again, and with Vanysha tucked safely under his arm, Kieran finally felt whole and complete.

T*hree months later*

A series of light taps against the door echoed through the dark chamber and dragged Kieran out of sleep's comforting embrace.

"Go. Away."

While he'd expected Vanysha's voice to join with his, it was her location across the room that had encouraged him to peel back his eyelids. Warm amber light filtered in through the domed steeleglass ceiling, announcing the start of another day on his new homeworld.

"*La'nen?*" he called out, squinting in his search for her. Soon, he spied her returning from the inset bathroom, a hesitant yet nervous smile on her pink lips. Concern chugged through his veins and he levered into a seated position, his brows knitting across his forehead. "Why are you up so—"

The door swung open, admitting the chieftain, his daughter, and his son, as well as other members of the Hexakan royal family, which halted any further inquiry.

"So, did you tell him yet?" Elsabet asked.

"Tell me what?" Kieran replied, leaning out as far as possible to reach Vanysha, while ensuring the sheet remained pooled at his waist. "That she's pregnant?"

Over the past several days, he'd had a feeling something was up. Between Vanysha's odd sleeping patterns and constant visits from the female members of H'reeh's family, Kieran had suspected the secret she'd fought to hide.

Her intoxicating aqua eyes flared as the first tear slid down her cheek. "How ... I mean, when..."

Kieran chuckled and, with a light tug, pulled her into his arms. "We're connected, remember? Besides," he whispered into her ear, "it's what kinda happens when you have a lot of sex."

"But, but, but," she stammered through her rough, shallow breathing, "what if ... Kier, I can't become my mother."

A scoff from someone at his back echoed Kieran's sentiments. "No one ever becomes their mother." Kieran smiled at Elsabet's spot-on assessment. His eyes fluttered shut as he touched his forehead to Vanysha's, while Elsabet added, "All they do is guide us to be more than who we are."

"You are going to be an amazing mother to our son, *la'nen*."

She squeaked out a strangled laugh, escaping from his embrace. "So sure it's going to be a boy?" she said. Though her smile had lost its earlier tension, Kieran still sensed her unease. He cradled her face, wiped away the silvery trails with the pad of his thumb. "What if it's a girl?"

Kieran arched a brow, a proper retort poised on his lips.

"What if it's both?"

H'reeh's voice froze Kieran's tongue, and he snapped his gaze toward group waiting just inside their room. Each member wore the same cryptic smirk, solidifying both the strong genetic bond and the powerful empathic skills of his adopted family. But the uncharacteristic bouncing of the burly princess, coupled with her beaming grin, cemented the chieftain's query.

"Twins?" He turned back to face Vanysha, elation and delight cramping his cheeks with a wide smile. "You're having twins?"

Before she had the chance to answer, he wrapped his arms around her, captured her lips with a passionate kiss, pouring all of his joy and love into their tender connection.

Voices rose and fell around him, and he was vaguely aware of hands clapping him on the back; his mind and his heart were focused on Vanysha alone. A life now grew within her, a life brought about by their love. As the door clicked shut, he broke the seal of their lips.

"Are…" she began softly, face downcast, "are you really okay with this?"

With a gentle touch under her chin, he led her gaze up to his, and he waited until she'd gathered herself and met his eyes.

"Vanysha, the main question is: Are *you* okay with this?" he replied. "As for me"—he trailed his fingertips along her jawline —"you have made me the happiest man in the entire universe." He tucked the shoulder-length strand of moonlit hair behind her ear. "And I cannot wait to see the faces of our children."

Tears melted into relieved laughter as Vanysha threw her arms around his neck, falling back with him onto the bed. "Oh, thank the gods! I've been so afraid to say anything. I … I love you and—"

"What?" His interruption had landed so quickly in the midst of her speech, he almost didn't believe anything he'd just heard. In all of their time together, her actions had always revealed what her words had not. He carefully wiggled out of her strangling hold, looking directly into her eyes. "Did … did you just say…"

Dawning rays gave her creamy skin a warm glow, and her smile blazed brighter than the suns miles above them. "I love you, Kieran. I'm sorry it took me this long to finally have the courage to tell you that."

"Thank you," he murmured, though whether the words had been meant for her or for the universe, he couldn't say. "Now," he added, "I truly am the luckiest man alive."

Smiling, Kieran pulled Vanysha into his arms, holding his precious gift tenderly against his heart.

ENTER THE WORLD OF THE
DANTARAN GALAXY

Need more steamy sci-fi romance? Join me in a journey across the stars and see what happens when worlds collide…

TO DISCOVER A DIVINE: RISE OF THE STRIA BOOK ONE

CHAPTER ONE

"Uhh, guys? Any idea why there's a girl in the hallway?"

Kahlym cal Jhuen skidded to a halt and blinked slowly behind the tinted visor of his battle helmet. Nope. His eyes were in proper working order. There, crouched at the feet of a pair of Rimmarian prison guards, was a female. Shock at the bizarre discovery froze his hand in place against the comm unit wired into his helm.

What the hell was a civvie doing in this part of the secure unit? All the intel placed this as the High-Risk Block, housing only the most violent offenders. Or, in his case, two of his crew. He had fulfilled his half of the rescue, discovering their ship's healer, and had sent him toward the landing bay when all hell had broken loose.

"I'm not sure if I heard you right, kid. You did say 'girl,' right?" Dhaerin's deeply accented voice buzzed in his ear, giving him time to scan the corridor one more time. Yup. She was still there, unarmed and bloodied.

His brain churned as klaxons blared all around him, screeching and jarring him back to his present situation. One of the guards raised his gun, aiming at the frightened young woman, and Kahlym sprang into action. Racing down the narrow passageway, he fired at the exposed back of the distracted soldier. The blast tore a hole through the clean white uniform and redecorated the wall in black and crimson.

"Is she cute?" Qaen, the primary reason for this side trip, chimed in. At least that meant the other team was successful and his navigator was not only back on the ship, but also back to his usual horn-dog self. The bastard might be the best damned nav in the entire Seventh Quadrant of the Dantaran Galaxy, but the man would screw anything on two legs. Hell, he'd even heard rumors of that rule being bent on more than one occasion if the prize caught his eye.

"Qaen, you ass," he hissed into the comm mic. "Leave it to you to think with your cock."

"Like he'd care if she was cute. I think his question is better translated to 'Is she naked?'" Kahlym's brother, Brel, chimed in. Kahlym had insisted he and Dhaerin, their two heavy gunners, remain behind on the ship to keep the potential violence to a minimum.

Hindsight was always such a bitch.

The op was supposed to be a simple snatch and grab. Secure codes were bought and paid for, the timing was perfect. Three-man team waltzes into one of the most highly guarded detention ships of the Rimmarian Thrall, pops the locks during a shift change, and just walks out with the two knuckleheads who got themselves nicked for a bloody transport violation.

With a growl half to himself, and half to the Fates, for his overly optimistic appraisal of the original situation, he shifted his focus back to the present. The second guard was slow as he turned, giving Kahlym time to fire off one more charge. The direct hit cleared the corridor, leaving him with quite a mystery on his hands. He knelt down to better study the terrified girl before him. A nasty bruise swelled along her ivory cheek, the hint of impending purples and blues contrasted with the deep brown of her wide eyes.

He let his hand fall from his helm as he stared. Her dark hair shone like a rich bloodwine, burgundy and mahogany tones blending and weaving through the thick mane tumbling past her shoulders. His gaze drifted down, finding lush curves shrouded in some unfamiliar thin fabric emblazoned with swirls of white, symbolic images on an inky background, her arms encased in the same lightweight, flimsy stuff. Her legs tucked beneath her, were wrapped in some kind of form-fitting black material and her feet were clad in bold and brightly colored short boots. The longer he stared, the more captivated he became.

He reached a cautious hand toward her, careful not to frighten her. His mind raced, and he fought to keep at bay the images of what she might have already endured.

"Are you okay?"

Her eyes flared wide as she scooted further away from him. He raised his hands, hoping to ease her fears.

"Don't worry. I'm not going to hurt you."

"You wanna step this up, Kahl? Things are getting dicey down here." Brel's normally calm voice shouted over the blasts echoing through the link.

"Working on it," he muttered. He turned his focus back to

the cowering female. Even in her fear-stricken state, she fascinated him. Everything about her was unlike anything he had seen in all his travels throughout the Dantaran galaxy. Her wide brown eyes transfixed him until all he wanted to do was pull her into his arms and kiss away her alarm.

Without warning, his frozen ward grabbed one of the guard's discarded weapons at his feet and fired a quick volley over his shoulder. Spinning, he drew his own gun, but not before the Thrall soldier crumpled in a mangled heap.

Holy crap. He rounded his gaze back to her, the blaster held out before her with trembling arms. This mysterious female just saved his ass. He blinked as the gravity of her actions sunk in.

Soldiers and warriors exchanged blood debts as easily as others exchanged handshakes. It was assumed when the time came, the thankful marker would be repaid in kind and no one truly kept track. But to have a civilian, unarmed and innocent, step into the fray and protect the life of a fighter, those rare favors were given the utmost reverence.

His life was now hers to command, a blood debt he was eager to honor with each passing second.

Author's Notes

Thank you for allowing my stories into your life and I hope you stay along for the ride. Without readers like you, my characters would only live in my own imaginations.

If you enjoyed this, or any of my works, I would love to hear from you. Drop me a line, send a DM on social media, or even some kind words on a review can make all the difference for an author.

Keep Believing in Magic!

Tessa McFionn has always had a love of all things unreal. Growing up reading Tolkien, Heinlein, and comic books, playing D&D, and watching *Thundarr the Barbarian* on Saturday mornings, she was immersed in worlds of magic. When her mother introduced her to *Dune* and *An Interview with a Vampire*, she was hooked on romance in speculative fiction, and after discovering Sherrilyn Kenyon, she realized love can share center stage in the story.

A very native Californian, calling Southern California home for most of her life, she grew up in San Diego and attended college in Northern California and Orange County, only to return to San Diego to work as a teacher. Insatiably curious and imaginative, she loves to learn and discover, making her wicked knowledge of trivial facts an unwelcomed guest at many Trivial Pursuit boards.

Her first novel, *Spirit Fall*, came to her as she looked over the edge of a very dark place. Since then, she's added three more tales to the world of the Guardian Warriors and *Spirit Bound*, Book Two in the series, was awarded the 2016 Write Touch award for Paranormal Romance from WisRWA. But she never lost her love for science fiction and began a space opera, The Rise of the Stria, in March 2018 with the release of *To Discover a Divine* and book two,

Divine Challenges, and book three, *A Divine's Retribution,* have been added to the tale.

When not writing, she can be found hiking all around Southern California or at Disneyland with her husband, as well as family, friends or anyone who wants to play at the Happiest Place on Earth. She also feeds her artistic soul through her passions for theatre, dance and music. A proud parent of far too many high school seniors and two still living house plants, she also enjoys hockey, reading and playing Words with Friends to keep her vocabulary sharp.

Also by Tessa McFionn

The Guardians

Spirit Fall, Book One

Spirit Bound, Book Two

Spirit Song, Book Three

Spirit Shattered, Book Four

The Rise of the Stria

To Discover A Divine, Book One

Divine Challenges, Book Two

A Divine's Retribution, Book Three

A Curse of Forever, a supernatural novella

ANTHOLOGY STORIES

Storybook Pub: "Wishes & Whiskey"

Storybook Pub 2: "Dangerous Attractions"

Tricks, Treats & Teasers: "Care to Dance?"

Caught Under the Mistletoe: "A Holiday Dream to Chase"